THE ASTRALS
& NOKTS

REALMS OF RUIN

NIKA McKINNEY

Realms of Ruin is a work of fiction. Unless otherwise stated, names, characters, places, events, and incidents are the products of the author's imagination or are used fictitiously. Any resemblance to actual events, locales, or persons, living or dead, is entirely coincidental.

Copyright © 2026 by Nika McKinney

All rights reserved. No part of this book may be reproduced in any form or by any electronic or mechanical means, including information storage and retrieval systems, without written permission from the author, except for the use of brief quotations in a book review.

No generative artificial intelligence (AI) was used in the writing of this work. The author expressly prohibits any entity from using this publication for purposes of training AI technologies. The author also exercises their rights under Article 4(3) of the Digital Single Market Directive 2019/790 and expressly reserves this publication from the text and data mining exception.

ISBN: 978-1-971198-00-2 (e-book, digital)
ISBN: 978-1-971198-01-9 (Paperback)

Cover design by OkayCreationsSH

CONTENTS

Author's Note	xi
The Definitive Guide to the Realms	xiii
Prologue	1
Chapter One	5
The Spy	
Chapter Two	11
The Spy	
Chapter Three	17
The Spy	
Chapter Four	26
The General	
Chapter Five	31
The Spy	
Chapter Six	36
The General	
Chapter Seven	40
The Spy	
Chapter Eight	45
The Spy	
Chapter Nine	55
The General	
Chapter Ten	62
The Spy	
Chapter Eleven	74
The Spy	
Chapter Twelve	85
The Spy	
Chapter Thirteen	95
The General	
Chapter Fourteen	100
The Spy	
Chapter Fifteen	108
The Spy	
Chapter Sixteen	115
The Spy	

Chapter Seventeen   123
The General

Chapter Eighteen   130
The Spy

Chapter Nineteen   137
The General

Chapter Twenty   146
The Spy

Chapter Twenty-One   156
The Spy

Chapter Twenty-Two   171
The General

Chapter Twenty-Three   175
The Spy

Chapter Twenty-Four   188
The Spy

Chapter Twenty-Five   201
The General

Chapter Twenty-Six   205
The Spy

Chapter Twenty-Seven   216
The Spy

Chapter Twenty-Eight   224
The General

Chapter Twenty-Nine   233
The Spy

Chapter Thirty   244
The General

Chapter Thirty-One   254
The Spy

Chapter Thirty-Two   261
The Spy

Chapter Thirty-Three   270
The Spy

Chapter Thirty-Four   276
The General

Chapter Thirty-Five   286
The Spy

Chapter Thirty-Six   298
The Spy

Chapter Thirty-Seven   302
The General

Chapter Thirty-Eight	307
The Spy	
Chapter Thirty-Nine	311
The General	
Chapter Forty	316
The Spy	
Chapter Forty-One	323
The Spy	
Chapter Forty-Two	332
The Spy	
Chapter Forty-Three	339
The Spy	
Chapter Forty-Four	347
The Spy	
Chapter Forty-Five	357
The Spy	
Chapter Forty-Six	362
The Spy	
Epilogue	367
Acknowledgments	373
About the Author	375

For the ones acquainted with pain and loss and live your lives as penance. May you find your freedom.

AUTHOR'S NOTE

Realms of Ruin is an emotional, new adult fantasy romance set in the volatile realms of Haluma and Yarit. It is intended for readers who are 18+ and includes elements of hand-to-hand combat, perilous situations, blood, intense violence, torture, brutal injuries, death, spying, death and injury to minors, poisoning, drug use, PTSD symptoms, graphic language, and sexual activities that are shown on the page. It includes mature themes such as physical and emotional abuse, trauma, anxiety, and grief.

Readers who may be sensitive to these elements, please take note, and prepare to be enchanted by the realms…

THE DEFINITIVE GUIDE TO THE REALMS

Terms to know

Astral: Creatures of light magic. Their existence is now myth.

Nokt: Creatures of dark magic. Their existence has been forgotten.

Dreki: The king's elite soldiers who retain reptilian features. To become a dreki, one must trade their humanity in order to gain greater magic than what you were born with. They are the highest rank in the military. To become a dreki requires an invitation from the King.

Wolvin: Large, solitary beasts, resembling wolves, that live in the Perellian Forest.

Vestal Anchor: Revered, specially chosen individuals, cloistered in the King's castle to serve the crown. They are provided every luxury in the realm. It is a high honor to become one.

Supreme Vestal: The head of the Vestal Anchors, chosen by the gods through the King.

Berine: A mineral mined from the Auren Mountains

Glint: A street drug circulating through the realm of

Haluma. It leaves gold dust behind when used and has negative effects on magic.

Dryad: Forest nymphs, ancient beings whose magic is connected to trees and the forest.

Hamadryad: Dryads whose purpose is to protect sacred groves, often violent with trespassers.

Nereid: Oceanic nymphs, which include sirens and mermaids/mermen, whose magic is connected to the oceans.

~

Places
- Aphellion: Uh-fell-ee-yon- the Liberation camp
- Haluma: Huh-loo-muh- the realm of King Nolan
- Lyrae: Leer-ay- the capital of Yarit, the city of waterways
- Maripol: Mare-ih-pole- the capital of Haluma
- Nereid: Nare-reed- the underwater realm of Queen Thaleia
- Perellion Forest: Purr-ell-ee-yon Forest
- Rivellan Wood: Ruh-vell-inn Wood
- Vorkut: Vohr-koot- a city in the north, near the glacial hinterlands
- Yarit: Yuh-reet- the realm of Queen Avery
- Zephyrus Sea: Zeff-eye-russ Sea

~

People
- Queen Avery: Ay-ver-ee
- Belham: Bell-uhm
- Bowen: Boh-inn
- Delah: Day-luh
- Dominus: Dom-inn-us
- Elyon: Ell-ee-yon
- Finn: Fin

Gemma: Jim-muh
Ilayah: Ill-aye-uh
Kaida: Kay-duh
Korin: Core-inn
Liora: Lee-oar-uh
Maelic: May-lick
King Nolan: Noh-linn
Ruin: Roo-inn
Sieren: Sear-inn
Queen Thaleia: Thuh-lay-yuh
Wes: Wes
Xuri: Zuhr-ee

PROLOGUE
SEVENTEEN YEARS AGO

The last time I saw him was the day my world exploded. Darkness stole us both. He disappeared into it. My mind became consumed by it.

My last memory, before everything blew up, played on a loop in my mind. I lay on the cool granite rock. A stream wound around our meeting spot, its steady gurgle offering a soft reassurance. He didn't always show, but I always knew when he was near.

My hair fanned out around me while I counted the stars. Absently, I scanned the sky for meteors. Dried tears carved out lines of salt down my cheeks.

At home, I had made the mistake of looking in the wrong direction. Or I had breathed too loud. I triggered my own punishment. My fingers still trembled as they tapped against the stone. The movement pulled on my wrist, where torn skin oozed blood. I hated the metal cuffs used to confine me. I hated my father, my jailer, even more.

I sensed my friend approaching. The frantic ache in my chest settled when lifeless shadows turned sentient.

Darkness rippled around me. "He did it again didn't he? Are you okay?"

I sat up slowly. My vision adjusted from the distant cosmos to the closeness of a dark-haired, cloaked boy. How did he know when I needed him most? His concern almost broke me. Almost.

"I'm better now. It was over faster than the last time." Because I blacked out. He lost control of his anger and his fist met my temple.

"Let me see." He leaned closer. With a featherlight touch, he shifted my wild hair back, the small braids behind my ears dragging with the movement. An angry sigh hovered between us. "When I'm older, I'll repay your father for every moment he harmed you. I'll kill him." Shadows speared outward, but none touched me. He shouldn't have any form of magic, not at his age—that came around puberty. They were as mysterious as our meetings.

His anger might have frightened me, but he was my friend. I wasn't scared. I knew real monsters. I lived with one.

"When we're older, I won't be anywhere near Maripol. Maybe when our magics come in, I will be a master hunter and you could build things. And we could live in a castle in the mountains." If only.

The side of his mouth twitched. "That might be nice. Except, I hate the snow and ice. I'm a fan of the sun and the heat."

"Then maybe your magic will be fire, and mine could be growing flowers."

He laughed then, gazing at me with amusement. "That isn't a very helpful magic."

I jumped up. "I could borrow your magic! And then I would burn my father into nothing. Nothing but ash." It would make my life so much easier. Then it would just be me and my mom, and we wouldn't have to practice masking our fear or hiding our bruises.

He touched my shoulder—an act of tenderness I didn't know I needed. "Even if I don't wield flames, I will incinerate him if it means you will find peace. I would scorch the earth to stop your nightmares."

If only my nightmares were confined to my sleep. I offered him a smile; he needed to see I would be okay even if we both knew it was a lie.

I grabbed my bow and two arrows. After my punishments, I found that moving my hands helped calm me. I was a master at twirling sticks and braiding flower crowns. The evidence of both remained behind as we went in search of rabbits.

Leaves and pine needles crunched loudly from behind me. "Dom! Come on! You're going to scare them all away with your clomping." I swung my arm around in my haste to shush him.

He hit the ground so hard leaves flew upward. Laughter spilled from me at his attempt to avoid my arrow pointed at his chest.

"Watch where you swing that thing!"

I lowered my weapon as he slowly stood, brushing pine needles off of himself. He shook his head in the wake of my lingering chuckle and we found a secluded spot to hunt.

We crouched behind a felled tree, quietly waiting for unsuspecting prey. I enjoyed bringing wild game back for my mother to cook. When you're nine, making your mother smile matters.

A tap on my arm had me searching for the rabbit he had spotted. I released the arrow and made a clean kill. We jumped over the tree trunk and snagged the body.

"Well, aren't you a menace." He quirked his brow and ruffled my hair. I flashed him a smile. His answering grin didn't reach his amber eyes. "I can't stay long this time. I snuck out to see you. My training is taking more time away. I had to check on you though."

It never occurred to me to ask about where he'd come from, how he got here, and what he trained for. I just knew that he made me feel safe. He showed up when I needed him. I twirled my bow in my hands as sadness cinched my throat.

"Hey." I met his gaze. Darkness clung to him. It didn't bother me because his eyes were kind. "I have to leave now." He dragged his finger from my left temple, across my forehead, and over the right temple. "For protection." I always giggled when he did that. If only it actually worked.

"I promise, I will find you." The earnestness in his parting words made me smile. I didn't doubt him because he always did.

We turned our separate directions. Him, toward the darkness of the forest. Me, back to my parents in Maripol. I dragged my feet the whole way, hoping with each step that everyone lay deep in sleep.

That particular night, when I faced my childhood home, acrid smoke filled my lungs. The rabbit's body dropped forgotten from my hand. Everything I knew had burned to the ground. Life, as I knew it, was reduced to ash. The curse I'd voiced earlier to Dom echoed in my mind.

My mother's favorite scarf mocked me as it draped across the embers. A charred hole sizzled at the edges, mimicking the hollowed out space in my chest.

I didn't even notice when a young wolvin prowled around me, nor when she nuzzled my hand as I stood paralyzed in shock. She sat down beside me and helped shoulder my pain.

A single tear fell. It was the last time I let myself cry. Dark rage clamped down, strengthening me. It severed me from my grief. In that moment, I knew everything had changed. And I was utterly alone.

I once had a friend. He promised he would protect me. But it was the last time I ever saw him. When I needed him most, he disappeared.

I've always wondered what happened to him.

CHAPTER ONE
THE SPY

A distant tremor disturbed my sleep, the tinkle of crystals from the overhead chandelier splintering my awareness. When the sharp scrape of claws coursed down my arm, I jolted upright. Maelic stared with his reptilian eyes and smug smile. I swallowed my hatred toward the Good King's second-in-command. Only he would have the audacity to enter my bedchamber unannounced. I lifted my chin despite my vulnerable position.

"There's been another earthquake. You're to report to the Rivellan Wood at once. Lock down the area and search for any rebel activity."

I managed a nod. He waited.

"United in Strength," I forced out the proper soldier's response before bringing my arm across my chest and thumping my shoulder in a deferential salute. The realm's mantra tasted sour on my lips.

Maelic pivoted on his heel. A piercing alarm sounded right before he exited my room. His chuckle echoed in his wake. I winced at the noise. Bastard.

I always slept in my fighting leathers when I stayed at the

Keep, for intrusions just like this. I raced to the alarm to turn it off, the sound pounding in my temples. I glared at the clock while I gathered my blades. Only three hours of sleep. Precise movements readied me for potential battle despite my lingering fatigue.

Leaning over the basin in my bathroom, I splashed water on my face. The mirror reflected the ghost of a woman. Black circles under desperate eyes. A bone-deep sigh escaped me. These earthquakes had been increasing in frequency, and I had been sent on numerous missions to capture the rebels involved. I needed to get ahead of them; I always felt two steps behind.

I finished putting my hair into a ponytail, the tiny braids behind my ears swept up with the rest of the mass, while water dripped off my jawline. The braids were the one thing I could not release from my past. They served as a perpetual reminder of my mother and all that I'd lost. I grabbed a cherry candy from my nightstand, before popping it into my mouth. With a deep breath, I squared my shoulders and left my room.

A soldier of lower rank met me outside. He thrust a canteen at me filled with water from the castle's spring—the only water soldiers were permitted to drink. I took it from him, single-mindedly focused on my objective. He raced to keep up with me.

He handed me a map, briefing me in the deserted hallway. "There's been a disruption to an incoming Berine shipment. A warden has a portal waiting." I glanced down at the map, noting the location within the wood. Frost built at my fingertips. I hoped I got there before the rebels scattered.

I emerged from the portal amid plumes of dust. They rose in phantasmic waves, mirroring the agitation radiating off me. Fog enveloped my movements as I surveyed the forest on the outskirts of my infected, though cherished, city. I absorbed every nuanced detail of the chaos before me.

The violence of another earthquake left cracks in the forest floor of the Rivellan Wood, set between Haluma's capital, Maripol, and the bordering Auren Mountains. Felled trees, like scattered matchsticks, obstructed the terrain. These earthquakes had the reputation of rearranging the topography of the land. New rock formations and relocated trees left a confusing aftermath.

Remnants of sleep clouded my eyes as dawn crept beyond the horizon. The eastern mountains' looming peaks and the spires of pines blocked out the meager light of morning. Wind rustled around me as I continued to scan for any signs of the Berine transport supposedly disrupted by tonight's tectonics.

I lived near this forest, and knew it well, but the rearrangement of the land kept me in a constant state of reassessment. We adjusted our maps weekly when landmarks disappeared and the forest reconfigured itself. Importing Berine from the mountainous mines proved trickier every month.

This was my fourth investigation where land movements thwarted a Berine supply shipment. Coincidence could no longer be blamed. Our realm relied on Berine—a rare mineral extracted from the depths of Auren's jagged peaks. The journey from the heart of the mountains to the arms of Maripol enticed only the most rugged of men. I knew the group in charge of this evening's transport, so spying out a rebel should be simple. If I could find one in this hazy darkness.

I refused to blink, waiting instead for my dried-out eyes to involuntarily water. When my water affinity had manifested, I learned my tears revealed auras. They wafted off of people like colored smoke. Too bad I had committed to never feeling grief again; true tears eluded me as much as the rebel group I suspected was behind the earthquakes.

The rebellion, flowing in from the neighboring realm of Yarit on the other side of the mountains, had tightened their grip on our supply routes. They stalked the Berine caravans, hoping to choke us out. I yearned to return the favor.

The rebellion had shifted tactics recently in an attempt to dismantle our power from the inside, led by their general—whom no one had ever seen firsthand. First they introduced the addictive drug Glint to our citizens, the telltale golden dust it left behind lending to its name. Now they sought to reduce our access to Berine.

My fingers clenched, my anger always churning right below the surface when I thought of Glint or the rebels. My steps grew more urgent as my bloodlust increased. Kaida's shadow trailed me, keeping other wolvin at bay so I had no need to protect myself against their vicious attacks.

The magic in Haluma had been decreasing across our realm and no one knew why. Magic entwined with our lifeblood; therefore, the loss of it was terminal, as evidenced by our teeming graveyards. When ingested, Berine would bind to the magic in blood, sustaining it. Unfortunately, it required daily ingestion to maintain, thus our need for a constant supply. It's one of the reasons King Nolan provided Maripolians with fountains throughout the city—they would never have to worry about sustaining their magic.

I hadn't noticed my own affinity being affected, but I worried nonetheless. Instinctively, I pulsed water magic out the tips of my fingers. My shoulders relaxed. Still there.

Enough tears welled in my protesting eyes that I finally studied the darkness between the trees. Glimmers of retreating auras beckoned me, and like a wraith, I stalked between the spindly pines cloaked in fog thanks to my water affinity. Fueled by my hatred for the rebels that got me up each morning, I stretched out my hands as ice crystals formed, leaving a shower of sparkling shards in my wake.

Several figures scattered after the dismemberment of the Berine caravan and the violent upheaval of the earth beneath our feet. Tremors continued to rattle the ground as I pursued the trail that I hoped might belong to a wayward rebel.

My mouth watered as the taste of vengeance surged. Duty to Haluma, my home, no matter how bleak and decrepit it had become, pulsed in my veins. Committed protection to my only friend, Delah, anchored me. Once my parents had been burned alive by someone high on Glint, Delah, a fellow orphan, found me. She had immediately become like a little sister, bound by our shared losses.

My commitment to the realm's innocents, like me and Delah, was the motivation that warmed me on my coldest nights. I was grateful that King Nolan shared my sense of responsibility toward those affected most by Glint's impact.

Ahead of me, a man in black clutched his hood as he ran, then stumbled. I caught a flash of his face as he hurried to right himself. His profile revealed a sharp nose and the absence of a beard. His aura surged the acid green of turmoil. He wasn't part of the transport crew.

"Found you." I pushed myself faster, and my magic harder. The surrounding fog condensed, glazing the forest floor in ice. The stranger slipped and fell, his hands and knees colliding with rocks. "Stay down."

A sharp whistle pierced the cold air. The man whistled back. Two short bursts echoed through the trees. He was warning his partners.

"Shouldn't have done that." I hurled a handful of ice darts at him; one pierced his neck through his woolen cloak.

He shouted in pain, groping at his wounds, and slowly turned to look at me. His aura was muted olive now: resignation.

I smiled bitterly as Kaida, my pet wolvin, emerged from the early-morning gloom. She was a massive creature—her head easily reached my chest—and her fangs glimmered with saliva.

"Is it going to eat me?" the man uttered. Pathetic.

"Only if I tell her to." Then I slammed my dagger hilt into his temple. He crumpled the rest of the way to the ground, and the woods fell into eerie disquiet.

Kaida took a small step forward, her nose twitching.

"Sorry, not this time." I rested my hand on her back. "I need you to carry him for me."

She glared at me.

"Now."

She huffed a sigh and sulked toward the slumped figure. She gripped his body between her massive jaws. His arm grazed the forest floor as she turned to me.

I rubbed the tension from my temples. Though adrenaline coursed through me in the thrill of the hunt, when it dropped, I'd feel the full effect of my exhaustion.

"To the cells," I directed Kaida. We strolled out of Rivellan Wood and through the deserted streets of Maripol toward a nondescript building, warded for sound. The rebel would remain there until I returned with the others to extract what information we could in order to annihilate our rebel enemies.

CHAPTER TWO
THE SPY

The gleam in Wes's eyes disturbed me. Not because they were glowing and his vertical pupils rapidly expanded into black pools. It was the excitement alongside his magic, throbbing, like he was getting off on the thought of torture.

We entered the extraction chamber. The rebel sat secured in the same chair I left him in, though now he was conscious.

I watched warily as Wes's body contorted, scales emerging from the top of his forehead, clicking, overlapping, cascading downward over his entire body, until he shifted completely into a dreki. The new magic he possessed pushed against my skin, goose bumps erupting. He had recently made the trade and embodied all the power and status of the dreki name.

Even though witnessing a dreki in person unnerved me, I looked forward to my own invitation. Worry started to grow with every day that passed without King Nolan offering me the opportunity.

I knew better than to intervene with Wes's violence. I attempted it once, revealing a crack in my soldier facade. Empathy was intolerable, a weakness that would disqualify me from the revered dreki status. I wouldn't forget that lesson again.

Feigned boredom settled in place of my discomfort. My mask of indifference became a second skin, especially in the midst of an information extraction. I swallowed. They needed me as their lie detector—auras revealed a lot about a person.

Wes's clawed hand gripped the man's hair, yanking his head back. Dag, he called himself, jerked and thrashed beneath the ropes that restrained his wrists and ankles. Belham circled them both, sneering. His fingers itched to release his own magic, but we needed information. Belham shot a quick glance in my direction, a hint of doubt in his gray eyes that I had found the wrong guy.

I knew I had not. My affinity allowed me to see motives and emotions as colorful auras. Dag reeked of secrets. His actions in the woods were meant to redirect the shipment of Berine. He may not have been the lead in this operation, but he was instrumental in its outcome.

Berine was sought after and sabotaged relentlessly, most notably by the rebels and their haughty general. Since my ascension to an elite, the final rank before becoming a dreki, all my missions focused on the protection of our Berine supply and searching for rebels in our realm.

Wes's claws etched lines across Dag's skin, splitting it open like an unfolding zipper. His blood dripped in rivulets down his arms, pooling on the stained floor. Belham bent over to look Dag in his bloodshot eyes. Dag whimpered. I leaned in. Belham straightened up and rolled his neck. "How are you redirecting these shipments?"

Dag stayed silent, averting his eyes.

"Where is the Wolf?" Belham's lethal tone echoed off the stones.

Dag's countenance iced over as he glared at Belham. "How should I know?"

"So he exists." Belham tapped his thigh in contemplation. "Interesting."

I noted Dag's aura waning.

Wes jumped in. "We will find where your family is." He glanced pointedly at the ring on the man's finger. "If you tell us how you reroute the Berine, we will keep them out of this."

Dag closed his eyes, a tear rolling down his defeated face. He took a stabilizing breath, clenching his jaw, his aura turning defiant once more.

He turned, spitting in Wes's reptilian face. "The General," he wheezed. "You have no idea—" He stopped as blood began dripping from the corner of his mouth, his ragged breaths echoing in the confined space. He collected himself as more blood oozed from his wounds.

I cocked my head in curiosity. The elusive general of the rebellion had stalked our realm for years. His ascension was the impetus for this drug war. I wondered how close Dag and the general were...

Wes didn't even wipe off the spit as he bared his sharp teeth. "Your defiance shields you from nothing. If you won't tell us what we want to know, I'll find it myself." Dag looked away, his spine straightening.

Wes seized Dag's head with both clawed hands, aligning his palms with the man's temples. Wes shut his eyes in focused contemplation, searching. Dag moaned, bordering on unconsciousness. Wes's scaled lids startled open, then relaxed with a satisfied grin. "There it is," he mused. Slower than necessary, he pulled out threads of silver from deep within the man's skull.

The guttural scream released from Dag caused every fiber in me to recoil; the shriek felt like my eardrums were cleaving in two. I glanced away, hiding my unease. Wes clutched the threads in his hands, deftly storing them within a warded leather pouch.

Belham watched intently, his eyes glittering in anticipation.

Several threads were removed as the man bled out, his hoarse voice fading to agonized groans, his last moments filled with unimaginable pain. Tearing out memories shredded the mind, but this guy's body was butchered enough to hopefully render him unconscious. I quietly exhaled.

"You're up." Wes gestured for Belham. Dag persistently clung to life. Belham's forefinger shifted into a scorpion's stinger. Now it was his turn for a sadistic release. He thrust the needle of the stinger into the man's side, jolting Dag's entire body. Dag started convulsing within minutes.

This felt unnecessary; the man was on the cliff's edge of death, and a soft breeze could easily push him over the side. But this was the game. And I had to play along. Sometimes the thrill of bloodlust pounded through my own veins when true justice was served. But this was not justice, and an idea prickled my skin, one that might open up a strategic opportunity.

I pulled the water in the air toward me, forming a blade of ice. The hilt molded perfectly to my hand; my fingers didn't register the frigid temperature. The blade sparkled under the dim lighting of this makeshift prison cell. I feigned a delighted smile for the audience observing me. The blade gleamed as I twirled it. "Back up," I commanded.

Wes and Belham retreated, their faces like rabid dogs unable to reach their bones. I swung the sword, making the killing blow. Dag slumped in the chair. The sword disintegrated, adding to the puddle of liquid accumulating on the floor. I replenished my stores of magic, reabsorbing only the untainted water back into myself.

The congealed mess threatened to stain my boots. "Did you get the information we needed? Or did we just kill the one person who could reveal the whereabouts of the rebels?" I barely contained my disgust and agitation.

Wes studied me, then shifted back into his human form. His reptilian eyes remained. "His memories named the Crimson

Wolf. It was the answer to our question that hovered at the surface of his mind. There was no image though, so presumably he'd never met him." He patted the leather pouch containing Dag's silver memory threads. "Pulling out more information was futile as he was strictly an informant, and only given minimal information. Probably in case he was discovered, as he foolishly was." Wes began licking the blood off his hands. That was new. Also, disgusting. I averted my eyes.

"Then let's get this intel to Maelic."

Belham turned toward me, his stinger protruding threateningly in the dank air. "You didn't have fun, Ruin? Did you need more blood?" He sauntered closer. My body tensed at his nearness. He dragged that ghastly stinger along the leathers near my collarbone. Why do men so often feel the need to showcase their superiority? I scoffed at his attempt to intimidate.

"Stop," Wes commanded, a hint of warning in his tone. "Get your thrills some other way, Belham. We need to get back to the Order. Maelic was probably expecting us an hour ago."

Belham huffed. Turning on his heel, he flicked his hand, opening a portal. Belham gained his poison stinger when he made the trade; originally, his magic was that of a warden—a person whose magic could fold space so you could step from one point to another, creating portals. The portal spun chaotically, a black hole waiting to suck them in.

Belham gestured for Wes to enter the vortex first. Wes's lip curled as he studied me, his disdain dripping like thick syrup. Finally relenting, Wes entered the portal, then Belham, while I stayed behind to use my water magic to clean the mess. I preferred riding my horse anyway. Belham's portals left me nauseous.

As soon as the portal shut, I got to work. I had not intended the sword I conjured to slit Dag's throat to truly cause his end. When Dag mentioned the general, a plan awakened. Dag's heart still beat, albeit weakly, and it stuttered and slowed. I moved quickly, using water to clear away the grime and blood. I released his fetters and tied strips of cloth around his wounds, staunching more blood loss.

I'd worked tirelessly to excel in all the areas that mattered—spying, weaponry, extracting information, hunting the rebels. I naively assumed my commitment and skill would showcase my loyalty and then I'd be able to negotiate terms concerning my fate; that I would finally become a dreki. Yet King Nolan had not extended me an invitation. I needed more to establish my value.

I was running out of time and ideas... until tonight. Though I held out hope for King Nolan's good graces, I still had Maelic, Nolan's gatekeeper, to report to, and he didn't seem keen on recommending the trade for me. Perhaps this extraction wouldn't be a waste after all. I threw a tidal wave of water around the room, washing away the crimson spatter now coating the plastered walls.

I heaved Dag's unconscious body over my shoulder, trying not to jostle his wounds. I laid him as carefully as I could on my horse. My arms shook with his dead weight. Kaida stood in the shadows nearby. We raced to my home, back near the Rivellan Wood where Delah might be able to provide a tonic to keep Dag alive long enough to send the general a message.

CHAPTER THREE
THE SPY

Delah clasped a hand over her mouth in disgust, or surprise. Probably both. My lips lost the battle to the smirk fighting its way out. I hopped off my horse and pulled the rebel's body off. Delah helped me lower the broken man onto a mat of hay.

"Would you grab something that would help him heal and stop the bleeding? Maybe something to help him regain consciousness?" I batted my eyes. Delah rolled hers, then turned brusquely to retrieve whatever elixirs matched my request. I slumped back on my heels, wiping hair out of my face. The earthy, wood chip smell of the stable was a stark contrast to the moldy copper scent from tonight's extraction. Torture was my least favorite part of this job. So messy.

I surveyed Dag. Guilt knotted my stomach, but I swallowed it down. What would make someone risk his own life and his family's livelihood? Where did the hatred for our realm and its people stem from?

Delah returned with several vials. We maneuvered Dag's body, sitting him more upright to keep him from aspirating all of the tonics. I held his mouth open while Delah poured the liquid down his throat. He sputtered, but involuntarily swallowed, a slight moan escaping his chapped lips. I eased him back down, waiting for the tonic to take effect.

"What are you up to?" Delah crossed her arms, eyes narrowing on me.

"It might be best if you don't know the full extent of it. I would ask that you keep this situation quiet, though."

"Of course, Rue." She gazed out the window, searching the shadows.

"Is everything okay?" I leaned toward her, picking up on a tension I'd been too preoccupied to notice before.

A smile that didn't quite reach her hazel eyes formed. "I've been conscripted to become a Vestal Anchor."

I choked on my own spit. "That's great news! I can't believe you've been chosen." I embraced her. This was one less thing I'd have to worry about if my plan fell through. Delah would always be provided for. No one had taken care of me when I had been young, and sometimes I wondered if my protection and duty to Delah stemmed from a desire to give her what I never had. This turn of events would allow her to be honored as one of the revered Vestal Anchors. I couldn't contain my grin.

"Yes," she half laughed into my shoulder, her voice muffled by my hair. She pushed off me, regaining her balance. "It is great news. I don't know why they chose me, but it's an honor to serve the realm."

I never interacted with them, only seeing the Supreme Vestal here and there among the castle grounds in his giant crimson cloak. Vestals were specifically chosen through divine selection via the Good King's magic. Vestals used their powers to protect Haluma and serve the king. There was no higher honor if you were chosen. Vestals took vows of purity and silence and lived in luxury in their own wing of the castle. Only King Nolan was more revered. I shook my head. How providential for this news to fall on the very night I sought to change my own future.

A quick glance at Dag confirmed he hadn't moved from his slumped position. Shifting my focus back to Delah, her fisted hands and tight smile seemed out of alignment with her words. Though they seemed genuine, her body betrayed an alternative sentiment. "Why does it seem like this isn't really good news for you?"

She threw off my concern with a wave of her hand. "It's been a long day and you dumped a rebel in our stable. We can celebrate later."

I didn't buy into her response, but Dag's eyes fluttered and he took a deep breath, interrupting our conversation.

"I'll see you inside." Delah took one last look at Dag, then hurried away, leaving me with the awakening rebel.

He blinked several times, taking in his surroundings. Confusion etched his features until his gaze landed on me. He clumsily scooted backward, his shoulder slamming into the wall. I granted him his space, lifting my arms in a placating gesture.

"I'd like to make a deal."

Dag paused his retreat, his attention fully upon me.

"I will return you to your family in exchange for information."

He glared at me, his brain clearly ticking through my proposition. Crusted blood cracked along his tightened jaw.

His hand reached toward the wound on his neck. "I have no way of contacting anyone in the rebellion. And I have no cause to trust you." He inhaled a ragged breath.

I prowled around him. "Ah, ah, ah! I know you can communicate with someone inside the rebellion. They wouldn't send you here without an exit strategy." While blades and battles could achieve many things, cunning and manipulation were equally valid weapons. I wondered if I could meet with their abhorrent general. Perhaps we could make a deal regarding either Berine or Glint; I'd be pleased with either.

I didn't know what motivated the rebels so strongly as to

destroy Haluma. Power? Greed? No one had seen the general in years, but I had to try. "Get me an audience with the general, and I will release you."

He winced, his hands now clutching his forehead, likely a residual effect of Wes pulling out his memory threads. His mind would be pitted with the loss, but Wes had removed relatively few. He'd be fine. Probably. "I'll see what I can do," he mumbled.

I arched a brow, waiting for him to continue.

"I have no way to reach out to them, but they'll check in later tonight. They have an oracle who can mind-walk."

I nodded, thinking. I maintained a mask of indifference. The excitement that flared in my chest had me pacing to expel the energy. I had no idea if the general would respond to my summons. But this was the closest I'd come to enacting real change. Perhaps I really could become a dreki, serve the king, rid our streets and alleyways of Glint, and turn the tide of this war. Gods, that sounded amazing.

"I can send the request. I can't guarantee the outcome."

"Tell them Ruin of the Scourge would like to barter. Then let's hope you're persuasive." I stood, dusting dirt and hay pieces off my legs.

"Where are you going?" His eyes darted frantically around. Kaida entered the barn, her massive body blocking any hope for escape. Dag's jaw fell open, his pale skin somehow losing even more color.

"I'm going to get some sleep. You should too. I'll check on you in the morning. Oh, and don't try to run, because there isn't a tonic that will heal ice-burn." I threw a saddle blanket toward my terrified captive, then surrounded him with a cage of ice.

~

MY VEINS THRUMMED, antsy for news from Dag. If I could secure a meeting with the general, it might be the key to securing my place as a dreki. I didn't trust the rebel leader. I detested everything he stood for. But if we could strike a deal, it might be the extra leverage I'd need to negotiate new terms for my position in the military.

No one was coming to my aid. My future was up to me. If I couldn't deliver, and they didn't ask me to trade my humanity for the power of the dreki, then I risked becoming dispensable. Drained. I shuddered.

I threw a new pair of leathers on, secured my weapons, and plaited my hair. Three small braids below my left ear and two small braids below my right, then I gathered the whole thick, wavy mass and twisted them securely together.

Walking into the living area, I grabbed two apples from a bowl on the table. Delah still slumbered in the room on the other side of our shared cabin as I quietly left, clicking the door shut behind me. My sisterly protectiveness appreciated we could remain in our little home, a reprieve from the madness of the military and its politics.

Moonlight glazed the ground in shimmering patches, lighting a path toward the stable. The rebel remained confined within the ice cage I'd constructed. A snore rumbled out of his parted mouth when I entered. Kaida wasn't here, most likely having returned to some dark corner of the woods. Wolvin were the things of nightmares, but she was my nightmare. I couldn't get rid of her if I tried.

Kaida's first appearance coincided with one of the worst days of my life. Even now, pain twisted my heart when I thought of how I had returned from hunting with Dom. But seeing her daily triggered my past less and less. My entire life had been reduced to cinderblocks and ash. The ground beneath me might as well have turned to lava and subsumed me.

Everything had changed in that moment. Losing my father wasn't significant, but losing my mother was devastating. But I lost more than just my parents, I lost my friend. He promised he would find me, he would protect me. Perhaps it was unfair for me to hold him to that. My heart raged anyway, in the same old tune it always did when thoughts of him came up. I rolled my shoulders and ignored the feeling.

With a flick of my fingers, the cage surrounding Dag dissolved into a puddle. Water soaked into his clothes, rousing him awake.

Startling to attention, he fixed his bleary eyes on me. I leaned against the wooden walls, lazily twirling my dagger. "Well?" I inquired. "Will you be returned to Yarit, or do I kill you now?"

His eyes widened. "The oracle mind-walked, just as I said. I got confirmation that the General will send someone to meet with you. It's the best I could do." He stared at his hands, twisting the ring on his finger.

It wasn't what I'd asked for, but it was better than nothing. "Fine."

"Fine?" Hope glimmered behind his trepidation.

"I'll release you to the woods. Hopefully your people will find you before the wolvin do. Rumor has it they have been hunting people now. But first, you'll drink an elixir to bind you to our deal. If the rebellion doesn't meet their end of the bargain, the tonic will turn to poison. If I get my meeting, you'll have nothing to worry about." He nodded slowly, twisting his ring more aggressively. I didn't actually believe the wolvin rumors, but he didn't have to know that.

I tossed him an apple on my way out.

AFTER LEAVING a note for Delah to provide one of her experimental elixirs for Dag, and explaining the parameters of our deal, I took off on my horse to the Keep. The king's castle, nestled at the base of the mountains, included a military barracks, training ground, and the great palace.

A cool breeze chilled my skin when I dismounted my horse. Shadows nipped my hands and swirled around my ankles, giving me pause.

"Good work yesterday, Ruin." His silky voice curled around me. I turned, finding King Nolan taking shape before me. His cold shadows receded to reveal his wavy, blond hair and a smile that could melt iron ore. The scent of smoke and steel accompanied his appearance. His presence roused my exhausted muscles. I stood at attention, facing the Good King, lapping up his compliment.

A few curious shadows coursed their way along my arms, sweeping back a stray hair from my face in a fatherly gesture.

"I seek to serve you, Your Majesty. I desire the protection of this realm from those that would seek to destroy it."

His shadows iced against my skin. Everything beyond the king blurred. I tasted the metallic zip of power, the sensation overwhelming my senses.

"You have become a formidable weapon. Your team is one of the best." He circled me slowly. "I hope you will take hold of the power destined for you. The dreki are my most trusted, the most revered warriors in all of Haluma. It is the highest honor you can hold. Once you align yourself with me, your world will be opened to innumerable possibilities."

I nodded, my mind clouded with the urge to taste more of this power and maintain Nolan's approval. His attentions calmed an aching part inside of me.

He scrutinized me, his face carefully blank. "Your next mission will determine the invitation you crave. You will have everything you could ever need. Together, we can finally destroy our oppressors."

I perked up at this. The king knew me well, having comforted me when I was brought in as a terrified child. Had always abundantly provided for me. Only he knew my secret, and he never judged me for it. His presence brought me comfort.

"When you take hold of this power, you will be trained in using it so that what you love will not be destroyed. Not like last time."

My shoulders dropped. The open sore in my soul festered despite my efforts to bind it. Had I not spoken the curse over my father, my mother would still be alive. This was my burden. King Nolan had helped as best he could, and now he offered me this beautiful chance at redemption.

His shadows coalesced around him once more. The sounds of the night infiltrated my senses as my awareness slowly returned. His stare bored into me as his body dissolved into a swirling mass of wild shadows. "You are very valuable to me. I'll follow up soon."

Then he was gone.

I shook my head to clear my thoughts. The king's presence often left me with a slight tremor, sometimes nausea. It was simultaneously magnetic and off-putting; his power pulled me in, transfixing me. I struggled to think straight when he was near.

My life transformed the day my house burned down, and a cavernous space remained. This opportunity felt like the missing piece. I made it to the highest level I could in the king's army, his elite force. It's what they trained us for. Becoming a dreki meant I would have full authority and power to divest our realm from the rebels seeking to subjugate it. And now that invite would be mine. Elation coursed through me.

I continued my trek with an extra bounce in my step, reflecting on what the king said and actions that needed to be taken. I still had one more mission. I had to make it count to solidify my place.

I committed to continue training hard, knowing my strength

in combat along with my magic would set me apart, even from the power of the dreki. If I had any hope of maintaining my position in the army, in the event I did not get invited to make the trade, then I had to be even better than them. I wouldn't let it come to that, though. The lesson of being twice as proficient was ingrained in me, as it is for every woman who dares to succeed in a man's domain.

The king was right; I had become one of his primary weapons. I smiled at the thought. I knew he wanted me to succeed, maybe even more than I did. I rubbed my hands together as hope ignited within me. I would prevail no matter what mission they gave me.

CHAPTER FOUR
THE GENERAL

Darkness settled heavier than my shadows. It bounced off the stone walls, as oppressive as any shielding ward. My soldiers crept behind me in silence, moving like mythical ghost leopards. No sounds, save for my own breath, broke the tension.

I'd spent months detailing our route—the map in Finn's hands testament to that. I had every hallway and stairwell memorized. Galea, our Prime Elixist, had created a glowing ink for this particular operation. I had painstakingly drawn each curve and path with my own hand. The ink led us like a beacon on the paper toward the prisoner. We had no need for King Nolan's floating light orbs.

My fisted hand swung upward. Everyone behind me stilled, awaiting my next command. An eerie quiet settled in the tower. Not one guard, one grunt, or even a distant bird call, could be heard. I assessed my team. We were ready for whatever lay beyond this door.

Stepping forward, my shoulders filled the doorway. My metal magic swirled into the iron locks. Several clicks shattered the quiet, making me wince. I threw my shadows into the room right as the door swung open. Cold metal formed within my grip, extending into double-edged, black blades that pulsed with my magic. Yet nothing emerged from the dismal room. The emptiness unnerved me.

We fanned out. Searching. Searching. We were here for Ilayah, our Prime Oracle. She had been taken several weeks ago, and our spies within Maripol only just unearthed where they'd confined her.

I had never stopped looking for *her*, though. Surely, even after all this time, I would recognize her. My eyes scanned my surroundings, as if I would see her as an adult and I would just *know*. An ember of hope would always smolder for her. My disappointment settled as familiar as the sun's rising. I instinctively searched anyway.

Hundreds of floating lights filled the space. The brighter ones hung low, while the dimmer orbs hovered close to the ceiling. The faint shimmer of magic coursed upward, as if drawn by a magnet, directly into the spheres. I grimaced at the scent of burnt sugar and acid that permeated the room. Glint and its residual dust lay thick upon every surface.

My team and I pulled on black leather gloves. Though Glint's power only worked when it was ingested or injected, there was no need to purposely subject ourselves to the golden poison.

"Here! She's here." Harrison waved his dagger in the air, the blade reflecting against the orbs' light.

My breath stalled as I rushed over. Ilayah resembled a mere shadow of herself, lying amongst wrinkled sheets. Every line of her once-healthy body had become sharp and angular. Each bone could be counted on her emaciated frame. The metal around us began to vibrate. A few soldiers spared me worried glances. Harrison took a subtle step away. I fisted my hands at my sides.

Her body remained motionless; her awareness obliterated by

the Glint in her system. The wrinkles around her eyes deepened in the dim lighting, and her sunken cheeks aged her well beyond her sixty years. Bruises peppered her arms in varying shades of blue, black, yellow, and green. Her once lustrous brown skin now ashen and dull.

My anger grew claws. It had taken us months to get information from our spies in the castle to determine where she was being held. I was grateful Xuri hadn't seen her like this. I hoped we weren't too late.

Harrison extended his arms, hovering them above her body as his magic seeped into her. He was dually-trained as a soldier and healer. "I can only numb her and keep her unconscious at this point. I don't have time to do much more. Nothing is broken, and she won't be in pain when we transport her."

Finn, my second-in-command, stepped forward. We exchanged a look, both of us grave in our assessment. I nodded to him. He scooped her up, holding her gently to his chest as her head lolled to the side.

A whine caught my attention as we turned to leave. I squinted into a dark corner of the room.

"We need to go," Finn urged me. I waved him off, creeping from shadow to shadow. A large crate covered by an oversized blanket sat against the back wall. Soldiers shifted on their feet. None dared to challenge me.

I lifted the blanket off the crate. Several wolvin greeted me with whimpers and fangs. They shoved themselves back against the far side of the enclosure, huddled around each other. Their fur bristled along their spines as they glared at me. I didn't deliberate my decision. My magic unlocked the bolts fastening the bars together.

The animals stilled at their sudden freedom. They bowed their heads to their feet in a show of submission. When they met my gaze, I froze. These were not normal wolvin. I cloaked the beasts in my shadow, blinding them with darkness until we exited the room. They snarled and bucked within the darkness, but I couldn't risk an attack on our team.

Finn rolled his eyes as I passed him. "Those could kill anyone."

I knew what was potentially at stake. If Nolan played with beasts like he played with Primes, then he deserved to have them unleashed upon his own people. "Then so be it."

We exited the tower into predawn darkness. Stars glittered above us, indifferent to our infiltration. I raced ahead, trusting everyone followed closely behind me. Not a guard in sight. My spies did not lead me astray with the intelligence they'd supplied us.

My shadows shifted, warning me of movement ahead. Our small group halted at my signal. Fear over Ilayah's condition had my magic itching to unleash.

Finn subtly cleared his throat. I ignored the insinuated directive. I probably should have melted into the shadows, but my ire begged for an outlet. Two guards strode past, unaware of our presence. Before they could blink, I pulled the two longswords crossed at my back. The blades sliced through the air as cleanly as they did the throats of the king's soldiers. Their knees slammed against the ground, blood gurgling out, staining their proud armor.

One of my men leapt forward and dragged the soldiers' swiftly draining bodies away from the open. He positioned them to appear as though they were leaning against one another in slumber or stupor. I arched a brow at the soldier, offering him an impressed nod. He almost smiled, then caught himself, saluting me instead.

I took us back to the location we'd entered the castle from. Under the cover of darkness, the back corner of the sparring fields offered a concealed space for Finn to open a portal. Finn entered first, holding Ilayah carefully. The portal's breeze fluttered her graying hair as he stepped through. I remained behind, making sure the rest of my soldiers made it into the spiraling portal.

When it closed behind them, I returned to the shadows. I had to meet up with Finn's newest recruit, and our time frame was brief.

A scream sailed through the night. I turned in its direction, locating the wolvin predators I'd released. They were known as solitary hunters, but this group must have bonded in their confinement because they stalked passersby in what appeared to be a coordinated effort.

Retribution warmed me from the inside. I hoped those beasts released mayhem. My satisfaction was short-lived when the oppressive weight of Nolan's darkness intensified. My shadows writhed beneath the assault. I peered upward into the night sky, squinting to differentiate the night from the veil.

That veil of darkness only meant one thing. The king's power was increasing.

CHAPTER FIVE
THE SPY

The shadowed spires of the Keep loomed in the distance when the rising sun halted, as if the night sought to pull it back under. I paused mid-stride, my thoughts about the trade halting. The thickening veil of darkness signaled the rebels were at work. My magic coursed through me at the sight, ready to obliterate any hint of rebel activity.

I quickened my pace toward the castle when the stench of smoke and burning wood assaulted me. I froze for a second, my hand wavering at Kaida's side. I would know that smell anywhere. Without thinking, I sprinted away from the direction of the Keep and toward the source of the fire. Smoke billowed like a flag in the dark-plum sky, directing me to the inferno.

Screams sailed on the breeze as I dodged early morning sellers heading to the markets, unperturbed, or perhaps numb, to the chaos around them. I raced through the cobbled streets, around small fountains and hobbling wagons. Kaida followed at a distance; she would only scare the citizens with her presence.

Horror seized me as I rounded the next corner, my hand flying to my mouth. The orphanage I had briefly lived in, before a scout from the Keep found me, was engulfed in flames. Again.

Women and children fanned out, fleeing. Some screamed, some cried, some struggled silently in shock as they were dragged away from danger.

I hoped this wasn't a repeat of the fires that targeted orphanages shortly after I had joined the king's military. The Night of Ash, where every orphanage in Maripol had been targeted in one evening, and every girl living in them had been killed or gone missing. My instincts flared and I catalogued every man, woman, and child in the vicinity.

Even more disturbing, though, were the three wolvin prowling in front of the door, refusing entry or allowing exit. Wolvin were wild animals that avoided the city and its people, preferring the Rivellan Wood. Attacks only came when provoked. This was something different, calculated.

My magic hummed as I pulled out the longsword from the sheath on my back. Ice crusted down the blade, elongating and sharpening it. My eyes darted skyward to movement in an upper-story window. A child screamed behind the glass, beating against it with small, frantic fists.

My instant fear for the boy had ice freezing the ground beneath me. The moisture in the air wouldn't be enough to draw from to douse the fire. I decided to conserve my affinity for the battle with the group of wolvin.

They sneered at me, exposing numerous gleaming teeth. A rabid energy pulsed around them as they twitched and pawed at the ground. Tiny hairs on the back of my neck prickled. My mother's words echoed in my mind: *"Do not be shaken."*

I circled them, not positive I could take on three at once. The wolvin stepped forward, a low growl following. Blood coated their muzzles and chests. Their claws scraped along the stone. And their eyes... I wouldn't have believed it unless I saw it firsthand. They had the eyes of the dreki. If the Good King was turning animals into dreki, there had to be a reason. These were not protecting Maripolian citizens, though. King Nolan would forgive me for putting them down.

I searched for Kaida. I needed her help.

She sidled up to me, heeding my call. The crowd scattered further at our approach. The wolvin stood several heads taller than me, their saliva dripping in large globs. One of them shuddered, and I watched in dread as scales clicked into place along its shoulders and across its chest. I swallowed hard, focusing my attention on their bodies. There weren't many exposed openings for me to exploit. My aim had to be perfection.

I didn't wait for the remaining wolvin to become fully armored. My magic lit up as I pulled water from a nearby fountain, forming bladed stars of ice. I cast them toward the eyes and bare throats of the beasts. One accomplished its goal of slicing a neck. A sharp bark severed the quiet air. Blood spilled as it collapsed in a heap on the packed dirt.

The armored wolvin prowled toward me. "Take the left one," I directed Kaida. She growled under her breath as she approached the deranged animal, her hackles rising.

The dreki-wolvin charged at me. I held my position, not daring to blink, until it was almost upon me. I crouched, thrusting my sword upward as it sought to leap onto me. I had observed the armor clicking into place on Wes and Belham so many times and heard their muttered complaints about places the armor didn't reach. I had to believe the same weak spot existed on these wolvin. I gritted my teeth and shoved with all the force I could muster. The blade embedded in its chest, at a small gap of exposed flesh, and threw off its momentum.

I rolled out of the way, but not before its claws grazed my arm. Blood coursed down my bicep and between my fingers, dampening the dirt. The beast recovered quickly, popping back onto its feet and stalking toward me. The fire raged on behind it and my skin tingled with the urge to bust through the front door and save the child in the window. But this damned wolvin blocked my entry.

The hilt of my longsword protruded from the beast's chest, glittering in the growing light of day as the animal heaved in ragged breaths. It lunged toward me. I withdrew two daggers with blood-slicked fingers before throwing them in rapid succession toward its massive face. One bounced off of it, but the other implanted in its cheek.

Its reptilian eyes narrowed with boiling rage. Blood leaked out of its wounds, but whatever power it had acquired sustained its strength. It shuddered and shifted on its large paws, standing taller.

Kaida wrestled with the other wolvin to my left. I quickly withdrew another dagger, glazing it in unforgiving ice, and threw it directly into its throat. The wolvin roared as Kaida finished the job.

I zigzagged around the dreki-wolvin. Its steps staggered, less precise. I summoned what water was left from the small fountain nearby. It was one of the few Berine-infused fountains littered around the city that Nolan had erected to help with the decline of magic. Gods, I was thankful for his generosity in this moment.

My magic drew the liquid toward me—there might be enough water to divert the wolvin. I thrust the water at the beast's face. A curtain of pain covered the wolvin in the form of a thousand icy needles. It shrieked at the barrage of tiny stab wounds.

In its distraction, I ran toward it and yanked my sword from its chest. A squelching noise rent the air as blood poured out in a macabre waterfall. I wasted no time swinging for its exposed flesh. My sword reverberated with every tear of thick skin and corded muscle. Dreki scales scattered like lethal leaves around us.

I swung my blade once more. The animal's head landed with

a thump on the ground, spattering blood across my boots. I moved before its body followed.

The front door hung limply as I raced into the burning orphanage. I yelled for the child while smoke filled my lungs. If I used much more magic without replenishing, I would be worthless. I crawled along the floor, blindly searching for the stairs, and what little oxygen, was left. The child stood shaking crouched at the landing and I heaved a sigh of relief.

I grabbed him and bolted back toward the front door, doing my best to shield his small body.

I crossed the threshold just as beams collapsed in a spray of sparks and ash. Stone bit my knees as we fell to the ground outside. All I knew was burning lungs and watering eyes. Someone grabbed the little boy and carried him to safety.

Blinded by a crowd of auras, I searched for Kaida until a black figure caught my attention. I squinted to make out its form. It appeared humanoid but with limbs longer than they should be. Dread dripped down my spine, paralyzing me. Its gaze locked with mine as it cocked its head. Inky pools of black studied me. Slowly, it retreated into an alley as I rasped a breath. Kaida sat at my side, nudging me with her nose. I wrapped my arm around her and she helped me to my feet.

My mind raced. Terror and confusion fought for dominance within me. What was that creature in the crowd? Why had wolvin been transformed into dreki? Blood dripped down my arm as the questions lingered, unanswered.

CHAPTER SIX
THE GENERAL

My shadows shrouded me, blurring my movements. My connection point with one of Nolan's own wasn't a far walk. My departure from King Nolan's Keep was a simple affair, especially at this hour. I strode through cobbled streets into the more decrepit side of Maripol.

Finn's new defector would be waiting for me, if she'd followed his instructions. Her arrival at the location of our meeting was a test in itself. I had yet to meet the girl, but Finn had scouted her weeks prior. She had been easy to turn. I knew Finn could handle this, but I wanted eyes on all of the people we'd recruited, especially defectors. I needed to make sure they were truly on our side now.

Howls cut through the night. The wolvins' escape from the king's castle was the least of my worries. I grinned. They would make for a welcomed distraction during this meeting. The building ahead sat abandoned and in disrepair; my men knew well how to construct a ward of illusion.

The tingle of the ward washed across my skin when I crossed the threshold. A few low-burning candles illuminated the entryway, casting dancing shadows from the disrupted flames.

I walked down a small hallway that led into an open space. Covered windows prevented curious eyes. The girl was already at the table, her fidgeting fingers the only tell of her anxiety. She tensed at my approach.

"Who are you? Where is Finn?" Confusion and wariness evident in her tone.

"You can call me General."

Surprise crossed her face briefly. Her eyes darted around, clearly uncertain about what to do next. She pushed back her chair, readying to stand.

"You can stay seated. No need for deference." She glanced around, still unsure, then slowly returned to her seat. I observed her every move, my shadows curling around her, scenting for any hint of Nolan's magic. My metal affinity hovered right below the surface, ready to weaponize at any moment.

Shadows flared around the room cloaking us deeper in secrecy. "I make sure every moving part of the rebellion is in working order, Delah. After this meeting, we likely won't meet again."

She flinched at my address. Or my shadows. I couldn't tell. She needed to know with whom she dealt with, but I also needed her relaxed enough to report and retain information. Too much fear would hinder her recall and impact our time. I needed to make this quick.

"You've been in contact with Finn. He apologizes for his absence. Were you able to get the information?" I pulled out a chair across from the girl. She was much younger than I expected. But Finn assured me she could be trusted. She had already provided vital information related to the drekis.

"Y-yes." She tried hard to master her trepidation. I didn't have the patience to coddle her. I assessed her, observing her subtle tells, her furtive glances. With my shadows so active, I knew the runes on my neck would attract her attention. I growled at her direct perusal. She would likely buckle under any interrogation by Nolan, so we would not disclose any more information than necessary for both of our sakes. And she would need training. I motioned for her to continue.

"They are experimenting with new strains of Glint to see how magic is affected. There are rumors that stolen magic is being used to feed something. They are just rumors though, no one has seen anything. King Nolan's second, Maelic, has me checking out Glint houses. I am testing elixirs on some of the addicts to see if it impacts the rate of magic siphoned."

She worried her bottom lip as I drummed my fingers on the table's worn surface.

"I'm also now on track to become a Vestal Anchor."

My head jerked up. We both knew what that would mean. "Do they normally conscript elixists? Can't your sister in the Scourge pull some strings?" Finn had mentioned Delah lived with an elite spy, another bonus to having her on our side. If Delah had been recruited, then our time would be cut short. Maybe I should have her feel out other elixists that would be open to defecting.

Delah shook her head. "Ruin is a delicate situation."

Ruin? Interesting…

"But do you think she could be flipped? If she knew what you knew?" I remained still, keeping my eagerness contained.

"Her hatred runs deep. I would have to tread carefully. But I will try."

I leaned back, hissing frustration through my teeth. I didn't want to blow our cover by becoming overzealous. All that we did was purposeful and methodical. Over the last several years, we had infiltrated Haluma, turning King Nolan's people against him, and planting our own. Right under his nose. We needed the foundations of his realm to crack and implode.

Ruin had fallen into my lap with her hope to bargain with

me. I'd meet with her this evening. This opportunity gave me an in that would have taken me months, if not years, to accomplish. Manipulation wasn't my preferred style, but Ruin could be the key to the king's final undoing. Her level of clearance, the stage right before becoming a dreki, was invaluable. I would do whatever I needed for my people. At the thought, the rings on my fingers flared. The black titanium melted around my fingers, waiting for my magic to form them into something violent.

"There's a festival tomorrow. Plenty of Glint should be floating around. And you'll be there." I didn't wait for her response. My chair scratched against the floorboards as I stood. Delah's fear had smoothed around the edges yet she shrank into herself as I reached my full height.

Whether she *wanted* to attend the festival or not didn't matter to me. She was involved now, and my command was law.

I pulled my shadows back into me. "Welcome to the Liberation."

CHAPTER SEVEN
THE SPY

"Don't ask questions, just, patch me up."

Delah stared at me, her mouth agape. I went straight to the elixist annex at the Keep, knowing I would find Delah. She hastily pulled items out of her bag, situating her workspace. *Had she just arrived?* She grabbed a blue tonic that she poured on a piece of cotton, then dabbed at the gashes on my arm. She handed me a wet towel and I wiped away the dried blood. She seemed flustered. I would be too if she had walked in with wounds like mine.

The pungent tonic bubbled on my wounds. A burning, then an overwhelming itching sensation overtook my senses. I gritted my teeth and stared at the edges of my torn skin as it slowly mended itself. The burn lingered but the itchiness dissipated, leaving behind pale pink lines. I released a breath.

Delah hadn't made it into the elite force like I had; her magic wasn't suited for it. Her ability to concoct potions, healing elixirs, and chemical weapons was unmatched. And this tonic proved it. I finally allowed myself to relax.

Orbs of light floated near the ceiling casting a dreamy spell upon the room. Most of the castle used torches, but King Nolan had introduced spheres of light to the buildings and homes throughout Maripol. Over time, they would become too bright, and workers would replace them for any Haluman citizen. Some hovered in the elixist annex still, where they had been invented decades prior.

Delah leaned back against a counter, corking the vial of tonic she'd used on me. Her eyebrow arched, waiting for an explanation. I offered none. Not here.

"Did you get our guest his tonic?"

Delah smirked, offering a curt nod. Candid conversation would have to wait until we were back at home. I glanced at the clock on the wall. I had to report to Maelic shortly. A wave of exhaustion hit me. I needed to replenish my magic reserves soon. I felt depleted after having used so much of it earlier. The rapid loss of my water affinity left me dry-mouthed and dizzy.

Delah handed me a glass of water, which I gratefully gulped down. It would refill my magic enough to get me through the next few hours. Since I had water magic, if I did not reabsorb, or get enough rest to recharge, I would become dehydrated and exhausted. My skin would crack and bleed and my dry mouth would prevent me from swallowing. Untrained magic wielders succumbed to death for their ignorance or carelessness around reabsorption. Many people had. I recalled an oracle who developed complete memory loss, and a sound manipulator who fell deaf shortly before their demise.

Delah's eyes darted around, despite us being the only ones in the room. I strained to hear her lowered voice. "Be careful, Rue. Things around here seem like they're at a boiling point. Rumors are swirling." Delah implored me. I offered a smile that didn't come close to reaching my eyes. If she only knew what I'd just seen.

She wasn't wrong about the rising temperature of the realm. War sat idly on the horizon. The realms of Haluma and Yarit were at odds ever since King Nolan took the throne. It all happened before I was born. There used to be Primes, the masters of magic, who taught their craft and helped hone the skills of younger wielders. Without Primes, magic declined. They all disappeared shortly after Nolan ascended. Some believed their disappearance was what led to the rebellion's attacks—that they sought after the Primes who were left. But I knew the truth: all had died.

The entire realm of Haluma teetered on the edge of outright violence between the loss of magic and the spread of Glint. Even the land seemed to cry out for mercy with its increasing earthquakes that rearranged the topography of the realm. And now, with those wolvin-turned-dreki, things seemed to be spiraling. I needed to find King Nolan. He would know what was going on. He would have a plan. But first, Maelic.

Shaking away my unease, I offered Delah a wan smile. I made my way to the exit, leaving her.

The hustle and bustle of the military grounds drowned out most of my thoughts. I trekked across the Keep, a completely walled-in fortress with the palace at its center. Maelic's office stood in some buildings near the Vestal Anchor's wing.

As my superior officer, Maelic held one of the highest positions in the Order. He'd already made the trade to become a dreki and remained one of King Nolan's closest advisers. Though I'd never seen him shift, his vertical pupils never allowed you to forget his underlying nature.

Light from windows and torches bent the shadows as I passed through stone corridors, the grays all mixing together. I stopped at Maelic's door and knocked sharply.

"Enter." The heavy oak door scraped against the stone. The scent of paper, sweat, and smoke assaulted me. I waited to be summoned further.

Maelic's reptilian pupils focused on me, his irises near glowing as he took me in. "Sit, Ruin." His feet were propped on his desk, disturbing eyes blinking in irritation. The king's crest adorned the wall behind him, three flames surrounded by the Haluman Viper. I noted several maps decorating the space.

I perched on the edge of the furthest chair. Its black velvet cushions offered little comfort in the presence of Maelic. He sniffed once in my direction, like the animal he now was. I waited. A prickling sensation trailed the back of my neck.

Maelic shuffled through some papers. "The rebellion continues to undermine our ability to acquire Berine. We have yet to discover the location of their primary stronghold, not even a scent on the breeze of them. King Nolan tires of our ongoing defensive posture. We fear they plan an attack on our realm, and we need to be on the offense."

My eyes found a missive on his desk detailing an explosion at a Glint house. He drew my attention as he continued.

"The Berine supply has been dwindling for far longer than we realized. Magic is fading in the realm. If we don't stabilize our reserve, we risk our people losing magic altogether. So, I need you to scout Yarit's capital." He flipped a map toward me, pointing at its location.

I harnessed my surprise at his directive; instead, focusing intently on the map. It was nearly law that travel outside of Haluma was restricted to all but the dreki. I had never been permitted to enter another realm. It underscored how precarious tensions had become.

"The memory threads I saw last night showed someone discussing peculiar tectonic movements outside of the city of Lyrae. They correspond to what the earthquakes here have done —interfering with our trafficking routes, likely related to the rebel known as the Crimson Wolf. We believe they hide out somewhere around Yarit's capital."

I released my breath, squaring my shoulders. "Let me find the Crimson Wolf. It would be my honor to return with him. I could not only weed out the rebel network, but also take out their primary weapon against us." I held his stare, unflinching.

Maelic pondered my response. "Your espionage skills are much more refined than Wes's or Belham's." He steepled his fingers, assessing. "Wes is a dreki, though, and he wouldn't stand out as much as you think because Yarit is the realm of nymphs. The oceanic nymphs and some of the naiyads display very unique features. This mission is too vital to not send a soldier with the bloodbond of loyalty and the power of the dreki to obtain the Crimson Wolf."

His words settled like iron in my gut. My magic and strength could rival either of them in dreki form. My insides twisted.

I held his gaze, wondering what more he withheld. My jaw clenched. "Let me do this." My hands itched to pull a blade, my instinct to protect myself in the presence of his power—it was also my urge to kill him for being a bastard. My hands fisted before my ice betrayed me.

Maelic's magic involved seeing through illusions. I wondered if he could sense my scheming. I abruptly stood. His vile eyes searched my body. I lifted my chin under his scrutiny.

He rolled up the map of Yarit and tossed it to me, "I'll think about it. Study this in the meantime." He continued his shrewd assessment of me. His lip curled as if finding me lacking. His vertical pupils narrowed before he finally turned his back to me.

Understanding my dismissal, I gripped the map tighter. My mind danced with the possibility of opportunity as I left his office. The Crimson Wolf was mine. I would not be denied.

CHAPTER EIGHT
THE SPY

My return to the cabin was a blur, as I lost myself in thought. I took the less-traveled route from the castle, weaving through the Rivellan Wood. Night descended faster below the evergreen canopy. I sensed, rather than saw, Kaida as I walked.

The wind abruptly changed direction and I stilled. Kaida's low growl sharpened my focus to my immediate environment. I extended my hand in her direction. Not yet.

Moisture from the air swirled protectively around me. Frost nipped at my fingertips. A figure emerged from the shadows. A heavy presence, but without immediate threat. Nothing like the wolvin or the black figure from earlier.

"Who are you?" My voice held firm as an ice dagger solidified in my waiting hand.

"You requested a meeting. My curiosity got the best of me." The tenor of his voice sent goose bumps down my arms. His broad shoulders blocked the forest out, strong and wide beneath fortified armor. His cloak billowed around him.

"It's you. The General." I barely contained my breathlessness. The raised hood concealed his face almost as much as the writhing shadows. I only knew two people with shadow magic. And this was not King Nolan, or *him*. I squinted through the darkness to glean a better view of his obscured face.

A subtle nod shifted the hood of his cloak. "Why shouldn't I kill you where you stand? Why should I make a deal with you, a member of the Good King's Scourge?" He spit the name like acid from his mouth. The clink of rings forced my gaze to his clenched fist. I swallowed, ignoring his disdain.

Duty to Haluma pulsed in my veins. But my lifeblood was fueled by vengeance against the source of my deepest loss. Glint killed my parents. Glint forged a generation of orphans, just like me. My voice did not tremble, though the hope inside me did. "Stop trafficking Glint into Haluma. In exchange, I can offer safe passage for the rebels I find. I'll send them back to Yarit, through the Rivellan Wood."

If I could change at least one facet of this war, the spread of Glint, it would be significant. It might even be enough to earn the king's favor. My heart raced as I waited for his response. I hardly breathed.

"We don't…" He paused, assessing. The shadows around his face shifted. A furrowed brow hinting at confusion flashed across his features. There, then gone beneath the twisting darkness. "I'll consider your proposition."

My magic relaxed. It was something. It was tentative. It was hope.

He cocked his head to the side. The silence between us grew heavy. "You do know, Ruin of the Scourge, that we are not the ones bringing Glint into Haluma. Your own king is responsible for that. It was he who opened the veil that's darkening your realm."

I scoffed. He stood disgustingly self-assured. The ice dagger crackled with frost as I twirled it. Did he think I was stupid? Whatever darkness he perceived was directly related to the devastation wrought by his army of thieves.

"How uninspiring that the ruthless General would imply the King's wrongdoing. I would have expected more from you. It is well-known that your following introduced Glint to destroy our people. Confident accusations don't change facts." The temperature around us dropped as the ice at my feet spread. My agitation made manifest.

He shook his head as though disappointed.

A twisting splinter of doubt dug into my mind. Questionable thoughts like these threatened the strength of our realm. I wouldn't let the vile general get under my skin. If anything, this made me more determined to become a dreki. Loyalty mattered. I shifted on my feet.

"My offer still stands." I twirled my dagger. The weight of his stare lay heavy on me.

His rings flared amidst the darkness. "Like I said, I'll consider it."

"What's your name?" I had to know. The swirling shadows felt familiar. I clenched my fingers to stifle a ribbon of water that sought to touch them.

"You haven't earned that yet. The General will suffice." He backed up, our conversation apparently over.

"Wait. How will I find you?" I gritted my teeth, hating what the question revealed.

Though his eyes remained hidden inside his hood, I could feel his intense focus on me. "You won't. I'll find you." He retreated further. The black swirl of a portal hovered behind his tall frame. In a blink, he walked through it and disappeared.

I stood motionless in the empty wood. The weight of my scheming settled in my chest. If Maelic or King Nolan found out what I just did, it would be viewed as a betrayal. I knew the king, though. I'd seen the way he cared for the people of Haluma, for me. He would understand my intentions.

Kaida stalked toward me, then nudged my arm. I ran my fingers through her fur, and together, we returned to the cabin.

Delah grinned as I walked through the door. "You're here!" She ran over and hugged me. I allowed my soldier's mask to slip as I relaxed into her embrace. I pushed aside my interaction with the general. The less Delah knew, the safer she would be. I knew I needed to tell her something, though; she would undoubtedly sense my turmoil.

"Maelic wants to send me to Yarit for espionage, but isn't entrusting me with rebel targets," I blurted. Her smile faltered.

"Well," she said, feigning optimism, "let's have a meal first and then figure out what to do about it." She gave me a wink and reached for the good cheese along with the grater.

"You're too good to me, Delah." One of my few joys was cheese, particularly aged cheese melted on anything. Tonight, it looked like scalloped potatoes were on the menu. I took the grater out of Delah's hand and began shredding. A gentle silence descended.

"Maelic has me checking out the Glint houses." Delah's hesitant tone gave me pause. "It has been enlightening; he has me testing elixirs on some of the addicts. My next trip is in two days."

I shot her a curious look, then remembered the report I saw on Maelic's desk. "I heard about the explosion at a Glint house in the Oleander district the other day. Be careful visiting those places."

"They don't send me into danger. That's your job." She winked. "Besides, King Nolan says it's important to keep some Glint in circulation because it helps control the population. It keeps the masses contained."

I barked out a laugh. "You're joking. The Good King would never say that. My entire role in the Scourge has centered around eradicating its existence."

Delah studied me, then resumed her focus on the food, shrugging. "I just have an odd feeling about it. Glint's reach continues to grow, and the way it's siphoning magic is getting worse." My eyebrows rose at the admission. "There have also been talks about the Supreme Vestal and his role with Glint," she volunteered.

I paused, straightening to attention, "What have you heard? Surely Glint isn't connected to Vestal Anchors." Vestal Anchors were selected by the king himself, to serve the crown. I shifted uncomfortably at the insinuation of malevolence. It was merely petty palace gossip. Spreading rumors like this could get you killed.

"It's probably nothing."

I chafed at Delah's veiled accusations. If anyone overheard her, she could be imprisoned for crimes against the king.

"Let's go out tomorrow! It's the Twin Moon Festival, when they're supposed to be at their brightest. Just me and you. Let's pretend we're not part of the Order for one night." I barely suppressed my eye roll. "Especially since I'm going to be a Vestal Anchor. It might be one of the last times we get to do this." A flash of sadness skittered across her features.

"Everyone is going to know who I am, Delah." It was a weak response. And we both knew I'd do it, especially in light of her recent recruitment. The block of cheese was shrinking and I adjusted my fingers to avoid slicing them on the small blades.

"They won't if you don't flaunt your weapons. And you wear *normal* clothes. Like a dress."

I glanced down at my leathers. "What's wrong with these?" Now it was Delah's turn to suppress an eye roll. I gave her a good-natured pinch to her arm, and we continued making our meal.

Delah worried her lip, her whole countenance heavy with concern. "You'll figure this out, then return just like you have after every other mission. And you're going to spoil the potatoes if you grate much more of that hard rind." She reached for the cheese and the grater, setting them on the counter.

"Something feels different about this, Delah." I stared out the window, wondering about the general. "Maelic said this mission needed a dreki on it. It's what they trained me to become. I want to do it, I really do." I sighed. "Dreki power could protect me. Could protect us both, maybe even give me the life I've craved. Perhaps I wouldn't care once I turned dreki."

But that didn't sit right either. I railed against the idea of submitting so completely to anything or anyone. Deep down I desired freedom, and a small part of me couldn't reconcile the trade with that tender dream. I shook my head. I had to squelch that down. There was no alternative.

Delah considered me. "Something about it does feel wrong. We don't know what happens to your soul when you make the trade. What if you become more like Wes and Belham? They use their magic to destroy and exploit. What if you turn into that? It's like they're slaves to animalistic appetites. They weren't comforting before the trade, but now they're absolutely terrifying. Do you think you would still desire to protect others?"

She raised a valid point.

"There's a part of you that still fights, Rue. If you're instinct says wait, then wait. The trade is irrevocable." That was true, and it added to the burden of my decision. "I've heard rumors recently among the elixists. Some have been assisting with the newer drekis. They've witnessed oddities among them. Some are having trouble shifting out of their reptilian forms. Some are being consumed by their power."

I hadn't heard of that but would add it to the list of things I would investigate. I knew becoming a dreki meant unlimited power, and the king had never let harm befall his elite. "I truly doubt that is accurate information." Even here, in the privacy of our cabin, voicing anything against the king felt like betrayal.

An emotion I couldn't identify skittered across her face. "If you're ever in trouble, there's a man named Evander in the north. He's a mercenary with unique gifts. We worked together on elixirs a few years back. He always told me to whisper his name in the winds if I needed anything."

"That's... a weird way to communicate with someone." Her insistence seemed a bit overdone. I laughed uneasily, batting the concern in her voice away. "Let's talk about something else. We have tonight and we have cheese. What could be better?" I diverted.

We ate our dinner in amicable silence, intermittently giggling at some inane thing Delah would spout out. The fire began to die down and Delah prepared for sleep. My evening, however, was just getting started.

I PULLED on my nice leathers, the ones that felt like butter across my skin, allowing me to move silently among the shadows. I filled the sheaths that sat on my waist and lined my thighs with freshly sharpened blades. I had a small job to take care of before I retired for the evening, but one could never be too prepared.

One of the ways I tried to stay true to myself, clutching at the last vestiges of the soul my upbringing had systematically shredded, was by enacting my own brand of vigilante justice. A small way I burned back the darkness.

Brushing my hair back, I twisted it into intricate braids. I paused at my reflection in the tarnished mirror, noticing how my lips' heart shape was identical to my late mother's, my purple-blue eyes just like my dead father's. The shimmer of lilac in my hair reminded me that I needed to put a coracite mask on it immediately; it was too much of a beacon of identification.

I never learned why I was born with hair the shade of the lilac-blush petals of the Lunar Peony. Along with my mother's persistent repetition to stay soft, clever, and alert, she drilled it into me that I could never reveal my natural hair. She taught me to use a common mineral, coracite, to bleach out the color. Not even my father was privy to my congenital anomaly.

I'd take care of that tomorrow morning. Tonight, I was violence.

I quietly opened our front door. Grabbing my faithful mare, I led her out into the night, clomping my way toward the city of Maripol.

I tethered the chestnut horse to a tree that allowed her room to graze, my eyes set on the Oleander Quarter.

The streets were mostly quiet tonight. Clouds obscured the twin moons, offering more darkness than light. The sounds of sin drifted by on the wind as it threaded through open windows.

I waited outside the Kitten Market, a brothel tucked away from the main streets. Its seclusion attracted wealthier clients who desired discretion along with their misdeeds. I'd tracked this particular man for a few weeks after learning about him during one of my previous missions, keeping him on my radar.

He favored a worker that he visited faithfully each Thursday, arriving between ten and eleven in the evening. He predictably departed sometime after midnight. I was willing to wait all night for this one, though.

As I was slinking around the realm, gathering intel for Maelic, I inevitably bumped up against many unsavory individuals in this city. This guy at the Kitten Market, Tavis, was busy collecting little girls. I didn't know where they were sent, but I would happily rid the world of his putrid soul. Tonight, all my planning will pay off.

I checked my watch, realizing I had at least another thirty minutes.

I paused as two men leaned on each other, stumbling toward the same puddle, adding their own vile piss to it. I blew out some air, averting my eyes. The hilt of my dagger crackled with frost.

My skin prickled with the unnerving awareness I was being watched. I searched the shadows. The darkness served as both a haven and a threat. I wouldn't discover the intrusive observer from my vantage point. Shadows, like smoke, swirled in the alley. Ice chips collected at my fingertips.

Nolan's shadows always seemed sharp and cold. These shadows twined languidly, without precision. Had the general returned so soon? I narrowed my eyes to peer into the depths of the darkened corridors around me, willing my eyes to water and reveal the aura behind the shadows.

Just then, the door to the brothel opened, stealing my attention, and Tavis emerged. I strode with predatory stealth, following him in the shadows as he left the building. I barely felt much these days, neither high nor low, but the thrill of ridding the world from even one heinous predator who lured children soothed some broken part of me. Perhaps I had turned into the monster I needed when I was a little girl.

He turned down another road, making his way back toward the nicer part of the city, away from the stench and grime that characterized this quarter. A subtle sparkle of gold wafted around him, the sure-sign of Glint. If he had taken enough of it, it would hamper any magic he might be able to use against me. He might even be hallucinating. I could only hope to add to his nightmare.

I flicked my finger, summoning the fog. It roiled and built, merging with the shadows, coalescing into a blinding wall. The man stopped, confused at how his environment had shifted so quickly. I gripped my dagger, positioning it at the perfect angle as I rushed the man. I grabbed him from behind and swiped it cleanly across his throat. He jolted, then staggered several steps. The sound of gurgling blood and breath echoed against the sleepy stone walls. His body crumpled against the cobblestones.

His eyes grew wide with terror as his heart rate slowed. He

wildly searched for his assailant. I bent over him, wiping the blood from my dagger off on his fancy cloak.

"Children are not a commodity," I whispered. Ragged breaths and twitching limbs were his only response.

I stood, twirling my dagger several times before sheathing it. I stepped over his body, humming as I stalked through the night back toward my horse, my home. As the fog convulsed with my steps, the trace scent of amber and leather drifted into my awareness.

I swear the shadows moved with me.

CHAPTER NINE
THE GENERAL

I hit the ground running before the portal behind me sealed shut. I had stumbled upon Ruin on my way out, and the way she stalked through the city piqued my interest. I had wasted enough time watching her, though. My shadows surged forward, clearing a path through the streets of Aphellion. The sound of my boots pounding the earth fell in time with my racing heart. I sprinted toward the bleached limestone that made up the healing quarter, intent on speaking with Ilayah.

I stopped short at the door, gathering myself. Finn's somber face met me at its entrance; what hope I clung to slowly disintegrated. With a fortifying breath, I stepped into the warded room. Soothing lavender and the sharpness of healing tonics permeated the air.

Xuri held her mother's hand, her dark eyes rimmed in red. She shook her head when she saw the question in my eyes, the woven beads in her hair clinking with the movement.

Everyone, save Xuri, shuffled out of the room, offering us privacy. Ilayah had taken me in when Xuri found me as an infant in the Perellian Forest. She had acted as my own mother in all the ways that counted. My shoulders slumped as I again beheld her withered body.

"They drained her of almost all of her magic. There's nothing we can do except help her transition peacefully into death. She briefly became conscious, but delirium overtook her—the side effect of a deeply depleted oracle." Xuri spoke calmly, softly. A tear followed the path of its predecessors down her cheek.

I took hold of Ilayah's other hand. I remembered when my own fingers used to fit snugly in her palm. Now my hand engulfed hers as I gently held it, the bones of her hand both sharp and frail. Her dark-brown skin, once glowing and soft like Xuri's, was now ashen and crepey from her immense dehydration.

She was our Prime Oracle. Had she known her end? Had she seen what would happen when she crossed that portal months ago? What was worth this outcome?

I knew these were questions borne of desperation and stark grief. Unanswerable. A way to channel a sense of control. But there was none. Only fuel for my anger. Another light snuffed by Nolan's darkness.

Ilayah's brow scrunched in discomfort as her body began to seize. The withdrawal symptoms from the amount of Glint in her blood were already beginning.

I called for Sieren, the Prime Healer, who rushed back into the room. She released her magic upon Ilayah, whose body fought against the calming force. A few stray twitches worked their way to the surface, but her physical agitation abated, her twisted features eventually relaxing.

After a few minutes, Sieren addressed us. "Her heart is failing. It won't be long before she passes. Now is the time to say your final good-byes."

Xuri stood and exited with Sieren, leaving me alone with the woman who helped raise me. It wasn't supposed to end like this. I clenched my jaw.

"I'm sorry I didn't get to you sooner." My voice cracked. I tried again. "Thank you for your dedication to me and Aphellion. You will be so deeply missed." I sighed. A young part within me broke, even as my eyes remained dry.

Her seizure had mussed her black hair, some strands lying haphazardly across her face. I swiped them aside, my finger grazing her forehead. At my touch, a vision erupted.

I no longer stood in the healer's room. Dread and inky midnight blanketed my sight. Streaks of blush pink pierced through the cold bleakness. A soft voice wafted through the vision.

"There is one you're tasked to find. Scales will fall and release the blind. When darkness wins and day recedes, peace will bloom and hope will bleed."

I blinked, returning to myself. My sight refocused on Ilayah, still silent and shallowly breathing in her bed. The voice and vision imprinted heavy in my mind, stealing my focus. What I saw meant little, as most visions do—flashes of color and strange words. I would write down the phrases when I returned to my study.

I leaned closer, whispering over her. "Thank you, Ilayah. Be at peace." I softly touched her hand one final time, then summoned Xuri. I squeezed her shoulder as she passed before leaving her to her final good-byes.

Finn walked in step with me as I left the healer's space. "I'll return to Maripol with you tonight for the festival. We will continue connecting our spies with Haluma's defectors. The veil deepens."

Finn nodded.

I raked my hands through my hair in agitation. "He will not win." Shadows seeped out of my knuckles. I would sooner lose my own life than allow the king to prevail. My steps grew leaden at Finn's leaked gravity magic. He tucked it away before I became anchored to the stone beneath my feet. The impact of our raw grief finding what small outlets it could.

"Sorry," he mumbled. I waved my hand in his direction as he peeled off to summon our troops and relay information. We were all on edge. Losing Ilayah was a tremendous loss, affecting us all.

The walk to the other side of Aphellion offered a moment for me to collect my thoughts from the last several hours. In the privacy of my home, I collapsed on the sofa. The reality that we had succeeded in getting Ilayah back, only to have her succumb to the horrific effects of Glint, settled heavy on me.

I never had dealt well with loss. The metal around my home writhed and vibrated. My rings melted down, forming lethal arrows that I impaled the nearby wall with. Grief slammed against the anger within me. I shook with the collision. I would give myself this rare moment. I could not afford to succumb fully to my grief. Evil didn't sleep, so I wouldn't either. The wave of emotions eventually, slowly, receded.

I called the arrows back to myself, reforming them into the rings around my fingers. Stalking up the stairs, I headed toward my study. Stacks of blank paper cluttered my desk. I pulled off a sheet from the top and wrote out the words melodically sung in my mind during my final vision from Ilayah.

I tacked the paper on my wall next to other sketches and maps, the words tumbling around as I sought to understand them. Like most prophetic visions, only time would reveal the truth of the words. But decoding them served as a persistent, if fruitless, pastime of mine, ever since I was young. Ilayah's voice rose in my memory, chiding me for forcing meaning onto things that would not be cajoled into revelation until its proper time.

I glanced around my office. Boxes of charcoal and containers of ink pens lay stacked on a shelf. Detailed maps of Lyrae,

Maripol, and other secretive places around the realms decorated the walls. I had the urge to draw something, any means to release some of the pain I carried, but time was not on my side to begin such an endeavor.

Drawing had always come naturally to me. It was not well-known that the Liberation's leader had a talent for art and cartography, and I intended to keep it that way. Commissions came from all over for my accurate renditions, including from King Nolan himself. I was more than happy to provide him with modified versions of the realm of Yarit, where the Liberation's location lay right under his nose.

Any way I could sabotage his efforts were thoroughly exploited. Shadows twined out of my knuckles, their sinuous movements matching the beat of my heart. Grief glazed my focus as I stared at the hypnotic movements of the shadows.

A bell chimed in the distance. The collection of long and short tones rang from one side of Aphellion to the other, signaling a death of one of our own. I gazed out the window toward the Auren Mountains. It was over. At least she was now at peace.

I sighed, my moment of reprieve melting away. Duty took precedence as I grabbed my ceremonial sword and quickly descended the stairs, making my way to the public annex. With Ilayah's death, Xuri would ascend to take the Prime Oracle's position. It would take place before her mother's body would have the chance to turn cold. Ilayah's death ceremony wouldn't occur for another several days.

A crowd had already gathered before a makeshift platform, with streams of people continuing to join from around Aphellion. This same platform had been erected under the same gnarled oak for my own ascension to Liberation leader when I had come of age. This ceremony would be significantly more somber. Death bells didn't happen often, but when they did, we came together as a community, dropping everything to lend silent solidarity to those most affected.

Xuri stood readied on the platform, confident and regal despite her loss. The crowd parted at my approach, all taking a knee or the soldier's sign of respect. Women gripped their children, affording me a wide berth.

At the chime of any death bells, soldiers would be released throughout Aphellion to spread the news, and gather our people. We would hold the weight of loss with the hope for our future in delicate balance. I nodded at Xuri, who briefly shut her eyes, inhaled, and offered a bow of deference.

The crowd hushed as I stepped forward. "We have lost Ilayah Prorociste, our beloved Prime Oracle. She served the Liberation and aided the realms at large with valor and virtue. We mourn her death."

Silence followed my pronouncement. All heads bowed at my words. I hit my chest with my fist in the soldier's sign of respect. Thumps resounded among the crowd. I turned toward Xuri.

"Xuri Prorociste." She knelt before me, her box braids draping across her face. A single tear trailed down her cheek. I took a deep breath. "You have been trained your whole life to assume this role. Though it has arrived sooner than any of us expected, you are fully qualified and completely entrusted with carrying the torch of the Prime Oracle. May your mouth only speak truth. May your heart only know hope. May your courage never lack no matter the visions you receive. Now, rise."

All eyes focused on Xuri. Xuri's gaze trained on mine. "My sister and comrade-in-arms." I lifted the ceremonial blade and released my magic. Thin tendrils of metal braided and curled into a semi-enclosure around Xuri, a metallic alcove of living vines, growing upward toward the oak tree's canopy. The enclosure was a symbol of protection and a visual of a gilded anointing. A child clapped.

"Do you willingly take hold of the position and task before you?"

"I accept the responsibility of the Prime Oracle. From now until my death." She held her hands out in acceptance and supplication to the people she now served, and the gods that granted her this ascended power.

I opened my palm revealing a nugget of gold. It melted down into thousands of fine strands that laced around her forearms in glittering, decorative vambraces.

Xuri watched, her arms outstretched. She spoke low out of the side of her mouth, "A bit gaudy, don't you think?"

"It's ceremonial. And you're welcome." A ribbon of gold pinched her skin. She glared up at me, a ghost of a smile flashing.

Addressing the crowd again, I bellowed, "I present to you Prime Oracle Xuri, the Liberation's source of wise counsel and our wellspring of prophetic predictions. Lead us well." I stepped back, giving Xuri prominence.

The crowd applauded with optimism and certitude. My time to mourn Ilayah would have to wait. The day was closing and a Haluman festival awaited.

CHAPTER TEN
THE SPY

The sun had reached its zenith and was well on its descent by the time I staggered to the bathroom to wash my face. A few sprays of blood from last night's foray dotted my cheek. The coolness of the water awakened my sluggish mind and perked up the magic in my veins.

Purple-blue eyes reflected back at me. Were they always this hollow? The sight of my pale-pink strands had me pulling out the container of coracite rock. I crushed it into a fine powder, then added a few drops of water. In moments, the thick paste coated the strands of my waist-length hair. Its effects muted out any other pigment and will render my hair a lustrous white, similar to many in the realm.

My mother instilled in me the importance of hiding my hair's true color. I didn't know the why, but I remembered her unwavering fear. I promised her I would never reveal it to anyone—even the king. I had made that promise shortly before her death. After washing the paste out, I secured my three braids behind my right ear and two behind my left. Since we were going out, I made them much thinner than normal in case Delah decided to do something crazy with my hair. Hardly noticeable, I tugged on them the way my mother used to, a habit I had no intention of breaking.

I startled when my bedroom door flew open. Delah had an extra shimmy to her steps as she burst into my room, getting herself ready and fussing over me. "Wear one of my dresses. The blue one! It'll make your eyes pop." Then she scurried away.

I chuckled to myself. We used to go out and flirt and dance until we could barely stand. The more I advanced in my training, the more I realized these events would have to be forgotten. Connections led to cracks in my armor. They opened me up to vulnerabilities.

I grabbed dark kohl and a thin brush, drawing a vicious cat-eye. Delah was right; blue would complement the gold flecks in them. Delah rounded the corner, bustling back into my room. Wearing a lime-green slip of a dress, she presented my blue outfit with a barely restrained giggle. I eyed it dubiously. The last time I wore it, I wasn't quite as filled out. My eyebrow arched as Delah thrust it into my arms.

"If it's a few inches shorter because your chest decided to outgrow mine, then that's your 'problem.' " She made air quotes and rolled her eyes playfully. I pulled it on with a groan. It was definitely a few inches shorter. I'd be yanking on it all night. It was tighter on my hips, and the halter style highlighted my toned arms. The material rippled and shimmered, like the water I so easily controlled.

Delah curled my hair into soft waves. After fluffing her own curls, she gave me a once-over, smiling in approval. I finished putting some color on my lips and took her arm in mine. Her lime-green dress glittered as we headed toward the front of the house.

"Let's do this."

Walking through the city at night left me equally elated and unsettled. I loved the meandering cobblestone streets, the sounds of laughter, and bustle of life. It reminded me of what I fought for. Why I sleuthed and killed and tortured. To protect this—families and communities.

I fought for the mother I'd lost.

King Nolan did his best to provide for the city's orphans, for me, and I was deeply grateful. In the immediate aftermath of my home burning down, because of the king, I always had a roof over my head and plenty of food. He built the orphanages that housed and protected all the children who lost parents to Glint. He provided free electricity and access to clean water.

Unease followed when I inevitably witnessed the golden shimmer of Glint on moaning bodies slumped in alleyways. There was a veil of darkness in Maripol that felt like a disease, a wet tarp weighing down the city's energy. The residual result of the rebellion's work.

Rage boiled every time another child was orphaned from an overzealous addict. Frustration gnawed at me when it seemed that all my efforts to dismantle Glint's power were a waste. I couldn't give up on the innocents, though. I was once like them.

I pushed my thoughts aside, intent on enjoying this time with Delah.

The bass emanating from the festival could be felt in every one of my organs as a circle of trees and stone came into view. The sound wielder behind the music must have had a powerful skillset for amplification. Delah's eyes lit in excitement as we entered. Ice sculptures in the shape of various animals presided over the crowd atop silver pedestals. My lip curled at the sight of the carved-ice drake. It reminded me of the dreki when they shape-shifted—all scales and claws. I looked away.

Aerial dancers hung from vines dropping down from the trees' canopy. Light orbs floated around them, their dim light pulsing. The walls of the festival consisted of ancient, twisted trees tangled together in an orgy of limbs. Swaying leaves created a strobing effect as the light from the two moons scattered downward, invoking a mesmerizing atmosphere.

Servers floated between crowds of people, various drinks in tow. Smoke wafted from the top of several glasses. I grabbed a purple mixture with a floating candied iris and a honey-colored libation with a twist of lemon for Delah.

She accepted her drink with a dazzling smile, and we *clinked* our glasses together. She took a big gulp, while I slowly sipped mine. I rolled my shoulders, shoving my discomfort aside. This wasn't my scene, but I was determined to have fun for Delah.

I surveyed the space, the people moving in stop-motion from the erratic lights while I continued forcing the tension and vigilance from my rigid body—old habits die hard. I downed the rest of my drink and allowed the alcohol to lull my nerves.

Delah, ever the optimist, snagged my wrist and pulled me into the mass of bodies that clogged the dance area. The tangy smell of Glint engulfed me like fog in the vale.

"Delah!" A feminine voice carried through the din. Delah turned and embraced the woman.

"Rue, this is Jazmina, a fellow elixist I work with." I nodded and smiled a greeting. Delah turned toward Jazmina, chatting. Their laughter rang in the air at some shared inside joke. I glanced away from their friendly banter. Delah deserved to experience the freedom and joy of friendships and thrilling nights out. It was for this very thing that I had fought in the Scourge.

I turned just as two unnaturally attractive, and very muscular, men sauntered over. Delah paused her conversation.

"Care to dance?" the blonde one asked Delah. She grabbed his hand as a devious smile formed. She repositioned herself toward her willing partner. He wore his long hair in a top knot, the sides shaved, like some god of the north. Just Delah's type. I kept her in my sights as they got acquainted with each other.

The darker man hovered near me. "You probably want to dance with that one." I gestured toward Jazmina.

"Actually, I would like to dance with you." He extended his hand.

I eyed him. Why not?

The scent of leather and amber tugged on the edges of my mind as I drew closer to him. I reflexively inhaled it. Darkness swirled around him as the moonlight flickered. His shadows blended seamlessly with the night around him to the casual observer. But I had experience with sentient darkness. Awareness shot through me. This was the general. Though he hid behind his shadows previously, did he think I wouldn't recognize him? Or did he just not care?

He lowered his face to speak into my ear. "You don't seem like the type to frequent these events." I suppressed a shiver. A little flirting wouldn't hurt my chances at gleaning some information from him. Two could play this game.

I peered upward, trying to assess his face. His eyes flared briefly, but the shadows obscured a clear view. "This isn't my scene. I'm here for my friend. And I could say the same for you. This doesn't seem like your idea of a good time." I arched my brow.

He shrugged one shoulder. "I told you I'd find you."

I narrowed my eyes at him before he sent me into a spin. I caught glimpses of bodies unfolding off of the thick vines dangling above us, arms extended in the air around me, in time to the beat of drums, and couples twirling in hypnotic motion.

He pulled me back into his body, moving with sensuous grace. My own body awakened. The revelry and my previous purple drink loosened my inhibitions. I felt like a flower leaning toward the sun, willing to be scorched by the heat of the temptation in front of me. I could set aside my hatred if it meant I got him talking.

It had been years since I allowed myself to indulge with a man. None had come close to the caliber of what stood before me. The heartless general. No one was more off-limits. No one I hated more.

I wondered how far I could push him.

His large hand skimmed down my arms, landing in the dip of my waist. He firmly commanded my body as we moved in time with the music. His touch seared my skin through the thin fabric of my dress, and I wondered if he had this effect on all the women he danced with. His forearms flexed as his hand devoured my waistline.

I casually draped my arms around his neck, playing with his cropped dark hair. He kept it short on the sides and longer on top. A few strands tried to fall across his forehead, begging for my correction. Dark, silvery runes cast a light shimmer from his jaw down below his collar. I blinked at the inscriptions, but they disappeared. I'd never seen a tattoo like that.

"Brazen of you to waltz into Maripol without a weapon," I ventured.

"Seemed pointless when I am one."

I scoffed. He might have been right, but I wouldn't let him know that. Rule number one when dealing with handsome men: never let them believe you find them attractive.

"Your confidence far exceeds your demonstrated performance." I smiled sweetly. "I could kill you right here." My affinity lanced into the hand at my waist—a blade of burning ice I made sure would sting, but not quite draw blood.

Shadows snaked around my throat, warm and velvety, subtly tightening. He leaned forward again, not even remotely affected by my threat. "Then do it." He pulled me closer, pressing my ice blade further into himself.

I released my hold on my affinity. I didn't want to get blood on Delah's dress.

"Have you investigated my claims that your king provides his citizens with poison?" The low rumble of his tone in my ear stirred my core, despite the treasonous words he spoke.

The neckline of my halter inched downward as my chest brushed against his own. "And why would that be true when my primary directives are to destroy Glint traffickers and find the source of its supply? What a waste of an elite soldier like myself if it hinged on a lie." I dragged my fingers along his neck and down his chest. Gods, he was huge. A muscle feathered in his jaw and his breathing tensed. Good. I affected him as much as he affected me.

"Illusionists pretending to be leaders know how to create immaculate distractions. Wouldn't you agree?" His eyes glinted.

"Is that not what you are doing in this very moment?" I held his gaze, biting my lower lip. He swallowed, tracking the movement.

The general moved me around other couples, ignoring my barb. "Perhaps you should ask yourself what might be in it for him. Or why he seems to collect orphans." My eyes narrowed. He knew who I was and probably knew my background. Now that I'd seen his face, I would be able to track him better and learn more about where he came from and what he was after.

"Seeking the low hanging fruit, are we? Hoping for a reaction? You have the confidence of a much taller man." He quirked a brow before a laugh burst out of him. The genuineness of his amusement transformed his face. I almost got a glimpse of the man beneath the bravado. To be fair, he was absurdly tall, but I'd hoped to knock him down a peg. His thumb traced circles at my hip, my body all too aware of his hands on me. He was relentless.

I pressed myself against him, restraining the urge to shut my eyes and just *feel*. "I didn't come out to discuss potential duplicity. Tell me, General, how does the Crimson Wolf divert our Berine shipments?"

One of his hands snaked from my waist around to my lower back, the other crept behind my head, tilting it upward. His fingers slid along my scalp, tugging at my hair. He leaned down, aligning his face toward my own. I held my breath, nearly forgetting my question.

I waited to see if those lips felt as warm and soft as they appeared. Would he crush me with them? I wouldn't mind if he did. My entire body hovered in reckless anticipation.

He tantalizingly grazed my mouth, teasing me with cruel lips. "The Crimson Wolf is a myth." He straightened up, releasing me from his thrall.

The loss of his touch almost made me whimper. Almost. Ruin, the spy, observed his every minute movement.

He hadn't been truthful.

I licked my lips, disappointed in more ways than one. I knew the Crimson Wolf was part of his rebellion. If he didn't want to acknowledge him, I'd try a different route. "Then why are *you* interfering with our Berine? You're harming innocent citizens of Haluma, General."

His gaze lingered on my lips. "Keep digging, Ruin of the Scourge. I have no doubt they trained you well. I'm just not sure they're pointing you in the right direction. And you can call me Judd." He had the audacity to wink at me.

I pushed him away at that. I'd had enough of his insinuations against the Good King. I cringed inwardly. I had just flirted with the general. The *rebel* general.

Resolve for my loyalty to King Nolan surged within me. Judd was right. I had been trained thoroughly in espionage. And I would use that skill to uncover what the rebellion was up to.

Somehow, I had blocked out the crowd around us. All my awareness had focused on him. The spell between us broke. The floating orbs pulsed brighter, and the mass of people flooded my senses.

A tray of waters lay nearby. I grabbed one and downed its contents in an effort to clear my head. I gripped the empty glass as my eyes locked with Judd, momentarily arrested. An indolent smirk spread across his bold features.

Something about him nagged at me. Besides Nolan, there was only one person in all the realms I knew of who had shadows. But he said his name was Judd. A hope I hadn't foreseen fell dashed before I could acknowledge it. I shouldn't have been disappointed.

I couldn't break my stare.

He leaned closer, his breath ghosting my cheeks. "Go ahead and look your fill, but trust me, anything more will only end in heartbreak." Shadows pulsed around his shoulders. I peered closer, searching beyond his arrogant warning. His eyes glowed as his pupils widened. He scanned my face with a mixture of desire and... anger?

His muscular arms dropped to his side as he studied me like a rare gemstone. He took a step closer, and though it was wrong, I welcomed it.

A sharp laugh from nearby punctured the moment, deflating it. I sat the glass down. The movement caught Judd's attention and he stared at the glass, his body stilling. I vaguely noted alarm filling his features. I wasn't going to get much more out of him. I increasingly felt the waters of our conversation rising, becoming more dangerous as we continued. Perhaps I should shut this down before I allowed something traitorous to happen. His allure would sweep me out like a riptide. I had to end this.

I searched for Delah.

Where was the woman in the lime-green dress?

Finally, I spotted her. Her mysterious companion stood an inch from her face. One hand rested on her backside and the other gently stroked her arm. I watched as she blinked coyly. He leaned forward and they began kissing—no, devouring each other.

I walked over, swerving through the crowds. "I'm heading out, Delah."

She shifted toward me, breaking her lip-locked connection, a dazed look on her face. "Already?"

"You aren't leaving now, are you?" Delah's partner asked her, his face showing a hint of amusement. He stood as tall and muscular as Judd, though blond where Judd was dark and stormy.

Judd appeared at my side. "You good, Finn?" His blonde friend nodded as he subtly pulled Delah closer to himself.

A wave of dizziness swept over me as I shifted on my feet. "I'm sorry, Delah. I'll meet you at home. You have fun." I paused, forcing a smile, "But not too much."

"I should come with you—" she started.

"No." I cut her off, taking hold of her hand. "Your friend Jazmina is around here somewhere and you two can look out for each other. I'll be happy knowing you're having a good time." I discreetly pointed out the security I had scoped out when we first entered the festival. "You know I'll just hover anyway." She squeezed my hand before letting it go.

Delah lingered a moment, while her companion, Finn, stood awkwardly behind her.

"I'll be a couple of hours at most."

I nodded, then turned and exited, leaving Delah, and the general, behind.

My vision blurred as I walked back toward the Rivellan Wood, the chaos of the festival receding behind me. My senses distorted. Stumbling, I leaned against a building. A tremor wracked through my body. Something was very wrong. I stared down at my hands, and there it was. Golden shimmer dusted my fingertips. My stomach dropped.

Dizziness crested. Shadows and light curled in threatening shapes around me. Crouching, I shoved my finger down my throat. My movements were sloppy. It was too late to throw it up anyway. Golden poison coursed through my system. I would have to let it run its course.

Fear crawled up my throat. I slumped, helpless to the intoxication of Glint. I could feel my magic separating from my blood, like I was being unmade with acid and fire.

My skin prickled as my body registered the presence of someone. I tried to speak, but my lips wouldn't move. Warm arms scooped me up, cradling me. My mind screamed. My body was no longer my own. A whimper escaped me.

"Shh. It's okay. You're safe now. The water cup. When you sat it down, I saw traces of Glint on the rim." Damn. Perhaps King Nolan's weird obsession with the soldier's water supplies was warranted. "I'll take you home."

Wind rustled across my face as I faintly registered our movement. My magic leaked out of me. Was I hallucinating? His lush smell surrounded me. It blunted the sharpness of my alarm. I dully wondered if he would try to kill me. Why would he help the king's spy?

I blacked out.

∼

A DOOR CREAKED. Familiar smells greeted me. My head lolled. Gentle hands laid me on something soft.

"You must drink this. It will help flush it from your system." Gods, that voice could tame a wolvin. Something cold and hard met my lips. A strong hand splayed at the base of my skull, tilting my head back.

"Try to swallow. Please." I wished I could open my eyes. I sputtered as liquid filled my mouth. I involuntarily swallowed. A trickle of it ran down my chin. A warm thumb wiped away the remnants. It lingered on my bottom lip. This must be a dream.

Silence blanketed the room. My tremors lessened. Lethargy and fatigue overwhelmed me. On the brink of unconsciousness, a whisper penetrated the fog. "I'll be in touch, Ruin of the Scourge."

CHAPTER ELEVEN
THE SPY

A raging case of dry mouth interrupted my slumber. Afternoon light slashed across my bed, where I lay haphazardly in the tiny dress from the night prior. My head throbbed, but I was lucid. Confusion laced through the holes in my memory. I sat up, expecting a wave of dizziness that never came.

My canteen lay on my nightstand. I didn't recall leaving it there. I gulped down the water inside it. Who brought me home? Could it have really been the general? I was lucky to have made it back safely. My hand shook as I set the canteen back down. Last night could have been so bad. I knew deep down that it was Judd who saved me. I didn't trust him, but I sat confounded, my foot tapping erratically on the floorboards.

The general had shadow magic, just like the king. It was a magic the king claimed only he possessed. Yet, in a secret part of me, lined with the fumes of betrayal toward King Nolan, I knew this was untrue.

The memory of Dom came easily. The last time I saw him, he'd promised me he'd return. After all this time, it was still an unhealed wound reeking of abandonment and the hollowness of hurt. I shoved it aside. There had to be a connection between Judd and Dom. I would figure it out.

My fingers still shimmered with Glint's residue. I ripped moisture out of the air and coated my hands, then wiped them thoroughly on my dress. The threat and effects of it ignited my rage. A singular purpose crystallized in my mind. I wanted to destroy every last person who spread the vile poison. I wanted to avenge my mother—the victim of a Glint addict. I wanted to protect the unprotected. And if I allowed myself to pause and truly look inward, perhaps I just wanted to protect myself, the little girl the world tried to break.

I hopped up, pacing my room. I would accompany Delah on her mission to the Glint house this evening. I walked over to my bedside, dug into the glass bowl full of hard candies, and popped a cherry candy in my mouth, focusing on its sweetness. A soul-deep sigh escaped. My exhaustion reached well beyond the physical.

As the candy dissolved in my mouth, my decision honed into a blade. King Nolan would not deny me the option to make the trade when the evidence of my loyalty and commitment to the innocents lay bare before him. I would do it with the blood and information of our enemies. I would carve my own way. And it would start tonight.

I THREW a quick dinner together before I shared my plan with Delah.

"You want to come with me to a Glint house?" Delah gaped at me, her fork hovering halfway to her mouth.

I grinned smugly in response.

"Don't be surprised if things are different from what you've heard. I think you accompanying me is long overdue. But, Rue, I'm supposed to be in and out, simply obtaining some of the

Glint being passed around so we can examine it and figure out how they are changing it. The plan doesn't include daggers."

"But you're bringing knives!" I gesticulated with my empty fork. I knew I was riling her, and I suppressed my amusement.

"I'll have them as backup, which I've never needed before." She set her own fork down, daring me to push back.

"I will lead with words first, okay? I won't bring them out unless there's a threat." I quirked my eyebrow and smiled. I feigned an innocence not even a child could be fooled into believing was real.

Delah groaned, and I knew I'd won.

"This'll be fun," I cajoled. "Besides, we haven't done a hit in the city since before the military officials caught two thieving orphans. It'll be like old times."

"You are so annoying sometimes. I hope I don't regret this." Delah sighed in defeat, even as a small grin quirked the side of her mouth.

THICK FOG HUDDLED in the corners of the stone walls we passed. Shadows mingled with the smells of rubbish and damp earth. Delah and I moved as close to the darkness as we could, homing in on a Glint house outside the Oleander district. It felt good to be out in the streets with her, pushing back the darkness in our own way.

Glint was the drug that connected all levels of society. In large quantities, it was hallucinogenic—the quintessential party drug for the wealthy. For the underprivileged, the enticement of numbness and reprieve from squalor was too much. I hated how our city was built in such a way that the line between wealth and poverty had stretched into an insurmountable chasm.

We weaved through the darkened streets, stepping over

puddles and waste that collected in scattered heaps. The few people we encountered kept their faces drawn deep in the hoods of their cloaks, desiring to avoid us as much as we did them. Dim lights illuminated the entryways of crumbling facades. Delah checked her map before pulling me down a side street.

"The house is up ahead. We need to get in, secure the Glint, and then we're out. Got it?" Delah shifted on her feet, antsy.

We kept our hoods up, two reapers in the dark. The deep thrum of music interrupted the stillness of the evening. We approached a nondescript door and pushed it open. Within the dark hall, the stench of mold assaulted my senses. The further we walked into the hovel, the louder the music became. We turned into a large open room, stopping at the entrance.

My eyes widened as I took in the scene. Men and women lay limp and disoriented atop every piece of furniture in the room. A child played in a corner. The saccharine smell of Glint sagged thick in the air. A man turned our way and sauntered over, his pupils dilated. "What brings you ladies here this evening?" he drawled, the golden remnants of Glint sparkling on his shirt as if he'd wiped his hands all over himself.

I let Delah lead as I continued scanning the room.

"We want three tags of Glint," she confidently responded, using the correct slang. The man took his time appraising us. "We have plenty of coin." She pulled out a bag, jingling it in emphasis. The man fixated on it.

"Wait here," he directed, then heavily turned away. A twitch rippled across his torso.

There were moans as people spasmed and attempted to move their lethargic bodies. I walked over to a young woman whose hollow eyes dragged toward me. "My magic," she wheezed. "They took it." She attempted to lift her arm but dropped it promptly, seemingly losing all energy in the process.

My shoulders tensed as my magic pulsed, on high alert.

Something wasn't right here. The fine hairs on my arm prickled with unease. I had observed Glint in action before, but this was something else. "How much did you take?" I asked the woman. She didn't register that she'd heard my question. My eyes met Delah's, whose concerned expression mirrored my own.

The child in the corner paused his nonsensical chatter and peered directly at me. His sharp gaze froze me in place. "Scourge," he whispered. I shook my head in a pleading warning.

"Scourge!" he yelled. He jumped up, pointing, electricity shooting from his open palm. It hit a man on the floor, his back leaning against one of the few chairs. The man's eyes profusely watered as his body seized in response.

Delah backed up, arms raised defensively. I drew water toward myself. Instinct flared my magic to life as I focused on the boy. Darkness enveloped him, and his aura convulsed erratically. He cast another cord of electricity in our direction. My hands shot up a wall of water, hardening it just in time to deflect the bolt.

"Get out of here," I hissed at Delah, shoving her behind me.

The boy cocked his head, a grimace melting his features. "I recognize you, Scourge. What are you doing here? Come to mock the plight of the poor? As if your king has not taken enough? We cope the best we can, and Glint gives us relief. Even if it feeds…" He paused, glancing upward, clenching his mouth shut. "Again, What. Are. You. Doing. Here?"

His face morphed before my eyes into that of the notorious Glint supplier, Thorn, the elusive shape-shifter on my shortlist of marks to dispatch. Our cover blown, I wouldn't get intel out of this excursion like I'd hoped, but perhaps apprehending Thorn would be an even better gift to drop at Maelic's feet.

"No judgment from us, Thorn," I pointedly stated his name. "Just here for a few tags of Glint. After we get them, we'll be on our way."

"I think not." He lunged, sending tentacles of electricity outward. They swarmed around his body in a protective shield. My sword formed, drawing from the dampness in the air, its gleaming blade crystallizing instantly. My daggers, enforced with Berine, would absorb some of his electrical magic. I drew one from my thigh holster with my opposite hand and threw it at his arm. He jolted, snarling as he grabbed his bicep.

The electricity flickered with his back step, and I seized the opening. Manacles of magicked ice formed around his ankles and wrists. I decreased their temperature to well below freezing, burning his exposed flesh. He dropped to his knees.

His electricity guttered. A bubble of water encased his hands as protection against his electrical magic. Should he try to unleash it, it would only serve to electrocute him instead.

I stomped over and grabbed him by the hair. My sword threatened his exposed throat. "Get up." Delah hovered near the exit. I eyed her. "Let's go."

She gawked at me, her eyes darting around the room. "I need those vials. And, Rue, some of these people are dying. We have to do something." The bodies littered around the room exhibited the effects of overused magic. Yet this was not a voluntary draining of their affinity. If Glint siphoned most of their magic, then they would soon stop breathing.

I glared down at Thorn, making sure my affinity securely confined him. "Five minutes. I'll help you get the Glint. There's nothing we can do for these people, though. There is no antidote." I hated that truth.

Delah searched the room for any leftover vials. She found one that was half full, its contents swirling inside. I ran to the back area where our original informant ran off to. The acrid stench of Glint overwhelmed me—a mixture of sugared syrup with the acidic sharpness of vinegar and shattered glass. A sharp headache pierced my skull. I reached for the wall, stabilizing myself. More had to be here somewhere. A glow from under a nearby door caught my attention.

I hastily lunged toward it, pushing the door open without regard for what lay beyond. Several wealthy-looking men hopped to their feet. Tags of Glint tinkled to the floor. I wielded my water into a cyclone. They backed up immediately, giving me an opportunity to grab wayward vials. I stuffed four into the satchel at my waist, bolting back out the door before the cyclone collapsed.

Thorn lay motionless on the floor where I left him. Delah kept cautious watch over him. "I have the vials. We leave. Now." I reached for Thorn.

"Rue!" Delah gasped. "What are you doing? You can't bring him."

"I'll keep him in the stables, and he's thoroughly disarmed." I gave her a wolfish smile as she cast furtive glances around the room.

"Let's get on, then."

We melted into the night, my water affinity pulling the meandering fog into a condensed wave that shoved Thorn forward despite his attempts to disobey.

Under the cover of darkness, we returned to our cabin. I secured Thorn within our stable much like I had with Dag. My adrenaline waned as I walked the short path to my front door. I needed at least a few hours of sleep before tomorrow, when my hunt for the Crimson Wolf begins.

LEATHER, blades, and armor adorned me. I slung my pack over my shoulder. It was dark. Silent. I knew Delah would want to say good-bye. But quiet escapes were sometimes easier than facing unknown futures under the weight of emotional good-byes.

I stuffed a small bag with cherry candies, and a few in my pocket, before leaving my room. Delah had left me a neatly folded note in the kitchen next to a teacup and some leaves. I gently sniffed, noting the strong scent of spearmint amidst dried black tea. I flicked my wrist and the water boiled. I poured it over the leaves, letting them steep. Of course, Delah knew I'd be gone before she arose. We always looked out for each other in our own small ways.

My mind wandered briefly to the fear of not being invited to become a dreki. The pit in my stomach that formed every time I thought of it dissipated as I recounted my plan. I would offer Thorn as a symbol of my allegiance to Haluma. It was my ticket out. The Crimson Wolf, my ticket back in.

After straining the leaves, I snatched Delah's note and stuffed it in my pocket. The door clicked shut behind me.

At the stables, early dust motes floated among the hay. Thorn was right where I'd left him—manacled and surrounded by a bubble of water. I walked over to my horse, pressing my forehead into her neck. I needed her calm to become my own. This had to work.

I nudged Thorn with my boot, and secured a tether from his cuffs to the horse. A sharp whistle had Kaida emerging from the wood. Her bared teeth would keep his legs moving. Taking one last fortifying breath, I shifted my focus forward and swung into the saddle.

Wes was already waiting with Maelic when I arrived at the Keep. They spoke in low tones while servants scurried around affixing packs of food and supplies to Wes's horse. I dismounted my own and walked over.

Maelic turned to me, cocking his head to the side in his reptilian way. I pulled in a breath, gesturing toward my captive. "My loyalty is only for King Nolan and Haluma, and I intend to prove it." I yanked Thorn's tether, bringing him to his knees. "Starting with a parting gift for you." My voice did not waver, but the silence that followed had my insides trembling.

Maelic assessed me. His vertical pupils narrowed on Thorn. A vicious smirk cracked across his face. He motioned with his hand and servants immediately moved to my horse to prepare her for travel. I released a held breath, willing myself to remain stoic.

"You each know your task here." Maelic addressed me and Wes but fixed his gaze solely on me. "As soon as the Crimson Wolf is found, preferably alive, return immediately. And if you come across the General, then by all means, remedy that problem by whatever way you deem necessary." Wes hissed a laugh.

Maelic slithered nearer to me, his power knocking against my own. I painted a bored expression on my face, my body unnaturally still. "I expect you will receive an invitation for the trade when you return, Rue. Perhaps Nolan will make an exception if you fail in this charade you concocted. In which case, you can make the trade or be dismissed." He bared his teeth as if anticipating my refusal. I nodded, not breaking my stance. He eyed me a moment longer, never blinking, then his gaze darted beyond me.

If he was trying to scare me, it was working. Nausea braided with fear. The urge to spin my dagger or pop a cherry candy overwhelmed me, anything to regulate my overwhelming dread. I felt like I was one step away from triggering a trap I couldn't see. I drummed my fingers against my leg.

Cold shadows heralded King Nolan. He arrived in a fitted black shirt that stretched tightly across his chest, his hair slightly windswept from the breeze of his shadows. He wore a velvet cloak with the king's crest embroidered in silver thread. We all knelt in deference.

Nolan's powerful magic pulsed as he beckoned us to stand. A soft smile graced his face. He took a step toward me, his hand extended in a gentle gesture. He traced a line down my jaw with his finger. Taken aback, I couldn't break my gaze nor could I understand this public display. Nolan had never physically engaged with me before. My heart rate ticked up as he slowly drew a trail back upward, his fingers skimming below my ear, leaving a chill in their wake. I flinched at a sharp piercing sensation. Swallowing a gasp, my hand flew up, cupping the side of my neck as I jolted back a step.

"Ah! I apologize. It seems my shadows got away from me." The king dropped his arm and his shadows retreated. He kept his dark gaze trained on me as I sought to recover from the startling zap. "I simply came to bid you all farewell. Good luck in Lyrae. I have no doubt you will find the Crimson Wolf, much like you unearthed the elusive Thorn. I look forward to your return, Ruin." I nodded, feeling dazed and determined. He flashed his charming smile, then faced Thorn.

Thorn glared up at the king. "I've done what you asked—" Nolan silenced him with a flick of his hand. Shadows flew toward Thorn, encircling his face and body. Thorn's eyes and mouth widened. Shadows swallowed the sound of his scream. They rushed into Thorn's gaping mouth, choking him. Agony left him writhing on the ground.

Horror arrested me as I stifled my own scream. Veins, previously invisible beneath Thorn's skin, became raised and black like poisoned tributaries. Boils erupted as he kicked against an invisible force. And then he stilled. The stark contrast of silence descended with an oppressive weight. A powdery black substance dusted the shell of what Thorn once was.

Nolan's eyes were almost wholly black when he fixed his gaze on me. He slowly licked his lips. The urge to gag overwhelmed me. "Haluma fails when loyalty goes unchecked. Do not disappoint me." I kept my face carefully blank. Fear ripped through me, stealing my response.

Maelic sniffed. "Ahh there he is!" He gestured behind me,

breaking through the intensity of the moment. Nolan and I turned toward Belham as he guided his gelding toward us. My brow furrowed, and the small hairs on my neck stood on end. His smile held the deranged slant of a feral wolf. Vertical pupils kept me in their sights.

My mind reeled. I had never seen that side of Nolan before. Judd's words burrowed into me. *"Illusionists pretending to be leaders know how to create immaculate distractions."* The thought ate at me. I shifted on my feet.

I turned back to Belham. I held out hope that I could confirm my loyalties, and perhaps if there was any hesitation, I could sway King Nolan by succeeding in this mission. If my gamble failed, I wouldn't be able to return. They would drain me. My confidence wavered after what I'd just witnessed.

"Is this everything?" I deflected. I shoved my hands in the pocket of my cloak, hiding their tremor. I had my instructions to find the Crimson Wolf. No need to waste any more time. Maelic reminded me of the ornate map of the Yaritian realm he'd previously given me. I had thoroughly studied it, focusing on its capital city, Lyrae, my final destination.

"Everything appears in order." He gestured to Belham, whose presence was both an act of intimidation for me as much as Wes and my ticket out of the realm. He tilted his head in concentration before creating a portal.

I pulled myself onto my saddle, taking a last look at King Nolan. His dark eyes bored into me as his shadows melded with the hem of his dark cloak. Wes mounted his tawny horse and sauntered forward. My last thought was of Delah and my relief at her appointment as a Vestal Anchor as I stepped through the portal.

The familiar portal breeze caressed my skin. Darkness enveloped me. In the next blink, my mare's muscles flexed, a wave of nausea hitting me as we propelled into the realm of Yarit.

CHAPTER TWELVE
THE SPY

We emerged in the Perellian Forest; it's so unlike the Rivellan Wood where thin pines yielded thick carpets of layered needles. The trees in Yarit climbed skyward, their thick and gnarled trunks blotting out most of the sun's rays. The scent of sap and swirling leaves suffused the air. Strange bird calls soared from the forest's canopy.

Wes and his horse strolled forward. His unnerving eyes assessed the foreign landscape. Kept in the dark on his goals for this particular mission, I wondered if it aligned with mine, or deviated into something else entirely.

"Have you ever seen someone drained of their magic?" he hissed.

"Not recently." I refused to make eye contact with him, though I could feel his stare groping me. I clutched my reins, ice crusting the leather straps.

"It's mesmerizing. They tie you down, and suppress your magic. Then they inject you with a poison that literally cleaves your affinity from you. Did you know magic has a smell?" He breathed in deeply. Gods, he was horrifying. "It smells like damp moss and sugary syrup. Or that's the smell of the poison," he whispered in my direction.

I glared at him, refusing to respond.

He laughed, licking his lips. "Some people seize, some of them scream. Magic is always tied to blood you know. It's supposed to feel like a fire boiling through you as it rips the magic from your essence. Leaves the veins bloated and rotting." A small moan escaped him, like he yearned to watch another draining.

"Good to know," I deadpanned, attempting to quell this one-sided conversation. My mouth turned dry, lingering dread planting itself in my stomach. I veered my horse away and, gratefully, Wes continued in his own direction until he disappeared into the mystical wood. If I didn't see him again, I might throw a party. I encouraged my horse to speed up, wanting to leave all talk of the draining, and the way Wes seemed erotically stimulated by it, far behind me.

A violent shudder wracked my body as I forced myself to think through bits of information about Yarit, while taking note of the sun as I sought a general trajectory north toward the city of Lyrae. I recalled geographical locations: the coast of the Zephyrus Sea to the east, the Auren Mountains in the west. The Perellian Forest in all its magical finery would extend toward the capital, ceasing at the edge of a meadow. It eventually led to the famed canals slicing through the city of Lyrae.

I made a mental list of tasks necessary for success in this final mission, the weight of it settling on my tense shoulders. I pulled a cherry candy out of my satchel, unwrapping the small treat in hopes to quell my unease.

My musings were interrupted by a low rumbling sound. Searching for the source, I noted trembling leaves below and swaying branches above. The earth shifted beneath us and my horse stumbled, both of us grunting. I jumped off the saddle crouching low to the ground, keeping hold of my horse's reins with one hand while covering my head with the other. A jagged, thunderous sound swelled around me.

Rocks jutted out of the forest floor spewing clouds of clotted dirt. Tree trunks surrendered their sturdy resting places, gliding across the earth to newfound plots. Leaves peppered the ground in an array of colors. The land shuddered once more before ceasing its erratic movements.

I slowly straightened, relinquishing my protective stance. My eyes widened as I surveyed my surroundings. The landscape was... utterly changed. The path I had been riding had disappeared. New trees created a new skyline. Was this what happened in the Rivellan Wood? I had never been present when the earthquakes had actually occurred. Slowly, my disorientation and erratic heartbeat lessened.

The common sounds of the forest resumed: a symphony of rustling leaves, bird calls, and insect chirps. I waited several minutes before continuing to walk alongside my horse. I was hesitant to mount her again in the event another earthquake erupted. I double-checked that all my weapons were secured, patting myself down.

I scanned the area, vigilant to any suspicious movement as I continued my trek through the woods, steadily relaxing with each movement forward.

As the sun lowered in the sky, and I was still no closer to finding my way out of this forest, a whimper broke through the woodland noise, my pulse spiking once more. A soft sniffle raised the hairs on my arms; a muffled cry followed. I deviated from my path, steps cautious, to seek the source of the distress, my instincts kicking in. I paused, listening intently. *Please help me find you.*

Pivoting toward the sound of a snapping twig, I carefully tread on leaves of every color—green, red, purple, yellow, orange, pink. I didn't want to spook whoever was there.

A mop of curly hair interrupted the backdrop of twisting

tree trunks. A young girl sat against a tree, her slender shoulders slumped over, while her tears silently dripped into her skirts. She looked around twelve years old. Several trees appeared to surround her, almost protectively. Ivy grew between the trunks creating a covering over her head, shading her. I stilled, observing the peculiarity.

"Are you okay?" I tentatively ventured. I softened my voice to appear nonthreatening, despite the rows of weapons secured to my waist and thigh.

She jerked her head upright and sank back further against the tree as if to melt into it. Her hands fisted with detritus.

"I won't hurt you. I just want to see if you're alright. I could hear you from over there." I absently gestured to wherever "over there" was, and gingerly stepped forward. She twitched like a sparrow, ready to bolt at the slightest movement. Something about her reminded me of Delah when she was a young girl. Perhaps the resolve in her shoulders, or the way she steeled her face to mask any fear. Really, I never interacted with other young girls, so maybe it was just her age and seeming innocence.

She assessed me as her throat swallowed some of her trepidation. "Who are you?" Her voice was much stronger than I expected.

"My name is Rue. Do you have a parent or a friend nearby? Are you lost?"

"I messed up." Her eyes darted around as she bit her lower lip in worry. Returning her gaze to me, she said, "But I'll be fine, they're almost here."

"Your parents? They are coming?"

"You aren't from Lyrae are you?" Her face morphed into one of perplexed interest. Absently, I noted her aversion to my questions.

Caution laced my response. "I recently arrived in Yarit. Can I help you back to your home?" I didn't exactly have a keen sense of direction myself, but I could protect her as we found our way out of here. Why had she been left alone? I continued scanning the environment for threats.

A rustling in the brush had the hairs on the back of my neck standing. I quickly moved to shield the young girl. I deftly unsheathed my sword, my senses sharpening for a scent, a sound, a movement. My affinity throbbed beneath my skin, awaiting my command.

A shuddering tree lurched toward me. I ducked and swung my sword in the direction of the limbs careening my way. A dryad. A *vicious* dryad. Its limbs sharpened into spears as it barreled in my direction. I leapt out of the way, drawing it away from the young girl.

I needed to distract it. But how could I defeat a nymph? It was incredibly fast, and more agile than I could have anticipated. I quickly sifted through the little knowledge I'd obtained regarding tree nymphs. They often turned angry when someone trespassed in their space. Well, that was obvious, and not currently helpful.

I attempted to bait it, calling it over to me, drawing its undivided attention. A bead of sweat dripped down my spine. Outmatched in speed, I had only my magic and wit as defense.

The tree scowled at me. I cocked my head, realizing it was a male dryad. "If we have trespassed, Dryad, please accept our apologies." Its roots coiled beneath the ground as it sought to encircle me. Its body contorted as a tree-warrior took shape.

Odds are not in your favor, I thought. *Not helpful.* I subtly bounced on either foot, shifting my weight in anticipation of his next strike.

"I'm a hamadryad, protector of this sacred grove," it sneered. Its bark sloughed off in tiny peels that swirled in the wind as it violently gestured to the group of trees we stood among. A spear-limb spiked downward, and I dove before it grazed my arm. It punctured the earth with enough force to create a hole that would have surely impaled me.

"Please, we are not here to harm. We're trying to leave." I hoped my gentle tone would calm the tree nymph's ferocity. Instead, it glared, further incensed. The frightened girl moved behind it, edging away from its towering glower, her mop of curls snagging on wayward branches.

My distractions for the hamadryad were not enough, and his attention quickly landed on the retreating girl. Instinctively, I threw a water shield around her, creating an impenetrable wall. A spear slammed down upon it and the girl screamed, gripping her face as her eyes clenched shut. But the shield did not crack. The girl peeped an eye open, perplexed and relieved.

"Run!" I screamed. Her frantic gaze met mine before she tore through the forest, weaving through the trees. When she was thoroughly out of harm's way, I would release the water barrier and turn it on myself. But until then, it was me and this very angry tree-titan.

Roots grabbed hold of my ankles, yanking them out from under me. My back slammed against the ground, air whooshing out of my lungs. I lay stunned for mere seconds, but it was enough for the dryad to stalk over, a small grin on his rough-hewn features.

I stilled, finding my center. I called to the water in the soil beneath me and the vapor in the air. But what could harm a tree? "Stop!" I yelled.

It paused, curiosity winning out over its rage. A veiled amusement glimmered across his features.

I sat up, and in that moment, another tree strode over. My shoulders slumped. I couldn't stand against more than one dryad.

"She is under my charge. Release her." The hamadryad scowled, rolling his seething eyes, but miraculously complied. The roots receded and the two trees communicated in a language I couldn't decipher. There was huffing and the ground trembled beneath me, but in the end, the interceding tree motioned for me to stand and run away. So I did.

I traveled in the direction I had last seen the young girl, wildly searching for her. "Hello?" I yelled, cupping my hands around my mouth. I never got her name. How would I find her?

Several yards away, huddled against the earth, I discovered the elusive child seeking to cover herself with debris in a vain effort of camouflage. Around her, the soil and leaves lay damp with the remnants of my magicked barrier of water. I caught her eye and her scrambling stilled, arms dropping in relief.

"Are you okay?" I asked.

"You saved me," she responded, dazed. I offered a curt nod. Of course I would protect her, she was but a child, not that she could have known that. "Where is the dryad?" Her eyes darted around, searching for the lumbering beast.

"I think we are free of it for now. We need to leave these woods, though; it isn't safe."

Her shoulders relaxed, though she continued searching the forest.

"I've been lost in the woods before." I kicked at some leaves as I moved closer to her, hoping to distract her from her fears. "When I was little, I used to make flower crowns to pass the time, until I found my way back home. Have you ever made one?"

Her eyes lit up. "I haven't! Will you show me?" She scrambled to her feet.

I pulled down a vine that had laced itself up a tree trunk. I flinched when I cut the main stalk, unsure whether it would shout at me. I had no idea what was alive among the trees. "Watch me." I began to braid strands of the vine together. It had been years since I last did this, but the action came back easily, my muscle memory taking over.

I found some small yellow flowers poking out from beneath

fallen leaves. "Gather some of those, but leave plenty of stem." I pointed.

She bent over and picked several flowers. "My name's Korin. Thank you for helping me." She stood, smiling, dropping the flowers in my palm.

I weaved them into the crown before placing it on her head. The saffron petals stood out against her dark hair. I braided a few of her own strands among the crown to keep it secure. I stepped back in shrewd assessment. She twirled for me, beaming. "Now you're a proper Wilderess. A lady of the wilds."

Her stomach interrupted our charade with a growling protest. "When I get back to Lyrae, I'm going to get the biggest plate of roasted rabbit, with fresh bread. And maybe even a chocolate tart!" She devolved into "mmms" and giggles.

The last of her trepidation disappeared and we began walking toward what I believed to be the direction of Lyrae. Darkness had crept upon us. The sun seemed to have set quicker in these woods than they did in Haluma. I strained to see within the increasing shadows.

A breeze tousled my hair, and Korin startled beside me. "Thank you for your kindness," she rushed out.

Her curly hair grazed her shoulders, a few strands getting stuck in her mouth from the same errant breeze. "Maybe you can teach me more about flower crowns. I'd love to learn how to braid—" Her words stalled as she peered beyond me.

I turned in the direction of her gaze as a man emerged from the shadows, stalking toward us. I covertly palmed my dagger while reaching for Korin, pulling her closer to me and away from the potential danger. Another dryad? I steeled myself at the oncoming threat. My iced longsword extended from my other hand, tiny crystal shards spraying into the darkness like flecks of stardust.

"Korin." The man's voice was iron and velvet, his gaze hard as flint. I barely made out his form in the shadows that engulfed us. But I recognized the swirling darkness, and the large man within them. My longsword dissolved into harmless drops.

As soon as he noticed my water magic he tensed. "Get behind me, Korin. *Now*."

Korin's brow furrowed. "He can be a little intense," she whispered. She offered an apologetic look before stepping toward Judd. I gave her an encouraging smile.

Judd's amber eyes glittered amidst the gloom, assessing me as I did him. His presence stalled me, filling me simultaneously with frustration and fascination. He carried himself with regal confidence, as if he owned the woods themselves. His aura pulsed a gentle midnight blue. Power pressed down on me. The waves of lethality and the gleam of the twin swords peeking over his massive shoulders severed my trance.

I glanced quickly away and toward Korin, "Do you know this man?"

She held her soft smile, nodding in affirmation. "Thank you again."

The gratitude was all mine. She was a part of the rebellion, and she could lead me straight to them. I didn't want to harm her, but I wasn't above using her trust to uncover the Crimson Wolf.

Black metal rings clinked as he enclosed her small hand in his own. Shadows hazed around him, obscuring his features. He tugged Korin to his side, her flower crown jostling at the movement. She gave me a reassuring wink, threading her slender arm into his muscular one. Then, offering me an imperceptible nod, they backed into the consuming shadows.

I blinked as light resumed its descent through the scraggly branches of the trees. I stood there for several minutes. The trill of birds again filled the ambient silence. I could only hope that Korin was as safe as she had led me to believe. I kept my dagger in my hand, lingering a few more minutes before finally trekking back to my horse.

Gathering the reins and recognizing my dehydration after expelling so much magic, I closed my eyes and threw out my affinity in searching ripples. My water called to any nearby streams or ponds waiting for a response. The gentle lap of a reply sang as I mounted my mare and followed the magical pull leading me to water. Floating leaves drifted lazily around me as if suspended by the magic of the wood.

I briefly wondered about the peculiar earthquake while I made camp. Under the silver light of twinkling stars, I rehashed the day's events. My mind strayed to haunting amber eyes before the exhaustion of the day hit me, and sleep pulled me under.

CHAPTER THIRTEEN
THE GENERAL

"Ow, you're hurting me!"

I immediately loosened my grip on Korin's arm. I closed my eyes and groped for patience. We stood in the middle of Aphellion, having portaled there from the middle of the Perellian Forest.

My simmering worry over Korin's whereabouts exploded when I saw her occupying the same space as the king's spy. *Foka*. Ruin was in Yarit. I would hunt her down before she had a chance to get near Korin again.

Korin massaged her arm. "That woman saved me from a hamadryad. Why are you so angry?" She stood rigid, her arms crossed against her chest.

I suppressed a snarl. I didn't want to scare the girl, but she had no idea the amount of danger she had been in. If I had shown up much later, things might have turned out significantly worse.

I swiped my hand down my face. "You can't befriend everyone you meet, Korin. The world is not a safe place." My voice emerged stilted through my clenched teeth. This child would drive anyone off a cliff of sanity.

She had the nerve to scoff at me. "You're way more worked up than you need to be. Everything turned out fine. She even made me a flower crown." She gently fluffed the braided circlet now thoroughly tangled in her hair.

I hadn't seen a flower crown in years. I peered closer, but Korin jerked back. Confusion and defiance bolstered her.

"Ahh, you found her!" Sonora swept over, interrupting us. She tsked Korin for disappearing right after their magic lesson. Korin had more mothers and fathers than she could count. Including me, I suppose. Her parents died when she was very young and we all stepped in to fill the gaps.

In moments like these, I wondered if we had missed some crucial developmental stage these last twelve years regarding common sense and an understanding of the world. Sonora whisked Korin away before we could finish our standoff. I continued to fume as I turned toward my home, sequestered near the base of the mountains.

Anger boiled as I marched up to my study. My spies in Maripol had not reported movement among the Scourge. The king kept them cloistered within his realm, allowing no one but his dreki to leave Haluma and see what lay beyond the boundaries of his realm. I could distract myself with adjusting the new map of the Perellian Forest, particularly after this most recent land shift from the earthquakes. By the time I reached the second floor of my home, my breathing had become labored. I ignored it.

The chaos of the last couple days settled in as I sunk heavily into my chair. Grief at losing Ilayah hung heavy in my chest. She was the last of the elder Primes. Ilayah had escaped the first round of recruitment into King Nolan's original Vestal Anchor program. But in the end, she had been abducted and drained anyway. I couldn't protect her from her end, but I wouldn't fail her legacy. Her death only spurred my resolve.

Then there was Ruin... who was no doubt currently under Nolan's orders to investigate Yarit. She had already been sniffing around about the Crimson Wolf. Her presence was a distraction, and one I would need to remedy. My purpose and focus had always been, and continued to be, for my people. I would not allow Ruin to jeopardize anything, especially if she posed a threat to us.

Frustration had my fist slamming against the wooden desk. Korin would need security now, and that probably wouldn't go over well.

I'll put Sonora in charge of it.

I unrolled the working map I had of Yarit. Carefully, I erased the area where I'd found Korin. I closed my eyes and visualized the topography. Slowly, I inked new lines along the paper, forming trees, hills, paths, and rocky outcroppings. The dryads could let me know what else had changed later so I could fill in pertinent details I might have missed. My hand trembled slightly with each brushstroke. I gripped the pen firmly, steadying the tremor. Eventually, I lost myself in the calming process of drawing.

I yanked out another piece of paper and sketched out the silhouette of a woman. It was always just beyond my mind's eye. I tried to add as much detail as I could. But as with all the ones before it, I didn't get enough of a vision to complete it. It was a compulsion to draw her. It had been ever since I was young. This time, I got a little more of her nose, a bit more of her hair.

It landed on the pile with all the others.

I stared out the window, and my mind wandered. I was no oracle, but I couldn't stop the recurring dream of me and Elyon, the great god. I had it again the night prior. The residual mystery usually lasted days before I moved on from it. Until it happened again.

He came as he always did—a study in contrasts. He loomed

tall and formidable with an air of violence, but his voice boomed with gentleness and care that loosened my defenses. His dark hair blew in phantom winds making the strands shift into multicolored hues as if it couldn't decide which color to commit to. His light eyes swirled and an indigo eagle flew overhead. His skin pulsed as if lightning flashed in his blood.

It was he who named me the Liberation's leader. The night after my first dream, my adoptive mother, Ilayah, had come to me with a vision of my future. It was from that moment on that I began training for my current role.

As with all of these dreams, this one held remnants of grief for a family I never knew. My interactions with Elyon left a residue of longing I couldn't place. The dreams solidified my purpose as the final Liberator. Too bad he couldn't just tell me how I was supposed to accomplish that. At least I woke with a sense of rightness for the path before me. Before I awakened, he drew his line of protection across my brow. I could feel the ghostly impression of his touch even now.

My heart skipped a beat causing me to cough. I had waited too long. I hastily moved maps and communications and tankards around, searching for one of my vials. A pen fell to the floor, rolling in a lonely arc toward the wall.

My eyes landed on a thin glass bottle, corked and full of my tonic. I popped it open and drank the liquid. It coursed thickly down my throat, leaving a familiar tingling in its wake, as if infused with too much spice.

My head fell back against the chair while I waited for the elixir to fill my blood. The effects from these tonics were steadily decreasing. My body slowly demanded more. I glanced down at my arms. My mouth went dry. Gray veins had formed darkened trails down to my wrists, now slowly disappearing thanks to my tonic—a new symptom I'd have to tell Sieren about.

Our timeline just moved up. I dropped my arms in my lap,

my shadows gliding around them. I had no desire to see the truth beneath my skin.

The veil was deepening, and Nolan was creating more drekis than ever before. The Liberation needed an alliance with Queen Thaleia to give us a true chance. I just had to figure out how to get into her realm and secure her support before time ran out.

CHAPTER FOURTEEN
THE SPY

He sneered at the tear rolling down my cheek, his voice mocking my misery. The stone walls surrounded me, closing in. Somehow there was still space enough for him to pace, a leashed predator. A multitude of weapons cast threatening glares. Each whip, spike, and point hanging menacingly along the wall. He slowed his pacing to graze his fingers across each one, intentionally accentuating each sharpened point. They swayed on their hooks at his touch.

He peered down at me, gripping my knees to my chest, trying to disappear. Sweat dampened my clothes. My feet turned numb as they settled on to the frozen, unforgiving stone floor. The waiting. That was perhaps the worst part. The psychological manipulations almost worse than the beatings. Almost.

I closed my eyes, trying to imagine my mom. Willing my eyes to suck up all moisture so no more evidence of my fear expressed itself. I imagined her comfort, her soft touch, her firm hugs. She always smelled of lavender tea, a mug of the steaming brew her constant companion. I jolted back to the present, unclenching my fists, eyes popping open, at the snapping sound of his chosen instrument. The small whip with splintered metal chunks embedded in the leathers that *extended like vicious tentacles. One hit and he would drag it down my back, creating four jagged slices at a time.*

I would likely pass out. I would need to find a healer when this was over. When he got his anger out of his system, I knew I would be left behind to figure it all out. If only I could disappear. My fear blanketed my thoughts. My rage fueled my resolve. There was no way out of this. One day, I would kill this man.

Bars slammed around me.

Caged.

Trapped.

Hate bloomed.

His violent gaze found mine, and I screamed.

My thrashing body pulled me from the nightmare. The soreness in my throat told me I probably alerted anyone in a five mile radius of my location. My blanket lay bunched at the end of my makeshift bed. Gradually, my breathing calmed as I reoriented myself to the current place and time, my body unwilling or unable to cease its trembling. I sat up slowly, rubbing my arms in self-comfort. I pulled a cherry candy out of my satchel, mechanically tasting its fruity sweetness.

I searched for my cloak, restless with the desire to move. I wouldn't be falling back asleep anytime soon. I reached for the woolen garment, a deep burgundy with no embellishments, securing it around my shoulders. I shoved on my leather boots and raised the hood over my braided hair.

The man in my nightmare, the ghost of my father, continued to claw at me. The vivid helplessness and inability to flee left the unnerving residue of paralysis. Anger, old and deep, festered. My military training drilled a calculated control over my rage.

Anger was a tightrope.

My hands clenched and unclenched. My body shook as I inhaled ragged breaths. Anger wasn't all violence. It could provide momentum where I'd otherwise be stagnant. But it also bared lethal fangs in an effort to protect tender parts.

I preferred my weak spots to remain divested from the light of day. Old pain tended to bubble up, making its inconvenient presence known, in the black of the night, the time when the demons roam, when my guard dropped.

I focused on a collection of leaves, admiring their many colors piled one upon the other in a mosaic blanket. In another life, I might have imagined they had the power to heal. A fool's thought.

I sat down, leaning my back against a tree, and closed my eyes. When I opened them again, the rising sun spilled downward in dazzling streams of oranges and pinks. I shifted and the crinkling of paper sounded. Delah's note. I pulled it from my pocket.

> Rue,
> Destroy this once you read it.
> I know you have a plan. And when you make up your mind, no one can change it. You're the most stubborn person I know. If you succeed in becoming a dreki, I will help you. If you change your mind, I'll support you in that way too. No one has gotten out of becoming a dreki without punishment though. But no one is as clever as you are.
> If you have any doubt about the trade, please look into it. I have heard how Berine can be used against us..."

"Your rest is uneasy."

I startled, jumping to my feet, an ice dagger materializing within a blink. The note fluttered to the ground, momentarily forgotten. I wildly searched for the source of the voice, but no person appeared. My eyes narrowed, combing through early morning shadows of ancient trees.

The trunk of a tree shimmered, then moved toward me. I stilled as I took in the sight. A woman with skin like flaking bark slowly glided toward me. Her hair swayed in a wild tangle of silky leaves and supple branches. Her amused eyes gleamed a rich golden brown.

"My name is Bex. I watched over you last night when you emerged in distress." She eyed me thoughtfully as my surprise turned to outright curiosity.

"I'm Rue. I… thank you. I hope I didn't wake you." I winced. Do trees sleep? Was I in her living room?

She chuckled, her trunk shifting into a curvaceous female form.

"You're a forest nymph aren't you? Were you the one who helped me yesterday with the hamadryad?"

She nodded. "I did. And yes, I am a dryad. My sisters and I guard this grove." Her leaves rustled with a casual gesture to our surroundings. Her mesmerizing gaze, rich like damp soil, landed back on me. "What haunts you, Rue?"

I shifted on my feet. Her question and direct eye contact peeled back my layers like her shaves of bark. I studied her. She had gone out of her way to protect me, and nothing about her screamed "threat" at the moment. I chose to answer her question, if for no other reason than to stay in her good graces. Maybe she would help get me out of the forest. A soft chuckle escaped me, brushing off her concern. "Things best forgotten."

"Hmm." Bex glided around me. "And where are you headed?"

"Lyrae. I got turned around after an earthquake. Can you point me in the right direction?"

Bex smiled. "I can help you through these woods. They are not all filled with kind nymphs. You would do well to remember that. Let me know when you are ready to depart."

I picked up Delah's note and started forward. Bex moved along the forest floor with unnatural grace. I assumed a tree would possess jerkier movements. Dryads were full of surprises.

I had no idea how large this forest was, and would have found myself continually turned around since the forest's canopy blotted out the overhead sky. We traveled in a comfortable silence. Flowers as wide and deep as soup pots swayed on their top-heavy stalks. The smell of jasmine and honeysuckle mingled with decaying leaves. Vines outstretched before my eyes, grabbing on to tree limbs as though sentient, following us. Perhaps they were.

Bex hummed a tune that attracted small birds with jewel-toned feathers. Their iridescent chests soared through the air like shooting stars made of delicate rainbows. Throughout our journey, Bex would lean over and pick some berries or mushrooms, adding them to a hole in her trunk.

After several hours, we stopped to eat. Bex unveiled her collection of foodie treasures. I gaped at the spread.

Bex laughed, causing her leaves to flutter. "Of course I have no need for food, these are all for you. I hardly ever see females in this part of the forest. It's always heavy-footed men with rank smells." I hid my smirk behind my hand, imagining the Berine suppliers from the Rivellan Wood and how they fit her description.

Grateful for the fleshy mushrooms and juicy berries, I ate them alongside a small bit of cheese. I lay back, reaching into my pocket for a hard candy out of habit.

"Bex, what do you know about the earthquakes?"

"They are new to us, as they likely are to you. I do know that the cause of them is in response to the veil..." She trailed off, offering nothing more.

I puzzled at that. The darkness of Maripol hadn't seemed to have reached Yarit, but it made sense that the veil would be heavier here if the rebels staked their claim in this land. I finished my candy, standing.

"You'll make it to Lyrae by late afternoon. It isn't far off." Bex gestured to the east.

I packed up my things and mounted my horse. Excitement bubbled within me. "Lead the way."

We trotted on through the green-tinged light of the forest. Wildflowers increased in number the closer we got to the forest's edge. Bright-blue cornflowers and yellow goldenrods carpeted the wood. Bees and butterflies danced among them.

I pulled out the note from Delah, now crumpled. I carefully smoothed it out, and picked up where I had left off:

> I have heard about how Berine can be used against us. It's well known that we need it to bind to the magic in our bodies, preventing us from losing our affinities, but it can also be used in the draining of magic. At this point, I am not convinced anyone should be ingesting Berine.
> From my experiments with Glint, I firmly believe Glint is a form of refined Berine. It is used purposely to drain magic, which eventually kills the person. I've been studying raw Berine and refined Glint to find an antidote for it. Be careful Rue. Keep investigating. The king may not be the person we've believed him to be. You're all the family I have.
> Delah

I stared at the page. Berine kept Halumans strong. Berine saved our people. I reread the letter again. And again. Delah should know what she was talking about. But she was also young, and enough people sharing the same rumors could sway her. I refused to believe her concerns. I couldn't. It was treason. I fisted the note, shoving it back into my pocket. She almost sounded like the damn rebel general.

The space between my ribs grew tight. My plan to abduct, or assassinate, the Crimson Wolf suddenly felt fragile. Hairline fractures threatened my confidence. I had to focus on my plan: Track Korin. Locate the rebels' base. Destroy the Crimson Wolf. I would authenticate my loyalty. And ascend to a dreki.

But what if I was wrong? Delah has never been brash with her words. Insinuating the king had ill-intentions left me internally tilted.

I picked up my pace, resolved to find the Crimson Wolf. My only salvation.

The trees thinned the closer we came to Lyrae. Bex paused and gestured for me to stroll forward. "This is where I leave you. Follow this game trail and it will take you to the western side of Lyrae." A soft smile relaxed her features. "I hope you find what you're searching for."

I dipped my head in gratitude. Bex assumed her more tree-like stature as her roots sent plumes of soil in the air. Within minutes she had been subsumed by the forest, and I was left with the chirping birds.

Ahead, the trees opened to a small field, and beyond that was the beautiful city of Lyrae. Waterways zigzagged in living ribbons of cerulean silk below a breathtaking city. Buildings connected by gleaming bridges paid no mind to the landscape below. They seemed to float above the water-carved land and the gurgling canals. They created an organized city despite the earth's attempts to command a different placement.

The buildings themselves were works of art. Some stood tall with spires and turrets, others revealed elaborate balconies. Almost all of them were several stories high, with intricate filigree detailing the sides and corners. Statues of vicious-looking naiads kept watch on the roofs and eaves of several structures.

Glass covered many of the buildings, gleaming and glittering with the passing of the clouds across the sun. Vines with magenta flowers meandered their way up stone walls, their petals, like bored confetti, hazily rained down to the streets below.

Many of the buildings appeared to be living quarters. The lower levels of several of them boasted signs for stores and businesses. Skiffs and small boats drifted through the waterways. Some carried goods, others carried people. The tinkle of laughter coasted softly on the breeze. Large fountains established roundabouts for efficient movement of boats and gondolas. Their geysers shot several stories into the air, with vaporous spray merging with the humidity.

I urged my horse on, descending into the field that separated the forest from the city itself. I scanned the outskirts, locating a stable. We trotted toward it so that I could house my mare while I sleuthed around the city. I found an empty stall and quickly changed out of my leathers and into a nondescript, dark-purple dress. I finger-brushed my hair, setting it half-up to keep clear of my face. I wasn't Ruin, the elite spy. I was Rue Vespera, sweet, unassuming traveler.

My search for the Crimson Wolf officially began.

CHAPTER FIFTEEN
THE SPY

The city bustled with oblivious people. Open windows brought snippets of conversations weaving among the buzz of the city's energy. I wandered around the cobblestoned paths and numerous bridges. Walls of limestone and iron bars prevented a careless pedestrian from falling into the waterways below, and I stopped periodically to peer over the sides. Everything about this city seemed brighter than Maripol, even the auras. Yarit was supposed to be darker. Perhaps my senses were off.

I manipulated the moisture in the air to funnel distant conversations toward me. I scoffed at the normalcy of the people around me. Petty gossip, business transactions, and frivolous shopping as if the world around them wasn't teeming with deceptions, drug trafficking, and destruction. They had no idea they lived in a delusion. The Good King held the reigns of wrath, and soon all that was wrong would be made right. My desire to apprehend the Crimson Wolf burned within me. I was my own savior in this traitorous land.

Korin had unknowingly offered me a bit of information that served as the basis for my search. I wandered the streets until I found a tavern. The bartender tipped his head at me as he dried a tankard in his hands.

"Do you know of any places around here that serve chocolate tarts? Oh and a good roasted rabbit?" I smiled up at him expectantly.

He set the tankard down with a grin. "Got a craving do ya? A lot of places around here serve rabbit. Only two I know of make chocolate tarts. I would try the Foxhole near the Topaz Castle, and maybe the Mud Pit. Both should have what you're looking for."

I left a small tip for his recommendations before pulling out the map Maelic supplied me with. The detail of Lyrae allowed me to move within the city with confidence. I started northward toward the jeweled beacon in the north. It sat overlooking the city of waterways where the queen of Lyrae resided. Queen Avery still allowed trade between our realms, but it was well-known that her realm was threatened by the freedom Haluma boasted under King Nolan. Yarit kept many secrets, particularly around the strange nymphs that resided here—dryads within their forests and sirens off their coast.

The waning sun brought the coolness of the sea air further inland. Stores closed their doors and shutters; lights slowly winked out. Auras that wafted off of passersby seemed calmer and lighter than I had grown accustomed to. Lyrae's very atmosphere contrasted acutely with the heavy darkness that veiled my homeland.

Curiously, I didn't see any obvious signs of Glint's circulation. It ravaged Maripol seemingly unchecked. I knew too many kind people whose bodies turned up in dank alleyways, the golden residue of Glint smeared across their lifeless faces. Maripol may not have sirens, but the temptation song of Glint lured just as enticingly. Everyone knew Yarit was a darker, dirtier place than Haluma, but as I strolled its streets, the evidence proved the exact opposite. It left me unsettled.

I caught sight of a familiar face, a rebel I'd tussled with back in Maripol. He walked purposely with another man. I followed at a discreet distance, casually window-shopping and using the reflections to keep track of them. They entered a pub ahead of me. I lingered a few minutes before following behind them.

Tugging on the moisture in the air, I drew their low voices toward me in subtle currents. Their auras pulsed erratically in shades of maroon and deep crimson, signaling agitation and concern.

"She might be getting better at reorganizing the land, but she's still not accurate enough."

"If she can't control the earthquakes better, she might destroy a part of Lyrae." The men exchanged knowing looks.

"The Queen will take her out before that happens. She doesn't put up with strange magic—too threatening." He absently toyed with the tabletop, his fingers skimming the worn surface.

"You know what *she* says about her?" the first man said, then took a deep swallow of his drink. "She foresaw her success, and the General believes in her abilities."

They grew quiet. "I hope they're right. If she succeeds it could change the outcome of this war. But if she doesn't…"

They somberly nodded.

I stowed their cryptic conversation away as the men moved on to more mundane topics. I wrestled with staying with them or returning to my search for Korin. I decided to risk losing both for greater gain and gambled on Korin. The night air washed over me when I left the pub and turned north once more.

The Foxhole loomed in the distance. Its white wooden sign swung casually from clinking chains. Lanterns illuminated the path to the entrance. Music escaped into the night as patrons opened its wooden door.

I entered the revelry, scanning the large room for a table. I gently edged around groups of people engaged in boisterous conversation. I zeroed in on a vacant table, positioning myself with my back to the crowd, while allowing a clear view of the exits. I ordered the roasted rabbit and an ale from the server.

The humidity of this seaside city easily fed into my affinity. I pulled some moisture from the air creating a simple looking glass of ice. I casually raised it, and began sprucing my hair. Tilting it surreptitiously, I scanned the other patrons behind me. A grin blossomed across my face and every muscle in me relaxed. There she was.

Korin wiped smudges of chocolate tart off of her cheek between fits of laughter. Her companions were caught up in their own conversations. I didn't recognize any of them, but I committed their faces to memory. Korin could lead me straight to the rebels. I suppressed the urge to destroy everyone she was with. The Crimson Wolf was my target. I couldn't get too hasty.

I sat the frozen mirror down and tunneled the humid air toward myself. I listened as Korin shared a story about rearranging the positions of some buildings. She relayed how a Prime Elixist had walked through the front door of what she thought was her lab, but in fact had been rotated around and was now a storage shed. The story seemed made up, and everyone laughed, some shaking their heads at the silliness of it all. I forgot how imaginative children could be.

The entrance of the Foxhole swung open, and a deep voice lassoed my attention. A breathtaking man entered the room, striding purposefully toward Korin's table. I tensed as the general scored his hands through his dark hair, mussing it in the process. A few stray waves settled across his brow. His golden irises seemed lined in dark bronze. His face was perfection. A straight nose symmetrically accentuated his carved jaw. *What was in this drink?*

I pried my eyes away. A faint blush heated my cheeks. I tried to refocus on the food in front of me and the conversation four tables away. I shifted in my seat to glean a better view.

A gray-haired man stood, clasping forearms with Judd. Several black rings adorned his strong hands. I zeroed in on them. Those were the same long fingers that had gripped my waist at the festival, that carried me home. The same lethal hands that orchestrated the spread of Glint. I gulped down air.

Their conversation continued to flow directly toward me. "You're wearing it!" yelped Korin. I flinched at her outburst. Her hands dug deep into her collar. She produced a colorfully braided necklace with interwoven beads, her enthusiasm an electrical current aimed right at Judd.

His startling eyes landed on the girl. A genuine smile softened his features. A dimple formed on his cheek, somehow increasing my blood flow with its appearance. He gripped an identical necklace from beneath his tunic, revealing colorful strands at odds with his monochromatic clothing.

I struggled to shift my gaze away from their interaction. The way he engaged with Korin vexed me. This stormy man held such a tenderness toward the girl that clashed with what I knew of him. Emotion welled upward, pricking my eyes and constricting my throat. It overtook me in its suddenness, from some long-abandoned space within me. Never had my own father gazed at me with such care and familiarity. With such tenderness.

I sat back, finally looking away. A confusing blend of despair and longing choked me. I swallowed it down, turning back toward them.

Korin beamed in triumph. "I knew you would."

He tousled her curly hair, leaving them curtained across her eyes. He addressed the rest of the group while Korin rearranged her hair out of her face. My body remained positioned toward my food, but my attention stayed on Korin and Judd from the corner of my eye.

A woman with a seductively low neckline approached the general. She leaned into him as if she knew him. A large swig of ale chased down my distaste. I tried to peel my eyes away, but seemed unable to control my gaze. Of course he would attract attention; how could he not? His strong posture and ridiculous height made it seem like he could command the wind.

My head cocked slightly as I covertly studied him. He appeared as self-assured and at ease as he did at the Twin Moon Festival. Everyone around him deferred to him, even as he easily smiled in an effort to diffuse the power differential. He politely dismissed the brazen woman. I ignored the gratification that followed.

Korin excused herself to use the bathroom. I finished off my ale and left plenty of coin to cover my meal, then hurried after her. I stalled a few moments outside the door before stepping inside. I froze the lock on the door, ensuring no one else interrupted our serendipitous meeting.

The spigot of water whooshed on, and I feigned washing my hands while I waited. Korin emerged from the stall and I brightened at her presence. It took her a moment to recognize me, but eventually she smiled back.

"Korin! What a surprise to bump into you here! Have you tried the chocolate tart? I hear it's delicious."

"I already ate two," she giggled, scrunching her little nose in the process.

"What are the odds I would find you again? I'm glad you are well and staying away from dryads." Lighthearted suspicion narrowed my eyes.

She waved her hand in the air dismissively, the colorful handmade necklace around her neck swinging with the movement. "Yes, yes; no more forest excursions unless a Prime is with me. Some people seem extra protective lately, so I can't do anything without an escort now," she huffed.

My mind reeled at the prospect of interacting with a Prime,

even if they were brainwashed by the rebellion. Korin was proving to be a very useful gateway to the rebel world. "I hope that's not on my account. I'd be happy to meet one of your escorts, or your Primes, and help put them at ease. If it would help, of course."

She glanced nervously around, her fingers toying with her necklace. "Well, I am supposed to practice my magic tomorrow. I have trouble with the reabsorption of it—sometimes I become super dizzy when I expel too fast. If you want, you could come." A twinge of remorse twisted my gut at exploiting her trust. But if that's what stood between me and the protection of Haluma, I would stomach it.

"I remember learning to control my own magic. Maybe I could offer some tricks of my own that I've learned over the years. Where should I meet you?"

Korin's face lit up like the Haluman sunrise.

CHAPTER SIXTEEN
THE SPY

Korin requested to meet right outside the city walls. I neared the stables where I'd left my mare as early morning fog hovered above the swaying grasses. I kept my burgundy cloak tied securely to ward off the chill.

Two women, Korin, and two other children clustered in the distance. When she spotted me, Korin waved her hand in the air, as if I wasn't plainly walking in her direction. Her long sleeves billowed with the effort. The sight made the corner of my mouth twitch. Gods, she was disarming.

The two adults stepped forward. The one with wavy, brown hair extended her hand in greeting, the other had thick raven hair pulled back in a collection of small braids with crystal beads woven through them and eyed me suspiciously.

"I'm Sonora. Korin warned me she had invited a friend; she was excited to have you join us this morning." Her soft tone belied the quiet strength with which she held herself. She gestured to her raven companion. "This is Xuri. She and her students will be practicing their craft as well." They both exchanged amused smiles.

"Thank you for allowing me to tag along. I couldn't resist Miss Korin's compelling invitation," I offered.

Korin smiled in triumph at having coaxed me into joining her magic practice. After the introductions, we carved a path through the trees.

I peered over at Korin, "You never told me what kind of magic you have."

She flashed a mischievous grin, "You'll just have to see for yourself."

We hiked through the brush for about twenty minutes, Korin skipping along, humming. She broke the silence. "What does Rue stand for anyway? Is that what your parents named you?" Her nose scrunched at the idea.

I chuckled at her directness. "It's a nickname. Only my good friends call me that. Do you have a nickname?" I replied, winking at her.

"I have a few nicknames," she responded before resuming her skipping.

We came to a clearing dotted with wildflowers. The rustle of grasses blended with the cawing of distant birds. Xuri gathered her two students and wandered further into the trees. Korin, Sonora, and I stood in the middle of a field—trees encircled us like eager spectators around our wildflower arena. I eyed them speculatively, wondering if a dryad observed us.

"Okay, Korin," encouraged Sonora. "You can do this. Channel your power into moving everything in this clearing in a clockwise direction. Just like last time. Find the core of your magic and mold it to your will. Are you ready?"

Korin nodded, shutting her eyes tight. She slowed her breathing and I noted her aura calming. It shifted from an excited magenta to a softer lilac. Her head cocked to the side and all childishness vanished with her concentration. Her eyes jolted open and she narrowed them toward the trees in front of her.

Vibrations stole up my calves as the ground rumbled, pebbles quivering. Suddenly, the land rotated. The trees themselves did not move, but the meadow we were standing in did, like some kind of possessed wagon wheel. My knees wobbled as a rasping yelp escaped me.

"You have land magic!" I sputtered.

Korin turned toward me, her face shining with elation. She waggled her eyebrows, reminding me she was just a child who was having fun. The thought of this girl wielding such a rare gift left me speechless. She was a wonder. A pang from somewhere old surfaced in my chest, the thought of what I could have been like had I been surrounded with loving, supportive adults knocked into my lungs. Who would I have been if I could have learned my magic without restraint or fear of punishment? I stuffed it away as quickly as it came.

Sonora broke in, "I am a Land Prime. I have expertise in rocks and other earth formations like mountains and canyons. I assist Korin in appropriately harnessing her power. She specializes in tectonics. But"—she sent a reproachful look toward Korin—"sometimes she overdoes it and faces the consequences."

As if on cue, Korin wobbled, reaching out for Sonora. She dropped to her knees, leaning over to regain her balance. Sonora observed her.

"She doesn't reabsorb after wielding like she should. It's her biggest liability. Since her magic is tethered to earth, she will lose her own groundedness. She becomes disoriented, losing her balance; at her worst, she faints. It's why I practice with her often. Land magic is very powerful and easily lost. She must draw it back into herself at much the same rate she expels it."

She crouched down next to Korin, stroking her back and moving hair out of her face. She spoke low, soft words to her. I stilled, observing them anew. Sonora was an actual Prime. My mouth went dry. I closed my eyes and took a deep breath. I didn't try to siphon their conversation with my magic, giving them, and me, a moment to recalibrate.

Slowly, Korin stood up, a clammy sheen to her smooth skin. She surveyed the area, frowning. We had rotated, but not the direction she intended. The trees were still within eyesight. She huffed and decided to try again. This time I stepped closer, just in case her loss of magic overcame her.

"I'm gonna move the trees," she mumbled with fervor.

Reminiscent of my experience in the Yaritian forest with Bex, the ground rumbled beneath me and tree roots writhed beneath the soil. Dust and debris kicked up from the forest floor. The gnarled observers glided and shifted around us. The movement persisted for several seconds. I couldn't tell if the land was moving the trees, or the trees themselves had uprooted, fleeing as if suddenly alive.

"Use the earth to reabsorb Korin!" Sonora urged.

Korin inhaled deeply, closing her eyes once more. A few more seconds passed. When they reopened, she jumped in the air, fist pumping as she did so. A bark of laughter escaped me, celebration filling my bones. "Look what you did! That was amazing!"

The earth continued shaking, and her eyes widened. We all lost our balance as an earthquake rattled the ground. Sonora yelled something about plate tectonics and aftershocks. Korin fell into me. The sleeve of her shirt bunched up at the elbow, exposing her forearm. My eyes settled on a small tattoo. Of a red wolf.

My breath stalled in my chest. Iron fear sank heavy and absolute. My mind reeled.

It couldn't be.

"Korin." I willed my voice into calm curiosity. My heart pounded in my ears. My palms turned clammy. "That's a unique tattoo you have."

She glanced up. "I just got it." She gestured toward the tattoo,

"Some people call me the Crimson Wolf." Her innocent eyes blinked up at me. "It's one of my nicknames," she added as an afterthought.

My stomach dropped. My ears rang in violent protest. Consuming dread filled the space where my previous elation leaked out.

"Rue?" asked Korin. She jumped up as the aftershocks downgraded to gentle vibrations. "Are you okay?"

"No," I whispered. "It cannot be." I looked around wildly. Sonora's brow furrowed in concern. "Give me a minute."

Korin backed up and walked over to Sonora.

Korin was the Crimson Wolf. She had the tattoo, the nickname, and the land magic to redirect Berine supplies. But she was barely of age, hardly a teenager. If I was to live, if I was to have a chance at a future, I had to kill her. I reached for my dagger, my fingers curling around the familiar hilt. I could make it quick and portal immediately back to Haluma.

My body crept toward the cliff of hyperventilating. My deepest values held my actions in a chokehold, refusing to align with the logic of my choices.

The familiar iron cage of entrapment closed in. Like the stone room I was "disciplined" in all those years ago. Like the steel cell they locked me in as an orphan. Like the gilded bars that detained my deepest fears. I closed my eyes, sipping shallow breaths of air.

How could I live with myself if I murdered her? She reminded me of Delah. She reminded me of *me*. Or at least the me I could have been, that I would have hoped to become. It wasn't her fault she was born with this magic.

But if I didn't, I would be a traitor to Haluma. Did I even have a choice?

"Rue? Are you okay? Can I get you some water?" This was Sonora now. I nodded, even though I could pull water out of the air. It would buy me some time.

I have always worked twice as hard to be the best soldier, to prove myself. Twice as hard to emerge at the top for the chance to steer the ship of my future. I survived my father. I survived as an orphan. I survived the training to become the Scourge.

My mind oscillated between my white-knuckled past and my quickly crumbling future. I knew what awaited Korin if I brought her back to Haluma. I couldn't do that to her. I couldn't be the weapon that stole her light.

I couldn't do it.

I released my hold on the hilt. My mind stumbled through this new predicament. I would be committing treason. The Good King would hunt me, would drain me. And if Delah's words held any merit, he would do it with the very drug that destroyed my parents and my life.

I could trade my soul to become a dreki and gain significant power. But power was never my goal. If I killed Korin, I'd be trading my soul in a different way—one I wouldn't recover from.

King Nolan had faith in me, and I would let him down. That realization hurt the most. Yet, the cost of betraying myself was something I wasn't willing to pay. Never again. Resolve hardened within me even as a piece of me died.

A flash of black caught in my periphery. I looked up just in time to see the last of the scales clicking into place. Two drekis emerged from the trees, prowling in our direction. I immediately recognized Wes and Belham. I nodded toward them, but they ignored me. Alarm heightened my senses.

"Guys." I gestured toward Sonora and Korin, my voice trembling. "Get away from here. Now!"

Korin stared at me in confusion and then her attention pulled swiftly away, searching the oncoming enemy, freezing at the sight of the drekis. Their eyes held a hypnotic quality that stunned most people for a few seconds.

Belham's eyes darted to me in surprise, quickly morphing

into revulsion. "I knew you were weak. I didn't expect you to betray your own, though. Nolan was wise to do what he did, he must have known."

I scrambled to my feet, bolting toward them. Wes lunged at the same time. I summoned my blade and deflected his as it swung through the air in a swift downward arc. Korin and Sonora were outfitted with nothing more than daggers. Their defenses meager against the power of the drekis.

Jagged rocks exploded out of the earth all around us. I hoped it wasn't Korin, or we would be carrying her out of the forest unconscious.

Belham's stinger lengthened from his extended hand into an angry wayward claw. His attention focused solely on Korin. *They knew.* I discharged my magic to fortify an encasement around Korin and Sonora, willing the barrier of thick ice to become impenetrable.

I fragmented my power between myself and Korin, never entertaining the idea that my connection to these dreki could be the reason harm befell them. Belham shrieked as he witnessed the barrier, understanding the impotence of his power against my affinity. His stinger dripped with anticipation, salivating for its prey. Wes needed to touch his victim to incite hallucinations, or remove memories.

My ice sword cut through the air in Wes's direction. His movements came swift, closing the space between us. He drew his blade and lunged. Flecks of gold reflected off the shards of ice that scattered in the air with every hit and deflection.

In the midst of the battle, a nagging thought burst forth: how did they know where I'd be? A wave of dizziness enveloped me. I licked chapped lips with a dry tongue. My depletion demanded repayment.

Korin yelled in my direction but her words fell unregistered, her voice muffled by the ice encasing her. Wes steadily pushed me backward. Awareness withered as I began fighting primarily from muscle memory rather than conscious thought. Failing to replenish my magic, I faltered.

"Get over here! Get closer to us!" Korin's voice broke through the melee. I ducked, narrowly missing Wes's blade. I swung my leg out, but he dodged it just as easily. We had been sparring partners for years, both knowing each other's moves and defenses. Deftly, I yanked out a dagger and threw it at him. He pivoted, but not before it lodged into his shoulder. He hissed at me as he paused to pull it out. It barely pierced through his scales.

Gifted precious seconds, I rushed toward the ice barrier. Sonora motioned purposefully with her hand. A thrum rippled through the air before a thunderous sound brought me to my knees. The land rapidly cracked, violently separating. The deafening sound of rocks breaking accompanied plumes of dirt that exploded into the morning air, obscuring the landscape in a thick haze.

Belham jumped, forced to retreat from the onslaught of cracked earth and protruding boulders. Monoliths angled toward his body, seething in their desire to impale. The calm morning fog now displaced with the murkiness of dust and disturbed earth.

A chasm carved a circle around Wes and Belham, stranding them upon a shrinking island. They were unable to cross the ravine Sonora summoned. My gaze locked on Belham. His responding smile, imbued with a disturbed knowing, made me falter.

He turned his back to me, forming a portal on their magicked prison. It was the last thing I saw before a sharp pain lanced through my body. I clawed at my ear, my throat. Pain blinded me. I collapsed, my body seizing in response. A scream tore through my lungs, emptying me of all thought.

Then everything faded to soothing black.

CHAPTER SEVENTEEN
THE GENERAL

The unmistakable remnants of death magic lingered on the bark. I peered closer. The residue gave the impression of obsidian granules, as if someone took the black stone and ground it in a mortar and pestle.

I cracked my neck.

I continued searching for any other signs of the scaled demons—drekis. Our turned spies alerted us to most of their missions, particularly those involving movement in our realm. I didn't expect to find any lurking about today, but evidence of char left me on alert.

The reptiles reeked of death magic—broken magic that leaches life. The kind of magic birthed from their dark king and bestowed to his dreki—his convoluted attempt at creating his version of Primes. The *Good* King. I scoffed to myself, and a puff of shadow expelled from my knuckles.

We were amassing a plan that would take him out, but I hadn't figured out a way to make it to the Nereids. I sighed. Deep down, I really felt the only way to rid the world of King Nolan was to find a cure, but the Nereids were the next logical step. Another problem for another day.

There would be an end to death magic, according to the oracles, but I had no way of knowing if it would be in my lifetime. Regardless, it didn't stop me from planning and plotting, doing everything in my power to preserve Aphellion, and the greater realms.

I may not currently be powerful enough to destroy death magic completely, but I knew well how to disrupt plans and, at the very least, be a pain in Nolan's ass. I chuckled at the thought. If that were to be my legacy, it wouldn't be the worst thing.

I resumed scanning my surroundings, my senses heightened, as I sent my magic out in waves to explore and assess.

My horse grunted, the ground shaking much more aggressively than normal for having a land wielder nearby. A faint scream sliced through the trees. Everything sharpened. I bolted toward the source of the sound.

A gentle ripple tugged against my shadows. Internally, I heard the distress call. Xuri. Had she encountered a dreki? My blood simmered in my veins, a slumbering viper awakening, poised to unleash.

I raced through the dimly lit woods on my horse, narrowly avoiding the whip of low hanging branches. Xuri's call grew louder as I zeroed in on her location.

Beyond the trees, I glimpsed their group in a deceivingly peaceful meadow. Wildflowers swayed indolently in the breeze, even as the land yielded destruction. Dust suspended in a silently hovering cloud around them. Broken earth, jutting rocks, and a chasm that surrounded a small plot of dismembered land, left the field in disarray. Char appeared to float on the swirling breeze, yet no threat presented itself.

I swiftly dismounted, then ran toward Xuri. She held a petite woman covered in blood. Her chest rose and fell in shallow pants. The ground around them darkened as if a bucket of water had been poured out.

I regarded the woman, who was impossibly too familiar, her

white hair almost lavender near the roots in the shade of the meadow. Her limp body retained an aura of strength despite her obviously unconscious state.

I stalled at the realization that Xuri held Ruin. My memory of our interactions painted her in bold colors. Seeing her like this, weakened and vulnerable, unnerved me. Her wavy hair fanned out along the wadded-up cloak her head rested upon, soaking up rivulets of blood. Her delicate face contorted in pain, the column of her neck slick with crimson.

My shadows swirled around me in restless agitation. They waited to defend or destroy, calculating, gathering minute details to make sense of the scene before me.

My gaze shifted to Xuri. Urgency lashed from her sharp caramel gaze as she held the woman in her lap.

Xuri's students stood by, awaiting direction from either myself or their revered teacher. Ruin bled copiously, the metallic smell filling my nostrils. As I absorbed the scene, I sensed the remnants of dark magic seeping out of her. Char flowed alongside her lifeblood.

My stomach clenched, unsettled. I had never seen that before. I furrowed my brow as I peered at Xuri. She shook her head as if to answer my unspoken question. She didn't know what was happening either. She spoke softly into my mind as only a Prime Oracle could, *"Death Magic."* Alarm flared.

Sonora squatted nearby. She embraced a stricken Korin. "Her name is Rue," she offered. "Korin had invited her to join us this morning. She fended off two dreki attempting to attack us." Her voice faltered with her final report. "They seemed intent on getting to Korin. Rue used water magic to protect us." Her countenance hardened as she relayed the chain of events. She darkened further recounting the dreki's interest in Korin. My metal rings flared.

"You must take her to the healer immediately. She will die

soon if we don't." Xuri extended her arms, barely lifting Rue's torso.

I hesitated. She had been hunting Korin and lured the dreki to our realm. Saving her seemed like the clearest form of stupidity. But Ruin had also protected Korin. I couldn't make sense of it.

Korin trembled, her voice squeaking through her shock. "We have to help her."

My lips pursed in a thin line. I better not regret this. I extended my arms toward Rue.

Her lips parted in a feeble groan, and I swiftly channeled my magic to staunch the flow of blood around her face. My shadows skimmed across her waxen skin to find any other wounds. The simple ministrations wouldn't be enough if she was to survive. I could clot some of it, but it was like her body was trying to forcefully expel the death magic's toxin, hindering my efforts.

With Xuri's help, we lifted her onto my horse. After settling her in my lap, we sped through the city of Lyrae toward the rebellion's warded camp. I gently clutched Rue's limp and fading body, hoping she would survive this nightmare. Not only for her sake, but I had *many* questions.

I stared at her—intrigue and distrust flowing in equal measure.

This was the second time I carried her unconscious, her fragility oddly moving. "I've got you, Ruin," I spoke into her hair. She remained unresponsive.

We bolted through the city, using back alleys and lesser-known roads to avoid a potential scene. My imposing gelding commanded attention from the few passersby we encountered. Pedestrians jumped out of our way.

Aphellion, the rebel camp, was less a collection of tents and more a city in itself. It was organized into sections for learning, living, healing, and training. Even Queen Avery herself was not fully aware of our location. We were nestled outside of the city proper. Our stronghold thickly veiled by wards maintained by Finn, which allowed us to stretch from the feet of the Topaz Castle to the base of the mountains in the west. Most didn't know it even existed.

To the average Yaritian, all that could be seen was more forest, overgrown with thorns and poisonous plants. A place to avoid. I rode straight for it, bursting through the ward to the other side.

A soldier on duty startled, then relaxed upon identification of their general. "Send Sieren." Without waiting for a response, I headed to the healing quarters, trusting the soldier would make haste to find the Prime Healer.

My heart raced as I considered the consequences of this woman dying. We valued all life, but beyond that, she might know something about the drekis, especially since she successfully fought them off. I briefly assessed her. Her skin had lost color rapidly as blood managed to leak out in thick globs, primarily from one of her ears. Small trickles of blood also trailed from her nose and mouth. I could find no other wounds.

"General!" Sieren hollered at me, racing in my direction. I halted my horse and several other healers came over to help us dismount. I carried Rue to a private space where her wounds could be dealt with.

I relayed what I knew to Sieren. With the other healers occupied, I whispered, "Xuri sensed death magic on her. These may not be straightforward wounds." Sieren nodded tersely and resumed her care, facilitating and directing those under her.

I stood back granting ample space to hopefully perform a miracle. Towels rapidly soaked up Rue's unceasing streams of blood. I peered closer, studying her features. A deep ripple of familiarity lapped at the corners of my memory. The feeling unnerved me.

Sieren closed her eyes, going inward, her hands drifting

slowly down Rue's body, hovering inches above her silent form. Searching for the source of the blood loss, her investigation came up empty. "A deep pulse strains around her neck area, but I find nothing physically visible. The ongoing blood loss will drain her if we don't figure this out quickly." She turned, searching, then grabbed a male healer, her eyes alight with purpose. "Logan, trace her for death magic."

He nodded, approaching Rue's side. The air shimmered beneath his fingers, the whir of his affinity wrapped around her chest and swept up her neck. The air coalesced into waves of moonlight right below her ear, the one that would not cease oozing blood. "A Surveille parasite, just here." He condensed his shimmering magic over the offensive area. "We have to get it out. It might harm her, but she'll die if we do nothing."

"I'll get an elixist. When I get back, I will cast the removal spell." Sieren scrambled out of the room, her departure leaving a wake of quiet tension.

I felt antsy in the weighted silence. Stepping forward, I addressed Logan, "What can I do to help?"

"Can you redirect the blood flow from this area? It will minimize the tissue destruction and create more space for us to remove the Surveille," the healer responded.

While I primarily wielded my metal magic in combat, I could also use it to maneuver the iron found in blood, to manipulate it for brief periods. It required gentle precision, or I risked bursting veins. Luckily, years of practice had honed my craft. "Let me know when you're ready."

Sieren returned, an elixist in tow. We positioned ourselves, each understanding our roles. She extended her arms. "Let's get this parasite."

Everyone stilled. The air itself held its breath. Sieren began chanting, and the temperature dropped as her magic absorbed into Rue's skin. I called the iron in her blood away from the parasite, focusing on both speed and keeping the pressure as low as possible so as not to strain her circulatory system.

The sensation of her blood with my magic was both excruciating and enchanting. The death magic burned against me. But whatever flowed in her veins gripped me—a living current that latched on to my power. The flavor of cherries washed across my tongue, catching me off guard. I doubled down on my task, refusing to lose focus.

The Surveille twitched and jerked, writhing against the thin barrier of Rue's skin. It strained against its confines, clearly pissed at being yanked out of its host, no matter how subtly. Its legs thrashed like a deranged spider.

Sieren's voice grew firmer, louder. The parasite broke through the skin in a sharp burst. The waiting elixist blew a powder over it. The Surveille violently resisted, jerking erratically, then stilled. Tongs grabbed it, transferring it to a waiting jar, the rim sealed with glowing magic. The elixist gripped the jar with wonder, then quietly exited the room.

I released my hold on her blood, confusion settling in. I rubbed my temples, unsure if keeping her in Aphellion was wise. The healers moved in to mend her damaged neck. They placed their hands around her, knitting her tissues back together. Blood finally stopped dripping from her mouth and ears. Pinkened towels littered the floor in a chilling reminder of how close death hovered. Rue's breathing receded into something soft and shallow, the line between her brows relaxing.

As I studied the soft lines of her face, I hoped we weren't too late.

CHAPTER EIGHTEEN
THE SPY

Low and incoherent mutterings droned beside me. A groan escaped as I attempted to shift. Pain pillaged my neck from jaw to clavicle. Unrecognizable surroundings greeted me as I pried my eyes open. My sluggish mind struggled to make sense of the bed confining me, the soft, blue blankets shoved aside. The light slanting through the open window attested to a late hour. My eyes flitted toward the sound of hushed voices.

The events leading to my lapse in consciousness slammed into me with fresh horror. I chose to save Korin, and Wes and Belham witnessed it. A guttural sound escaped me, unbidden. My choices pioneered this fresh hell. Unconsciousness sounded intensely appealing.

A dark-haired woman not much older than me startled me as she walked closer, her kind eyes assessing. She bowed in greeting. "I am the healer here, my name is Sieren. You've been out for three days."

I froze. Three days?

"Where am I? Do you know what happened to me?" My dry

mouth croaked. I must have lost a lot of magic. Or blood. Probably both.

"You are in Aphellion, the Liberation camp. It's warded; don't worry, no one can find us. You are lucky to still be alive." She offered me a glass of water alongside her gentle reproof.

I gratefully took it, my hand trembling, and gulped it down. I felt it flow all the way into my stomach, which growled aggressively in return. My neck throbbed with every swallow. I tenderly brushed my neck.

"We weren't sure you would wake up after what happened," Sieren continued.

"What *did* happen? I remember fighting off drekis, and then… nothing." I groped for a memory, but none arose.

Sieren pulled over a leather chair, a brightly colored pillow warming its utilitarian form. She adjusted the sheets and blankets covering my exposed legs. "May I help you sit up?" she offered.

Carefully supporting my back, she edged me forward, repositioning some pillows to brace me. I leaned against them, fighting through the sharp pain emanating from below my left ear. After assessing my overall comfort, she took a seat beside the bed.

"From what I was told, when the drekis escaped through a portal, you collapsed. You fell unconscious and blood began pouring out of your eyes and ears. It was an unusual amount of blood since there wasn't an obvious wound. Our Prime Oracle, Xuri, sensed the char within your blood. When you got here, we found a Surveille parasite lodged in your neck. How do you suppose that got there?" A note of suspicion laced her words. The hairs on my arm prickled.

Taken aback, my mind coursed with information that barely registered in my overwhelm. "I'm sorry, can you please explain the char, and the…" My mind searched for the word. "The surf…"

"Surveille," she supplied. I distantly nodded in affirmation.

"The char is residual leftover from the use of death magic. It mixed with your blood; it became obvious because you lost so much of it. Surveilles are parasites that act as an eye for someone in another location. One was implanted beneath your skin, below your ear. It observed you and your surroundings, reporting to whomever placed it in the first place. It feeds on the magic in your blood." The information settled heavy in my chest, stealing my breath.

"I had no idea," I whispered. I stared into Sieren's eyes, willing her to believe me. "I didn't know it was there."

She stared at me for a beat too long, determining the truth of my confession. After a moment, she resumed, "Who do you think gave it to you?"

I closed my eyes, recalling my departure from Haluma. The graze of Nolan's fingers along my jaw—a caress, I had thought at the time. But, no. It was no tender farewell. It was a branding, a leash to keep watch over me.

He had expected my betrayal, or at the very least, harbored extreme mistrust. Belham's words echoed: *"Nolan was wise to do what he did to you."* They all knew he had inserted the parasite. Nolan didn't have faith in me—that hurt. He was waiting for my misstep. Only dreki were allowed to leave Haluma, and I was an exception. Not because I displayed more prowess, but rather to expose my weakness and have an excuse to drain my power. I never would have become a dreki, nor could I have won my freedom. I sank further into myself, withering under my whirlwind thoughts.

"King Nolan," I rasped. "He put it in my neck." A tear pricked the corner of my eye. I forcefully blinked it away. I wanted to disappear.

Delah's note came back to me. If Nolan betrayed me like this, he was not above betraying his realm by stealing their magics bit by bit, framing the rebellion in the process. I reeled as puzzle pieces fell into place. It made perfect sense. If I was busy hunting the rebels for interfering with our Berine supplies, then I would never have discovered who was ultimately behind Glint's distribution, and Nolan knew I would stop at nothing to find the truth. He used my pain at losing my mother against me. Why had he trained me if it was all for a lie?

A knock on the door interrupted my revelation. A young man scurried in with a tray of food. I nodded in thanks as he set it on my bed. A full spread of breakfast greeted me: crisp bacon, soft eggs, pungent cheese, and a fluff of bread slathered in jam. I inhaled the scents as my stomach again made its presence known.

Taking a bite, I absently chewed as Sieren asked the young man to fetch the oracle. He left us in silence, the door clicking shut behind him. I carefully swallowed, the movement a cascade of pain along my throat.

"I would like for you to speak with Xuri. I believe you met her the morning you went with Korin to the woods. I can also have a bath set up for you after. And—" She paused. "we will need to discuss your place here at this camp once the General arrives. If you are to have one at all." She added this last part without malice, just a simple statement of fact.

I understood the implication of it. And I didn't blame them for it. I had entered their world with the intention of murdering the Crimson Wolf, and potentially infiltrating the rebellion to report back their secrets and whereabouts to the Good King. I was found with a parasite that relayed my every move.

But I had made my choice. I defected. I couldn't return to Haluma, even if I'd wanted to. Not now. Not as a traitor. My stomach lurched. Nolan would go to great lengths to find me too, if for no other reason than to prove a point and make an example of me. I would likely become a public spectacle using his preferred mode of slow torture.

Grief at what I'd just sacrificed, what I'd just lost, lapped at me. I curled into myself. King Nolan had been my biggest champion. He had showered me with gifts and gave me a chance when I was a homeless, motherless child. He gave me a purpose, and I'd lived according to his directives for years. He was the hope of Haluma. And I had foolishly put all my hope in him. My grief was a weakness that ignited my rage.

I was abandoned. Again. King Nolan never intended to come for me, to protect me. He used me. Manipulated me in my grief. And for what? What had he really wanted from me? My emotions roiled in violent conflict. My breaths serrated the air.

Shame spiraled around me for having purposely exploited Korin. It got me nowhere except to lead me to the choice of betraying myself or my realm. I had entrusted everything to the king. But he had never believed in me. I clutched at my stomach as it threatened to bring forth the breakfast I'd just eaten.

In the end, I did betray my realm. And I collapsed under the discovery that after all this time, I had betrayed myself the most. It left a vise tightening around my battered throat.

My world splintered around me as I lay frozen on a bed in rebel territory. At the mercy of my enemies.

I was a liability. And I couldn't blame these people for not trusting me. But now I belonged nowhere. Anger clawed across my skin, heating it. I needed a plan. I was good as dead if I returned to Haluma. But could I find purpose here? What could I possibly offer the general? My mind sifted through my options, processing through my skills.

I never intended to join the rebellion—the group I fought against my entire life—but perhaps sharing an enemy could form the basis of an alliance. I desperately hoped it would.

A large part of me longed to make up for what I'd subjected Korin to. And maybe, I could use my affinity to further their cause long enough for me to get Delah out of Haluma. Perhaps I could atone for every choice that led me to this moment. Fear scraped against me. I choked back my swelling shame. My trust in my own judgment collapsed through my fingers like grains of sand in the wind.

Maybe Delah and I could finally start over, away from both Haluma and Yarit, away from this battle threatening to erupt into a full-blown war. My current weakened state gnawed at me. I could have used another few days to recover before I made my case to these people. I knew time was not on my side.

The door creaked open and Xuri entered, accompanied by the same two students she brought with her to the woods. She offered a tight smile as she entered, the mirth not quite reaching her eyes. "I'm glad to see you have awakened. That was quite a harrowing adventure you had us on." She paused, gaging my response.

"I'm glad to have made it through."

Xuri paced the side of my bed, strategically thinking through her next words. "We scanned the rest of your body for other Surveille parasites. Thankfully there was nothing else related to death magic coursing through your blood, or implanted beneath your skin. But someone with death magic put that parasite into your neck." An involuntary shiver skittered down my spine. "We know who you are. So, what I say next should stay in this room, and not be relayed elsewhere." Her eyebrow arched in a silent challenge, untrusting. She stopped her pacing and faced me, her students stood back, observing.

"I am the Prime Oracle here. I have helped lead the rebellion since its inception. The General wanted to be rid of you as soon as you recovered. And while I don't fault him that, I would like to get a glimpse of who you were and what you will be. I assume since you fought against the dreki, you might have compromised your own mission, which leads me to believe Haluma will not receive you with open arms. Do I assume correctly?"

I stared down at my hands which had become clammy with every mounting statement Xuri spoke. My words formed slowly. The reality of my actions remained difficult to process.

"Yes. I did not follow through with my orders as planned. I am sure my future in Haluma will be short-lived if I do return." I envisioned the walls closing in, my magic being drained. My choices were indeed limited; it was no use pretending otherwise.

Xuri nodded. She edged closer to the bed to address me. "Then you don't have many options. If you would permit me, I would like to use my power to glean a vision for you. It might get you the leverage you need to gain a second chance with the General, seeing as how you put a cherished member of our community at risk. He isn't used to offering them, but my input may sway him. It could also damn you." Her gaze searched me. "Are you willing?"

I reached for the glass of water that had been left on my side table. I gripped it, willing it to stabilize me. Fear and lingering dehydration parched my mouth. I gulped the water down, the fluid splitting around the hard lump in my throat. Steeling myself for whatever outcome awaited, I gave my consent.

CHAPTER NINETEEN
THE GENERAL

Sweat mingled with the agitation on my brow.

Sching. I clenched the hilts of my longswords, sweeping them in controlled arcs toward Finn. I needed this outlet, and Finn was my strongest opponent. Neither of us went easy on the other.

He spun, easily avoiding my blades, then lunged toward me. My elbow made satisfying contact with his chest. He grunted with the force.

Xuri asked me to stay away until she viewed Ruin's life threads. She knew where to find me when she was done. I had been sparring for most of the morning, and my restlessness crept into my combat. Finn delivered a swift punch to my shoulder. I turned to find his weapons lifted and a self-assured, if tired, smile. We both heaved from our exertion.

"Water break."

Finn nudged me as I bent over to grab my canteen from the ground. I glanced in the direction he gestured toward and straightened at the sight of Xuri coming our way.

I jogged over to meet her, the canteen forgotten. "What did you find out?"

She silently led the way to a nearby bench. My arms crossed taut across my body. The last several days had sat heavy on me, one that sparring relieved, though barely. The suspense of Rue's recovery left me tightly coiled. Even my jaw wasn't immune. A light breeze ruffled across the fields as we sat down.

"May I show you?" The transfer of her visions to others was a newer skill. I'd hoped this time I wasn't left with a pounding skull.

I shifted toward her and nodded, waiting, teeth gritted in anticipation. Xuri placed her palms flush against my temples and shut her eyes.

My mind exploded in an assault of visions. Light flashed. Emotions seared. Images flared in vivid color as if projected in front of me. I sped along a thread—both strong and delicate. Lilac hair, a stone room, the dripping of blood. Angry fists, sparring fields, inner conflict. A friendship deeply forged, sinister reptilian eyes, a desire for home. An unmoored ship, searching. Grief that made me double over.

Then the thread split into several strands. Many futures. One stood out, thicker than the rest, and I followed it. I coursed down a magenta thread. Xuri's power coaxed it to reveal its secrets. Softening, it released hazy images of a gathered army, destruction, a glowing cure. A tether. Thick desire and depthless love thrummed through me. My breath caught, and I centered myself amidst the overwhelm as the vision sped on. Healing. Death. A catastrophic loss. Consuming darkness. Then, a veil shifting into brilliant starlight. A kaleidoscope of colors consumed my mind, shifting and merging. I gasped for air, groping in the ether. Then abruptly, it ceased.

My eyes jerked open. I gripped the stone bench beneath me, seeking balance. Xuri's rich, brown eyes remained glazed as she slowly came back to herself.

She cleared her throat, then placed her hand on my shoulder. "I think she might be the key. She knows about things we do not. And those images…" Her hand dropped to her lap as she gazed toward the Auren Mountains. "I think she can find the cure."

I tensed at her words.

"You know I wouldn't try to sell false hope. And she can't go back to Haluma. You could help her see what's really going on; she might be open to it."

I frowned toward the ground, tasting the veracity of her words. "Does this align with what your mother foretold?"

"She doesn't fit the profile, but looks can change. Maybe she's the one foretold, maybe they're two different people. But what I saw in her life threads… I really think she's the one we've been waiting for."

"Is she trustworthy? Or could this be a double-cross type situation? Something to make it look like she defected, but truly didn't?" I needed more than sketchy reassurances that moving forward with Rue wouldn't implode everything we had worked for. Visions were open to interpretation, after all.

"I wondered the same thing at first. But after my vision, and seeing her reaction to the news of the Surveille parasite, I believe it to be authentic. Perhaps you should speak with her and judge for yourself. And… I gave her a vision of my memories as well."

My eyes widened at her disclosure.

"We need her on our side. I thought she should see what her king has truly been up to. How he has brought destruction and destroyed a generation of girls. What he did to our mother…"

I swiped a lock of hair away from my brow, my eyes unseeing as my mind churned—creating scenarios, predicting outcomes, daring to hope. "Fine, I'll speak with her. Please notify me as soon as she awakens." I stood, gripping her shoulder. "Thank you, Xuri."

"Of course. But…"

I glanced up at her, my focus sharpened at her cautionary tone.

"She's been trained as an elite soldier, fully indoctrinated. The Liberation is depending on you to free us from Nolan's power. My memories might help her to see the truth, or she might view them as a ploy to convince her to join our side. Stay on your guard with her. She might be the one to lead us to a cure, to getting rid of the veil, but she should be nothing more than that."

I bristled at her directive. I could make up my own mind. Destroying the king, and thus the darkness, was my only focus. I offered a terse nod before turning on my heel.

SHE CALLED HERSELF RUE, an uncommon name and one I felt confident wasn't her given name.

I curled my fingers inward, the comforting weight of my black titanium rings cutting into my circulation.

I scowled at the thought of her having gotten so close to Korin. But she had put herself in danger in order to protect the endearing land wielder. Shadows seeped out of my knuckles. *Foka,* I didn't trust her at all, but if she could aid us in finding a cure... I shook my head at the mere idea of it. Ludicrous.

The thought chipped away at me. If there stood a glimmer of a chance...

I stalked my way across Aphellion, leaving the common areas behind. The bustle of the dining hall and elixist gardens faded. A breeze whispered down from the mountains to the west, colliding with the humid air from the Lyraean waterways.

The healers' buildings came into view, their white limestone almost blinding in the afternoon sun. Without blemish, the hewn stone stood proudly, the healers' magic mending even the rocks used to house them and their patients.

The door remained shut and I debated knocking. After a beat, I opted not to. Respect was earned, and I hadn't decided if she leaned more prisoner or ally. The door swung open and I filled the threshold, hardening my gaze, even as my eyes adjusted from the blinding light of day to the dim glow of her room. My anger churned with suspicion, barely restrained.

Rue turned toward me, eyes widening. She lay ensconced in her bed. The light-blue coverlet scrunched haphazardly at her waist. The thin tunic provided by the healers barely concealed her small frame. Her white hair fell in ripples over one shoulder, exposing the area of her neck where the Surveille parasite was extracted, now nearly healed. Fading bruises diffused across her skin.

She adjusted her body in an attempt to sit upright. I watched her cover a wince with the movement, then brought up the blanket as if to shield herself from me.

Good. Let her feel fear.

As I drew closer, she subtly tensed, steeling herself. Her face remained carefully blank as she bored into me with arrestingly vibrant eyes. In expectation. In challenge. She lifted her chin, radiating a resolute strength. Well, damn. Her eyes were the strangest shade of blue, almost purple. Perhaps a trick of the low lighting? I released my shadows, banking my curiosity. A quiet threat.

Clearing my throat, I leaned against a dresser, its frame creaking in protest. "Seems you were in the right place at the right time." My words emerged flat. A slight shrug her only response. "We keep running into each other. What brought you to Yarit?" I shrewdly assessed her every movement.

She tensed, but didn't flinch, her expression unmoved. Her ongoing silence spurred me onward.

"Did you summon the drekis that entered this realm? The Scourge?" I stalked forward a step, letting my size fill the space, allowing my metal affinity to rattle the iron shutters on the walls.

Her shoulders slumped a notch, and she avoided my gaze. "I *was* a part of the Scourge. Obviously, I'm not anymore." The last part came out as a whispered afterthought. She took in a deep breath, rallying her words, facing me again. "I was sent here to find the Crimson Wolf. Then I did…" Her breath hitched. "And I couldn't do it. I've betrayed my realm." Her hand absently drifted to her neck as she spoke. It wavered before she dropped it back in her lap.

I tapped my finger on my leg, my rings softly *tinging* at the movement. I sensed her heart beating rapidly. Her fingers clenched to stifle a tremor, but she spoke truthfully. My mouth opened to ask another question, but she beat me to it.

"I would like to make a bargain." Those piercing eyes met mine, expectant. Her sharp edges called to my own, a honed warrior in both physique and spirit, and I had the sudden urge to spar. Or take a cold shower. Her gaze fixed like a bolt of electricity—magnetic and unflinching.

"You aren't in much of a position to do such a thing. And right now, I don't think you can be trusted. You had a change of heart after meeting Korin? Bravo. And now you're aligned with the rebellion?" I scoffed. Waves of anger radiated off of me.

"I realize what this looks like," she forged on. "Which is why I want to strike a deal with you. I'm an elite spy. I can see auras, and weed out traitors, dissenters, liars. I can proficiently wield water. I am willing to help you. King Nolan is not who I thought he was." She stopped talking, seeking to control the tremble in her voice. Her breath heaved, "In exchange, I would like for me and my sister, Delah, to be given safe passage. Far away from here. Where we cannot be found. King Nolan won't let me live. And after what Xuri showed me, I don't want to return to Maripol anyway."

Surprise warped my thoughts. Her boldness and fear equally prominent as she recognized her bleak situation. I chewed on her words, contemplating. Unconsciously, I resumed drumming the same finger against my leg. She glanced down at the movement and I abruptly stilled. "Thank you for letting Xuri observe your life threads. If it weren't for that, I would gladly have killed you myself. The safety of my family and my people are paramount. But you might prove very useful to me. And for that, I'll consider your bargain."

She nodded once, a tinge of relief softening her brow.

"How do I know you aren't truly spying for Haluma?"

Indignation prickled and she crossed her arms. "I guess you don't. Unless you have someone who can pull memories. But I can assure you I am not a dreki. I have not made that trade. I have little else to offer beyond my word, and whatever your oracle saw." She could throw daggers with that challenging stare. Not many would dare to respond so audaciously. I perked up at her defiance, swiftly chiding the curious beast inside.

But her magic. That's what really gave me pause. The last water wielder had perished decades ago, and I had no means of reaching the underwater realms without one. But with Ruin, I could gain access to what I desperately needed.

"You will have round-the-clock guards. I would like to train with you to determine your strengths. Lucky for you, I'm in need of a water wielder. One wrong move from you, one whiff of treason, and our bargain is void and I will dispatch you myself."

"Yes, you said that before." She pointedly glared at me. My shadows swirled around in warning and she blanched.

I studied her, seeing past her bravado to the fear beneath. My power subtly relented. "Things will go easier for you if you're open to ideas that might go against the stories they packaged for you. You might be surprised to find that what you thought was true may not be. When you're ready to learn more, come find me."

She appeared to wilt before my eyes. "Like what? Tell me one thing you think I don't know."

Her words were tangible, deflating things. I wanted her to understand, but I didn't want to completely demoralize her; I had worked with many orphans from Haluma who struggled intensely at the outset of learning their lives were a lie and they had been brainwashed. And Ruin was technically still in recovery from a parasite; I really did need her for her power. I would have to tread lightly.

"I already know that Glint is refined Berine. And Nolan uses it on his own people. My sister suspected his treachery. Xuri revealed the deepening veil and the effects of how he drained your previous oracle. There is nothing left for me in Maripol." She shrank beneath the admission. Whether due to her physical recovery or the emotional output, I wasn't sure.

Somehow she had pieced together the distortions despite Haluma's consuming propaganda. Perhaps Delah was able to convince her after all. I offered a curt nod.

"We will start training tomorrow." I didn't wait for her response as I took my leave, the door slamming at my exit.

She unnerved me. She dared to make a bargain with me after leading drekis to our doorstep. Was it really Korin that made her defect?

I pinched the bridge of my nose. I had barely gotten any sleep in the last several days. Not with sorting through newly recruited spies, Ilayah's passing, and making sure no other assassins portaled in. Then there was the issue of Queen Avery's request to dine. I had yet to respond.

Multiple loose ends dangled in my periphery; it wasn't the wisest time to go traipsing to the coast. But seeking an alliance with the Nereid Queen might shift the tide of this entire war.

I closed my eyes as the idea burrowed into my bones. I let that persistent weed of hope peek through the cracks. It had shriveled to near nothing. But with a water wielder on our side, we could take one more step in the right direction. Because I couldn't meet the Nereid Queen without one.

CHAPTER TWENTY
THE SPY

I awakened from anxiety-riddled sleep. Glancing around the room, I noticed training leathers, my boots, and—oddly, but thankfully—the cherry candies I'd had stashed in my pockets and satchel when I'd gone to the fields with Korin.

Guilt coiled in my stomach at the thought of the young girl. I had to make recompense for putting her in such a dangerous situation.

The urgent desire to move had me getting out of bed. My neck remained stiff where the parasite once lived, but overt pain had dissipated leaving a wary, dull ache. I leaned my head back, my fingers gently grazing my neck wound. The worst of my recovery was now behind me.

I secured my braids—three behind my right ear and two behind my left—then tied back the rest, hoping that whatever awaited at the sparring fields would be painful enough to numb the effects of my choices.

As prepared as I could be, I followed a silent guard through the rebellion's domain. We weaved through houses made of varying types of stone. The healing area consisted primarily of sun-bleached limestone; scrolling copper details suffused the facade, creating ornate window borders as well as practical beams that gleamed in the twinkling pre-dawn.

Other areas housed tall stone buildings, some with chimneys where curling black smoke spilled into the sky. An area further off included a great hall and other larger facilities. We eventually came upon an open area of sectioned-off fields.

I took off in a sprint, running along the perimeter of the sparring area. My feet pounded against the ground, dew spraying off short blades of grass in twinkling explosions I felt rather than saw. A few tears streaked down my face. No one, save for my watchful guard, stood by to distract me with their auras, so I let them flow.

A gaping hollow spread within me. How could I have grown up in Haluma and believed in the lies so thoroughly? How did I miss the truth staring me in the face? I had trusted the king, the one who knew the worst about me, and everything he did and said had been a lie. There *were* Primes still alive. And he hunted them all to harvest them for their magic. I wanted to puke. I could hardly trust myself.

I pushed my body well beyond what I should have exerted in my current state. The site of the Surveille extraction had slightly reopened, and a small trickle of blood dampened my collar. I slashed the back of my hand across my eyes smearing my tears. Whatever pain I experienced, was pain I deserved. For my blind trust. For my stupidity.

An old ache scraped against my ribs. One that whispered my lack, imprinting my isolation on my skin for all to observe. I had again lost everything, and I only had myself to blame. Just like with my parents. My breaths heaved and I slowed to a stop, dizzy, leaning over my knees to draw air into my lungs.

Again.

I resumed my frenetic pace, blood and sweat mingling with hatred—at both myself and the king. I followed my worn trail along the outskirts of the sparring fields over and over, welcoming the sharp burn of my muscles, the sting in my lungs.

The scent of leather and amber broke my concentration. When my path led me away from the base of the mountains, I caught the general watching me with keen and curious eyes. I slowed, breaths jagged in the cool air.

The morning had opened its indolent eyes revealing hues of cerulean and coral, clouds growing brighter with the reflection of the sun's rays. I forced my anxious thoughts to dissipate, imagining the space left behind being filled with a golden strength. Like Judd's eyes, damn him.

I proceeded over to where weapons lounged against a gray stone wall. I grabbed a simple, dull broadsword. This thing couldn't cut through a soft piece of fruit, but it would make do for simple drills.

The general met me at the collection of swords and battle axes. He seemed as large and solid as the stone wall I had gathered my sword from. He blatantly assessed me, his face yielding nothing. "You started early. Let's see how you fight, Ruin of the Scourge. But no magic."

I assumed my fighting stance. "It's Rue," I corrected him.

He merely shrugged, removing his own sword from its sheath and took up his position opposite me. He lunged, our dance beginning. He displayed the clever, graceful movements of a man well-trained. His footwork and feinting, his strength and power calculated and deliberately impressive, even to me, an elite soldier. But I was eager to prove I would not be a liability, but rather a formidable fighting ally in whatever he required of me. We parried and twisted, ducked and lunged.

I settled easily into combat, armoring myself and embracing the lethality of my body. I twisted away from his blade, my own narrowly missing his chest as he tactfully avoided contact. His stance faltered, and I swept my foot under him, ready to take him out. He caught my movement with breathtaking speed, turning my attempt against me.

In a heartbeat, he was on top of me, his weight dispersed enough for me to choke on my dignity. Muscular forearms held him up in an effort to avoid crushing me. That maddening mouth twitched in a deviously taunting smirk, mere inches from my face. "Your confidence far exceeds your demonstrated performance." He jumped up, beckoning me with a cocky summon of his hand. "Again, Scourge."

I cracked my neck, ready to wipe that smug grin off his face and make him eat the words he'd thrown back at me. My feet planted, balance restored, we went again.

After multiple draws, two wins, and mostly getting my ass handed to me, we finally took a break. I regarded the mountains, breathing in the piney air swooping down from their rugged peaks.

The thought of Haluma on the other side of those leering pinnacles was a slamming reminder of the enemies now hunting me. A warning of the retribution sure to come. The worst was that I deserved whatever came for me. I closed my eyes when that familiar feeling of being caged breached my defenses. Deep breaths.

In.

Out.

Judd sighed. "I can't imagine the difficulty of aligning with who you once believed was your enemy."

I was still sorting through the maze of truths and distortions. I chanced a look at the general. "I still don't know that you're *not* my enemy. But you're a lesser evil than the King." I pulled a few long blades of grass, twisting them in my hands. "I always thought you brought in Glint. Delah only recently revealed the connection between it and Nolan." How many times had she tried to expose the lies, only for me to silence her?

"That's the twisted story Nolan uses to further his own

interests." He sat down beside me, his shoulder near my own. "In the beginning of his reign, he started the Vestal Anchor program—a way to harvest magic. He has a refinery where he synthesizes Glint from Berine. It's connected to the water treatment system so he can pump Glint into the water supply."

Hells. The fountains throughout the city. My breaths wavered.

Pity softened the hardness of his words. "Berine absorbs magic, but refined, Glint siphons it. He incrementally drains his own people. The purpose of his light orbs is to absorb the siphoned magic. When they become saturated they sink lower and burn brighter. It's why he sends workers to replace them. They're collected and the stolen magic creates the dreki."

I tore at the weeds and grass beneath my fingers. A tremble stole through my body and I couldn't speak. I had to hear this though. I needed to. I did not sense a lie.

"Vestal Anchors were once all Primes. They were the ones with the strongest magic, the richest resource to siphon from. The King stood to gain the most from them. They were rounded up and drained. He wanted Primes of his own, so he created the dreki from them."

My understanding of the world tilted on its axis. I thought of Delah next in line to become a Vestal Anchor, my stomach bottoming out. Judd kept speaking.

"The Liberation established itself as a haven for escaped Primes. Our numbers increased as more people filtered out of Haluma and wandered into Yarit. They sought safety, away from the thrall of Glint and the threat of Nolan. We built up and warded Aphellion, and the Liberation has worked subversively ever since to try and undermine the King and prevent more Berine from flooding into his realm, strengthening him. Xuri's mother narrowly escaped that first recruitment." He paused, gathering himself, his eyes glassy. He spoke of Xuri and her mother with such fondness. They clearly had a history.

I stared down at my fingers as he spoke, absently braiding long blades of grass. Xuri had offered me a glimpse of her dying mother, the pain of the memory sharp and bitter as if it had been my own.

"Primes almost never leave Aphellion. She insisted on entering Maripol again, to search for the girl in her visions. Unfortunately, her presence was swiftly discovered. We didn't get to her in time and the withdrawal symptoms of Glint destroyed her mind and eventually her body."

This information settled like land after an earthquake. Everything had rearranged, the topography forming new shapes, though the ground itself remained the same. Something itched, writhed beneath my skin. Something I had compelled to stay inside all these years. I had ignored my intuition. I had colluded with a deceiver. I avoided the cracks in Haluma's recorded history because they threatened to break the dam of King Nolan's carefully constructed lies.

The Good King had covered his bases so well, twisting the story so that the populace revered him as savior. His version showed him victim to the rebels. Hero, rather than villain, to the realms. And I chose to believe him.

Hollowness swelled. Anger consumed to the point of desolation. It's a special kind of torture to face the lies that let you sleep at night. If I were being honest with myself, pieces of my beliefs had been fragmenting and falling apart for a while now. I had stitched them together to keep me under the banner of loyalty. The deceptions across the realm had burrowed as deep as my own heart.

I shuttered the black hole yawning inside me. I had to get back to Delah before they made her an official Vestal Anchor, my fear for her dramatically surging. I moved away from the general, despite a deep desire to remain near. I was overwhelmed, untethered.

"Nolan is a master of illusions. His expertise is deception."

I put my head in my hands, restraining a scream that threatened to sever the air. "I had no idea. And Xuri..." I shook my head. Perhaps we had both lost a mother to Nolan's Glint. If my lies were what previously kept me warm at night, then my anger would now do the job.

"She has handled the loss of Ilayah with much grace. Though the grief still aches," he responded. His care for Xuri pointed to something much deeper between them. A pang of disappointment layered onto my overwhelm.

The general assessed me before responding. "I know this truth is painful. It's a lot to take in. You of all people have the right to rage."

Yet, anger could be directed and used. Mine went toward planning my retribution and Delah's escape.

Delah was likely safe for now, but she wouldn't be for long. My only hope at rescuing her was to keep my end of our bargain and use my magic to strengthen the Liberation. The effects of the lies coiled around me. Nolan had let me believe the Liberation was behind my parents' demise. It was him all along. I wouldn't let him take any more from me.

"Well, well, well!" A boisterous voice slashed into the moment. A man as tall as the general sauntered up, his arms crossed genially across his chest. He stopped next to Judd, facing me, oblivious to his intrusion. I welcomed the distraction.

Where the general's dark coloring aligned with his perpetual scowl, this man's blond hair matched his lighthearted air. The sides of his shaved head faded into a messy top knot, like one of the ice hunters from the glacial hinterlands. The hint of a grin showed through his neatly trimmed beard. His blue eyes held a spark of amusement. "You must be who everyone's talking about, causing all the chaos around here. The defecting Not-Dreki." He held out his hand. "I'm Finn, the General's second. You can call me Finn." He said with a wink.

My mouth twitched, trying not to smile. I shook his hand against my better judgment. "The name is Ruin, or Rue actually."

He took a halfstep back, assessing me. "That's not your real name. What is it truly?"

He seemed vaguely familiar, but the feeling passed with the onslaught of his rudeness. "I see the rebels live up to the rumors of being mannerless heathens."

He smiled broadly. "I've been called worse. But I can't call you Ruin, also known as Rue. How about Rebby? Still in the *R* family, but has a better ring to it. Now that you're a rebel and all."

"You might find a dagger in your back if you call me that again."

"Have to have your daggers for that to happen." He clapped the general on his back. "I see you are getting our newest recruit in shape. Can't believe you'd start without me." The general rolled his eyes as he rolled up his sleeves. His exposed forearms flexed as he casually gripped his canteen. I swallowed hard, looking away, anywhere but in their direction.

"We just finished an hour of sparring. If you care to join us next time, you might want to wake up earlier."

"I had a late night!" Finn's eyebrows rose suggesting the antics of the night before. I had to suppress rolling my own eyes at him. "Well, in that case, tomorrow we can see how talented you are with a blade, Rebby. We won't have much time before we head to see the Nereid Queen."

The general sheathed his swords and turned to me. "Not bad this morning. Especially in light of the Surveille."

I warmed under his praise and began gathering my things. "Where are the Nereids?" I inquired.

The general quirked his head to the side. "They never let you leave Haluma did they? You've never heard of the Nereid Realm?"

Shame needled me, but I stood straighter. "Will you answer my question?" I arched my brow.

A lopsided smile bloomed across his jaw revealing a shadowed dimple. "It's the underwater realm of ocean nymphs and sirens. You are going to be the means by which we get there."

I stopped breathing.

He took a halting step toward me. "What is it?"

I fiddled with the edge of my leathers, anything to avoid eye contact when I admitted my deficiency. "I can't swim," I mumbled.

Finn's guffaw had a family of birds taking flight. I winced.

The general threw his wooden sword at Finn, who retreated at the assault.

"How does a water wielder not know how to swim?" He gently pried, no mockery in the question.

I still couldn't look him in the eye. "I grew up in Haluma, and as you already noted, I was *not* permitted to leave. It's a realm surrounded by mountains and forest and hills. Not... water."

He wiped a hand down his face. I could almost hear him groan. "I'll teach you."

My neck twinged from the speed at which I jerked to meet his gaze. My shock and confusion lay bare across my face. I scrutinized his expression, yet I detected no annoyance as I'd expected.

"One of our Primes, Gemma, can assist with making sure you know how to keep us breathing. I will ensure you know how to swim." His sincerity destabilized me.

I swallowed my embarrassment, grateful for the small kindness of his offer. I busied myself with my canteen, seeking to hide the grin that fought its way forward. Working with a Prime and expanding the use of my magic had me feeling like a little girl on her birthday.

"If you have any books on the Nereids, I would love to read them." Having been sequestered in Haluma, and my entire education biased toward the Good King and his agenda, I knew little about the rest of the realms.

Judd softened, thinking. "I'll have some dropped off for you this afternoon. And if you're anything like Xuri, I'll get you some of her pining-maiden stories as well."

I internally flinched at his mention of the Prime. What was the nature of their relationship? I forced the muscle in my jaw to relax. "I do enjoy a little romance to pass the time. Especially if there's a single-bed situation," I coyly responded.

He stared at me with a knowing twinkle. "Consider it done."

I took a swig of water at the same moment hairs on the back of my neck prickled.

Darkness captured my attention as shadows swam across the fields, blotting out the gleaming sun. The air around us stilled and my body responded before my mind understood, freezing beneath the cold power that draped across Aphellion. We slowly peered skyward. My canteen dropped to the ground, water gurgling out of it.

Dread leached from my bones as I beheld the monsters.

CHAPTER TWENTY-ONE
THE SPY

"Run," I breathed. There were three of them, heralding a darkness beneath their waxen wings. Their leathery bodies traveled close to one another, searching the grounds with intrusive eyes. Their bodies were human in shape, yet their limbs elongated well beyond what was normal. It resembled the same creature I had seen in the alley back in Haluma. I stumbled in my hasty retreat.

A screech pierced the air, forcing my eyes shut with its sharpness as if the sound had talons. The general ran beside me, his double longswords flashing in both of his hands. The rings on his fingers flared like embers waiting to catch fire.

A bell rang feverishly across the Liberation's territory. Streams of soldiers poured outside, dressed in their scaled leathers.

The beasts dipped toward me with outstretched hands. Long claws extended, sharpened into razor-sharp blades. As they descended, I saw thick spikes along their backs and smaller spines down their limbs. Their heads were as bald as a vulture's. I ducked to avoid its grasp, narrowly missing a claw.

We zigzagged through the fields, leading them away from the rest of Aphellion. The cold sweat of fear dampened my top.

Another creature dove at us. The general's rings immediately shifted into arrows. Several glanced off of their bodies. They returned to the general's waiting hands, and he cast them toward their inky eyes. One hit its mark and the creature hissed, retreating back into the sky.

A second beast changed tactics, landing on the ground in front of us. It's grotesquely long limbs moved with unmatched speed. It strode straight toward me, reeking of rot and decay.

The general fought back the third creature, sprays of metal arrows sailing through the sky. It cocked its head toward the general and its pupils widened in a flash of fear.

"Don't provoke us. We aren't here for you," it uttered with feigned bravery.

Judd advanced on it, ignoring its plea. Soldiers were still racing in our direction, their weapons unsheathed, Finn leading their attack.

The creature before me loomed, unperturbed. "Ruin of the Scourge, you have betrayed the Good King. Come with us and face your punishment." Its voice was grinding and sharp. I blanched at its words, my courage curdling inside me. My pause opened an opportunity for abduction.

The beast lunged for my arm. I twisted out of its reach, but it closed the space between us quicker than I could recover. A scream tore out of me as the ground melted away. I suppressed a gag as the rancid scent of death smothered me. I clenched my eyes shut, focusing on my magic. I had never summoned the clouds before, but I was frantic to try anything to destroy these monsters.

I pulled on the water in the air, imagining the clouds condensing at my call. My fear slowed me down but I fought through it. *Do not be shaken.* I would die before I allowed this vile creature to win. Below me, I watched as the general yelled skyward, his voice stolen by the winds.

Finn and an army of soldiers surrounded the remaining beast. Manacles of magicked metal appeared on its wrists and ankles. Chains coiled around its body, tightening until it collapsed into the dirt. The clouds around me turned dark. The beast would not return me to Haluma. Not today.

Hail responded to my call, descending mercilessly upon the creature, beating against its bat-like wings. I forced my body to freeze until it burned the claws that bound me. It snarled and lurched, discharging an acid that burned through my leathers, but released me from its clutches. My scream twined with the air as I plummeted toward my doom. The flying creature above me writhed and hissed against my magic's effects.

The general shoved Finn, pointing at me. Finn raised his arms and my descent slowed until my feet kissed the ground. I fell to my knees, recovering my breath as the weight of true gravity returned. The creature above retreated.

The general's attention on me allowed the beast at his feet to gain ground. Its claws slashed at Judd's armor, shoving him into dirt and hailstones. The repeated blows finally tore through the scales, sundering the flesh across his chest. The sight viscerally impacted me. A scream tore loose as the beast leered over the general.

My body grew desiccated— lips chapped, mouth parched. I gathered small hailstones in my hand, reabsorbing my essence. I had just enough affinity for a final blow. I dug down deep, yanking a thread that tethered me to the clouds above. Hailstones formed into lethal blades, this final beast their sole target.

Acidic poison dripped from the spikes on its arms. Malice coated its features. I unleashed. Rain and hail descended in a torrent, aiming exclusively for Nolan's creature. The deluge of ice froze the poison beading out of the monster's body, crystallizing it. Hail razored through its leathery hide. Black, tarry blood oozed and spattered the ground. It screeched and wobbled on its feet before finally succumbing to its injuries.

I dragged myself toward the general on shaking hands, the acid on my leathers still burning through my flesh.

Judd locked eyes with me. I rolled onto my back, weakly trying to pull my leathers away from my burning skin. Soldiers and healers swarmed around us as my awareness flickered.

"Dom!" Finn yelled. I fought for lucidity, looking around for the person he addressed. Finn knelt in front of the general, assessing his wounds. His shadows hovered around him. Dizziness washed over me and I closed my eyes. *Dom?* No, his name was Judd.

A man named Bowen knelt beside me searching for injuries. The healers and elixists had arrived. I reached for Bowen in a desperate bid to help me with my leathers, the smell of my burning skin consuming me.

"Get it off. Get it off," I begged. He began trying to remove my clothing but fumbled with the clasps.

A large hand pushed Bowen back followed by a domineering growl. The flash of a dagger made me gasp. The blade sliced down a seam in my leathers, relieving me of the acidic compression against my skin. Someone covered me with a cloak, and I was lifted off the ground. The burning against my skin immediately receded.

Strong arms enclosed me. I sagged against a broad chest. It smelled of safety. It smelled like the general. My mind churned as if through marshland. The king had sent acid-spewing flying monsters to hunt me. I shivered in the aftermath.

"I will repay the King for all the harm he has caused us. What he has done to you." His words penetrated my haze, echoing a similar threat made long ago to a frightened girl in the woods. But could it be? The pieces clicked into place. I blinked to clear my vision and regarded the grim-faced warrior who protectively held me with fresh eyes.

Human blood and monster ichor mingled with the stubble of his cheeks. He had the same dark hair. The same honeyed eyes that glowed with a piercing luminosity. All the signs were there. *Was it really Dom?* Anger at all the years of his silence crouched on the fringes, but the truth was I had missed him. I sank into his protection. For just this moment.

He held me tight against his chest the whole way back to the healing quarter before reluctantly laying me on a bed. Concern marred his tired brow as he backed away. He used his broad shoulders to push the healers back, ripping their salves from their hands and tending to my burns himself.

I dared a glance at my wounds. Char crusted the borders of my seared skin. The soothing pressure of his hands relaxed me and I dropped my head back on my pillow. Despite his obvious distrust for me, his calloused fingers applied a gentle balm. His touch was careful, unhurried. I didn't understand why the leader of the rebellion would stoop to a healer's station. I didn't contemplate the effect it had on me.

Finn interrupted my care, gripping the general's shoulder in agitation.

"Dom, you're fading. You've waited too long." His second didn't back down from the general's violent glare.

My vision focused long enough to notice the darkened veins beneath his skin. What had those monsters done to him?

Sieren ushered the general out of my space. Her brow furrowed in concern as she urged him into the other room. He glanced back at me, lips pursed, as if reluctant to leave my side. The door shut firmly behind them, sealing me away from the general's fate.

I watched through murky consciousness as a flurry of healers entered and departed Judd's—no, Dom's room. An elixist hurried by, and I flagged him over. He stopped short, inclining his head with impatience.

"Is the general okay?" I asked.

He shifted on his feet, agitated. His hands were full of multiple vials whose contents sloshed with his jerky movements. "He'll be fine by tomorrow." The man hustled away, the glass vials rattling in his wake.

I fell in and out of sleep, and I eventually felt strong enough to sit up. My wounds became numb, and my tissues had already started to mend back together. I was even able to eat and drink. I observed as the Prime Healer departed from the general's room.

I had to speak with him. I had to hear his name from his own lips. I shuffled over to his door. A guard I had somehow missed inserted himself between me and the door.

He held himself straight, slightly threatening. "The General cannot see you."

I bristled. "I just want to check on him."

"No one except the Prime can enter until tomorrow." He puffed his chest and subtly gripped the hilt of his sword.

Alarm coursed through me. Why this show of force? What was happening?

"Let her in," the general yelled from the other side.

I arched a brow at the guard who immediately obeyed.

The general's eyes remained closed as I entered. Candles flickered in the darkened room lending a peaceful atmosphere. A thin sheet covered his exposed chest, while a heavier white quilt lay across his hips and legs. The carved muscles of his shoulders and chest glistened with a sheen of healing oils. It did little to diminish the oddity of his veins—darkened tracks beneath his pallid skin. Glass vials littered his bedside table.

"I can feel you, Ruin of the Scourge. Come to end me in my weakened state?" He didn't even bother to open his eyes.

I trained my magic on him, his aura glowed stable, not a flicker of pain. A small sigh escaped me.

He slowly opened his eyes, though they remained at half-mast. His lip twitched to one side. "It'll take more than this to bring me down." His hand lazily gestured toward his torso. "Don't think this gets you out of training with me tomorrow."

"Are your healers so gifted that you would be recovered by dawn?" I scanned his body, not giving my eyes a chance to linger on the way the sheet clung to his rippled muscles.

"They only have me staying here to monitor me. And then they gave me a restorative elixir to force me to sleep and allow their mending to complete." As if on cue, he yawned.

The elixist Bowen burst through the door. "Dom, here are two more vials. I'll work on creating a more concentrated tonic." He stopped short, eyes darting wildly between the two of us. He deposited the vials, removing the empty ones, then ducked out.

I surveyed the general. Judd. *Dom.* "What did he call you?" Deep down, I already knew. But the truth needed to be stated. Ice chips hardened along my arms, flaking from my fingers onto the floor.

The general inclined his head, confusion forging a line on his brow. "Dom. My name."

The floor began to freeze. "I thought your name was Judd."

A weak laugh huffed out of him. "That's the name I use as a cover. I couldn't go through other realms announcing my identity. I'd say you've earned the right to know it, at this point."

My world rearranged as another lie fell exposed. "One more question for you, General. What are your thoughts on snow and ice?"

He assessed me like I'd lost my mind. But I needed to know his answer. "I hate them. Who wants to be cold all the time?"

The air stilled. It was him. It was always him. And he didn't know who I was. I realized all at once that I represented everything he hated: His enemy-king's groomed spy, and a wielder whose core magic, ice, was everything he despised. Whatever ember existed between us flickered out. I couldn't afford to remain in a delusion. We were allies under a bargain borne of my need to survive.

I forced a smile that was more a grimace. Slumbering grief and the repressed sting of abandonment threatened to devour me. I swayed on my feet, needing to escape.

My words cut the silence from a tight, pressurized place. "I hope you feel better."

Dom blinked slow, a small smile quirking the sides of his mouth. He turned on his side, showcasing his massive back, tattoos swirled in intricate patterns and ancient script I couldn't read. "I'll see you at dawn." And with that, he relaxed, his breathing slowed into the rhythm of quiet slumber.

NIGHTMARES PLAGUED me and I awoke in the disorienting in-between feeling young, exposed, and vulnerable. Reality's horrid blanket settled upon me, smothering me. The king had unleashed monsters, and they had found Aphellion. The general was Dom, my oldest friend, and I felt overwhelmed with conflict over it. My distrust for my own judgment lurked like a demon in the rafters.

I absently felt around in my discarded leathers for a cherry candy, grateful to have overstuffed my pockets with them from the day prior. The process of fully tasting it dulled my spiked nerves, even if only a fraction. I inhaled, and inspected my chest from yesterday's battle. Pale-pink skin replaced the angry burn marks as if tiny carnations had burrowed into my flesh. I pulled on a tunic and trousers, and stalked to the sparring fields, my dedicated night guard close behind.

Dark-velvet sky yielded to the sun's honeyed rays. My rage

sang like the notes of a drum, thrumming with every pulse of my heart. Rage at the king. Rage at Dom. But mostly white-hot rage at myself. I started my sprints around the fields. I wanted to feel pain. I wanted to feel nothing.

I pushed myself until I collapsed. Sweat dripped down my spine, drenching my clothes. I welcomed the sting of jagged rocks piercing the flesh of my knees. I lurched forward, vomiting. My stomach emptied itself, leaving me depleted. Hollow, save for that persistent ache.

I remained there, staring at the ground as if it could yield answers to the questions that wailed their beating fists against me. Then the general's boots sidled into my field of vision. I leaned back on my heels, not caring about the contents of my stomach staining the dirt.

The general crouched before me. "You're going to drain your magic just by sweating it out if you aren't careful."

I flinched.

"I've been watching you train. You push yourself too hard." He paused, regarding me. "You don't have to punish yourself, Ruin. We all have regrets. You don't have to kill yourself to make up for yours." He had no idea.

I couldn't look at him. I was angry. I was hurt. The truth was I still missed him, well, what we had. I didn't want his kindness, though. I needed space, or a good fight. I pulled a candy out of my pocket to help wash the sour taste from my mouth. Standing, I brushed past Dom, ignoring his concern.

At the fields, Finn paused his conversation with a guard. He marched over, giving a hearty pat to my shoulder and an awkward side hug. I twisted out of his embrace, aiming for the weapons table. Dom picked up some folded leathers, offering them to me.

"I have my own, General," I spat.

He exchanged a glance with Finn. "These are better." My gruff demeanor clearly confounded him. I glanced at the proffered leathers, then did a double take. These were scaled. My gaze flicked upward as he cocked a haughty eyebrow at me. I rolled my eyes and reached for them.

My fingers caressed the material. The scales weren't made of leather, and yet they were not quite metal. Their color shifted in the light from bluish-black to a sheen of silver. They held a unique tensile strength that belied their thin construction. Each one shimmered with subtle magic. The scales overlapped just like a dreki's, but were flexible enough to allow swift movements.

The general interrupted my assessment with his deep timbre. "These leathers are the lightest we have created so far, while maintaining the strength of a shield of steel. They have saved me from countless ambushes and attacks, though they aren't impenetrable. I want you to train in them this morning. Get used to how it feels, how they move." He turned on his heel and grabbed a sword, gesturing for Finn to join him, effectively dismissing me.

I grabbed the clothes and walked to a nearby building. I admired myself in the mirror, begrudgingly observing the perfect fit, the placement of padding and pockets and holsters for all manner of blades. I'd never worn anything so skillfully made. I pulled my boots back on, tightening all the buckles and straps, and headed back to the field where Finn and the general sparred.

Bowen intercepted me on my way back. He wore his long hair in a knot on the top of his head. His arms swarmed with tattoos in the ancient Sarulien language of the gods, something I'd noticed several people in Aphellion sported. I knew nothing of the runes and glyphs.

"I'm glad to see you're feeling better," he ventured.

I slowed my pace to offer a moment of brief conversation before reuniting with the general. Anything to delay my return.

"Thanks for your help yesterday. You're a healer?" I asked him.

"I'm an elixist, but I work very closely with the Prime Healer and Prime Elixist. Hence my presence in emergencies." He smiled down at me. I perked up at the disclosure of his magic.

"My best friend, more a sister really, she is an elixist back in Maripol. One of the most accomplished. I know very little about what elixists do, but the way she created medicines and tonics was impressive." I knew I was talking too fast. But, it felt good to discuss Delah, one of the few things from my life in Maripol that wasn't a disgrace. I even spoke with my hands, an embarrassing habit I'd mostly squelched. I shoved them into my pockets. My excitement in connecting with someone else here, who didn't judge me, left me with a modicum of hope that softened the harshness of my current reality.

"Maybe I can show you around the elixist quarter and introduce you to the Prime there. She's taught me everything I know. And whenever your friend visits, I'm happy to do the same with her. If you're ever bored, I have some elixirs that make you hallucinate in neon colors." He flashed a boyish grin.

A laugh bubbled out of me. "That's the last thing I need." I patted his arm. "Thanks again for your help yesterday." I turned, startled to find Dom watching me. His shadows pulsed around him darkening the glare on his face. The wooden sword he held cracked in his hands. Gods he was a moody one.

Finn, taking advantage of his distraction, pushed him aside. Their swords clanged, melding with the whistle of the wind and the early songbirds. He pinned Dom, who reluctantly conceded. Dom stood, brushing dirt off his clothes, and they both turned toward me.

Finn, again, had a smile so wide his teeth gleamed. He let out a low whistle. The general assessed me with indifference, holding his heavy stare a beat too long.

Finn mock bowed before me. "Leathers fit for a water-wielding queen. Care to train with me?" I bowed my head in response, searching the weapons area for the same dull sword I used the previous morning. The general stepped back, quiet, watchful. The heat of his observation prickled the small hairs on my neck. I wanted to swat him away.

I didn't wait for Finn to set up his stance before I came at him. I ducked and spun as he deflected and slashed. He was good, but I had leftover angst from my night of bad dreams, my coiled rage fueling my attack. Ice coated my fingertips. My sword crackled as frost slowly combed its way down the blade, elongating and sharpening it.

"Enough!" The general's booming voice broke through my focus. I gasped at the realization of my ice-crusted fingers. I dropped my sword, stepping back. The general cocked his head at me, curiosity and concern in his eyes.

"There are easier ways to get me to yield than freezing my balls, Rebby." Finn winked.

"I'm sorry, I didn't realize…" I closed my eyes taking a deep breath. I needed to calm my volatile nerves.

"It happens. Collect yourself, then let's continue." The general unsheathed the two swords crisscrossing his back, setting them aside. He grabbed two dull ones, giving them elaborate test-swings in the air. He grunted in approval and turned to face me. "No magic, just weapons."

I nodded in understanding, then took up my position.

I kept my attention on my adversary, watching the general's footwork, both purposeful and graceful. I fell into a rhythm with his sparring, like a natural dance. He feinted left and caught me off guard. He moved with unnatural speed, spinning me so that my back was flush against his chest.

I sought control over my short breaths, my body noticing all the places it was pressed against this towering man. His unyielding form stood solid behind me. He leaned down, whispering in the shell of my ear, "Stop watching my feet." Then he pushed me off of him as he raised his sword. "Again." A small shudder slid down my spine even as I glowered at him. I hated his arrogance.

My eyes narrowed. Gathering my focus, I harnessed my training into that small quiet place, the place I went to as the Scourge. The general adjusted his stance, picking up on the shift in my demeanor. Good. Let him wonder.

I lunged, slashing, twisting. My useless blade threatened his exposed right side. My movements landed swift and confident. I edged close enough to fake one direction, then swiped with my dagger from the other. He faltered for the second I needed to get my blade across his throat.

Finn stood across the way, his mouth hanging open. I started to lower the blade as the general met my eye. His strong hand enclosed my own while I gripped the hilt of my sword. He kept the blade at his throat, his amber eyes glittering.

"Well, aren't you a menace." My breath hitched. Memories drifted upward in my mind, of all the times he'd said that in the past. He stared at my lips for several beats.

A small muscle in his jaw feathered. I was staring. My chest constricted. I wanted to tell him. I wanted to know why he never came for me. The words lodged tight in my throat.

"General!" A young soldier ran up, interrupting our training. He bowed in deference to the general. "Another body was found. We need you to assess it."

Another? How many bodies had there been before this one? The threads of Nolan's evil wound discretely across the entire kingdom. I had been too sequestered, too deceived to have recognized it. But his illusions hold no sway over me now.

The general accepted his report, his face stern and contemplative—the face of a commander. He dismissed the soldier and turned his attention to me. "I told you we would have the dawn. But duty now calls me elsewhere."

My guilt and desperation wouldn't allow me to stay silent. And I knew that the more useful I was, the more the general would owe me when it came time to get Delah. "It's the king isn't it? I can do more than just get us to the Nereid Realm. I know of a mercenary with powers that could bolster your defenses against the King. He has unique weapons. I can help you dismantle it all." I needed to do this for Korin. For myself. It was a small way I could right some of my wrongs and help secure a better future for people like Delah.

The general regarded me. "I would accept any allies and assistance you can offer." He drummed his fingers against his thigh.

It hit me that the movement was the same from when we were young. I always knew he'd retreated into his mind, deep in thought, when he did that. A pang of sadness filtered tight across my chest.

"The queen of Yarit, Queen Avery, sent a missive requesting a meeting. You can come and show me what Ruin of the Scourge is capable of."

I raised my eyebrows. "Does she know who I am?" A thread of panic slithered around my throat. If she knew of me, she could report my whereabouts to the king.

His softened gaze penetrated mine. "No, but it wouldn't be unexpected for me to bring a companion. She requests my presence quarterly, with other leaders from Lyrae. I am gathering my army as Nolan gathers his. This is movement in that direction."

"Then I will summon my contact, and accompany you to visit Queen Avery." I sincerely hoped that Delah's information regarding the man from up north in Vorkut held true.

"I'll provide you with the proper attire for our evening with the queen." He sheathed the previously discarded twin swords across his back, then left to deal with the body, Finn falling in step beside him.

The wind swirled around me at their departure. I closed my eyes and whispered Evander's name into it, sharing who I was and what I needed. The sound of his name dissolved in the breeze. I only hoped the wind would carry my voice to the mercenary's ears in time.

CHAPTER TWENTY-TWO
THE GENERAL

Why did she smell of cherries? I scowled at the memory. When she had that dull sword pressed against my neck, her face so close to mine, my body couldn't decide if it was ready to fight or poised to... I silenced the rest of that thought. She was a woman with too many secrets, a woman who was using me as much as I was using her. I cracked my neck.

She had seemed surprisingly angry at the fields. I suppose if I were stuck in a foreign realm and hunted by bat creatures, I'd have an attitude as well. Maybe I should get her more romance books. Women loved those.

I took a deep breath and let my rings melt down around my fingers. When I saw her falling from the sky, fear had consumed me. If Finn had not cast his gravity affinity toward her, slowing her descent, I would be burying her instead of sparring this morning. I didn't have time to examine the emotion that surged at the thought.

My brisk pace increased. The way she fought those creatures off, and the way she desired to fight for Aphellion, had a kernel of respect growing between us. And *foka*, where had *Bowen* come from? The elixist needed to keep his distance from her. He had plenty of ladies fawning over him.

My rings formed blades as my emotion sharpened. It wasn't my concern. So why did I want to make it my business? My blades darted around me in a swarm of angry bees. I clenched my hands.

The sound of my boots reverberated in the afternoon's silence. The soldier that interrupted our training needed me to identify a body that had been found in the woods. I was curious if it would match one of the bodies recovered from Nolan's mine.

My forces had recently discovered a Berine mine within the Auren Mountains. We were in the process of shutting it down to staunch the flow of the drug. There were many fronts we were fighting.

Time was of the essence. King Nolan was amassing an army of drekis. The Yaritian ruler, Queen Avery, was alerted, but as usual, she stayed in her jeweled castle, turning a blind eye. She stayed preoccupied with the prophecy. Many years ago, an oracle shared the vision that the queen's own magic would be drained by a child of the gods. Her paranoia consumed her.

The Liberation stayed under the radar, behind our wards, moving in the shadows. The erratic queen kept a small army, but her loyalties to the king were unknown. Her inaction bred questions.

Finn and I stepped into the great stone building at the edge of Aphellion. It was three stories of granite with four levels below the ground full of guarded cells. Some rooms were used as a mortuary, some for imprisonment, others for extracting information by whatever means necessary. The cell we headed to now was in one of the subterranean rooms. It was brightly lit with numerous torches.

A stone table sat in the middle of the room, a limp figure upon its surface. I covered my nose and mouth with the cowl at my neck, stifling the rancid odor that emanated from the body. The soldier in charge of the corpse lowered the sheet covering the man. Innumerable small holes covered his graying skin. It appeared as if his body broke out in boils that erupted all at once. The capillaries beneath his skin shone gray and black as though flushed with char. I cataloged the body, then nodded at the soldier to return the sheet.

We exited the room. The queasiness that settled at the sight of the corpse made me grateful for my empty stomach. This was the fourth body we had found in the last month. Finn and I moved to the upper levels toward my office.

The soldier who summoned me and brought us to the dead body followed close behind. "Have an elixist come in to test the body for death magic." He nodded in affirmation and left with his orders. I glanced up at Finn whose glazed expression indicated his own thoughtful processing at what we witnessed.

The scent of leather and parchment greeted us as I opened my office door. The window on the far wall lay cracked open, barely reducing the stifling heaviness these granite walls imposed. I slouched into a worn leather chair that faced a vastly underused fireplace.

Finn nestled into the opposite chair, his foot tapping in thought. He turned to me, "Do you think this is a warning? A practice run? Or a random act from a random creature?"

I stared, unseeing, out the window. "This is the fourth body. The same wounds. The same stench. The nymphs have not seen anything, but these bodies keep appearing in their midst. Alert our soldiers and spies. They need to be informed and prepared."

Finn nodded. "We did hear back from Delah, the elixist defector. She reported a new sweep on the citizens. Nolan is targeting orphans again. Several have gone missing. Most of them girls. I've already sent out some of our own to search for them, and bring them back here. Sieren and Xuri are preparing the old space. It's like a repeat of when we were kids, when you used to go in search of them."

It was how I found *her*. She wasn't an orphan and I couldn't just steal her away from her family, even if her father was a monster. But I visited her every chance I could, just to make sure she was alright. Until she actually did disappear. I still harbored hope that she was alive. Somewhere.

Nolan's collection of children had always been subtle and easily dismissed because they belonged to no family. No one to care about their absence meant they could vanish without any outcry; it was one less mouth to feed. But to have a large-scale operation with obvious missing persons... His desperation did not bode well.

Finn moved on. "Preparations are in place to destroy Nolan's mining operation. We also attempted to send one last message to Queen Thaleia in the Nereids. But who knows if she will have received it."

I began pacing. "I want the wards fortified around the whole of Aphellion. Extend them skyward if at all possible. With yesterday's incident, we have likely been discovered. Make sure guards are doubled around all entrances, and around our Primes."

"I already have a plan in motion. Most of the commanders have been briefed about our departure and their orders. I will make sure to reiterate before we leave." Finn's eyes sharpened as he slowly smirked. "That was some interesting sparring this morning. Maybe I can find a defector to 'train' with."

I shot him a warning glare. Even if I wanted to be the only one who made her smile, it wouldn't matter. She was off-limits. Maybe it would be better if she did forge a connection with Bowen. My mind was becoming too preoccupied with thoughts of her. I needed to figure out a way to silence it.

I swept out of the room to the echo of Finn's annoying chuckle.

CHAPTER TWENTY-THREE
THE SPY

Two small scraps of clothing, my expected swimming attire, were all that stood between me and mastering a new magical skill. I would have done it naked if I had to.

Gemma, a Prime Chemist, greeted me with a warm hug and an invitation to practice my magic in a discreet emerald lagoon. It was nestled among rocks and thick, gnarled wisteria vines. Tiny purple petals fluttered downward into a gentle mist that hovered above the water.

"What do you know of water wielders?" I inquired.

Gemma explained, "Magic is an art, but it's also something you can study. Once the base parts of it are understood, you can transform or create anything with it. Like how you can form ice from water. The dryads spoke of a water wielder long ago who could transform water into breathable air. I can help you channel your affinity to do the same." Her eyes glinted at the prospect, her excitement contagious.

"I've done a lot with my magic, but I've never understood the mechanics of it."

She waved her hand in the air. "No, no, of course you didn't. You simply made it happen. But the why is important to know as you grow and expand your magic's reach. If you can harness that power completely, there is much more that you could do with it. For now though, let's practice breathing underwater."

Gemma guided me in the process of threading my magic with the water, separating and transforming it, until it became a stable pocket of breathable air. My affinity rushed around and within me with silken fingers. She offered pointers for swimming, but with the ability to breathe underwater, the threat of drowning receded. We held on to rocks at the bottom in an effort to remain submerged.

I broke the surface, unable to contain my grin. "Next time, we need a rope to keep us underwater, so we can really test my endurance."

Gemma smiled, continuing to instruct me. She mentioned the importance of visualizing my intentions. Ultimately, my magic would be as restricted as my imagination. She reclined on the shore as clouds skittered above us.

My confidence grew with every challenge Gemma gave me. I dove to the bottom again. The effort of maintaining the bubble proved easier and easier. My muscles loosened as I drank in the reverie of wielding and replenishing my magic through the very pores of my skin as if I had done it a million times. My body slowly floated to the surface. With a bubble of air encased around me, any urgency to breach the surface fell away in the comfort of my magic.

Above me, the water violently rippled. A burst of bubbles knifed through my relaxed state. My body collapsed in on itself as I flailed my arms, unsure of the source of the commotion. I moved like a confused bird trying to fight and fly at the same time. Something firmly gripped my wrist, stilling me, then gently and swiftly pulled me upward. My chest hit a wall of rock.

Breath whooshed out of me as I threw out my hands for balance, splaying them to find a stable grip. My fingers didn't realize the stone beneath them was actually a warm body. Of solid muscle. The bubbles fizzled along with my pride as I stared into amused amber eyes. Gemma was nowhere in sight.

I lost my hold on my magic, the oxygen bubble instantly forgotten, vaporous droplets glittering back into the lagoon. Startled, I sucked in a breath, accidentally gulping down water in the process. I devolved into a fit of coughing.

Dom bit his lower lip, restraining a smile. He eyed me with mock concern as I hacked out whatever miserable amount of water lodged itself in my lungs. When at last I quieted, recovering my wits and my breathing, I glowered at him. "You might have warned me."

Dom peeled my hands off his chest. He eased his arms through the water, his shoulders and forearms tightening with the motion.

"I thought I'd follow up on those swim lessons."

I wasn't sure if I was ready to face him. The opened wound from my past was bleeding out and I hadn't staunched the blood. "Gemma is a great teacher. I feel confident I won't drown with my magic. We can forgo the lessons, *Dom*." I couldn't repress my sneer.

He quirked his head at my tone. "Magic isn't always a given. I need to know you could swim to the surface if necessary; if you ever became depleted underwater."

My eyes narrowed. I would rather teach myself. Surely it wasn't that hard. I didn't want his concern. I knew I was his ticket to the Nereids. He was my way out of Nolan's clutches. It could only ever be that simple. I had one friend here I could connect with. "I'll ask Bowen to help. I'm sure you're busy doing 'General' things. Don't worry I won't die before getting you to Queen Thaleia." His whole body tensed and his shadows spun around him.

I dove into the water to get away from him. My arms and legs jerked in uncoordinated movements. My defiance and persistence buckled down. I would not yield. I refused to use my magic, even as I sputtered and thrashed.

Dom scooped me out of the water. I shoved against him, not caring how belligerent I seemed. I struggled like a desperate fish in his hands. "What's going on, Rue? I'm trying to help you." I slammed my elbow into his ribs, a tiny whoosh of his breath my only reward. He tightened his grip to stifle my movements. I didn't want his help. I didn't want anything from him.

Emotion, long-coiled in my chest, erupted through my weakened shields. "You never came back for me!" I blurted, unable to hold back any longer. The nakedness of my words in the misted air left me raw. I tried to squirm out of his grip, only to end up facing him directly when he refused to release me. I trembled with the effort to keep myself together. The fissure that released my words threatened to widen.

Dom studied me, the golden flecks of his eyes burning into me. I didn't hide my anguish, locking onto his gaze so he could see what pain he'd caused. His eyes darted to the scars on my wrists, then back to my face. His mouth fell slack. Like a flower blooming in reverse, I watched as his confusion shifted into bewilderment. How recognition melted into understanding.

"Liora." If hope had a tone, it was this.

"That's not who I am anymore." I was numb, resolved. I tried to swim off, but damn him, I had to remain in his grip or I'd flounder to the bottom of the lagoon.

"I searched for you. Everywhere. Every time I returned to Maripol." His words were desperate, cracking through the space between us. I wanted to believe him, but my pain was a writhing vicious thing, and his words cut into my raw wounds. "What happened that night?" Slowly, Dom eased me to the shore, where my feet met sand and rocks.

I kept shaking my head, too afraid to speak. My jaw clenched in an effort to maintain my composure. Every question he posed threatened to unravel me. The air stilled around us, as if it too held its breath. "That was the night my parents died, because of... from Glint. I lived in an orphanage for only a few days before King Nolan found me." The king who saved only to deceive. The king who made me his puppet-weapon.

"Liora, I never stopped looking for you."

"Stop calling me that."

As if bespelled, our eyes locked. "Every trip to Maripol since that day, I have searched for you. Every. Time. Even when I thought you were dead."

Stillness settled around us, the only movement the drowsy descent of wisteria petals and the gentle lapping of the lagoon. What I knew of Dom clashed with my experience of every male I'd ever known. They lie. They take. They forget. I wanted to trust. I couldn't. Turmoil churned in a tempest.

I didn't know what to believe. "You aren't who they said you were," I whispered. It would have been so much easier if he was. Hate could bolster me, grant me solid ground. Whatever this was felt like aftershocks from an earthquake. Like quicksand.

He reached for me then. I wanted to believe him, but I had been deceived before. My shields locked down, severing me from my overwhelm. My skin frosted over.

Dom's hand slowly returned to his side. "I promised you I would find you. I never gave up. I can't believe you were right under my nose in Maripol, twice, and I didn't even realize..." He clenched his fist as his voice trailed off.

His apologies fell at my feet, years too late. And yet, their weight settled undiminished by the lost time, as if the words themselves held a magic all their own. They sunk into my cracks despite my misgivings. My fight seeped out of me.

A chill breeze brought a shiver to both of our bodies still

dripping with water. I pulled the dampness off of our skin, drying us instantly. Resigned, I held out my hand—a tender truce. Trust was too terrifying to approach, my walls not ready to lower, but perhaps we could start from a more honest place.

He took my hand, sandwiching it between both of his, warm in light of my frosted fingers. Grief and regret bracketed his amber eyes, and the weight of our past hovered between us thicker than the water's mist.

I squeezed Dom's hand. "I need to move or I might explode."

His gaze snaked down my body, to my swimming attire. Or the lack thereof. His pupils widened. "What are you wearing?" His voice cracked.

I glanced down, shrugging. As if he'd never seen a woman in swimming attire before.

A deep growl sounded as he turned away. The rings on his fingers flared and he tossed a cloak in my direction.

"Put this on and let's spar. I won't rescue you from drowning a third time."

I threw on my clothes with a roll of my eyes, and followed him to an open space beside the lagoon. Purple flower petals carpeted the grass, having blown over by the mountain's chilled breeze.

"Remove your blades," he commanded.

I flatly stared at him, no interest in following his directive. He sighed, "We're practicing with elemental magic, not swords or shadows, Ruin of the Scourge."

"Is that how you will address me with Queen Avery this evening?"

He scowled. "It might leave a bad taste in her mouth if I do. I suppose, if I cannot use your true name, I'll be forced to introduce you as Rue." He nearly spat the name. I raised my hands in surrender.

"I assume they know *your* true name?"

"They do." The black rings adorning his fingers began to

glow, then melt. They floated around him—an army of metal locusts. Ice prickled at my fingertips as he stalked toward me. His hovering rings morphed into arrowheads, all aimed at me.

My ice sword appeared, elongating in an extension of myself. It crackled and gleamed, solidifying into a double-edged blade of defiance. He projected his arrows toward my chest. I threw up an ice shield right before they made contact. One embedded itself into the thick sheet, the others bounced off, summoned back to their master.

The buckles of my armor began to heat, burning my skin. I winced, dousing them with water to cool them down. They'd melted, but no longer burned. The now-liquid metal skated up my arm, twisting around my throat in a lazy threat. I swallowed, not breaking eye contact with Dom.

I jolted as the metal tightened. Icy needles flew through the air, spearing toward his stupid smirk. His rings flattened around him, effectively repelling them. Ice exploded as they attempted to pierce his defenses. My breaths came in shorter gasps as the collar tightened, when suddenly it released. The liquefied metal enclosed my wrists, locking them in place. Magicked metal manacles.

Trapped. Again. A guttural scream left my lips as instant terror gripped me. I focused my affinity into the locks, freezing the metal until it cracked. Black spots dotted my vision. I ripped my hands free, lunging toward Dom. The desire to crack his pretty face overwhelmed my rational thought.

Dom could win this fight out of sheer body mass differential, but footing was just as crucial. I slammed my boot into the ground. Ice splintered outward, coating the earth beneath his feet. He broke his concentration by glancing downward. I rotated my hips, thrusting through my shoulder. My fist grazed his ear with the turn of his face, enough to impair his balance further.

I barreled into him, still seething from my body's automatic response. We hit the ground. Hard. My wheezing lungs couldn't inhale. I barely sipped the air around me.

"Wow. Impressive," Dom grunted. I didn't respond. He reached out, gripping my shoulder. "Are you okay?"

I blinked down at him, disoriented. Distantly, I registered that I had him straddled. "Don't ever bind my hands again."

My body took its time to regulate and recognize it was not in true peril. Dom sat up, bringing me with him, keeping me close.

We sat cross-legged, facing each other. He exhaled loudly. Deeply. Purposefully. My own inhales slowed, seeking to match his calming rhythm. He kept his firm grip on my upper arm, his thumb gently tracing circles. I closed my eyes, finally drawing in a complete breath. He leaned back, releasing me. Tension eased out of his shoulders.

I studied the Auren Mountains. Their peaks stood stark against the glowing blue of the morning sky. "I don't respond well to confinement, or feeling caged."

The heat of his gaze warmed my cheek. His eyes fell to my wrists, head tilting as he observed the scars across them, remnants of childhood cuffs and silent screams.

My eyes wandered down to my lap. I lacked the courage to meet his scrutiny, unwilling to discover the truth I might find.

"If I had known, I never would have used that on you." His gentle tone prickled with an icy edge. I folded my arms across my chest, nestling my exposed wrists into the crook of my elbows.

"It's been a long time. I wouldn't expect you to remember," I mumbled.

He ran his hands through his tousled hair. "It's not that I didn't remember. There is nothing forgettable about you. *Foka.* If your father was still alive, I would gladly sever his hands first, before slicing him with my blades, and make sure he could feel every sting of pain." The intensity in his low voice stroked the monster in my chest, leaving a satisfied sigh in its wake. "You have my word. I will never confine you like that again."

I could feel his desire to press, to ask more questions. Relenting, he diverted the conversation, sparing me. "Your skills with both combat and magic are impressive. If we worked together, we'd be quite the force."

I half-heartedly scoffed, finally meeting his eyes. The golden flecks churned like a storm-ravaged sea. "Isn't that what we're doing? At least for a time?"

"I suppose we are." Dom stood, offering his hand to help me up. I accepted it, his large fingers engulfing my own. Despite the time that had passed, a glimmer of our historic connection still pulsed.

"I'll see you this evening for the queen's dinner."

XURI ARRIVED LATE in the afternoon, zinging with enthusiasm. Hanging delicately from a golden hanger, swayed a magenta gown. I struggled with my opinion of the oracle, but the dress called to me, overriding my guardedness. I rushed over, my fingers eager to explore the beautiful dress.

The bodice consisted of artfully designed lace. Lilac-colored crystals wove throughout effecting dimensional movement with each glittering catch of light. It dove into a deep front V. Satin ribbons purposely draped across the back, connecting with the gossamer and chiffon skirts that would undoubtedly rest at the lowest point of my hips.

Xuri lifted it to my body with elegant fingers. The fit provided a figure-skimming silhouette. The thigh-high slit ended in a slight train. Nothing about this screamed subtle. She whirled away with it, hanging it up until it was time.

I grinned at her flitting about the room. She offered me tea "for awareness and joy." I stared at her above the rim of my mug, sipping the floral brew.

"At least you showered!" she chirped eventually, holding the dress up to my body. I winced; I had "showered" in the lagoon.

"Okay. Step out of those clothes and let's get you dressed."

She clapped her hands, the sound spurring me into action. I wiggled into the finely made gown, its impeccable tailoring conforming to my soft curves. Xuri circled me, inspecting the fit with an expert eye.

"I thought you were the oracle?" I asked.

She waved her hand dismissively, "I am a woman of many talents. And I hardly get to use this one. Don't burst my bubble."

I threw my hands up. "I would never dream of such a thing."

She curtly nodded, her finger tapping against her chin in contemplation. She drew to her full height, then twirled her finger. "Turn around for me."

I slowly rotated. Xuri snagged the satin ribbon at my back, pulling on the straps which served to tighten the bodice. The lace cinched back, further accentuating my ample chest. She tied the ribbons into a graceful bow at the base of my spine. Any lower and I'd be exposing much more than I'd ever allowed the public to view.

Facing Xuri again, she squealed with delight, nearly floating. "This color brings out the purple in your eyes. Dom was right." She squinted her rich-brown eyes, leaning into my personal space to really study my irises. Her warm smile transformed her face and she clapped again, startling me. She was a beautiful woman. I could see why Dom would be interested in her.

Xuri expertly braided my hair, securing it half-up in a golden clip. She provided me with makeup and heels. "I'll wait outside for you to finish, then I'll escort you to your carriage. Dom will meet us there." She turned on her heel, flitting out like a hummingbird.

I sipped more of my tea, then applied a thin line of kohl to my eyes and a pink stain to my lips. I examined a pot of shimmering silver powder before dipping in my finger and swiping it across my eyelids. The effect was subtle but striking. I dusted more along my shoulders.

Slipping my heeled shoes on, I took a breath and walked outside. Xuri stood waiting, her arm outstretched to assist with my balance as we walked across uneven pathways toward the carriage.

We strode silently, save for Xuri's ongoing humming, toward a sleek black carriage. I traced the lines of it with the tips of my fingers, leaving remnants of silver dust behind. I startled at the realization that it was crafted entirely from metal. The ornate design swirled and twisted in an array of metallic birds, flowers, and creeping ivy.

Dom stepped around the carriage, his hands casually in the pockets of his fitted black pants. The cut of his leather jacket molded to his broad shoulders, highlighting his biceps. The black brocade V-neck showcased his chest just enough to invite an extended perusal. He paused when he caught sight of me, his jaw tensing.

Xuri cleared her throat, releasing my arm. Strolling over to Dom she clinically assessed him. "You clean up nice. Take care of Rue for me. Try not to start any fights."

I bristled at her familiarity with him. She cast him a warning glare, offered me a wink, then sauntered off. I needed to get a hold of myself. I was here because of a bargain, and I would do well not to forget it. Whatever complicated relationship Dom and Xuri had, I needed to stay out of it.

I straightened my shoulders, schooling my features. The air settled heavy between us. Dom's piercing eyes stayed riveted upon my own.

"I suppose we don't want to be late," I voiced breathlessly. Dom tilted his head, heat flaring as he took in the entirety of my body. Slowly, he extended his hand, beckoning me into our flourished transport.

The passenger door clicked shut as Dom's magic locked us in. The metal designs on the interior walls curled, flowers actively blooming and ivy unfurling hypnotically as though breathing. Dom sat back, satisfaction deepening the dimple on his cheek. "About tonight." His deep voice cut through the thickening moment. He tapped his fingers on his knee, his rings clinking with the movement. "These dinners usually involve leaders from around Lyrae. There's a man named Oster who joined a few months ago. Information from our spies suggests he might be a trafficker, and I don't trust him."

"Do you trust anyone?"

He leveled me with a flat stare. "Very few." After a breath, he continued, "This evening should be a simple affair. Queen Avery is a paranoid woman, believes some mysterious entity is stealing her magic. This is one of many gatherings she uses to subdue her wild suspicions. I am included because I'm her mapmaker and I understand every corner of her realm."

"You're a cartographer?" My gaping mouth could catch flies.

A lopsided grin eased out of him. "I have a talent for it, and with the ever-changing landscape across the realms, I'm quite sought-after. I also don't try too hard to highlight Aphellion."

"I'd like to view your work one day." I wondered if King Nolan used his maps.

"Hmm. Perhaps." He crossed his ankle over his knee, leaning further back into the seat. "There are some people in attendance, besides Oster, that we have our eye on. If you see anything suspicious, tell me immediately, and I'll take care of it."

I nodded absently as I traced the metallic ivy on the carriage's walls, their ongoing movement as calming as the swells of the ocean. "Do you not trust me with the enemy?"

"It's not about trusting you. It's about protecting you." The ivy ceased its undulating motion.

Annoyance prickled. "That's what Nolan claimed as well."

Shadows surged from his fisted hands. "I do not operate on manipulations and deceptions. I am not *him*."

His earnestness settled me; I relaxed further into the seat. "I'm beginning to think you might not be."

Along the carriage walls, the flowers resumed their blooming.

CHAPTER TWENTY-FOUR
THE SPY

The Topaz Castle glowed as we approached. The walls climbed upward like a giant slab of luminous marble. No lines marred their smooth surfaces. Windows dotted the upper levels, glimmering in the draining light of dusk. The amber topaz diffused the light borne from within its walls, rendering torches unnecessary. The deep sound of rushing water beckoned my gaze eastward. Snowmelt ribboned down from the lavender mountains, flowing through the castle before emerging as a waterfall that tipped off the edge of the palace's foundations. It rushed gracefully down, merging with the waterways and canals that flowed below the elevated city of Lyrae.

It was rumored that magic from the nymphs aided in the castle's elaborate construction. Its many carved facets, along with the makeup of the gemstone itself, allowed the castle to retain an ethereal glowing translucence, rather than the transparent quality of mere glass. The sea carved a thin blue line beyond it, kissing the horizon.

Armored men barred entry, their chest plates and gauntlets ornately crafted from a topaz-colored metal. Only the finest for the jeweled queen. Our transport curved around to the entrance of the castle. Dom exited the carriage first, extending his hand to me. He pulled me to his side, the scent of leather and musk filling my senses. His lips brushed my ear. "I haven't told you, but you are stunning this evening." A shiver skated down my spine.

Before I could respond, we were moving, following armed guards into the palace. The sound of my heels clicked along the white-marble floors. My arm threaded through Dom's, his stride easing to compensate for my slower pace. His arm tensed as the doors to the dining room opened.

When I stood this close to him, the shock of familiarity resounded despite our years of separation. My mind felt jumbled, as if a mind manipulator hovered nearby. But I felt confident no outside intervention had unleashed the flutter in my stomach. I shouldn't indulge it. But for one night, it wouldn't hurt, right?

Chandeliers sparkled overhead, casting their crystalline radiance throughout the polished space. The golden walls shimmered with intricate carvings and ornate moldings. Gossamer curtains swayed in the sea breeze from the open windows. A large rectangular table with legs carved into the shape of lion's feet showcased richly prepared dishes with delicately stacked fruits and colorful cakes. Servers streamed from a discrete door, bringing in plates of braised meats, roasted vegetables, buttersoaked lobster, and fragrant rice.

Dom led me to an offset table made entirely of crystal. Effervescent liquor filled a swan chiseled from ice. It streamed from its hollow body out of its mouth into a bowl beneath. Dom grabbed two goblets and filled them both, offering me one. I politely sipped its contents. Bubbles sweet and chilled fizzed across my tongue. I had never tasted anything like it, and I tipped the glass back for more.

"Careful," Dom tsked. "Nymphian wine goes straight to your head if you aren't used to it."

My lips pursed into a brief pout, but I relented my consumption. I scanned the other people milling about. Focusing on my sight, I willed my eyes to water just enough to glean their auras. Several people hid their nervousness, their auras ranging from the pale orange of amusement to lime green indicating worry.

A woman entered the room and assumed a chair in a far corner, pulling down a gilded harp. Her fingers floated across the strings, composing a mellow melody that swept along the currents, softening the ambiance.

Dom leaned into me, his body warming my space. I involuntarily breathed him in, scolding myself in the process. "Oster just walked in. He's the one in the vest."

I casually scanned the room, landing on the man with the dark-green vest. His sandy hair was pulled back in a smart tail at the nape of his neck. He reclined lazily against the wall. His shrewd eyes noted the other guests, appearing to size them all up. His perusal stilled, a note of surprise lifted his brow as he glimpsed me. It vanished as quickly as it appeared, his curiosity instilling a vigor that energized his approaching steps.

I glanced away, feigning boredom, and took another small sip of the nymphian wine.

Oster's hand clapped the side of Dom's shoulder. "Good evening, Dominus," he boomed. A few others glanced our way, a roll of their eyes returned them to their previous conversations. "Who is this striking beauty you have with you?" His leering gaze left my lip curled in distaste. My fingers itched to pull a blade.

Dom placed a steadying hand at my lower back. "This is my... companion, Rue." I met his stare. Dom didn't turn away as he finished his introduction. "She's pretty, but she bites." I nearly choked on my wine. Dom chuckled as he sipped from his glass, unhurriedly returning his attention to Oster.

"The pleasure is truly mine. If this brute becomes a bore, come find me." His eyes glinted conspiratorially. He leaned toward my other side, indecently close. I held my ground as his tacky breath heated my face. "The name's Oster." He pulled away, straightening his vest.

His nasally voice grated on me. Dom's hand now gripped my waist, and I leaned into his side, relishing the comfort of his presence. Oster offered a licentious wink before strolling away, meandering through small clumps of other guests. If only it were appropriate to douse myself in my water magic to remove the tang of his presence.

A server rang a tinkling bell, and the harpist paused her music. "Please welcome Queen Avery. You may find your seats."

The room shuffled with a flurry of steps as we made our way to the table. Steam unfurled from the extravagant feast layered upon a crimson runner. Double doors swung wide and Queen Avery appeared. Her navy dress swished with elegant flourish. The velvet bodice shimmered with embroidered sea serpents, Lyrae's oceanic sentinels. The off-shoulder sweetheart neckline accentuated her chest. Her brown hair, liberally streaked with gray, swept upward into a simple twist, highlighting her delicate cheekbones. She glided into the room, a warm smile across her lips. She assumed the chair at the head of the table. At her nod, we all took our seats.

Dom sat a seat away from Queen Avery, while I sat to his left. She surveyed her guests, cunning in her assessment. "Any news on the earthquakes, Dom?" I vaguely wondered if she was aware of the rebellion stronghold's name, or its warded location.

Suspicion colored her indifferent tone. Dom leisurely buttered a fluffy roll. The yeasty smell made me salivate. He sat the roll down and inclined his head to the queen. I quickly grabbed the roll and took an impulsive bite. A small moan escaped me. The thigh brushing against my own tensed. Queen Avery suppressed her grin.

Dom cleared his throat. "My team continues to monitor the Perellian Forest and all of Yarit's borders. No concerning reports."

She nodded, taking a bite of roasted fennel and spiced carrots. She leaned back in her ornately gilded chair. "What do you suppose brought dreki to my doorstep?" I held my breath. The queen waited, eyebrow arched.

"It is what we intend to find out, Your Majesty," Dom responded, his answer seemingly satisfying the queen.

She addressed the whole table, "Any leads on the prophecy?"

Eyes averted the gaze of the formidable queen. A woman at the end of the table spoke up, "No, Your Majesty. Nothing has emerged."

The queen's mouth hardened into a displeased line. "My patience wanes. I expect much more from you all. Any news, no matter how small, needs to be reported immediately. Someone continues to harness my power without my permission." She slammed her fist onto the table, causing me to flinch. "I'd hate to align any further with King Nolan than necessary. The realm depends on you all." She paused, gathering herself. Her impassioned speech seemed to drain her.

"And you, Oster, what news?" She shifted her spotlight to the tall, lean man. I quirked my head, taking in his build. A pulse of familiarity lit as I surveyed him more intently than I had upon first meeting. The hairs on my neck prickled as if my body understood what I had yet to conclude. I straightened up, feigning interest in his response.

I trained my vision to his aura, yet I couldn't find one. I glanced around. The queen's flared a sharp, alert tangerine. Her aura gave a curious flicker, then switched to an ominous black, but before I could blink it transitioned back to tangerine. I glanced at Dom, whose aura crested in smoldering, protective blues. Other guests varied in their colors, some more prominent based on the intensity of their emotions.

But Oster...

I busied myself with my food, surreptitiously focused on the slimy man. I watched as he gesticulated wildly in response to the queen. His aura flared, black as a dreki's. Oster met my gaze.

Coldness washed over me and I returned to my food, finding it suddenly very interesting. Dom placed his arm around my exposed shoulders in response to my shiver. His warmth anchored me amidst a sea of sharks.

"Where are you from, Rue?" Oster asked me. The table lent their attention, forks and knives stalling. Even the queen appeared interested in my response.

I schooled my features, mixing some truth to my lie. "Up north. I was traveling through when I met Dom at a festival." I turned to him, his amber eyes flared at my lavender gaze. "Remember that? What an enlightening evening." In fact, he had taken me home after I poisoned myself with Glint, but that was beside the point. I bit my lower lip, containing my amusement.

Dom briefly flattened his gaze, appearing like he wanted to give me a good shove. "A night of dancing so memorable, I wonder if we could recreate it." Challenge accepted.

I lingered in his stare for a heartbeat more, then addressed Oster, returning his original question, "Where are *you* from?"

He waved his hands in the air. "Oh here and there. Mostly Lyrae, sometimes the Mountains."

Dom raised his eyebrows, "The Mountains? Not very hospitable."

"What can I say? I like my space." He eyed me once more, like I was a lock he was trying to pick.

A prickle of dread cut across my chest. Worry of Oster's influence in both Yarit and Haluma increased my anxiety. As a trafficker, he would need people in both realms in his pockets. If he had Nolan's ear, my appearance at this dinner would get back to him. I briefly wondered about sharing my concerns with Dom. This was my mess to fix, though.

I dabbed my mouth with a silk napkin, folding it discretely. "Pardon me, Your Majesty, but I'm not feeling well." She waved me off, apathetic to my plight. I whispered to Dom, "I'll be right back; I just need to use the bathroom." He eyed me warily, but acquiesced. His stare burned into the back of my neck as I retreated from the table.

A servant led me to a room removed from the festivities. I closed the door behind me and leaned against it. My reflection revealed my panic. I adjusted my dress, spruced my hair in the ornate mirror, and thought through my options. Did Oster recognize me? His eyes weren't slitted, so he couldn't have been a dreki. Was he one of Nolan's spies?

A knock on the door startled me. I yelled to the outside, "I'll be out—" The door opened. Oster strode in, smugness lining his features. I tried to speak, and he held up his hand, silencing me. "Ah, ah, ah!" he chided. "You're King Nolan's lost bird aren't you? Whoring with the rebellion now?"

I searched for a weapon, cursing my revealing dress and its severe lack of blades. His long fingers gripped my wrists, claws splitting my skin. I fought against his binding arms.

Tendrils of his magic warmed along my throat, encircling my chest. "Hard to scream when you have no voice. I'll let them know you became too ill and embarrassed to return. I'll take you home. Your *true* home." He sniffed my neck, his nose grazing a line toward my ear. Bile rose in my throat. I could not scream even if I wanted to.

He pulled out a vial of Glint. "This should help your transition."

I bucked against him, his magic having stolen the sound from my mouth. Clenching my eyes, I urged my skin to freeze. He jerked away, giving me just enough time to kick him in his chest and summon ice blades. The wall shook as he slammed against it. The vial clattered to the floor.

He slowly straightened. Brown eyes shifted into pits of inky black. Spikes poked through his clothes. My mouth went dry. What was he?

I propelled an ice dagger toward him. He darted to the side, the blade only nicking him. He maintained his arrogant smile as blood beaded along his jaw. "You can't kill me. I'm too vital for the queen. You would have to add her to the list of people tracking you down."

"Perhaps you're right. For now," I rasped, voice still compromised. I cuffed his wrists in burning ice. The chains wound downward from his shackles toward the floor, but Oster moved faster than my magicked links could form.

His movements blurred as he lunged at me in a potent rage. He fisted my hair and yanked it backward, forcing me to the floor.

"You should have died for what you did, but Nolan saved you, and this is how you repay him? Did you think we wouldn't find you? You're worthless without him."

The Glint vial popped as he uncorked it, and I bit down a silent scream. I tried to twist out of his grip, but I couldn't move with my head at his mercy and his spikes oozing poison.

He snarled down at me. "We have eyes and ears everywhere. An enemy to the King is as good as dead, but the Good King has unique plans for you."

Strands of hair blew into my face as the door swung open. The doorway seemed to shrink in the shadow of Dom's imposing form. His rings were already flying when I met his wrathful gaze.

They spun toward Oster, impaling him. Around us, copper and iron and gold began vibrating, then melting. The metals pulsed with Dom's rage, scaling up Oster's body in a shroud. I spun out of his grip, snagging the vial of Glint from his hand.

Retribution burned through me as I forced it down his throat. He sputtered and cursed, involuntarily swallowing its contents. His magic slipped and I regained my voice. "Let Nolan know I fight back," I seethed.

Instead of securing his wrists with iced manacles, I cuffed his dick instead. He blanched as I tightened it. The concentration of Glint would likely knock him out, if the burning in his crotch didn't first. I stood, wiping the wrinkles from my gown.

I turned toward Dom. "We can't kill him. Let's notify a guard and they can take care of it."

Dom stood rigid beside me. I placed my hand on his shoulder feeling the power of his magic still hovering around us. My water affinity caressed ribbons of warm water along his arms.

He slowly blinked, then took hold of my hand. "Let's go."

We left Oster on the floor, shutting the door firmly behind us. Dom pulled me to his chest, clutching me as if I'd dissolve in his grip.

"I'm okay."

His clenched jaw was the only response.

Dom ushered me into the shadow of the hall. I barely kept up with him. He caged me in his arms with my back pressed against the stone wall. "You knew. You knew who he was and you didn't tell me. He could have killed you." He grabbed my hand and placed it over his heart, eyes shut in a bid to gather himself. He flattened my fingers firmly against him as if I had the power to calm.

I could feel the erratic beat hammering in his chest. He took a shuddering breath. I kept my hand pressed against him, our breaths syncing. Slowly, his pulse steadied.

I gazed into gold-flecked eyes, my hand holding firm. His anger should have frightened me. But his eyes were kind. "You came for me," I whispered.

He exhaled, dropping his forehead to my own. We stood there, sharing breath, a hundred words left unsaid between us.

"I'll always come for you." His words were a salve to my tattered edges. I realized then, in the space between breaths, that a part of me was healing. Some long-distant, forgotten piece of me felt a little stronger when I accepted his strength. And maybe my strength fortified him in return.

And that distant piece dared to believe his declaration.

He eased away from me then, raking his hands through his hair. We needed to return to the dinner. He straightened his jacket while I smoothed down my dress.

The sounds of revelry were caustic in the wake of our return. It was too bright, too loud. The harpist had resumed playing and dessert replaced the meal. Fluffy clouds of whipped cream dotted small tarts and pink squares of cake. A piano and stringed instruments emerged, their accompanying musicians appearing behind them. The music turned lively, the guests swaying in the reverie.

He led me to a small space near the harpist, where other couples already waltzed. "One dance, then we leave."

I took his hand.

Dom towered over me, my heels adding scant height. He pulled me close; I momentarily tensed as one large hand rested open on my exposed back. The satin ribbons did little to shield me from his touch. His other hand encased one of mine.

This dance was different than the last time. At the festival, we had been strangers to each other. I saw him more clearly now, even if I still wasn't sure I could trust him. But I was willing to try.

I may as well have floated as he led me around the marble floor. The chandelier above us shimmered down shards of color as light flowed through the crystal prisms. The lilac gems in my gown glittered out of the corner of my eye with Dom directing my steps. I was struck by the luminosity of his amber eyes.

He slowed our speed, the hand on my back now toying with strands of my free-flowing hair. He lowered his lips to my ear. "Are you okay?"

I shivered. My dress trailed behind me, gossamer and chiffon ghosting the polished floor. "I'm fine. I thought Oster could be a dreki with his aura. But, he was the other beast, like the ones that attacked us in the fields."

Dom stilled. A candelabra near us melted.

I tugged on our clasped hands, spurring him back into motion. "Tame your metal, General. Oster is busy hallucinating on the floor of the women's bathroom. And I might have put a ring of burning ice-fire around his..." I waggled my eyebrows and pointedly glanced in the body part's direction.

Dom stuttered before throwing his head back in unbridled laughter. His delight at my disclosure coaxed a true smile from my own lips. The sound of his laugh washed over me like the relaxing warmth of the sun. We resumed our fluid steps and I tentatively rested my cheek on his chest.

"I'm sorry, I should have armed you." The hand at my back tugged me closer. He spoke into my hair, "I'll kill him."

"You will not." I lifted my face to his, my tone firm. "It's taken care of, but we shouldn't stay much longer." He nodded in reluctant agreement, the song nearing its end. His hand gently held my own despite the tension and rage tensing his broad shoulders.

"We can bid our farewells to the Queen and head back." He lifted our clasped hands, extending me into a twirl one final time. My hair and the layers of my skirts both lifted as a laugh bubbled out of me. Dom drew me against his body as I completed the spin.

My back lay flush against his chest as his fingers trailed down my upraised arm. The deep V-shaped neckline did little to hide my breathlessness, my chest heaving in the confines of the lacy bodice.

I peered up and back, meeting his solemn stare. The lingering melody of the song curled through the air in lazy tendrils. The glowing topaz walls became a dreamscape background flaring the same hue as Dom's eyes. I could hear the distant roar of the waterfall that emptied over the ridge into the sleeping arms of the city beneath us. A thrill of danger and a thread of peace wove around me.

The music ended and the thrall of our connection diminished into the hum of surrounding chatter. He kept my arm tucked tightly in his own, and we bowed and curtsied our goodbyes, respectfully making our exit from the queen.

The coolness of the night air tamed the heat surging through me. Dom assisted me into the carriage, lifting my gown enough so my shoes didn't snag.

Alone in the carriage, I released a full breath. Dom's large body stole the majority of the space, as if he commanded both our transport and the air I breathed. He waited patiently for me to gather my thoughts, studying me.

"I can see there's more. Tell me."

"Oster shape-shifted in the bathroom, not completely into one of those creatures, but enough to identify him as one. He planned to take me back to Nolan. In the dining room, I could see everyone's aura but his. He was able to suppress it somehow. Until I caught him off guard, then it flared."

"What does that mean?" Dom leaned forward. I could make out the dark fringe of his eyelashes, even in the shadowed confines of our coach.

"It flared black. Just like the drekis. Queen Avery said she didn't want to align any more with Nolan than she already had. I wonder why she's allowing it all." I turned, locking eyes with Dom; "He must have had an illusion spell or something. It would make sense if he was under one, it's the only thing that could have also hidden his aura."

Dom leaned back, contemplating. He drummed his fingers on his knees. "You're not safe," he blurted.

"I've never been safe." The metal vines in the carriage writhed, morphing into jagged edges and menacing points.

"I'll do whatever it takes to keep you protected. And I'll keep my end of the bargain and get you out of the realms." His rings glowed in the darkened carriage, highlighting the strain of his clenched fists.

I didn't need his protection. But some small part of me lapped up the vision of the towering force in front of me and the threat he posed at the suggestion of my suffering. Even if I knew deep down it related directly to our agreement and his need of my magic. We were both using the other. I could stop pretending we weren't when the night was over.

"You're just saying that because I'm wearing this amazing gown," I chirped. My half-hearted smile barely cut through the intensity of his stare.

The scowling face of the formidable general stared back at me. "I am not a man of idle words. I would never speak lightly of your well-being," he replied.

Our carriage came to a stop. The rebel city of Aphellion appeared in our loosely curtained windows. "Get some rest. We'll leave for the Nereid Realm tomorrow," he commanded.

We exited the carriage, a slightly softer air having settled between us.

I watched as he receded into the darkness.

CHAPTER TWENTY-FIVE
THE GENERAL

The brisk wind from the mountains did little to cool my agitation. I shouldn't have allowed myself to get that close to her. Her scent overrode my better judgment. Some mix between those cherry candies she's always eating and fresh snow. And I hate snow. *Foka.*

I needed to stay the course. My people depended on me, and despite the wider ignorance to the veil that spread across all realms, even the people of Haluma would soon cry out for help. They just hadn't realized that their king was no savior.

Liora was the key to my success. She would take us to the Nereids, and I would finally be able to call on my allies beneath the sea. With Liora's aid we would strengthen our army and fortify our weapons cache. I just needed to stay the course.

Finn appeared at my side, keeping pace with my pressured steps.

"Tough night?"

I grunted, not ready to discuss all that had transpired.

Finn didn't prod. "We have a situation you need to come see."

I glanced at my second. He wore his scaled leathers, all his weapons in place. I sighed. Evil never slept. The portal opened with a whir, and we stepped through.

We emerged in a barren area high up in the Auren Mountains. Pickaxes, shovels, and hammers lay discarded around us. A faint acrid smell hovered in the air.

We stepped around mounds of dirt and shattered rock. "This was one of Nolan's mining operations. My spy reported a massive Berine supply here, and the intensive underground extraction brought in significant numbers of dreki. I had been working on a way to get us in, but now…" He gestured to the scene before us. Deserted. The entrance to the mountain had been demolished as if it had collapsed in on itself.

Why had this shut down so abruptly? The twin moons offered just enough light to reveal char, the residue of death magic. Although with dreki abounding here, that wasn't a surprise.

"Surely they hadn't cleared out all the Berine in such a short amount of time. It's usually embedded in kimberlite magma; extraction is tedious." I kicked at one of the mounds of dirt, sending plumes of sand into the air.

Finn froze, staring at my feet. I followed his gaze to a part of a hand protruding from the land. My shadows whirled out of me, leveling the mounds around us.

In the eerie silence, the weight of dread pushed down on us. My shadows responded before the clouds of dust had settled. All around were bodies, or their parts. We stood among the dead.

One of the dark creatures sprawled lifeless and mangled, its spikes still dripping with acid. A child with blackened veins lay exposed beneath the starlight. The bodies were mostly children. Some had dreki scales and all bore blackened veins. The smell was overwhelming. I suppressed a gag.

Nolan had unleashed death magic throughout the realms and most were completely oblivious. The descent into darkness was slippery and subtle. Few had their eyes open. The land was the first to wither, and there were many logical arguments to explain it away. His prolific accumulation of orphans, these new acid-wielding creatures, not to mention his army of dreki, were all signs of horrors to come. I squinted toward the collapsed entrance of the mountainside. "How do you know this was a place of mining extraction if you had never seen it before today?"

"I had taken our spy's word for it."

My rings flared. "Nolan is experimenting on children. There's no other reason for them to be here, and with their veins infused with char. Either they shut it down, or they tunneled far enough to close this entrance and continue their work elsewhere. I assume your spy is still alive?"

Finn nodded in affirmation.

"We need to know everything. What he saw, what he really knows."

Movement caught our eye. The dark creature opened a charcoal eye, moaning toward the sky. A metal sword formed in my hand and my shadows poured out. I was at the monster's side immediately, blade to throat.

It curled in on itself in fear, but its injuries prevented it from fully retreating. "Dominussssss," it hissed. Finn and I exchanged glances. It continued its weak attempt at crawling away from us. "Don't send me back to him."

"What happened here?" I demanded.

The beast fell limp, giving up on its effort at self-protection. "His army grows. He will conquer what is his." It coughed up a glob of black blood and fixed its beady eyes on me, studying. "He will do whatever it takes to get her back."

Liora. Seeing her at the mercy of Oster had unleashed something within me. I would destroy the realms before I lost her again. Nolan's obsession with her disturbed me at the deepest levels. The blade in my hand flared and sharpened, turning glassy. Nolan used stolen power, and I knew mine would be enough to take him down. It was up to me to stop him. It always had been. Ilayah prophesied it, and Xuri confirmed it. I would go to whatever end to protect Liora from further harm, and free our world from his dark clutches.

"Why does he want her so badly?" I asked.

The creature trembled. "She belongs to him. He covets her power."

"The King has his water refinery. What does he need a water wielder for?"

The beast cocked its head at me, a small smirk forming along its thin lips. "Surely you have felt it, Dominus. Your shadows should know." It began coughing again. Its use of my name unnerved me, and his cryptic words seemed more baiting than truth.

"I've heard enough. End him."

Finn snuffed its life before the breath from my command had dissipated. I turned away.

"We have to be strategic about this. They're hunting her, Dom." Finn eyed me warily. "We could use her to lure Nolan from his guarded castle."

My teeth clenched at his words. "We *are* using her. Her magic will get us to Queen Thaleia. She has a connection in Vorkut for unique weapons. I *am* being strategic."

Finn's somber tone was laced with concern. "We don't know how much time we have left, and we can't lose sight of our goal."

He was right. I knew he was right. But I couldn't shake how wrong it felt.

CHAPTER TWENTY-SIX
THE SPY

Dawn, the heinous witch, came too soon. It felt like I had just closed my eyes. I groaned as my guard rapped on the door, yelling that it was time to wake up. I bet the general put him up to that. Heinous brute. I rolled off my bed in a heap of agitation and yanked my scaled leathers on.

The night guard wordlessly led me to the stables where horses were being loaded up. Saddle bags of food, tents, bed rolls, blankets, and weapons already secured. Our journey would take us through Yarit, around the outskirts of the city, and to the coast that would deliver us to the depths of the Zephyrus Sea.

Xuri emerged, dressed in her own fine leathers, with books and journals peeking out of leather satchels. Finn sauntered around inspecting his tall gelding. Finally, the general arrived with a servant who brought in plates of warm food for us to shovel down before we departed. Lastly, Bowen entered the stables. He gave a slight, reverent bow to the general before finding his own horse.

Xuri leaned in. "That's the Premier Elixist, Bowen, the most accomplished student our Prime has trained." He glanced toward me, smiling as he confidently mounted his horse, his long, brown hair artfully arranged in a top knot above his head, his arms covered in tattoos. I tried again to decipher them when I felt the tingling burn of someone staring. I searched for the source, catching the general's eye. He walked over to me, huffing as he proffered a large duffel. Definitely not a morning person.

I accepted his offering, the bag clinking as I grasped it. "Careful," he warned. I opened the mouth of the bag to reveal my swords and daggers. Their hilts mirrored the glitter in my eyes. A rush of relief surged through me as I sheathed my weapons. The general's mouth twitched in a depressing attempt at a smile.

The familiar weight of my blades relaxed me. I mounted my horse and scanned the area, quickly noting Dom's absence. I missed his retreat amidst the bustle of our departure. I finally caught him genuflecting in the shadows of a distant tree. I urged my mare in his direction, pretending to carelessly drift toward him rather than an obvious display of nosiness.

I angled my body toward the group, my head tilted slightly to keep Dom's form in my line of sight. He kept his head lowered, his arms resting on a propped-up knee as he mouthed silent words. He finished speaking and made the sign for the god Elyon, a simple drag of the finger from one temple to the other. The sign established as a symbol of the all-knowing nature of the god. The same gesture he had placed on my own forehead when we were kids.

I had forgotten he used to do that to me before he departed from the Rivellan Wood. Hardly anyone followed the old ways anymore, and yet Dom continued to do so. I tucked away this curiosity and maneuvered my horse back into the bustle of travel preparation.

My horse stood impatient, much like myself, when Dom

finally returned. His presence overpowered the rest of us, and my gaze annoyingly strayed to him.

"Careful!" Bowen hopped backward as Xuri froze in confusion. "That's my lucky pine cone."

Xuri cackled. "You have got to be kidding me."

Bowen cupped the small pine cone in his hands protectively. I peered at him closely, then back to Xuri. My hand clapped over my mouth to suppress my laughter.

"Aw leave him alone, Xuri. You know I have an emotional support rock." Finn removed a smooth stone from his pocket. Bowen's face lit up. My jaw dropped.

Dom stopped short, his mouth slightly open. He groaned, wiping his hand down his face. *"Foka."*

Finn caught Dom's muttered curse, his face contorting in offense. "What!? You could use a support rock or two, Scowling Shadow Man."

Dom rolled his eyes, shaking his head. He hopped onto his horse. "Secure your precious cargo and let's go." Still suppressing my laughter, I grabbed my horse's reins. Our journey beginning before the early morning stars winked out.

We made a brief stop at an apothecary in Lyrae. Bowen emerged with some vials, exchanging a brief look with the general. By nightfall, we had moved through the city of waterways and entered a copse of trees on the outskirts of the Perellian Forest.

An outcropping of rock extended from the earth creating a natural wall nearby. It was as enclosed as we could hope for. Tents went up swiftly. I stood by, observing Finn make use of his gravity magic by turning heavy loads into manageable work. I wasn't sure how to lend my services, so I held out tools and supplies in meager assistance. The general took to setting up a small fire.

"You're good at that, General. It still takes me at least twelve attempts to get a fire going. Perhaps my water magic fights against my efforts." His eyes glinted in the flickering flames.

"Dom."

I paused. "What?"

"My name is not General, it's Dom." He held my gaze, his face indecipherable. "And what is yours?"

Why did this matter so much? "You know my name."

"Ruin is not a name, it's a title meant to instill fear."

I scoffed. "I have been Rue since I was taken in by King Nolan. It is my name, *Dom*." I resumed setting up the food supplies, moving things around with unnecessary force. Busying myself, I was no longer interested in this conversation. Liora died the day my parents did. Why couldn't he let this go?

A grin barely ghosted his face, "And what were you before then?"

I stumbled a beat, my anger rising to protect, to destroy. The tips of my fingers frosted, the only sign I felt anything. My expression remained flat as I firmly retorted, "I was nothing." My magic surged, a roar in my ears, ice chips flaking off my fingers.

Shadows swirled around him. One extended, warm and soft as it gently swept back a lock of hair that had fallen out of my braid. I tensed. The shadows retreated, gathering in rippled waves toward the fisted hands at his sides. A sad smile softened his jawline. "Names have meaning, and you are not what they call you, what they have made you believe."

He turned then, disappearing into the cluster of trees. And I stood there, questioning my understanding of myself, perhaps for the first time.

~

WE RODE HARD the following day and arrived at the southern coast of the Zephyrus Sea where the Lyraean Shelf extended, and the great underwater trench beckoned. I had kept to myself, chewing on the words Dom had thrown at me. I found myself acutely aware of where he was at all times. His presence irritated even as it calmed.

Xuri informed us that she was staying behind, to await our return and care for the horses. A sense of relief I didn't dwell on followed her announcement. Finn, Bowen, Dom, and I prepared to enter the frothing deep.

This was my moment.

I had never been to the ocean before and the sight of the sea overcame me. I wished I had more time to savor it, but our mission took precedence. Concern that I could sustain our group crested higher than the waves before me. If my magic slipped, I would lead us all to inglorious deaths.

The ocean's pulse soothed my apprehension. Waves broke at the shoreline, and I chose to leave the remnants of my doubt with them. I wouldn't fail.

Dom inspected the horses, then spoke quietly with Xuri. I leaned in, trying to eavesdrop, but couldn't decipher their words. Agitation crept over me and my mouth went dry. She knew him better than I did, his history with her much less sordid than my own.

Xuri had only been kind to me. There was no reason for me to act on this overwhelming urge to destroy her. I would leave as soon as this journey was complete and the sooner I accepted that, the easier this would go. Dom turned and took hold of a vial from Bowen that he downed in one swig. I forced myself to turn away, glaring into the horizon.

Our little group gathered and I explained my magic, more for my sake than theirs. "The Prime Chemist taught me how to enclose us in bubbles that will allow for oxygenated air to flow. We will be able to breathe and communicate normally. I won't let us drown. I'll also manipulate water currents to push us deeper, faster." I was as prepared as I could be. While my control of the current helped in moving us quicker, it was really to compensate for my weak swimming skills. No one needed that detail, though.

Dom kissed the top of Xuri's head and my stomach dropped. "We hope to be back by week's end," he said. "If there's any way to send a message, we will. You will likely be too far for us to mind-walk." I groped at the vestiges of my dignity and tried to pull them together, shoving my ill-placed possessiveness far below the surface.

There was no future here for me. I knew this. Whatever I felt for Dom was one-sided and fruitless. I could not have a divided mind when it came to what I was about to do. I sucked in a deep breath and reviewed everything Gemma had taught me, slamming any errant thoughts of the general firmly into some dark, crusty corner of my mind.

The weight of our lives rested heavy on my shoulders when the moment finally arrived. It was not a foreign burden, though; I'd carried similar for years with me and Delah. I dipped my toes into the sea, stepping toward the unknown.

The water parted at our entrance, our boots leaving wet prints behind us in the sand. I drew my magic upward, feeling its familiar hum beneath my skin. I used what I had practiced with Gemma in the lagoon, calling forth the power of the surrounding water, envisioning what I needed. Our bodies submerged as an oxygenated bubble encircled us. The current swept us outward toward the great trench.

Water muffled sound in our descent. Wonder coursed between us as we glided through the water, passing swarms of glimmering fish. The water turned darker as we dove deeper and deeper down the slope that would lead us to the trench. We could see it in the distance—a darkness separate from the rest of the surrounding sea. Our entrance to the Nereid Kingdom.

Wielding my affinity felt like breathing. The air bubbles and the harnessed current didn't drain me. The easy cycle of release and reabsorption of my magic dissolved any lingering fear. Magic tingled in my veins and flit around my fingertips in silky ribbons.

A small smile formed, and I glanced to the side, accidentally meeting Dom's eye. He offered a subtle, lopsided smile of his own, a small dimple shadowing his cheek. I could have sworn his shadows pulsed, or simply a trick of the undulating water and the rippling light. His nearness made me feel like I could conquer anything. In another life, what might we have been?

Ahead in the trench, two men emerged, or rather two fully armored oceanic nymphs. Their tails were weapons themselves, large and powerful. Each man held a glittering trident. I slowed our descent, pushing against the current, until we halted a respectful distance from the warriors.

Dom swam forward, introducing us and explaining our request.

A whirlpool appeared, spiraling next to one of the mermen, growing larger and larger. One of the warriors stood guard, while the other led the way. My heart throbbed hesitantly in my chest as we followed him into the abyss.

The whirlpool sucked us in instantly. My focus clenched as I sought to hold my magic tight over me and my companions. A scream tore from my mouth, silently disappearing among the frothing waters. I groped for anyone near me, and as quickly as we were sucked in, the chaos abruptly stopped. My chest heaved as I searched for Dom, Finn, and Bowen. Our hands all hovered at the hilt of our weapons in preparation for potential battle.

"A warning would have been nice." Finn grumbled, his voice only slightly muffled in our underwater environment.

One of the mermen chuckled. "This way," he commanded.

A brilliant castle, like a great mountain, emerged from the depths of the sea. Underwater vents expelled steam that warmed the water around us, lending a comfortable temperature despite the depths we swam in.

We floated under archways, passing turrets and towers connected by parapets. The water glittered with the bioluminescent light of deep-sea creatures that flickered in shades of blue, white, and purple. Collections of worms with brightly illuminated bodies were packed every few feet—living torches along the walls.

I kept careful watch over all of our surroundings. Some merfolk swam around purposefully, others casually strolled, and some outright stopped and stared. Their hair floated around them along with the sheer material that did little to cover their toned bodies.

We were led swiftly through the palace directly toward the great hall, and throne room. I took note of every corridor and door we passed.

Brightly colored coral decorated the palace as both art and hardware. It wound around the doors and archways acting as a twisted, breathing molding. The walls and floors shimmered in opalescent hues as if made from the insides of thousands of oyster shells.

The doors to the throne room swung open and the queen herself rested on her throne, speaking to a guard at her side. Upon our entrance she straightened, her glowing eyes surged with curiosity. A sly smile curled her full lips. She wore a sheer, light-blue dress, tight at the bodice and flowing gracefully behind her tail in a translucent train. Her tail fins swayed languidly in the same motion as her gown. Her shoulders, arms, and cheeks shimmered with tiny iridescent scales. The queen's blue throne twisted upward into a threatening piece of spiked coral. It mimicked the queen, radiating both beauty and violence.

She gestured with her hand, translucent webbing catching in the light. "Welcome to Nereid, the oceanic realm of sea nymphs, or as you like to call us, mermaids. Your determination to meet me in my own lands is impressive." She eyed us all, inclining her head toward Dom, and a curious smirk toward me. "It has been a long time since another realm has ventured to our own. I assume you will be here a day or two, no? Let us get you settled in your rooms."

Though we had just arrived, I wasn't keen on getting comfortable, but we were clearly at the queen's mercy, and out of respect for the royal before us, we had no choice but to leave her presence and retreat to our assigned rooms.

I struggled to view auras with my magic spread so thin and sea water washing away my summoned tears. Dom believed this realm would aid the Liberation, yet he had never met them before. I worried his faith had been ill-placed. He likely wouldn't approve of my spying, but surely I could glean some information to increase our chances of assuring a Nereidian alliance.

Shame continued to batter me, an ever-present haunting in my mind. It stacked its heavy weight on the collection of repellent secrets from my past. If I was caught spying, I wasn't sure if Dom would understand, or if he would return me to Nolan. I was willing to take the gamble in my desire to prove my worth.

A mermaid with silvery skin approached, her hands began to glow as magic rippled out.

The queen addressed us, "This is Aydrielle, a lady of my court. She will allow you to move and breathe during your time here without concern for your safety." Aydrielle's magic caressed my face. I gasped with a sharp intake of breath as my nose tingled and my lungs filled with what felt like fresh air. A glance at Bowen showed gills had formed behind his ears.

"You may drop your own magic, Water Wielder. You and your companions are safe." I relaxed my hold on the bubble surrounding our group, and immediately my muscles unwound. The dual attention of maintaining enough air to keep us all alive had taken a toll.

"I can show you to your rooms." Aydrielle's voice was

melodic, her lithe body moving seamlessly out the throne room doors. We stirred up small bubbles as we moved to catch up with our escort. We coasted through several hallways with flowing tapestries. Weapons adorned the walls as well as collections of glowworms that suffused the palace with a surprising amount of light.

We entered a private area with tables and sofas arranged in a semicircle. Several doors surrounded the living area and Aydrielle led us to the first door, which was to be my room.

A bed and simple furnishings created a simple yet cozy setup. "When we sleep, our breathing stills, and the lack of air creates enough weight to make us sink. There are also kelp cuffs on the bed, should it be used for *other* activities aside from sleep." She arched her brow in Dom's direction, and I tensed at the gesture. Dom refrained from responding, pretending not to notice her attention.

"Feel free to relax. There are clothes in the closets for you to wear for this evening's dinner. I will send for someone to escort you from here when dinner is readied. Please, make yourselves at home." Her hips swayed as she exited. Finn, Dom, and Bowen trailed behind her.

I hoped that we would be in and out of here. Perhaps we would have an audience with the queen this evening. Maybe after dinner.

It wasn't like we had brought bags of clothes—there was little to unpack. I explored the monstrous piece of furniture akin to an armoire. Carvings of ancient sea dragons, sharks, and squid adorned it. The door clicked open revealing a large assortment of dresses. They were varying sizes, all of them sheer. I stared at each swath of fabric, my mouth slightly agape.

I assumed the queen expected me to wear one of these. The only piece of clothing I wore beneath my tunic and leathers was a silk chemise, and that wouldn't work beneath any of these gowns. I did still have the swimming suit from Gemma. The light color wouldn't be too contrasting with the sheer dress fabric. My sigh emitted a barrage of bubbles that tickled up my face.

My attention returned to the kelp cuffs at my bed. The idea of exactly how to spy on our hosts came to me when I learned of their purpose. I lay on the bed and secured my arms through the loops of the elongated leaves. Closing my eyes, I called to the water around me, reaching for it. I stilled my breath, fully concentrating on my affinity, envisioning my silhouette. A gentle disconnect from my body caused a ghost of a smile to form on my lips.

When I opened my eyes again, it was not to gaze at the ceiling in my room. My vision merged with the water around me. I glanced at my body on the bed, then stared at a mirror on the wall, the outline of my body shimmered and blended with the water. I had created a projection of myself through the power, and base material, of my affinity. I could spy anywhere.

CHAPTER TWENTY-SEVEN
THE SPY

I didn't know how much time I had before the dinner summons. My water-projected self might be recognizable if one stopped to assess the glimmering outline of my body's shape, but the constant undulation of the water blurred even that. The exhilaration of having accomplished this feat of magic left me buoyant.

I cracked my door open and leaked out of the room. Though I surged confidently down the hallways, I was not arrogant enough to storm down the center and risk detection. I stayed pressed against walls and tapestries, stilling when Nereidians passed by.

Servants, guards, and members of the queen's court flitted about. The throne room beckoned and I peered inside. The queen remained on her throne providing direction and idly speaking with those around her. I swam beyond it, intent in my search.

Recalling the other passages and guards from our initial journey through the palace, I turned down a hall with promise. It led to storage and kitchens and other service rooms. I backtracked, meandering along the corridors.

I spotted a warrior and tracked him. He followed a winding path that eventually opened into a large atrium. I bit my cheek to stifle my surprise. Thousands of muscled, armored warriors filled the area. A sigh of relief escaped me. Perhaps an accord between our realms would truly solidify our chances for success.

I stayed only briefly to observe what I could in regards to numbers, their division of organization, and general hierarchy. The atrium was several hundred feet wide and twice as tall. Levels were separated in ways I couldn't understand, but there were five that I could count, stretching toward the ceiling, where warriors sparred, weapons were tested, and forms were practiced. It was impressive and encouraging to witness.

I finally retreated, rushing back toward my room, acutely aware of the passing time. My movements involuntarily slowed the closer I came to the entrance of the throne room. Curiosity overcame me at the majesty of Queen Thaleia. I entered her space wary and watchful, lingering in the corner, observing. Everything about this realm captivated me—the colors, the movement, the beauty.

A creature of nightmares swam by, leashed and controlled by a handler. Its body ribboned through the water and its mouth featured long, protruding teeth—two on top and two on bottom. Several more followed behind the first. They innately horrified me. The queen clapped upon seeing them.

"The eels have arrived! It's been too long since we shared our fun with foreign dignitaries. I do love a good surprise. Make sure they are well-fed." The handlers maneuvered the beasts into cages. I noticed several other caged eels surrounded by a cloud of blood from the fish they consumed.

They exuded a violence that left me entranced. One of the eels completed its meal and was directed to sink its teeth into an empty container. The teeth oozed out a dark-purple liquid that collected at the bottom.

"They are magnificent, don't you think?"

I froze. How had she seen me? So engrossed with the hideousness of the eels and what they were doing with them, I failed to notice the queen's approach. Hells, this was bad.

Slowly, I turned to her, a sheepish smile on my face.

"These are vampire eels. They provide endless entertainment, as you will experience later this evening. Do you have a question for me? I much prefer direct confrontation over this sneaking around bit; though I commend you on your cleverness. I don't recall the last water-wielder having such power, or at least using it so brazenly."

Queen Thaleia did not face me directly. In fact, she did not openly acknowledge her conversation with me at all. If she had, surely guards would have surrounded us. I swallowed down my phantom throat.

"I had hoped to learn more about your kingdom. I did not mean any disrespect. The general is unaware of my actions," I mumbled.

"I am pleased to share about the Nereid Realm; we are a people who have fought valiantly for what is ours. Now is not the time to discuss this, though. Feel free to join the General and I when we meet tomorrow. For now, it would be best for you to return to your rooms."

I curtsied and began my retreat.

"A warning to you, Water Wielder." I paused at her address. "I can taste secrets. And yours are bitter on my tongue."

Good to know my history preceded me. I raced back to my room where my body remained on the bed, lying in repose as though asleep.

My awareness merged back with my body, and I gasped as air filled my lungs. The small gills below my ears fluttered with the intake of water. I removed the kelp cuffs and left them floating listlessly above my bed. I couldn't dwell on my embarrassment at the queen herself catching me.

Hells.

I entered the main living area where I'd breezed by Finn on my way in, hoping for a distraction.

Finn reclined on a velvet couch; Bowen sat on the other end reading a book from the coffee table. Finn threw out his flirty grin and patted the space next to him. "Take a seat, Rebby."

I rolled my eyes as I nestled into a spot on the sofa, still catching my breath and grateful for the invitation. Bowen sat on my other side, seemingly annoyed at my intrusion. "I told you that you'd find a dagger in your back if you called me that," I addressed Finn.

"I like to press my luck. How was that whirlpool portal for you? I thought my balls were going to explode."

I chuckled, recalling the experience. "It was a very uncomfortable feeling. I feared we would all be separated right until it stopped."

"I knew it! You would have missed me terribly."

"No one would miss you that much, Finn." Dom interrupted, his eyes dark in the ambient light. I avoided his gaze, feigning interest in Bowen's book. He perked up at my attentions and began explaining what he was reading. I hardly listened.

Shadows pulsed around me, and I peered up at Dom. A muscle in his jaw ticked as he stared down the space between Bowen and me. I frowned at him. Why the hells would he care if I was interested in Bowen's book?

Those shadows were as moody as its master. I reminded myself of the bargain I initiated. Once it was fulfilled, we could leave this realm and I could connect Evander with Dom. Then, I was leaving. The sting of my nails in my palm grounded me. This couldn't be over with sooner. I really needed to spend less time around Dom so I could keep my emotions in check. I flexed my fingers to ease the tension.

Dom noticed the movement as he pulled his shadows back toward himself. His voice flowed firm, if slightly detached. "I will make sure we get an audience with Queen Thaleia tomorrow. Tonight, let's just glean whatever we can about her and her kingdom and try to rest."

I wondered if I should tell him about my spying attempt, and the vampire eels, but caution kept me silent. Dom shifted to stare pointedly at Finn. "And eat whatever food they serve us, even if you have to pretend to like it. Don't insult them." His tone mirrored a mother chiding her son.

Finn appeared affronted at the remark. "How was I supposed to know that awful stew was Lord Fallon's dead wife's favorite meal?" He leaned toward me conspiratorially, pulling me closer than necessary. "I swear it looked like pig brain floating."

Dom clenched his jaw as the room appeared to darken. I smothered a smile, putting some space between us. "I'm sure we can all stomach whatever is served. We might even be gone by tomorrow. One night of foreign cuisine won't hurt us."

A knock interrupted us. A servant appeared to let us know they would lead us to the dining room when we were presentable. I peered down at my scaled leathers and softly sighed, not excited about changing into one of the provided gowns.

A young mermaid with mint-colored hair followed me to my room. "Will you need help dressing?" she asked.

"I suppose I might." She floated to the closet and emerged with a lavender dress, tiny shells sewn into the hem to help weigh it down. The material was soft and thin, and almost entirely see-through. I held it up, swallowing my future embarrassment.

The servant pretended not to notice. The girl opened a jar, and tiny flecks of glowing lights swam out, burrowing into the material. She softly smiled. "These are microjellies. They won't sting you, but their tentacles, which you can hardly see, cast a silver glow. Living glitter. They are used in our finest gowns."

She held it up, the dress now sparkling with the twinkling lights of a thousand jellies, nodding in approval.

I removed my leathers and searched for Gemma's swim suit. The little scraps of cloth barely covered my most intimate parts. The gracious mermaid averted her eyes until I beckoned for her, and then she pulled the dress over my head, affixing it securely to my body. The sheer fabric shimmered with a sweetheart neckline and fitted bodice. The gossamer grazed my hips before flowing delicately to my ankles. Even staying still, it glistened.

"If you intend to wear this stringed underthing, I would recommend only the bottom. The top detracts from the beauty of the dress. Our culture believes that the forms we inhabit are to be celebrated. I could rearrange the microjellies to cover more of your chest if that helps." I gulped, nodding.

The young mermaid beamed as she worked her magic with the dress, repositioning many of the jellies to at least cover my nipples. I would not allow this mortification to affect our mission. In and out. I did my part to get us safely into this realm. We could secure the queen's support and be done. If this dress brought me success, and a way to fulfill my end of the bargain, then so be it. The knot in my throat didn't agree. Hells, I did not sign up for this.

The mermaid gently combed my hair, which thankfully continued to maintain its whitened color. She created a coronet braid with half of my hair, affixed with a simple shell. The rest of my hair, including the small braids behind my ears, flowed in a curtain of silver behind me.

The servant searched through a drawer until she found some tiered earrings to compliment my gown. She offered them to me as she appraised my outfit, "Now you are most presentable for the Queen. Let's meet the others and I will lead you to dinner."

Reminding myself I was a highly trained murderous assassin

did not help my humiliation. I entered the living area to face the group of very male rebels with my chin held high.

Everyone stopped talking, the proverbial air sucked out of the room. I took in their outfits as they took in mine—the fabric of their shirts clung to their chests emphasizing every ripple of muscle. I noticed them all, but my gaze glued to Dom. The shirts lacked buttons on the top half revealing everything from his throat to his chest. His pants billowed with the current, intermittently adhering to his powerful thighs.

Bowen elbowed Finn and they immediately busied themselves with their hands. Dom stilled, a muscle in his jaw feathered as his eyes affixed to mine. Slowly, they raked down my body, then carefully back up. Warmth spread from my core, and the knowing heat of flushed cheeks radiated, but I refused to balk.

"I hope I don't have to kill anyone this evening. Might ruin the mission." His words cascaded over me, glass sharp and tempest black.

Swallowing hard, I flashed a coy smile. "Are we ready to eat or are we going to stare at each other all night?"

He took a step forward, meeting my challenge. "Perhaps I'm not hungry for food."

I didn't move, still unable to peel my eyes off of him. His pupils overpowered his golden irises, darkening his powerful features. His voice came out hard, gravelly. "I'll escort you. Take my hand. Please."

I had no desire to disobey.

"Good girl," he murmured.

My breath caught. His arm tensed beneath mine as he sensed my reaction.

"Good to know," he muttered.

"I could eat something," Finn suggestively responded, waggling his eyebrows, effectively throwing ice water on the heated moment.

I swear I heard Dom growl.

CHAPTER TWENTY-EIGHT
THE GENERAL

Finn shot me a warning glare as I struggled to compose myself. The curves of her body demanded my attention. And I wasn't in a sharing mood. My shadows betrayed me by responding to her presence, and I allowed them to restrain Bowen so that he followed far behind us. I held firmly to her arm, my glare threatening violence toward anyone who dared look in her direction.

We wound through hallways and under archways; mermen with tridents and sharks at their sides hovered every few feet. Queen Thaleia had done well for herself, and that boded well for me.

Entering the great room, we approached the raised dais where we were seated at a high table with the mermaid queen. I sat to the queen's left. Her consort reclined on her right. Rue sat across from me, next to Bowen. *Foka.* My entire body tensed at their proximity. It was going to be a long night.

I ignored the agitation simmering beneath my skin. Finn sat on the other side of Bowen, next to a mermaid whose dress left even less to the imagination than Rue's. I recognized the swim suit that Gemma had provided Rue back in Yarit. I was grateful she had brought it, but I refused to let myself explore why it mattered.

Most of the food laid out was a variation of fish or mussels or clams. The flavors ranged from briny to buttery. I ate my fill, while keeping an eye on our hosts and our surroundings. Rue's presence was a complicated, though not entirely unwelcomed, distraction. The queen reclined at my side, asking polite questions about Lyrae, avoiding the true nature of our visit.

I studied the room, noting the guards and the multitude of merfolk that filled the space. It seemed Queen Thaleia's court was well-ordered and relaxed. It was said that Queen Thaleia had once been cursed. Once she was able to break it, her realm had expanded as her power increased.

The queen raised her glass. "Tonight, we toast our guests. It's been too long since another realm has made the journey to us. May the evening be filled with the best delights the Nereids have to offer." Glasses clinked and my gaze caught Rue's. I wanted her beside me. I forced myself to study my food instead.

The queen leaned toward me. "We may discuss your concerns and requests tomorrow morning. Bring your water wielder as well. Tonight, General, is for merriment." I nodded, setting my glass down, resigned at having to wait longer for potential answers and curious at Rue's inclusion in our meeting.

Musicians began to play a haunting melody. Above us, purple smoke hazed through the water. It spread among us, fading to a pale lavender. Several people at the dinner erupted in applause at the sight.

A tingling sensation traveled through my magicked gills and a metallic taste hit the back of my throat. I vaguely noticed myself unwinding. Sounds became increasingly muffled as my ears attuned to the melody of the musicians.

Rue's laughter speared through the haze of my thoughts. What brought on her unabashed delight? And why wasn't I the source of it? I watched her leaning toward Bowen, her arm brushing his. I smoldered as I observed the touch. I shouldn't watch her. But I just needed one more glance. She was a vision of beauty so striking and fierce, I felt paralyzed by it.

Something inside of me opened, possessiveness bleeding out. My fork began to melt. I restrained the metal magic that punched beneath my skin. Finn shot me a warning glance, then disappeared with the mermaid that sat next to him, his intentions abundantly clear.

I shifted in my seat, willing this predatory feeling to subside. Shadows began leaking from my knuckles, swirling in the water around me. I shoved my fists under the table. If Rue desired Bowen, I would not interfere. Even that thought had my rings forming tiny blades.

I wanted to be the one to tease out her laughter, her sighs. My mind grew sluggish, and I focused my concentration on my erratic magic. But I couldn't pry my eyes away from Rue.

Queen Thaleia's lady in waiting, Aydrielle, came forward, brushing her hand down my arm. I turned toward her; the sensation of her caress tingled, warming me. I struggled to keep my thoughts clear. Something felt off. There was nothing that we had eaten or drank that could have affected my senses so sharply. And still, Rue pulled my attention harder than the tides bending toward the moon.

As if she could feel it herself, our eyes locked. I was riveted by the soft lines of her face, the graceful slope of her nose, and her dark lashes. Her dress shimmered, and the shadow of her breasts beneath the ethereal fabric made it difficult to focus on anything else. I bit my tongue until I tasted blood, a futile attempt to cast away increasingly volatile thoughts. *Foka.*

Aydrielle's fingers trailed along my shoulders, and unwelcomed warmth followed as I instinctively leaned in her direction. Her sultry voice drifted toward me. "I hope you're enjoying the venom of the vampire eels."

My attention swayed toward the queen's siren. "Vampire eels?"

She smiled knowingly, still dragging her fingers along my arm. "Their venom lowers inhibitions and creates a thrall. Think of it like a truth-telling aphrodisiac, or a more potent form of nymphian wine. It's a unique gift found only in our realm."

I jolted. No wonder this dinner became so much more charged. My words came out pressured, now actively seeking to resist the enticement of the venom's control and the allure of the siren next to me. "I must take my leave," I blurted, standing quickly. I barely prevented my chair from toppling to the floor.

The pull on my emotions and my body created an irresistible trance. Aydrielle put her hand on my arm, gently coaxing me closer to her. The scales on her cheeks shimmered and her hungry eyes locked on mine. My body pulsed with desire, even as my magic revolted against it; the object of my desire was not the nymph in front of me, it belonged to the enchanting woman beyond her.

"I would be happy to accompany you to your rooms. It would be a shame for you to get lost." Her sensuous tone pressed in on me. The musicians continued their hypnotic melody, weaving their lusty invitation throughout the room. My heart pounded as longing grew in my stomach.

Gritting my teeth, I reflexively searched for Rue. Still leaning toward Bowen, Rue allowed him to touch her. Yet, her fiery stare bored into me. Was that jealousy blazing under her piercing gaze? The water around her fisted hands crystallized. My own possessiveness responded.

"Excuse me," I forced out. Aydrielle released my arm as I lunged toward Bowen and Rue. A growl had Bowen backing off, making himself scarce. Rue gazed up at me. The purple in her eyes shone brightly in the glow of the sea, exuding a hunger that incinerated me.

She licked her lips, and I barely contained my groan. "We need to get back to our rooms. Now." My voice came out sharper than I intended, harsh in the growing din. Every muscle in my body strained to hold myself back from grabbing Rue and tasting her right there. My mouth watered at the thought.

My mind played out multiple scenarios of my body pressed against hers, pinning her wrists above her head. What would she sound like when I brought her to the edge? I blinked hard, the muscles in my clenched jaw ached. This was for her own protection. I think.

She backed up a step, her eyes half-mast. It took every drop of will to keep my focus on her face and not look down to the sheer veil of her dress and the seductive curves it clung to. Her body may as well have been made from a siren's song.

I implored her, "We are under the influence of a drug. We need to get out of here before..." She reached toward my face, her focus on my lips. I grabbed her wrist to stop her, my chest tightening with the self-restraint.

Undeterred, her other hand brushed my cheek. Her soft touch splintered me. "Sometimes, I find myself wondering what we could have been in any other life than the ones we have. I would have liked to have been a woman worthy of your affection." I could barely swallow. Her words struck me like no fist ever could.

She couldn't know how much my soul had always called to hers. She couldn't know that there could never be an "us." The fate of the realms rested on me alone, and Elyon had spoken through my dreams, through Xuri, regarding what the cost would be. It was my job to protect her. Even if it was from me.

My control eroded. "Rue, let's go," I begged her, my arousal unyielding.

Hurt clouded the water between us. The sound of a disappointed kitten escaped her lips. I couldn't dwell on it.

She reluctantly followed me out of the dining hall, her hand clasped in mine. Heat coursed up from the place where we touched. The further away we walked from the luring melody and the venom-saturated dining room, the more clarity took its place.

My anger hitched at what nearly happened. We should have been warned. I clutched Rue's hand for fear she would bolt back to what was very soon to be an orgy. I did not want to let go of her. But she wasn't mine to hold on to. I laced our fingers together anyway.

By the time we made it to our wing of the palace, the lustful haze had nearly vanished, though the tension in my shoulders remained and my aggression toward Bowen hadn't wavered. I couldn't bring myself to release our entwined fingers. I glanced down at our clasped hands. The scars on her wrists contrasted starkly against the rest of her skin.

My desire to protect and consume her swelled within me. The urge to abscond with her and hide her away from harm and pain overwhelmed rational thought. The melody of possession still sung through me. I wanted to lick every inch of her body and seal her as mine. And I wasn't sure I could blame eel venom for the urgency of that longing.

As if she read my thoughts, her cheeks flushed. "That could have made for a very awkward morning. One I know Xuri would not approve of." Had she heard Xuri's warning to me? She disentangled herself from me. Her hands fidgeted with her sparkling dress, drawing my eyes to her peaked nipples. I inhaled a shaky breath while Rue hugged her arms across her body.

"I prefer my partners to be a bit more lucid and consensual." My voice emerged broken, pressured. She peered up then, assessing.

She held my gaze longer than warranted. The blood in my ears rushed as the venomous smog slowly released its final grip on me, though my arousal persisted. Determination hardened her features. "I feel like I should apologize for what I said, but my words were true."

She fell silent, no longer willing to meet my eye. My thumb twitched to smooth the crease between her brow, to soothe away her concerns. I bit my cheek instead.

She huffed a mirthless laugh. "Anyway, we both know the leader of the rebellion and the king's spy could never work. And you had a life before me; I would never want to intrude. I'm grateful fate found a way to reestablish a friendship between us despite the direction our lives have taken."

An errant shadow shot out of me at her mention of friendship, the word curdling inside me. She only thought of us as friends. For her, the venom really had made it seem as though she had interest in me. Her attentions truly were toward Bowen. I couldn't think straight.

Duty clamped down, anchoring me, when all I wanted in this moment was to press her against the wall so I could lick and suck that word right out of her sensuous mouth.

I held still, my thoughts at war within me. A sad acceptance weakened her trembling smile. Turning away, she quietly entered her bed chamber. It was for the best.

With a frustrated sigh, I adjusted my pants and locked myself in my room.

IF ONLY IT had been possible the night before to take a cold shower while in the depths of the ocean. I had finally fallen into a fitful sleep, trying to avoid intrusive, lurid thoughts and smoky venom-infused dreams. The ornate clamshell, which served as a clock on the wall, displayed a pre-dawn hour.

I groaned into my pillow. Rue was the girl I had lost. She was the woman I couldn't keep.

As a child, I was sent out to search for orphans before Nolan could collect them, and instead, I found *her*. I kept her a secret from the Liberation, my protectiveness for her overpowering even then. She was always alone, always cloaked in her own shadow of grief. Until the day she disappeared. I had feared the worst when I couldn't find her. That bottomless feeling of dread and desperation still tormented me.

The urge to learn everything about her dominated my thoughts ever since I realized Ruin was Liora. But she still didn't trust me; not like she did with Bowen. I had no doubt I could sway her my direction, but it wouldn't be fair to open that door when I knew what was to come. We were raised to be enemies. Maybe I still was. I rolled over, groaning again.

I forced myself to think through our meeting with the queen. The Liberation needed the Nereids as allies. Xuri foresaw our future alliance. She also made it clear that if I die, there would be no hope for the realms. It would be subjugated as darkness devoured it. This alliance was the next step toward our success.

Hope was a fragile thing. A dangerous thing. I had seen its loss devastate some of my strongest soldiers. I was wary to give it too much weight. Putting your hope in the wrong thing... that's what destroyed spirits. I had let Xuri's enthusiasm rub off on me. I tried to reel some of it back in, preparing myself for the worst-case scenario. But what would that even be? I suppose Queen Thaleia could offer me nothing, and then I'd be no worse off than before. But that would certainly seal my future fate. There were no other options left—outside of the queen— nowhere else I could turn.

The clock finally displayed an acceptable hour to start the day. I shifted off the bed and pulled on my tunic and leathers. I wasn't completely comfortable peacocking around without a shirt. Though I wouldn't put it past Finn to "align with the culture" and have an easy excuse to flaunt himself.

I sincerely hoped Rue wouldn't try to. I growled internally.

That sheer gown last night viscerally unsettled me. Watching so many males peruse her curves had left my jaw so tight from its clenching that I wouldn't have been surprised to have cracked a tooth.

I popped my neck and shook out my arms, refocusing on the task at hand. A spread of food lay artfully displayed in the central living area where all our rooms connected. Bowen glanced up from his bowl, offering a drowsy nod. Finn strolled in from the main hallway moments later, disheveled, still wearing last night's clothes. He arched an eyebrow daring me to ask questions. When I didn't offer any, he shrugged and strolled to his room, yawning.

I grabbed a plate, loading it up with food that deceived with its beauty. I popped the delicacies in my mouth, the salinity of it all confirming my suspicions. The saltiness made me grimace but I swallowed it down.

Rue finally emerged; her hair plaited back, the glow of the light giving it a strange lilac hue. She nodded her greetings toward Bowen and me, carefully aloof. "This is salty. And this is saltier," I warned her.

She unsuccessfully restrained a grin as she piled food on her plate. She took a deep breath to steel herself, then after several attempts at chewing, made an audible swallowing sound. I stifled a laugh. She didn't hide her glare, though a smirk chased after it. I struggled to turn away from her.

Before I had a chance to bring up the morning's meeting with the queen, Aydrielle entered. "Good morning. I hope you all enjoyed yourselves last night." Her voice dripped heavy with innuendo.

She piled shrimp onto a plate alongside pickled sea cucumber. Her shoulder grazed mine as she proceeded to languidly eat her food. She sucked on her fingers as her gaze lingered on me. I shifted to put some space between us.

"If you are ready, the Queen awaits."

CHAPTER TWENTY-NINE
THE SPY

Aydrielle's gaze knifed into Dom's, boring into his golden eyes as she greeted our group. My chest tightened. I directed my focus on a teapot. If he had entertained her last night, it was none of my business. My heart raged. I took a deep breath, willing myself to ignore their interaction, pasting a blithe smile on my face.

My breakfast nearly choked me when she seductively licked her fingers. I swallowed my rising temper. If I possessed claws they would have extended. Instead, I ground my teeth as frigid ice threatened to spear out of me. What Dom chose to do and who he chose to do it with shouldn't concern me. My mind conjured an image of Dom's hands all over Aydrielle's voluptuous body. I could almost hear her moaning his name. My mouth turned dry. The floor beneath me started to freeze.

Aydrielle spun toward me with a calculated smile. I bared my teeth. I had to get a hold of myself before we met the queen. For a moment last night, I thought he might have held more than just respect for me. I had been wrong. I had misread his behavior. He had the chance to make a move and chose not to. Even under the thrall of that venom. Disappointment made a home in my chest, constricting it. Jealousy burned on the fringes. Dom's presence called to me constantly and it took everything in me to stay away. Gods, I needed space.

Dom cleared his throat. "Shall we?" He gestured for me to go first through the doorway. I felt out of place, my fingers fidgeting with the hilt of my daggers. I shoved my hands in my pockets. Between my confession the night before, Aydrielle's blatant desire for Dom, and my attendance with the queen, agitation and anxiety threatened to overwhelm me.

Aydrielle led us up a set of stairs to a room with an intimate seating area. Coral adorned the walls and framed the doorways in a kaleidoscope of color and texture. The queen reclined in an antique settee, gilded and covered in midnight-blue velvet. Tapestries softly billowed along the walls, depicting mermaids in various geological locales. Dom and I bowed upon our entrance and the queen waved her hand, dismissing Aydrielle and the other servants.

"Please, do sit," she directed us. My relief at Aydrielle's departure was palpable. My murderous thoughts dimmed. Dom shot a curious glance my direction that I chose to ignore.

We sat down on two ornate chairs with high backs and matching ottomans facing the queen. Dom started, "Thank you for meeting with us. It's an honor to have a moment of your time, and a privilege to learn from your experience."

The queen inclined her head in appreciation. "What do you wish to find here, Prince?"

Confusion bristled my brow at her address. Dom moved on without correction. "A darkness consumes the land, and it withers. King Nolan's power grows as he harvests more magic from his people. We have come seeking an alliance. I know you have won wars in your past against powerful realms. Would you allow your armies to fight again, alongside us?"

Queen Thaleia assessed Dom, her mind rapidly processing before carefully responding. She slowly stood, her finger tracing the outline of the settee as she swept around it. "It has been a very long time since we have seen war. But rest assured, we have remained prepared. The lands have been dying for a while now. But it's getting worse. The glacial hinterlands, north of Yarit, are an ancient area most sensitive to magic and its fluctuations. There is a darkness that has come, and as it consumes, it sucks out life and light. The evidence is laid bare in the glaciers. But it spreads.

"We have been separated from the realms of Haluma and Yarit ever since the last water wielder was purged by King Nolan. With Ruin involved, we can bridge the chasm that has separated us. We share a common enemy, General. I will lend you my army, that together we might destroy King Nolan and his Nokts."

Dom and I exchanged a glance. "What are Nokts?"

"They are the embodiment of darkness, created to combat the original guardians, now long gone. Their magic goes against the created order. They are dark creatures with distorted features and membranous wings. Many release acid as a defense. There are Nokts and there are Astrals. The words themselves imply their origin of allegiance—darkness and night, light and stars. Everyone in the realms aligns with one or the other. This is greater than King Nolan. This is a war between the gods we are all caught up in, and there is no neutrality."

I started. If this was true, then what was I? What was Dom?

"We've encountered Nokts. They are hunting Rue." Dom lingered on me. His jaw tightened—in anger or fear, I couldn't decipher.

The queen faced me, drumming her fingers. "Of course the King would covet your magic. Your proficiency of your elemental magic is not common, and your mastering of it without a Prime is impressive. But there is much more to you than what you know up to this point. I sense that there is light in you, but there is a similar veil to that which covers our world. It smothers you. For your sake, I hope you figure out how to break through it." Sadness lined her eyes when she turned abruptly, causing hundreds of bubbles to cascade around her shimmering body. Her cryptic words settled heavy between us as she paced.

"And you, Dominus, the prophesied General of the Liberation. Your curse is an acrid secret that burns in my throat. Even now, your blood is poisoned." She softened her tone further. "You are dying."

Dom tensed, then closed his eyes as he bowed his head. He did not refute her.

My heart buckled. The room shrank around me.

Her three words lanced through me. I stared at him, disbelieving. I just found him. My friend and comforting anchor from when I was a little girl. Until this moment, I had not realized he had become that to me again. Her seismic words threw me off-balance and shoved me toward a truth I'd refused to acknowledge. I swayed, hollowed out.

This whole time he'd shouldered the weight of his impending death and pursued freedom for his people at the expense of himself. I understood the sense of duty, even if I wanted to stab him for it. How long had he suffered in silence? My pulse thundered in my chest. I could not lose him again.

"What is the nature of your curse?" the queen asked. I scarcely breathed.

Dom shifted in his seat. "It happened shortly after I was born. We believe my shadows are a result of the blood curse. My blood is progressively being subsumed by it, turning it black, like char. My metal affinity has helped keep it at bay, but it's getting harder to contain. I have been told by my healers that my heart won't be able to handle the poison once it hits a certain threshold. And I believe that level is close to being reached." Regret and grief replaced the light of his amber eyes, dulling the life within them.

It all made sense. The reason they sent us out with an elixist. The vials of tonic. His veins that darken, then disappear. Why he had shadows before his metal magic emerged. It was his greatest secret and shame. The powerful general of the Liberation was quietly dying.

I dared not move for fear of breaking apart completely. I couldn't find my breath.

The queen regarded me. "You didn't know."

Dom turned to me then, his eyes glazed with pain, his shoulders dropping in resignation.

I didn't think. I simply moved. My heart took over where my fears roared restraint. I refused to leave him any longer in his isolation, in defeat. He had stayed with me in my anxiety, empowered me in my own weakness. He could have abandoned me to the lies I had swallowed. I would fight with him. I would destroy for him.

My affinity reached out as my arms embraced his body. As soon as we touched, his shadows flared, enveloping us in a warm and tender darkness, shielding us from the queen's observation. We clung to each other as breath demands air—committed, inseparable, unflinching.

I wanted to scream. I wanted to weep. Nolan had stolen everything from me. He would not get Dom too.

"You never told me," I rasped into his neck. I didn't know who was shaking, but it made me grip him tighter. The runes on his throat and collar appeared on his skin, shimmering in dark silver. The darker his shadows became, the brighter his tattoos shone. They were hauntingly beautiful.

"I didn't want to burden you. My life has been mapped out; I've always known I'd die. I'd just hoped to defeat Nolan before it happened." He rubbed my back. His strong hands belied his weakening state. I intended to console him, yet instead he comforted me.

"I'll help you find a cure. There has to be one." I would destroy Nolan, the realms—even myself—trying.

"There is none, Liora." Anguish dripped off of him. My old name on his lips tore me open further, exposing a raw vulnerability I wasn't ready for.

"Actually, there might be a cure you have not discovered." The queen's voice sliced through Dom's shadows. Immediately, they dissipated, reabsorbing into his hands.

We both stared expectantly at the siren queen, rebounding from the brief moment of intimacy. I clutched his hand in my own, unwilling to release our connection.

Her smile was soft, sad even. "This can help guide you toward your cure." Her elegant tail swept her toward a side table. She opened a drawer, emitting a few bubbles along with a tiny shrimp that pumped its body racing for cover.

She pulled out a small velvet bag, then extended her hand toward Dom. "This is a magically-imbued compass, a relic gifted to me for the curse that once plagued me. It will glow brighter and brighter the closer you come to your cure. I hope it leads you directly to that which you seek." She spared a glance my way before releasing the compass into Dom's possession. Its curvature of pale gold softly reflected the glowworms' ambient light.

"You must first put a drop of blood here." She pointed out a small compartment in the back of the compass. Dom unfastened the cover and removed one of his daggers. He sliced his finger and blood pearled, floating. He managed to catch a droplet in the compass's waiting chamber.

Dom held the artifact in his large hand, turning it over to assess the ornate filigree. It appeared as any other fancy compass—true north precisely situated with a delicately carved golden needle. It emitted a faint glow. He pocketed it and stood, bowing again to the queen. Thank you seemed like too small a response, but it was offered nonetheless.

"If there are revelations as to the origin or remedy for your curse, the Nymphian Library would have them. It's an ancient, hidden place that houses the world's oldest knowledge. Located in the Perellian Forest outside of Lyrae, it is inaccessible without nymphian magic. I will notify them that you seek an audience with the hamadryad who protects the library. It's where I would go first in a search for your curse's cure. It would be the one place that could have the knowledge needed in overcoming dark magic, which is the only thing that can cause a blood curse." She paused, sniffing the space between us. Her perusal of me left a glint in her eye. "And it might reveal more of your own mysterious heritage, Water Wielder."

Dom straightened his spine. "Any assistance for my cause would be greatly appreciated, and remembered."

"I am sure in the future, I will have need of aid, and when I call upon you, you will no doubt answer."

"You have my word, Queen Thaleia." Dom hit his fist across his chest. A soldier's sign of loyalty. Hope and determination flashed in his expression. I had the sudden urge to bottle it for him.

"How can I assist with reopening a path between our realms?" I was still discovering the extent of my magic, but I would offer whatever I could.

"We would need to create a bridge with your magic and our portals. The last water wielder created the way, and maintained it with some of her blood."

I reached for the hilt of my dagger. "Then I'll need a vial."

The queen smiled, and sent out a pulse of magic. A servant entered the room with a rolled map and a glass vial. She handed them to Queen Thaleia who passed off the vial before delicately unrolling the map and securing it to a low table.

The queen pointed out our approximate location in the sea, then dragged her elegantly webbed hand with its vicious nails upward, beyond Yarit. She outlined an area with her finger, tapping the place where the glaciers lay dying. It was very near the town of Vorkut, where we planned to venture next so that I could connect with Delah's mercenary friend and secure more weapons.

Queen Thaleia explained that Vorkut is more of an outpost for travelers, but there are many residents that maintain a market, apothecary, an inn, and other vital resources. The entrance to her realm had once been established in the glacial hinterlands, north of Vorkut. Once the bridge was established, she would combine her blood to mine and reopen the path between realms so that communications could resume.

"If a door previously existed there, my magic might take more easily to reestablishing it, rather than creating an entirely new entrance. I'm not even sure how to do it." But I had mastered transporting a group of people underwater without drowning. I had projected my consciousness through the sea. Perhaps there was much more I could do with my affinity, like the queen indicated.

"Like calls to like, and your magic should be able to pick up on the previous magic's pulse. It is degraded, but all magic leaves a residue—either shimmer or char. And similar magics echo with the same frequencies."

"Then lead us there." Her belief was contagious.

"I will send you out with Trent, a brilliant navigator who knows the terrain well. He will guide you down the path where the last bridge once stood. You will be portaled close to the coastal glaciers and fjords, but not directly. There are underwater sea caves you can enter, then travel through old lava tubes which will have you surfacing near glacier-fed inlets. Pay attention to your magic, then unleash it when the time is right. You must focus your intention and connection to the water. Do not be afraid of the power."

I became Ruin of the Scourge precisely because I moved forward despite my fear. Fear had always been a constant companion, and I would not shrink away now—too much depended on me. Dom stood close, his towering presence bolstering my resolve. His shadows thread around my wrists, whispering through my fingers. I was not alone.

We decided to leave that afternoon. The queen excused herself, her regal tail leaving ripples of power in her wake.

Dom and I turned toward each other. My mind was muddled with all that lay ahead of us. Of whatever was revealed between Dom and I. There was much I wanted to say.

"How long do you really think you have?" I couldn't speak the rest, but I had to know. My magic surged, defying the thought of his death.

"I'm not sure. Weeks? Maybe months? I require more tonic than I've ever needed to keep the effects of the curse muted." He started to say more but stopped himself. "I'm sorry I let you down."

"What?" No. I fisted my trembling hand. "You have done nothing but protect Aphellion and defend against the darkness. You will defeat Nolan. We have this compass, the Nereid Army, and I will open a bridge to our allies. You will overcome this curse. You will have a life."

"Perhaps... And what of you?" His shadows swam around us as if they listened with their own ears, awaiting my response.

My throat swelled thick with guilt and grief, with all the things I wanted but couldn't have. I had the sudden urge to reach out to Dom. My hands clenched instead, willing the pain of my nails to inject me with clarity. "I will help you accomplish your goals." It's all I could offer. I had done too much, and this was my opportunity for retribution, for penance. Was I darkness or light? Not even the queen could tell.

"Liora—"

"I am not ignorant enough to believe the King will stop at nothing to find me. My time is likely much less than yours in these realms. But I would rather die than see darkness prevail.

We made a bargain that I wish to extend. I will secure weapons in Vorkut, and beyond that, I will help you find your cure. There is no escape from my past, no realm where Nolan can't find me. From one old friend to another. Let me do this, and then let me go."

He jolted as if I'd punched him. His gentle touch tucked my hair behind my ear, his tenderness sharper than any blade against my heart. "I will only let you go when my final breath is torn from my lips. And even then, *m'est kisertes*, I will find you. As I have never stopped searching for you. I accept your bargain. But I do not accept your fate."

My lips parted with a gentle intake of sea water, and he tracked the movement.

When our eyes met again, I spoke low, tentative. "Then I suppose we should prepare to depart. Time is not on our side. And I fear the longer we delay, the more Nokts will be unleashed." It's not what I wanted to convey, but it was pertinent, safe.

Anguish stormed in his gaze. "As you wish."

My overwhelm silenced my response. My insides felt raw at the reality of our situation. We were the walking dead, and we both harbored hope that the other would live. The irony was not lost on me. I remained holed up inside my mind—planning, reeling, longing—as we walked through the castle's corridors.

Had my display of concern and affection revealed too much? He hadn't recoiled at my touch, but that didn't mean he felt the same for me. Something smoldered between us, but I could have misread it. My emotions slammed chaotically through me, my frosted fingertips the only outward sign of my distress.

We returned to our wing of the palace to apprise Bowen and Finn of our plans. We would travel to the surface where I would rebuild the bridge between realms. Finn would continue south to meet up with Xuri, while the rest of us entered Vorkut to meet up with Evander, Delah's mercenary connection.

"So Nokts are known even in the Nereids?" Finn asked.

Dom nodded. "I believe that moving forward, we should be on our guard for them, even as far north as the glacial hinterlands."

I interjected, "They are hunting me. So, wherever I am, we can expect their presence."

Dom took a small step forward, his voice unyielding. "I don't want you in harm's way. You have my word that I'll protect you."

"I don't need protecting." I scoffed.

He hesitated, pupils flaring. "I know. But I hope you'd let me anyway," he softly responded.

I did want that deep down. But we both knew it was an impossible expectation. I inhaled a shaky breath, momentarily forgetting our audience. I lived on borrowed time; happy endings were for maidens without blood on their hands. Not for people like me, with a man like him.

Fate had bound us together, ripped us apart, and offered me a chance to right my wrongs. Oracles had foretold a future of tragedy. I would do well to remember that. For him, though, I would do whatever it took to see him live. I would defy the prophecies.

Finn cleared his throat and exchanged an amused grin with Bowen. I glanced down at the realization that the floor beneath my feet had frozen in a path headed straight toward Dom. Heat crept up my neck, and I threw a dark glare toward Bowen, whose smile only grew. Dom studied our exchange in my periphery, a pulse of his shadows momentarily darkening our room.

I cut off my renegade magic and entered my room to pack my things.

CHAPTER THIRTY
THE GENERAL

As soon as Rue left, I stalked out of the room, suppressing a growl. I'd been a dying man since the day Xuri found me. As solid a truth as the beat of my slowly poisoned heart. Letting someone in now, when I was so close to death, was a stupid, selfish thing to do. Bowen's familiarity with Rue scraped away at my resolve. It revealed a possessiveness I couldn't restrain. The growl emerged anyway.

I turned a corner and barely missed running into a warrior. His powerful tail stalled as his cobalt-blue hair floated forward, slightly obscuring his face. He swiped it aside and offered a respectful bow. "I'm Trent. I'm ready when you and your companions are."

An array of blades outfitted his torso. A trident lay secured to his back, the strap stretched tightly across his chest. The trident's iron prongs formed octopus tentacles that wound around each other at the base, extending out into triple lethal points. His body carefully honed into its own deadly, muscular weapon.

"I was just coming to find you. We're ready."

Aydrielle emerged from behind Trent and offered food for

our trek. Likely various fish, maybe some kelp in varying states of brininess. I accepted it with thanks, though my taste buds recoiled. She slowly grazed her finger down my arm.

"I hope we meet again, General," she intoned.

With all politeness, I offered a respectful nod. *Foka*, I was glad to be getting out of here.

Queen Thaleia arrived to see us off and informed us that after we portaled out of her realm, her and Aydrielle's magic would no longer protect our air supply. Rue would have to take over to keep us from drowning.

We secured our weapons and bags to belts and straps. Daggers lined Rue's thighs. I stole glances at her as she absently traced the hilts, her shoulders softening with the movement. The siren queen wished us well, and then the portal appeared as a menacing whirlpool.

Rue reached out and my hand found hers. She peered at me gratefully, her brow furrowed in concern over the swirling water before us.

"I've got you," I whispered. She steeled her shoulders as we moved to the portal, Trent leading the way.

An onslaught of rushing water consumed us. Rue's fingers made a viselike grip around my hand as I felt the pull within the portal seek to rip us apart. I gritted my teeth, suppressing my own apprehension. And then it spit us out.

The light from the surface reached our depths, even though we were still far beneath the sea. My lungs and nose tingled as the last of the nymphian magic dissipated. Rue kept her wits about her and immediately had a bubble of air around our heads, offering a seamless transition from Aydrielle's power to her own.

She slowly relaxed and released my hand. Though my fingers were relieved at the reprieve from her panicked grip, a tendril of disappointment wound through my chest at the loss of our connection.

She pulsed the current around us to assist with her search, her eyes narrowed in concentration. Finally, she stilled, a smile slowly transforming her face. Her hand extended and magic rippled outward, twining with shimmering threads that were barely visible in the streaming currents. She rotated in her position, stopping after she found me.

"I found it! I found the bridge. More of it is intact than I expected. It'll take me some time to mend, but I know I can." Her joy rivaled the warmth of the sun. She laughed, and I knew in that moment there was nothing I wouldn't do to hear that sound again.

Her magic swirled through the seawater and a walkway took shape. It formed an ensorceled bridge that was more tunnel than open path.

"How are you doing that?" Bowen asked her.

Couldn't he see her magic? I glanced at Finn who also appeared perplexed at the formation of the bridge. Rue simply cackled at their confusion and continued pouring her affinity into the path between our realms. I hovered in the ocean, transfixed at the beauty of Rue creating something amazing with her power. She was so much more than she realized.

Bowen startled beside me as a blur of bubbles and shadow streaked across my line of sight. Trent unsheathed his trident in the turbulence, its menacing arrowhead points casting a purple glow. I lunged for Rue, but the watery environment slowed my movements. She floated beyond my reach.

The figure came into focus right as it slashed its way through the water. It used its filmy wings to thrust itself forward, acting as both propeller and rudder. Blackened scales covered its body, similar to the dreki; however, this had limbs far too long, like its body had been stretched into grotesque proportions.

Rue shot forward, placing herself between me and the Nokt,

distracting it from its advance toward me. My magic flew out as my stomach dropped. I wouldn't reach her in time.

Acid hovered around the Nokt's body in a gray-green fog. It did not dissolve into the water, but rather lay suspended in tiny droplets of toxic oil. They fizzed when they made contact with her leathers. My shadows surged faster.

She did not back down.

Alarm crashed through me at her bold recklessness. Her movements turned frantic when her magic didn't respond as she expected it to. The ocean's salinity slowed the formation of her ice shield, and she threw her arm up in defense at the beast's thrashing claws. It attacked with unnatural speed.

Rue's scream flipped a switch within me. Her blood clouded the water, smoking upward in an inky, crimson haze. She gripped her leg as her ice shield finally formed an enclosed defense around her. The Nokt howled in response to the barrier.

Rage consumed me. I pulled my longsword and slashed at the creature as its claws rent the water. My sword eased through its skin like butter, releasing black ichor, but not before his other razored hand cut across my chest. The scaled leathers prevented their penetration, but the drag of its claws near my side and across my bicep punctured the skin of my arm in a stinging laceration. Tiny droplets of acid singed my arms and face.

Distantly, I registered that Trent had cast his trident toward the beast's chest. It struck true. The Nokt thrashed, frantically removing the weapon. It searched for its attacker, its black eyes seething.

"Dom," Rue's pained voice pierced my concentration, reaching out for me in a desperate plea. The weakened state of her drew all my focus in her direction. I whirled toward her, trying to determine the severity of her injury. My heart pulsed erratically as fear for her threatened to overtake me. Her shield fell away at my approach.

I scanned her purple-blue eyes, unfocused and dazed. Her long hair haloed around her. Blood spilled from a gash across her thigh, cut nearly to the bone. Strips of torn muscle and ragged flesh drifted in the current, barely attached to her body.

Unsheathing my dagger, I cut away a part of my tunic. My adrenaline and fear surged to a feral level. Using the strip of fabric, I wound it tightly around her leg as both a tourniquet and bandage. I channeled my magic to her wound, calling on the iron in her blood to clot and stifle the rapid blood loss. I pulled her body to my own, shielding her in my arms. She didn't even try to fight me on it. *Foka.*

"Why did you throw yourself toward the Nokt?"

"Better me than you," she whispered.

I shook my head in disbelief, clutching her to me like she might disappear in my arms. Did she believe herself invincible, or worse, disposable?

Finn and Bowen had their swords extended as they closed in on the monster. Rows of jagged teeth flashed. Violence radiated off of it in suffocating waves. Trent whistled and his trident returned to his hands as though sentient.

"That's a neat trick," Finn muttered.

The creature's movements turned sluggish, yet no less lethal. Trent served as our best chance of overcoming the monster, his powerful tail whipping through the water like a coiled cobra. His weapon acted as an extension of his body, moving swiftly and gracefully in methodical attack.

I expelled my shadows to surround and comfort Rue, then extended more in an effort to blind our adversary in thick darkness. Several shadows formed scythes, slicing and hacking at the beast.

It paused at the sudden darkness, confused by my bladed attacks, just long enough for Finn to attract its attention. Finn shot his gravitational affinity toward the monster, attempting to sink it, but it swerved away from him with preternatural speed. It veered dangerously close to Liora and me.

Without hesitation, I tucked Liora into my side, using my body to protect her, and swung my sword downward, effectively decapitating it. Trent's trident once more pierced the scaled creature through its shredded chest. It crumpled in on itself. The demonic body floated limply as black blood oozed from its wounds. Its wings drooped in deathly surrender. Its death did not impact my need to keep Liora at my side.

"I need to finish the bridge," she panted. My shadows swarmed her, upholding, supporting, shielding. She sent me a grateful look and refocused her magic into the bridge despite her weakened state. It gleamed silver as it took shape. Determination fortified her as her affinity aligned with faintly shimmering threads—remnants of the old magic last used.

It dipped into the deep and would connect the surface to the Nereid portal, which would remain open with the bridge's completion and once the queen combined her magic with it.

The bridge solidified as though constructed of marble. Liora slumped deeper into my shadow's supports as she emptied herself into the final pieces of the bridge.

A blast of power blew us all back. My shadows cushioned the impact and tethered her to me. She sagged against my chest having expelled most of her affinity. The bridge between realms had been reestablished. There was little time to celebrate.

Trent beckoned us toward a shadowed area in the murky depths. As we came closer, a collection of underwater sea caves came into view. We followed as quickly as possible, having no more interest in open water. We entered the cave where small bioluminescent jellies twinkled throughout. Several holes dotted the roof and along the walls.

Trent assessed us all, his trident still clasped tightly in his hands. "Are you okay, Rue?"

She had regained her color, but barely contained her wince of pain. "It got my leg, but I should be fine," she gritted out.

Trent nodded gravely, then addressed me. "The portal won't be usable until the queen does her part. She will want to make sure the bridge will hold and the door is stable. Be watchful as you continue to the surface. I won't follow beyond this cave." He pointed toward one of the holes. "Those are old lava tubes. The water rapidly drops in salinity, which is why I must leave you here. Follow this path; it will take you to the surface. From there, you can head south to Vorkut."

"Thank you for assisting us." I made a fist and hit my chest. He returned the gesture.

"Safe travels." He departed, tightly clutching his weapon.

A smooth current swept us upward, powered by Liora's magic. The lava tube allowed for two people at a time to pass, a relief since I was assisting Rue. Her breathing came out ragged, and I instinctively clutched her tighter.

"I never would have thought the rebellion general would have it in him to assist a member of the Good King's Scourge," she huffed out.

"Ah well, I heard she's now a member of the Handsome General's Liberation. Don't worry, it'll be our little secret, *m'est kisertes*."

She quirked her brow at my use of the old language. I could see her mind trying to figure out what it meant. "I do enjoy torturing myself with vile things, *General*."

I smirked. "If you want to be tortured, all you have to do is ask." Her cheeks flushed and she fell silent. My shadows heated around us.

We weaved around corners, passing schools of small silver fish. Subtly, the water took on a bluer hue, light gradually filtering in. As soon as I noted the change, the water levels decreased, and our feet finally rested upon solid ground.

Rue nearly collapsed when she released her magic on our

group. We raked in our first breath of real air. Relief radiated across our party now that we could use our lungs again.

"I have no desire to revisit the Nereids anytime soon," Bowen stated. Finn grunted in agreement.

"Can you walk?" I asked Rue. She attempted a step, her knee buckling.

Bowen rushed to her side helping to support her. She leaned into him, resting her head against his shoulder, his arm wrapped protectively around her body.

Oh. Hells. No. I blazed.

My shadows moved without my instruction, and I scooped her up and away from Bowen, shoving him in the process.

"What are you doing?" she gasped.

"I can't do this," I responded through gritted teeth.

"Then put me down." She began to wiggle in my arms. She didn't know that not even my death would stop me from releasing her.

"I can't have you in another man's arms," I growled. "Not when you belong in mine."

She stared in disbelief for a long moment. Then she whispered into my chest, so low I almost missed it, "I like this better anyway."

Her body gently melted against mine. Her nearness calmed the possessive predator inside me, and my shadows eased with each intake of her breath.

I addressed Finn, who not so subtly held back his deranged enthusiasm at what he'd just witnessed. "Head straight for Xuri, and bring back our horses."

He waggled those disconcerting brows but was wise enough to remain silent.

Bowen turned hesitantly, his voice uneasy. "I lost my pouch of vials in the scuffle with the Nokt. I was going to give you one more dose of the tonic, but now I have none. They might have what I need at an apothecary in Vorkut, but I won't know until we arrive. I'm sorry, Dom."

I sensed the curse thickening in my veins. I needed more tonic. "Okay, then Bowen head straight to Vorkut. Rue and I will meet you there. Queen Thaleia said it was a small town, so there is likely only one or two inns. We will find you."

They surged ahead without us. Rue remained relaxed against me and my magic hummed with her in my arms. I walked for another hour before I laid Rue down on the cave floor for a brief break. Sluggishness from the char in my blood demanded I rest.

I sat next to her, surrounding us both with warm shadows to ward off the cold.

"Let me check your leg." It wasn't a question. I shook with the need to assess her wound.

She outstretched her leg in response, and I unwound the strip of fabric from her thigh. My fingers grazed her soft skin with its removal. I swallowed hard at her responding shiver. My fingertips begged for more, but I was intent on her wound. Other explorations would come later.

Her flayed flesh reminded me of her impulsive decision to get between me and the Nokt, surging my anger anew. Smeared blood streaked around her leg. I closed my eyes and pulled on her blood to clot it further. She sighed as my magic blended with her lifeblood.

"Never put yourself in danger like that again." I scarcely breathed the words.

"You didn't have to intervene. You would have made it to the surface just fine."

Foka, this woman. "I didn't care about making it to the surface. That wasn't even my concern." My shadows wrapped possessively around her even as my anger flared against her.

She bristled. "Gods, I'm sorry. It's fine. Why are you so pissed off?"

I turned her chin to face me, so she had no excuse when I addressed her defiance. "Do you think you don't matter? That losing you again wouldn't destroy me? Never. Do. That. Again."

She nodded slowly, holding my stare and peering deep into my soul. Not that it mattered; I'd bared it willingly.

I could feel my magic dimming with the curse's effects as I rewound the makeshift tourniquet, satisfied with how it fared. My shadows continued offering their meager warmth, and a faint smile graced her lips. She reached up and touched my neck with tentative fingers.

"What are these? They look like tattoos." She strained to read the glowing script.

"The runes show up when I use shadow magic. Ilayah thought they caused the shadows. Xuri thinks they feed them. They are ancient Sarulien." I savored her exploratory touch, tracing the lines that scrolled from my hairline to below my collarbone, encompassing the entirety of my neck.

"The language of the gods."

I nodded. Her hand dropped to her lap, and she nuzzled into my shadows like a cat in the sun.

I managed to get both of our cloaks out of our satchels. I leaned against the cave wall and she laid her head in my lap.

"Just rest. I've got you." Her shoulders released with a long exhale, and I smoothed wisps of hair away from her beautiful face.

Listening to her soft breathing loosened something knotted in my chest, and I wondered how deep I had already fallen for the king's spy.

CHAPTER THIRTY-ONE
THE SPY

The stone room was the same. The sound of the chains whispered torment. I gritted my teeth against the fear. My father walked in, his scowl oozing with disdain. The sound of dripping water echoed throughout.

"You don't have to do this," I pled. He smiled cruelly. I knew better than to beg. It just whets his appetite. He held a weapon as his wings extended. Scales began cascading down his head, over his shoulders, and down his body.

Click.

Click.

Click.

Was he always a dreki? Is he a Nokt? I couldn't remember. His feral eyes zeroed in on me. A helpless prey. I writhed against my bindings, moaning my fears. "Father, please don't. Please."

He raised a weapon in his clawed hands. The metal reflected the moonlight from the small window.

"No!"

I jolted upward. My eyes opened, searching wildly for my captor. Confusion and fear gripped me until a familiar voice enveloped me. "You're safe. You're safe."

Dom cautiously extended his hand, moving tendrils of hair from my face. I flinched, but forced myself to settle. He softly regarded me, tenderness radiating as he slowly inched backward, offering space. I attempted to stand, my leg screaming out in a shock of pain. I'd forgotten about that injury.

"How long was I asleep?" I asked, attempting to deflect from my clear distress.

"Not very long." He hesitated, studying me. "You still have nightmares."

His statement unnerved me in my raw state. Our shared history left me exposed to things I normally hid, and I warred with my desire to lean into his comfort. I chose to bind my embarrassment with thick ropes, shoving it into a dark closet.

I casually waved my hand in the air. "I'm used to them. Although this time a Nokt showed up in my dream, so that wasn't pleasant." I shrugged and forced a weak chuckle. My tapping fingers agitated the ensuing silence.

His gaze burned against me. "You don't have to be the strong one when you're with me. Nothing about you diminishes because of vulnerability."

I met his earnest, amber eyes. "Weakness can be weaponized."

"Then you have used it to slay me. And I would willingly subject myself to more of your blades. I might be the enemy in many people's stories, but never in yours."

Emotion threatened to overflow—for daring to believe him left me frayed, unsure. To open myself up to the possibility of... anything really, felt terrifying. I diverted. "Thank you for letting me sleep. We do need to get out of here though. We'll freeze to death if we don't make it to the surface."

He merely nodded and didn't push further.

I didn't think I could put my full weight on my injured leg, but I no longer wanted to be carried. "I believe I can limp well enough. I don't know how much further this tunnel goes before we're out. You should probably conserve your energy. Let me try to walk as far as I'm able."

He stood first, extending his hand to me. His large palm gently enclosed my own. The warmth where our hands joined comforted despite my misgivings. I straightened, unable to conceal my pain.

"I might need a little help," I muttered. Dom silently waited. Tentatively, I reached around his torso, using his body as leverage for each biting step.

He wrapped his arm across my upper back and beneath my far arm. "Is this okay?" he asked.

I should probably just let him carry me, but I rebelled against weakness. I hated that I couldn't do this on my own. Anger smoldered with all my grief and regret. Our tentative alliance went beyond our duty and common enemy. The connections from our past had been incrementally reforged over these last few weeks. And now the truth of his curse stripped every quiet hope away.

I was angry he'd kept this secret from me. I needed space. I didn't want to rely on him any more than I already had, but I required physical assistance with every smarting step. "It's fine." He tightened his grip on me and I reluctantly leaned into his embrace. I couldn't deny how my magic seemed to calm with his nearness.

We hobbled onward. Eventually, the floor became more and more slippery as the trickling water underfoot shifted to solid ice. I used my magic to suck out the water from our clothes and hair, which nominally reduced the shivers wracking through me. My awkward gait left me slipping far more than I preferred.

Dom finally turned to me. "You're stubborn."

I noted his skin seemed paler.

"The rest of the way might go faster if you let me carry you."

I knew he was right, the concession bitter on my tongue. My wound had stopped bleeding but my thigh throbbed with a deep, sharp pain. Despite my misgivings, time was of the essence.

"Fine." I surrendered. He seamlessly lifted me to his hard chest. What was this, the third time he's had to carry me? Gods, I needed to stop getting injured.

The exit from the ancient lava tubes finally appeared in the distance. We emerged in blinding sunshine surrounded by magnificent glaciers. They stretched before us in an array of blues—crystal clear, bright cerulean, and creamy teals. It was a wild, arresting beauty. Dom followed the direction of my swiveling head, both of us stalling.

To the west of us, a line of demarcation separated beauty from desolation. The landscape blackened as though a fire had swept through. Nothing but darkness remained. Ash hovered like a fog above the ground.

"Char," Dom stated, more to himself than for my benefit.

"From death magic?" I asked incredulously. He nodded in affirmation. The land withered, as though actively dying or already dead. I glanced up at him, startling again. His skin had nearly lost all its color. His veins contrasted sharply with his pallor. "Are you okay?" I whispered, withholding the urge to touch him.

He peered down at me, shutting his eyes, exhausted. "It's the poison in my blood. My tonic keeps it under control, but—" He gasped a breath. "—I couldn't take it underwater. Bowen lost the supply that he had in our fight with the Nokt."

A screech cut through the howling wind. In the distance, several Nokts circled. Dom grabbed my hand. I searched wildly around. Glacial caves surrounded us in almost every direction.

With my leg and his waning energy, we would not make it to Vorkut without being spotted. Dom subtly swayed. Both of us were far too drained to take on more than one Nokt, and maybe not even that.

"We need a cave. I can use my magic to help us stay warm so

we can recover enough to make the trek to Vorkut." Dom lacked the strength to protest, spiking my worry further.

We ran toward a nearby cave with an entrance large enough to accommodate Dom's height. My leg protested, but panic and survival masked the pain. Somehow, the Nokts had not seen us.

Dom's consciousness held on as tight as the last brown leaf on a winter-barren tree. He pushed through, using all of his strength to hold himself upright. His glazed eyes slowly blinked, tears accumulating at the corners in the frigid air.

We slowed to a hobble inside the cave, grateful to be out of the wind's assault on our unprotected faces. Dom slumped deeply into me, his surrender revealing the precipice he teetered on. I tensed in an effort to hold both of us up, my thigh demanding reprieve.

We limped toward the back, past water-carved walls. The path sloped sharply downward, threatening both our balance. The majesty of our shelter glossed over us in our haste toward safety.

A loud crack had us jolting to the side as a chunk of sharpened ice narrowly missed spearing my shoulder. It shattered in a plume of powder and crystalline shards. Above us, countless icicles, some needle-like, others as large and honed as my longsword, threatened to dislodge from the glacial ceiling.

Hoping to avoid any further interactions with skyborne weapons, my magic snaked throughout the cave to fortify its structure. Walls and ceilings hardened and puddles evaporated from the icy floor. I focused my attention on removing all cold from beneath our feet, while keeping the water solidified. I tightened my arm around Dom, summoning the water out of our clothes, drying us thoroughly.

"That's helpful," Dom slurred.

Urgency quickened my pace.

We reached an open space in the back of the cave, which seemed good enough to make our resting place. Despite my injured leg, I hurried to prepare a dry space for us. The light from outside diffused through the thick ice in a calm, bluish glow. The glimmering water-carved walls mimicked windswept sand dunes. Rippled lines etched along their surface as if a master calligrapher had drawn them.

Dom sagged to the floor, his breath turning ragged. His shadows released in an attempt to warm us, but they acted as mere licks of smoke, flickering quickly out of existence. His head dropped back against the wall, the action having spent what energy he had preserved.

I bit my lip. Though we weren't exactly sitting on freezing cold ice blocks, we were still in the north, in a glacial cave. And it was very cold. When the sun set, we would need a plan. I crouched next to Dom.

Relief flooded me at taking weight off my leg. I stretched it out to check the bandage, reassuring myself the wound hadn't reopened. I kept the cloth secured for now, my skin resisting movement from the residue of sticky, dried blood.

A line formed between Dom's closed eyes. His dark lashes fluttered in obvious discomfort. I beheld his face, more unkempt with days of stubble peppering his chiseled jaw. I noticed traces of the boy I once knew, buried beneath the powerful man he now was. He inhaled a shuddering breath.

"Are you sure rest is all you need?" I spoke softly, shattering the quiet of the cave. I didn't know how to help him.

His chin lifted slowly, as if weighted down. "The poison has never progressed this far before. I don't know what happens if it overwhelms my heart." He offered a false smile. "You might need to head to Vorkut on your own. Find the inn so you don't freeze to death." He half-heartedly shoved me, encouraging my departure. His arm flopped heavily back to his side.

My mouth thinned. "How embarrassing for Ruin of the Scourge to simply leave the general of the rebellion here to freeze. I prefer grander rumors of death and destruction over my enemies."

He didn't take the bait of my weak ribbing. "You're so much more than the rumors they spread about you." He shifted in discomfort. Then he gently tugged at my small braids, first on the left and then the right, just like I used to do when we were kids before we did something risky. Just as my mother had done to me in private moments in our garden.

"You remember?" My heart swelled, though my voice trembled.

"I could never forget anything about you. Except what you'd look like after seventeen years apparently." He let out a mirthless chuckle as his fingers ghosted over my own. He sighed. "Perhaps this is how I go. It could be worse."

Our fingers laced together. My breath stuttered in my chest with his words. "Not on my watch."

His thumb drew back and forth along my hand. It had been a long time since someone tried to comfort me. Since I allowed it.

"You were never my enemy you know. How could I despise someone so embedded in my veins?"

The question hovered in the air between us, as solid as the walls of our glacial tomb. His words scraped against my resolve, cracking it open to reveal a hope I did not dare voice.

"At least." He paused, gathering himself while his strength leaked out of him. "At least, I finally found you. I will always find you." His hand raked through my hair, teasing the strands. He quirked his head to the side, perplexity furrowing his brow. "This cave makes your hair seem almost lavender. How strange."

I tensed at the observation. But my concern was short-lived as his shoulders relaxed and he closed his eyes again. He grimaced before his slump turned more pronounced, his body folding in on itself

"Dom?" I squeaked. Yet he didn't stir.

CHAPTER THIRTY-TWO
THE SPY

I couldn't differentiate the hum of my magic with the rush of panicked blood in my ears. Had the Nokt caused an injury I didn't know about? Had he underestimated the amount of poison in his blood? Surely he wasn't dying now. I didn't allow myself time to dwell on it.

I untied my cloak, folding it into a makeshift pillow for his head. I pushed his own cloak aside, yanking up his shirt, searching his body for any lacerations. I discovered one across his right arm, char skimming the corners of the wound. My eyes grazed his torso, pausing momentarily. I refused to acknowledge the muscles that glistened in the ambient light, how hard they still were despite his sagging state. There were no wounds on his chest that I could find. I exhaled a modicum of relief, though Dom's current condition didn't lend itself to comforting reassurance.

There was nothing I could do to help him. I had no supplies, no healing training. Noting the amount of filth we both were in, I melted a portion of the wall, soaking a rag from my satchel in glacial water to rinse off his body and cleanse his armor.

Focusing on a task allowed my fear to drop to the icy floor amidst our blood and grime.

I absorbed the fullness of him, raking my eyes over every angle of his face. His full lips parted, spilling forth soft, uneven breaths. I tentatively brushed his cheek, and his lip twitched as though meaning to smile. I jerked my hand away. He continued to lay unmoving, but his breaths remained consistent. I covered him with his own cloak and assessed our temporary hideaway.

Perhaps we could rest for a day or two here in relative safety, away from any predators or Nokts. We might have enough food if we rationed it. I used the same rag to clean my own dried blood off my leg and my leathers. The char had not gone deep into either of our wounds and I easily rinsed it away.

Checking Dom once more, I dabbed at the small cuts along his arms where the Nokt's poison had burned. His eyes remained closed as his hand gripped my wrist, stalling my work. He opened his eyes taking a minute to regain his bearings. Adoration warmed his gaze as he regarded me. "I'm still alive, huh?" he asked hoarsely.

"You passed out, but it hasn't been long. I think your body took its opportunity to get the rest you've been denying it." The puddle of water I formed absorbed back into the wall of ice, having completed our ministrations. I set the rag down.

"This cave seems like a good place to lay low for a while. Might take more than a few minutes to regain our strength, though." His voice came out strained, rough.

Dom studied me, his penetrating stare as thick as his shadows. The air between us grew charged.

I busied myself with folding the rag. He assessed his body. His veins webbed darkly against his ashen skin. "Where's all the blood?"

"I washed it off." I shrugged one shoulder. "There hadn't been much to clean."

He scoffed. "I decapitated a Nokt and held you while your leg bled out. I think that's an understatement."

"Not much more of a mess than you normally look." His responding dark chuckle echoed in our confined space, the strength of his voice easing some of my concern over his physical state.

I couldn't suppress my weak attempts at humor. It allowed me to maintain some semblance of emotional distance. I blamed the cold for my shivering. Yet, even I could not deceive myself enough to avoid the truth of it. The fear of fully embracing hope and emotions I had spent years separated from chafed against me. My awakened feelings at the revelation of his blood poisoning scared me most of all.

There was little to do while we rested, reclining in comfortable silence as the sun descended. The realization of the dropping temperature slammed into us both, entombed as we were within a cave of ice. Dom carefully stretched his aching body, our eyes locking. I broke his stare, suddenly aware of all my limbs.

"It will get cold and we don't have many supplies." He peered upward toward the cave's ceiling with its waning light. His lips twitched and his dimple briefly appeared. "I have an idea for heat if you're willing."

Heat filled my face. Oh, my traitorous body was definitely willing.

"Body warmth is the best we can do since we don't have enough blankets," he continued clinically.

I nodded.

He took my nonverbal assent and sat forward, removing his cloak and tunic. His abs glistened in the glow of the glacial cavern, highlighting every ripple of hard muscle, every cut and bruise from our tussle with the Nokt. His loose-fitting pants hung low enough to showcase the V-shaped muscles at his waist.

This is for self-preservation only. Turning away, I removed the cloth tourniquet on my thigh, carefully extending my injured leg. I peeled off my filthy clothes. My tunic and leathers fell into a heap on the floor. My lavender silk chemise, which served as my undergarments, barely reached mid-thigh. It clung unrelentingly to all of my curves. I didn't trust myself to get completely naked, and the silk left little of my body to the imagination.

I retied the cloth over my wound, hoping it wouldn't become infected before we made it to Vorkut. Dom froze when I straightened. His eyes slowly, painstakingly, devoured my form before collecting himself.

"So we don't freeze to death," I forced out.

"For the greater good," he imperiously responded.

He lay back, beckoning me to do the same. A part of me wanted to resist, should have in fact. But another part awakened at the image of this beautiful man before me. He had only ever offered me choice and protection. Even now, he didn't force me one way or another. His broad shoulders took up most of the space, and I knew I was the missing puzzle piece that would fit perfectly against his chest. A mixture of grief and desire braided through my chest.

I knelt down, easing my back against his welcoming body. Our breaths synced as his warm hand roved to my waist, slowly circling around my body, gently pulling me flush against him.

"Is this okay?" he whispered.

"Dom..." My voice cracked. His body stilled at my hesitant tone. "What about Xuri?" I resisted arching into him further. My soul craved his touch. A deep wanting breached the surface of my carefully constructed shields. But I couldn't play pretend any longer. The haunting jealousy of what I'd witnessed between them plagued me. I had to know. I was grateful I faced away from him, conserving what little dignity I had left.

His thumb resumed tracing circles at my waist. His warm

voice ruffled my hair. "Xuri is like a sister to me. Nothing more." He wrapped me further into his arms, his magic spilling over us. "And you are *nothing* like a sister. You are so much more. You are the thoughts that keep me awake at night, the power that calls to my own. You are the water that quenches my soul. You are who the Great One foretold. Who I knew in part and drew from visions, but now I see in full. And you are everything beautiful."

His breath disarmed any remaining resistance, soft and warm against my neck. The urge to have his powerful hands on my body, around my throat, consumed my mind.

Relief suffused me. I could have wept.

"Li—Rue?"

Why did his voice have to be so delicious? "Yes?"

"How did you become Ruin?"

Tensing, I turned around to face him, his hold on my waist loosening.

"What happened that night?"

I stared up at a small patch of ice. My nerves attuned to the heat of Dom's body, so close to my own. What would it be like to surrender this part of my past to another? My breath quickened into shallow sips of air. Some secrets held their own form of death magic, infecting from deep within.

I swallowed hard. "Only Nolan knows what truly happened. I've never told anyone." The words floated between us, as fragile as the frost on my fingers. The weight in my chest hardened. I opened my mouth. Closed it. It was not the cold that had me shaking.

"You don't have to tell me," he soothed, smoothing my hair behind my ear.

Gods, his tenderness held the power to loosen bonds I'd long kept wound around me. Now, as when we were kids, he held a space of safety that I wanted to burrow in.

In the comfort of our glacial nest, my deep protections

relented. Perhaps moments of weakness weren't contemptible. I sensed a different type of strength borne of the ashes of this released pain. A strength that wasn't a white-knuckled armor, but rather a softer more resilient version. The energy of harboring this secret had drained me for so long. I decided to trust him with it.

"It was my fault my parents died." The confession fell like a stone in still water. My words hung heavy and oppressive. It was too late to pull them back. Silence stretched on for what felt like hours, and shame consumed deeper than the veil upon the land. I began to retreat. I'd rather risk a Nokt than sit in his disappointment, his rejection.

Dom gripped my arm, pulled me closer, and gently tilted my chin in his direction, forcing me to meet his stare. "How could that even be true?"

I studied his shoulder, unable to hold his gaze for fear of his judgment. "I said it to you that very night. I cursed my father and wished to destroy him with fire. Because of that curse, I returned to a burned down home and became an orphan. King Nolan knew what I'd done. He helped me keep it a secret, allowing me a chance to redeem myself as his spy." My tightening chest warned I had shared too much. I rallied my resolve, preparing for a long walk alone in the dark toward Vorkut.

His jaw tensed. I deserved his wrath. "Li, you were a child. You don't even have fire magic. What happened to your parents was not your fault. Nolan used that belief to manipulate you."

My eyes clenched shut. I wanted that to be true, I really did. I knew the story that had spread reported a person high on Glint started the fire, but would that have happened if I had not voiced the words? Confusion filtered in. In my bones, I understood this really was my fault. It was my burden to carry, to atone for.

His eyes reflected a winter storm. They softened as he beheld me and all the broken pieces of my soul. "Words have power, but not like that. You were just a child. You don't have to keep punishing yourself. You are a light, Liora. Don't let Nolan's lies diminish you."

His earnest words, warm as liquid gold, filled the ache between my scars. His anger was not toward me. Was the veil that Queen Thaleia saw in me this secret that I'd swallowed whole my entire life to darken my understanding? Had I allowed the king's lie to invade and debilitate me?

A part of me knew Dom spoke true, even as that young girl inside wrestled with fear-infested what-ifs. The more I entertained the veracity of Dom's words, the more a sense of freedom lightened me.

Perhaps I could stop punishing myself. I was struck by the thought. I had lived so long under a shroud of shame and convoluted responsibility. My time with Dom had begun to heal places I had stamped as incontrovertibly irredeemable. His thumb traced my bottom lip as he angled my face back up to his own.

"You're a light, Liora. You're *my* light." His lips brushed mine, warm and tentative. My body responded instantly, melting against him, gripping his shoulders. Tears dripped down my cheeks as our kiss grew hungrier.

Dom pulled back, softly kissing away each of my tears. His hands cupped my jaw and his shadows whispered along my arms, comforting me. Healing me.

"I can't lose you again." My words came out in a plea, a prayer against his lips. A dam ruptured and decades of unshed tears silently streamed. Fear and hope and pain coursed out of me. Dom, my anchor, reverently wiped them away, as if he sensed the weight in each sacred drop.

His teeth grazed a sensuous trail along my jaw until his mouth covered mine again. Desire blended with desperation as his tongue traced my parted lips. I needed this. I needed him.

His breath turned ragged and he studied me with quiet

reverence. "*M'est kisertes*, knowing this curse would end me eventually, I've kept myself shut off. My duty to the Liberation and our realm drives me." He exhaled slowly, his whispered words amplified by the icy walls. "But since I've found you, I feel a different duty superseding them all."

My breath hitched. He traced a line down my arm as his eyes searched mine. A question loomed in the depths of his honeyed irises. Goose bumps followed in the trail of his touch. A fissure in my armor took root, breaking open. Too many emotions flooded me—betrayal by my king, shame for my collusion, desire, grief, fear, and when I drank in the vision of Dom, I felt hunger. I felt healing. I felt hope.

I closed my eyes, reveling in his warmth. A violent shiver wracked his body, and his halting breath serrated the air.

"Li..." My name came out breathless, the tone slightly off, then Dom sagged backward, his arm falling listlessly to the side. I grappled for his wrist. It took me too long to find his heartbeat.

Assessing him more clinically, I realized his skin had turned grayer, the curse thickly coursing through his veins now. Their lines ran black beneath his flesh. I had nothing in my satchel that would help. And I wouldn't make it back in time from Vorkut if I attempted to seek assistance there.

I stared at falling water droplets, mocking the tears that desperately sought escape. My magic buzzed as I focused on the ice around me. An idea bloomed. I could use my magic to dilute Dom's blood, as he used his magic to clot mine. I had no idea if this would work, and it could potentially cause more harm. But I had to try. My breathing turned erratic as panic tightened my throat.

I placed my trembling hands on his chest. His shallow intakes of breath bolstered the urgency of my magic. I closed my eyes and imagined my power entering his veins and attacking the poison that feasted on his blood. My affinity gathered in a tidal wave of power, poised for release.

Curses were tangible things made with dangerous and distorted magic, manipulated with words and dark intent. Something malevolent created this, so I would send the light of my water to fight it back. Vapor rose from my fingertips as power threaded from me to Dom. My eyes welled with tears that fell toward his body. I vaguely registered that they absorbed into his skin, sizzling when it hit char leaving a shimmer in its wake. I could feel the tarry curse fighting against my affinity.

Dom's blood pulsed like silk through the fingers of my magic. The taste of acrid bitterness spilled across my tongue as I plunged into the depths of the toxin. My affinity pushed back the darkness in his veins, softening their contrast against his sallow skin. The sweetness of honeyed raspberries slowly replaced the flavor of poison in my mouth.

Tension eased from his body. His heart rate steadily grew stronger. Before my eyes, his skin took on a peachier hue, the anemic pallor fading away. I yielded everything I had into him. My stamina drooped with the effort to expel undiluted magic and control it with such a fine-tuned precision.

He didn't open his eyes, but his breathing leveled off. I halted my stream of magic, removing my hands from his chest. I wasn't sure if I'd succeeded, but my apprehension eased.

Sleep clawed at me, my own energy reserves deeply depleted. I used a tremendous amount of power and needed to replenish it. I wrapped us in my cloak with halting movements, then lay snugly against him. I pulled his leaden arm around me. As I closed my eyes, I hoped we would both awaken come morning.

CHAPTER THIRTY-THREE
THE SPY

When I finally emerged from a dreamless sleep, the comforting weight of Dom's arms was the first thing I sensed. He was warm, his chest swelling with inhales at my back. Alive.

The second thing I noted with certainty was that Dom was awake, and a smile inched its way across my face. I tried to turn toward him, but he tightened his grip, preventing any movement, keeping me caged and close. My thigh protested in a shot of pain at my half-hearted attempt. I relented, allowing myself to relax in the incandescence of our ice nest, giving myself this small moment to feel a sliver of peace and calm. We made it through the night.

As the early glow of morning illuminated the milky blue walls of our cavern, the movement of hundreds of fish brought flashes of light dancing around us. I glanced back at Dom as he too sat enthralled by the strobing silvers and pinks. Shadows and light flitted around us like luminescent butterflies. His eyes roved to mine and he stilled.

"Your hair. It's pink."

Hells. "Your observational skills. They're masterful."

He offered a half-hearted glare. "Xuri's mom, Ilayah, had a vision where the one who would find the cure for my curse had hair the color of lilac peonies. That is almost the shade of yours." He reached out to touch my hair but I started backward. He dropped his hand a few inches.

"My mother taught me early how to hide my hair. I have never heard of anyone else having such a reprehensible shade of springtime hair." Maybe I could get some coracite from the apothecary in Vorkut. The salt water must have stripped the color faster than normal.

"Did your mother ever tell you why you had to hide the color of your hair?"

"She didn't. But she made me promise to never reveal it to anyone."

"But you told me." He quirked his head. I startled again as Dom reached forward to touch a few strands between his fingers, but forced myself to still. He clearly couldn't resist. I just needed a warning to calm the alarms that tended to sound when I received unexpected touch, especially with my hair. "It has been said that those born with this are blessed by the gods." I scoffed as he stepped away from me, pausing. "Why does it feel like my curse was pushed back?"

I stood to stretch, letting my nerves recognize Dom was no threat. Exposing the color of my hair almost felt more vulnerable than my confession the previous night. Almost. "I wasn't sure what to do when you passed out. I remembered how you helped me by clotting my blood, and I wondered if my magic could dilute the poison in yours."

"Thank you." The sentiment was solemn and filled with a fragile hope. But then his face shuttered, a mask of neutrality taking over. I could feel a distance forming between us. Despite our kiss and the previous night's declarations, awkwardness settled. Did he regret what happened? Did the reality of my confession finally hit him? The rejection left me dizzy. I would feel the true pain later.

I quickly put my clothes back on, the lavender silk a poor protection against the chill of glacier ice. I retied the tourniquet around my thigh. The wound ached, but the support of the tied cloth lessened the weakness in my leg.

"We need to get to Vorkut today." He offered me some of the food from the Nereid realm. "Bowen will be waiting with my tonic. And we'll have to find Delah's connection quickly."

I nodded in between mouthfuls of chewy fish, gnawing on it just enough to swallow it down without gagging. As I ate, he pulled his own tunic and leathers back on. He affixed his cloak and gently draped mine across my shoulders.

After finishing our humble breakfast, we secured our belongings and prepared to head to Vorkut. Whatever last night had been left an uncomfortable flavor to our interactions. I kept to myself. I understood his response. It was a risk to share the truth, and it didn't pay off. I bit the inside of my cheek, the blood a warm distraction from the ache growing inside me.

My leg had lost some of its throbbing pain, and I could walk without assistance as we hiked upward toward the cave's entrance back into the exposure of the glacial hinterlands.

Leaving our sequestered hideaway, we silently trekked toward the small town of Vorkut, away from the char-encrusted landscape north of us. The skies remained void of Nokts, a small blessing.

Wind whipped at my hair, stinging my eyes. Dom remained quiet and hesitant with me. It made my anxiety buzz like ants beneath my skin. Abruptly, he turned toward me.

Haunted eyes searched me. "You know I'm dying, Rue. I shouldn't have given in to my desire for you. I've always known my end. It isn't fair to you." I blinked at him, trying to read through his words. He turned around and resumed his march toward Vorkut.

I stared open-mouthed at his retreating back. Anger fumed within me. I could smell his cowardice and it incited me. I hurried to catch up, my thigh stinging in a rope of pain with every bit of force I put on it.

I snagged his arm, breathlessly casting out an ill-thought-through barrage of words, "So you want to shut me out. I get it. Why try to live if you're just going to die? But don't you dare use me as an excuse to keep yourself in some sort of self-righteous prison."

He stopped short, causing me to trip and throw out a curse upon the uneven terrain. He gently gripped my arm, steadying me.

He pinched the bridge of his nose, clenching his eyes shut, searching for patience or restraint or another opportunity to distance himself from me. As if he didn't know about the prisons I had been kept in. About the prisons I'm still trying to break out of.

"Li, it isn't wise to open this door when it will likely cause us both great pain." Gods, it was about protection. I inhaled. Not rejection.

"Let me make that choice for myself," I whispered, stepping closer. I had to tilt my head up to maintain his gaze. His towering frame swallowed me in shadow.

His jaw clenched, a muscle feathering as he did so. I waited for his rebuttal as he took a breath through parted lips. The power in my veins surged, as if it could leap out and straddle him in the middle of this barren tundra, forcing him to choose something. To choose me. Traitorous magic.

He stared at the horizon, appearing tortured and conflicted. Longing flashed in the golden flecks of his eyes when he finally returned to my expectant stare. I bit my bottom lip, not trusting myself. Craving unfurled from the depths of my soul and he was the object of its relief.

Without a word, he turned on his heel stalking away from

me. My shoulders sagged, now burdened with the weight of disappointment, embarrassment, and confusing unfulfillment. The locks on my shields clicked back together. One at a time, they snapped into place, creating that familiar barrier. Even if it did feel like the armor was becoming too small for me to wear. But I didn't know another way to protect the fragile parts of me.

Ice crunched underfoot as I placed one boot in front of the other. I tried to harness my thoughts as my magic escalated to the sting of tears in my eyes. It was simply the letdown of unrealized hope. He would never let his own desires override his commitment to his cause. Fate was cruel that way. He warned me in the beginning this couldn't end well. This dam would not crack even if my heart did.

Lost in thought, I hadn't realized Dom had ceased walking. I halted, not ready to walk alongside him. I was prepared to follow him from a wide distance until we reached Vorkut. I needed to gather myself if we were to continue working alongside each other. I needed space and some time to recover.

I could sense the battle he waged against himself. He started to turn toward me again, but thought better of it. He wiped his hand down his face, a muttered *"Foka"* sailing in the wind as he faced me fully.

Lashing gusts disrupted my hair, the pink strands tickling my forehead as they swirled around me. The movement caught Dom's attention as his gaze locked on mine. I didn't know what kind of ground we were on, so I trusted the glacial environment over my emotions, and stood frozen. He took a few tentative steps, both determination and resignation wafting off of him.

"My whole life I have been chosen to lead. I am the hope of the rebellion, the prince of redemption for what has been stolen. I have been obsessed with finding a cure for my curse and overthrowing King Nolan. I long ago accepted my isolated existence. Yet, since meeting you…" He faltered, imperceptibly shaking his head. "Something has awakened within me." He raked his hand down his face. I saw too clearly the battle of responsibility against longing. He refused to advance toward me, holding himself back.

Words would not form. My magic writhed, urging me forward. I cautiously grasped his hand, the air chilling my skin to the point of numbing. He did not push me away.

"I am willing to fight for you as your friend and ally if that's what you want. Nolan's power threatens everything; I understand we fight for something greater than ourselves. I made you a promise, and I told you when it was fulfilled I would leave." The truth soured in my mouth. If this is what he needed from me I would do it, even though my heart rebelled against it.

His whole body went rigid. "I hate that word in your mouth." His pupils dilated, rimmed with a ring of glowing amber. "I cannot simply be your friend, *m'est kisertes*. I fear I need much more than that."

He reached out to hold my face, his thumb brushing against my cheek. He leaned forward hesitantly, pressed a soft kiss to my cheek. I stiffened as my magic responded to the electrical pulse that lanced through me. I could not deny the strange magnetism he had over me.

He pulled back at my rigidity, his face no longer readable. "Our bargain still stands. Whatever you choose to give me will be enough."

I needed some time to myself, away from the attraction that overrode both of our senses. The truth of Dom's curse, my feelings for him, and the lies of King Nolan weighed on me. Whatever grew between Dom and I settled confusingly on my cautious heart. The promise of an evening to process and plan next to a hearth at an inn sounded divine.

He released my hand, then with an aching tenderness, secured the hood of my cloak, before gently urging me on.

CHAPTER THIRTY-FOUR
THE GENERAL

The truth sprawled before me as exposed as the surrounding tundra. Next to me, Liora tightened her cloak as we trudged past glacial caves, the fabric doing little to ward off the chill. Her presence never left my awareness, and I'm not sure I wanted it to.

I really did fear I needed more of her. All of her. I tried to shut her out, remind myself of my responsibilities, but thoughts of her infiltrated my every attempt at focus, and consumed every one of my thoughts. Plans long established now shifted to accommodate her place in them. Her scent left me distracted. Her sighs made my fingers curl in their desire to find the places that would coax more of them out.

I glanced at her from my peripheral. Ilayah had gone in search of a girl in Maripol before she was captured. Xuri had visions of one with lilac-pink hair who would lead me to my cure. Ilayah's last vision to me included the prophetic words of "one I was tasked to find." Was she one and the same? My magic pulsed in affirmation and I nearly tripped.

She stared at me questioningly, and I offered a reassuring

smile. The punishing wind howled too loudly to sacrifice words.

The thought of losing her, of letting her go once the bargain was complete, clamped a vise around me. I couldn't allow it. But I felt her tense when we touched and though I wouldn't force her, I would dedicate my life to convincing her otherwise. I could give her time, even knowing I had little left.

I kept pace with her, lightly supporting her elbow to guide her over chunks of ice. Childhood memories of holding her hand when we jumped across streams in the Rivellan Wood filled my mind.

I remembered how she laughed when we were little. I always thought she had the most beautiful sing-song response to joy, sure that she had exercised her delight on a regular basis. But she had confessed that only when she was with me in the secluded forest did she feel the freedom to release her joy without fear of her father's retribution. I tried to coax it out of her as often as possible.

This particular day, we were practicing throwing daggers in the woods, only she kept hurling fistfuls of leaves at me. At one point, I threw my dagger too high, and it knocked a bee's hive off of a limb. It plummeted to the ground with a muted thump. We both stared, stunned. Then the bees came in earnest, and our young legs pumped like the wind to outpace the angry stingers aimed threateningly in our direction. I cupped her elbow then as I did now. Our laughter joined the buzz at our backs. Exhilaration fueled our retreat.

Our legs burned, but we didn't dare look behind us. I had grabbed her hand and she laced her fingers with my own. Together we jumped over a stream. In our minds, in the seclusion of the forest, we could defeat anything if we were together. Could that be true again?

With the cold, and Liora's injured thigh, we maintained a creeping pace. Flurries accumulated along our shoulders and pelted our cheeks. She struggled to keep the hood of her cloak up, concealing the mysterious color of her hair. There would be no laughter on this journey.

Both Liora and I barely contained the chatter of our teeth. One step in front of the other. The city couldn't be far ahead.

After what could have been hours or interminable minutes, the looming forms of buildings finally emerged from the sea of ice. Their presence brought a relief so strong I huffed a delirious laugh.

Queen Thaleia spoke true when she told us it was a small village. There were only a few prominent streets, and finding the inn was a simple affair. Blessedly warm air greeted us as the door shut at our backs, a few stray flakes of snow trailing us inside.

Liora snaked through crowds of people, heading straight to the roaring hearth. She nestled next to the heat, her shivers still visible even across the room. My shadows hovered near her, keeping watch. I scouted the tavern for signs of Bowen. My own body slowly thawed, and I found a server to inquire about lodging and lunch.

I almost argued when the server explained our room, but I was too cold and exhausted to put up a fight. I offered a handful of coins before finding Liora in the crowd. She was strong and capable, but I'd always thought myself her shield. As long as she was in my care, she would have my protection.

Her eyes found mine and I wordlessly beckoned her over. Her disappointment at leaving the fire's heat was subtle but evident. I'd make sure the hearth in her room would keep her warm through the night.

My shadows wisped around me, intimidating enough to encourage the crowds to part and a table to reveal itself. I led Liora over to it. The chairs creaked as we settled into them and the table wobbled with our arrival, the grain of the wood softened by years of leaning elbows and raucous card games.

Liora extended her injured leg, releasing a soft groan as she did. My jaw tensed at her pain. A nearby fork melted in the heat of my renewed anger; I needed to lay eyes on that wound and make sure it wasn't infected.

Rich stew and steaming bread arrived, interrupting my fierce concern. The smell of fresh food stoked my hunger, and we promptly devoured it. In the absence of fish or brine or any hint of seaweed, this was food for royalty.

I leaned back allowing my food to settle, then cleared my throat to capture Liora's attention. "The barmaid said Bowen had a room here. She hadn't seen him yet for lunch, though, so I assume he'll show up momentarily." While I hadn't committed on a way to break the other news to her, she grew suspicious at my tone.

Eyes narrowed, she laid her spoon down. "Say it, Brute."

My mouth twitched at the name. "You know those books you read where there's only one room to be had?"

Her entire face fell slack. The satiation that filled her features after a hearty meal shifted into comical disbelief.

"You've got to be kidding me." She appeared to be waiting for a punchline. I offered none.

My grin broke through. "The weather is turning and no one wants to be caught outside. We rented the final room here. The realms have conspired to torture us, Ruin of the Scourge."

She rolled her eyes. "The royal title can be dropped. You're allowed to call me Rue."

"I'll call you by your name when it's your given one."

She huffed like an indignant kitten. A bellowing voice knifed through the din, sweeping away her response. "DOM!"

Bowen jogged over, joining us at our table. "I was getting worried something had happened. Didn't know if I needed to send out a search party. A blizzard is on the way."

He assessed me critically, in a way that I could guarantee Xuri instructed him to do. Satisfied with what he saw, he acknowledged Liora with a warm smile. He ordered his lunch and addressed me. "I found what I needed at the apothecary. The tonic is in my room. You wouldn't believe some of the things they have here. For it being a remote outpost, they see a lot of travelers who bring in some unique items for trade."

Liora shifted in her seat, scanning the boisterous space. "If a storm is on the way, then I need to locate Evander. He might already be here." The inn bustled with the lunchtime crowd and travelers anxious to get out of the worsening weather.

She waved her hand in our direction. "You guys catch up; I'm going to… use my skills." Without waiting for a response, she threaded through the crowd.

My entire focus narrowed onto the headstrong, retreating woman. I followed her hooded head as she weaved through throngs of people like one of my shadows. A few heads popped up, observing her movement—even cloaked she demanded attention. My rings flared and my shadows pealed out, slithering along the floor toward the curious onlookers, ready to subdue should they become threatening.

She eased onto the last available barstool, surreptitiously assessing her surroundings.

"She's entirely capable of protecting herself, you know." I'd forgotten Bowen was still here, still talking. The glare I sent had his mouth promptly shutting.

"Grab my tonic, Premier Bowen." My obvious reminder of his station had him stiffening. Without response, he too disappeared into the crowd. At least with him gone I could focus on the other patrons and keep an eye on Liora.

One of the men stood, edging his way closer to her. My shadows picked up on the wrongness of the man. It was a feeling I'd grown to recognize. Dreki.

I finished my ale and abruptly stood. My fingers flexed with the tingling warmth of my magic and the heat of a room full of bodies. My affinity heeded my will, melting down the dreki's weapons. Every metal buckle and button turned to fiery liquid, dripping down his leathers. He stopped and patted himself down before reaching for his nonexistent sword hilt, alarm and confusion clouded his expression.

My attention divided between my spy and the dreki. Liora sat with her back to us, sipping a steaming mug of mulled wine. I verified her safety, watching as she offered a stack of coins that caused the barmaid's eyes to widen. The barmaid gestured toward the other end of the bar before tending to another customer.

Similarly to when she had sent out her magic to reinstate the bridge between realms, I could see the faintest shimmering threads reaching toward a burly man with red hair and a trimmed beard at the end of the bar.

My shadows flowed along the floorboards, out of sight from the crowd, rolling thick as fog to surround my unsuspecting prey. He had pushed himself out of the way, into a corner, so that he could continue removing the final articles of clothing that smoked with the remnants of melted metal.

The shadows lengthened, sharpened, positioned to strike across his exposed throat. The cut landed clean and the shadows caught his collapse. I reformed the melted metal into braces to hold him upright in the darkened corner, stabilizing his lifeless body. He was just another nameless patron keeping to themselves in the shadows. Until his blood caught someone's attention. But the smells and the sounds and the thick crowd of people would cover my actions for a long while yet.

I searched for Liora. She tensed as the redheaded man spotted her. Her threads of magic fell apart as he paid his tab and slowly stood, approaching her. Impulsively, I closed the gap between us, working my way through knots of people.

I wasn't the type to strike first and ask questions later, but with Liora, I would become whatever weapon was necessary to ensure her safety. The thought startled me, but settled like an unshakable truth in my bones.

My shadows edged close, listening, readied for attack.

"I thought you were a water wielder." His gruff voice made her jump, and her ice dagger was pressed against his stomach instantly. I smiled at her quick reaction. Such a menace.

His hands flew upward. "Whoa! I mean no harm. You're Delah's friend?" Evander. I released my own breath. Her dagger lowered.

With Liora relaxing, my own shadows thinned, returning to coil around my hands. Liora led him back toward the table that Bowen now reoccupied, and I followed behind. She peered into the crowd, her nose slightly scrunched in concentration. Her shoulders fractionally dropped when her eyes met mine. Her gaze traced from my hands to the air above me.

Her grin was almost wicked when she tracked my missing rings to the space above our heads. They floated aloft, aimed at her companion, ready to become whatever blade or defense she needed. She bit back her smile.

Introductions were made when I assumed my seat next to Bowen. The sight of my tonic next to his hand on the table brought a small relief to the tension in my chest.

Sound distorted as a faint hum slowly replaced the noise of the tavern. Pressure made it feel like my ears needed to pop. "We may speak freely. I have a silencing shield around us."

"I had hoped you'd received my messages," Liora quickly began.

"I did. I've been waiting for you. Delah had told me about you when we worked together. Her knowledge was invaluable to my success in making elixirs for her realm. Your king paid me well for my services."

"He's no longer my king," Liora forcefully interjected.

Something like pride sparked in my chest, and I had the overwhelming urge to embrace her.

"What is your power that the king should seek you?" she asked.

He grinned and pulled out several vials, identical to the one Bowen brought to the table. They rolled around in front of him. "I manipulate sound waves. It's how I noticed your magic funneling my conversation—it distorted the waves around me." He winked at Liora. "I can manipulate sound like in the use of this barrier. But my specialization is in tonics. Since there are no Primes to develop magic, I have sought out nymphs. They've lived far longer, and have kept meticulous records on magic and its uses. They taught me how to transmute sounds into liquids. When the vials are broken, the stored sound is released. To great effect."

He picked up a vial. "This one would emit a sonic boom, deafening anyone in its radius, efficient in stunning an adversary." He gestured to another. "This one harnesses the shattering of broken glass. Everyone ducks when it's used." He chuckled.

He placed the first vial down and raised the final one as if it were a treasure. Rotating the vial in his hands, the light sparkled through the clear liquid. "This one holds a siren's song. Its effects are... significant." He set it back down and leaned back, crossing his arms across his chest.

Liora's face remained a blank mask as she attuned to everything the sound wielder shared. The hood of her cloak had slipped down, partially revealing her hair. Instinctively, I pulled it forward for her. "Does Haluma have access to these?"

"No. My work for King Nolan focused on tonics that produced widespread silence."

I immediately tucked that information away. What was he hiding?

"Can you provide us with vials like this for a battle?" she asked, motioning toward the first two tonics.

Evander nodded. "I can do anything for a price. How much do you need?"

She didn't even glance in my direction. "As much as you have, along with your discretion, and a vow that you will not sell these to Haluma."

Seeing her take charge was like staring at a work of violent, sexy art.

Evander leaned forward. "Is Delah still there?"

"She's in Maripol. But I'm going to get her out."

Around us, people moved and laughed and yelled. But in our little bubble, silence hovered. My heart beat in my ears, awaiting his response.

Evander inclined his head. "I work for no realm. But if you get Delah to safety, then I will provide you with weapons. I fucking hate the dreki."

The mood shifted to one of relief. These vials could significantly aid our storming of Nolan's castle. They could distract, alarm, create confusion and chaos. Plans and hope built in my chest. We lifted our mugs in a toast. The sound shield dissolved around us and the noise of the tavern flowed again.

"Bowen will iron out the details and get you payment," I told him.

Evander stood and stretched, his knuckles skimming the crossbeams at the ceiling. He returned to the bar with his empty mug.

Bowen faced me. "How are you so energized right now? Why aren't you begging me for the tonic?"

I glanced at Liora, then back to Bowen. "Rue was able to dilute the poison in my blood with her magic. I still need the tonic, but for the time being, that seemed to stave off the curse's effects."

Bowen studied Liora, slowly chewing. "Impressive work, Ruin. Let's hope it doesn't come to that again once your bargain is fulfilled, or dear old Dom won't stand a chance."

Liora's answering smile didn't reach her eyes.

She shifted in her seat, then bent over to pick up a piece of trash that had stuck to her muddied boot. Concern flashed briefly before she crumpled it in her hands.

My suspicion roused at her response to whatever she'd seen. Before I could inquire, she yawned, then stood, discreetly scanning the tavern's patrons. "I'm going to clean up."

I wanted to follow, but relented. As much as I wanted to invade her space, she probably needed a moment to sort through the last few days. Bowen and I remained downstairs, planning our trip back to Yarit to meet up with Finn and Xuri. Travelers and locals shuffled in from the increasingly violent blizzard to grab a meal, or warm up with a cup of ale. Evander returned and Bowen engaged him with numerous questions related to his craft.

I politely remained at the table, but couldn't focus on their words, needing to check in with Liora. I grabbed my vial of tonic and ascended the stairs two at a time.

CHAPTER THIRTY-FIVE
THE SPY

Our attic space seemed small due to the sloped angles of the roof. The bed was large enough for two. If two people lay like sardines. A table and two chairs were positioned in the back corner of the room, near a frosted window. A small fireplace at the end of the bed released just enough heat to combat the chill creeping in from the outside.

I pulled out the piece of paper that had crunched beneath my boot in the tavern. The words leapt off the page, punching me in my gut. It was a recruitment poster for dreki. Nolan was spreading his tentacles to the furthest reaches of the realms in an effort to create more scaled fighters. That meant some were already here.

I startled at the knock on the door. A young boy brought two buckets of steaming water; apparently the pipes didn't make it to the attic floor. I shoved my unease about the dreki aside. Two trips later, the tub was filled and I stepped in the bath, luxuriating in the warmth. My muscles eased as I used the jasmine-scented soap to clean my hair and body, careful to wash around the gash on my thigh. It was deep, but it wasn't infected.

The walls of my world were closing in around me. I wanted

to make sure Dom could find his cure, and apparently, I was the foretold guide. I needed to get Delah out of Haluma before she became a Vestal Anchor.

Water sloshed up the sides of the tub with my anxious movement. Nolan would not stop hunting me until he found me. The truth of that broke something within me. I would never get away from who I was before. I put everyone around me at risk. Whatever future I'd envisioned crumbled. I would do what I could to give the Liberation the best chance at defeating the king. I would do whatever it took to protect my general.

I leaned back in the tub, submerging my face beneath the surface. The dull fuzziness of sound did nothing to mute my grief. I exited once the water had dropped to an uncomfortable chill.

The soft shirt and loose pants provided by the inn marked a refreshing change from the cold restraint of my leathers. I fished around in my satchel for a cherry candy, grateful I thought to protect them with my magic while visiting the Nereids.

As usual, focusing on the texture and burst of juicy flavor served to anchor me and still my thrumming heart as I thought about next steps, including the most immediate one: sharing a room with Dom. My jumbled mind raced with conflicting thoughts and desires, fears and hopes. Once I had Dom's cure secured, I could get Delah out. I didn't want to think about what might happen after that. But I understood what was required of me.

The door to the room opened and Dom entered, sniffing at the air. He subtly stiffened as he eyed me, then quickly turned away. The same boy arrived behind him to replace the water in the tub.

"If it's alright with you, I'd prefer to be clean before falling asleep tonight. I'll keep the door shut." I nodded, fighting back a vision of Dom's chiseled abs. He half turned toward me, hesitant. "There was a small selection of books downstairs. I thought maybe you would enjoy reading one on"—he held the book up to read the title—"*Legends of the Gods.*" He shifted on his feet, seemingly nervous. "Or I can take it back."

"No. It's great." I reached for it as he offered it to me, stifling my grin.

"Good. Good," he mumbled. Then quickly shut himself into the bathroom.

My smile refused to be restrained as I curled up on the bed in a nest of sheets and blankets, settling in to read the first few pages. The whisper of clothing being removed and splash of water brought awareness to my body. I closed my eyes to drown out the effects such sounds had on me. This was going to be a long night.

I turned the pages, most of the sentences breezing through me as I attempted to refocus on the words in front of me. It was a story about the beginning of all things, how an ancient god punished his second-in-command for trying to take the god's power for himself. My nerves buzzed as the words "Astral" and "Nokt" jumped off of the page. All noise fell away as I leaned closer, greedily reading every bit of lore. In all stories there are grains of truth, even if cloaked in embellished myth.

The story went on to describe Astrals as heavenly creatures, whereas Nokts were borne of darkness. Each type of being had a base magic, and each had the ability to attain a higher magic. I reclined among the pillows as the words sank in. Questions billowed forth like the blossoming sails of an armada. I turned page after page.

It discussed how no magic could survive in its host without a link—it must always be fed. The importance of a consistent source in order to maintain higher magic was a non-negotiable. I knew that when magic was wielded now, it had to be reabsorbed somehow; otherwise, it would drain the wielder, the source being the wielder's own body.

Basic magic was linked to physical organs or bodily processes. The energy from the wielder fed the power used. It was essentially a process of recycling the magic. The book described how when the use of sound went unreplenished, then hearing loss ensued, my own water magic caused dehydration, prophesy led to memory loss, and land manipulation resulted in vertigo and confusion.

These were common understandings that all people knew about. But I had never heard of higher magics. Did that even exist anymore?

My reading sped up in my excitement, devouring the words. With higher magic, a living source is required. A *couerdiae*. I paused at the phrase, clearly derived from the gods' ancient language. I had never heard of it before, but it resonated as my own water magic zipped inside me.

A *couerdiae*, the book described, was a bond made in blood. The bond becomes the source of the higher magic. If a bond does not exist, or is broken, there is no source to prevent the body from being drained from higher magic's use, leading to an agonizing death. Higher magic cannot exist apart from its source. The question was, could one access higher magic now? And if so, then how do you establish a bond?

A creak of the bathroom door and a spill of light interrupted my thoughts. Dom stood in the doorway, a towel slung low on his waist. One hand held the towel as the other slicked back his damp hair from his molten eyes. "Did that boy return with some clothes for me?"

My cheeks flushed as I tried unsuccessfully to look away. My mouth opened, then closed, suddenly dry. I took a breath and tried again. "He did not. I can go find some." I jumped up right as Bowen knocked on our door.

Dom called from behind me, "Bowen, could you grab a change of clothes for me from downstairs?"

"Of course, I'll be right back." He handed me the vial before descending the stairs.

The contents of the glass could have easily been water, the liquid inside a simple clear tonic. I handed it to Dom. My eyes strayed to the V at his hips, his abs flexing with each intake of his breath. Dom's gaze narrowed on the vial. "I grabbed my tonic before I came up here," he muttered.

He retrieved both vials and opened the bottle he had grabbed from downstairs. A song, sweet and delicious, flooded our room. I swallowed hard; my hands gripped the fabric of my pants, twisting at them. Dom's pupils blazed and his breath stuttered.

"Cork it." I forced out the words. He moved in slow motion, blinking away the power that swallowed us. The stopper silenced the spell, but the effects lingered heavy between us.

A wave of lust engulfed me.

Bowen blew back into the room, tossing clothes at Dom. He caught them deftly, then retreated back into the bathroom with leaden steps. He emerged in a loose-fitting top that cut deep at the neck. The sleeves had been shoved up to the elbow revealing his honed forearms. He looked way more delicious than should be humanly possible. I wanted to rip the clothes off. I licked my lips.

"Are you sure the vial you brought me is my tonic?" Dom directed at Bowen.

Bowen quirked his brow. "Of course. Let me see it." Dom handed it to Bowen. Bowen released a tendril of magic to test it. "This is yours." He handed it back, confused.

"Then this belongs to Evander," Dom pressed the other vial forcefully in Bowen's hand. "Do not open it."

Bowen looked from Dom to me. If a whole body could wince, then Bowen's just did. He pointedly addressed me. "Do you need my help?"

Dom tensed, and something almost inhuman snarled. "Leave."

The door shut behind Bowen before I could exhale.

Dom stood motionless, his muscles taut in a fight against the siren-song between us. The spell seemed to strip all pretense and filters. My mind hazed with its potency. Only raw, unfiltered emotion remained. Guilt at my choices convulsed into pain. Grief at Dom's curse bent into rage. Anger conflicted with consuming desire.

Determination flashed in his honeyed eyes. "You need to know I want you, Liora. I've been pulled to you since the day I stepped into Maripol. Even as a child I felt connected to you. When I lost you, I never once stopped searching. I would easily burn this whole place down for you. I stand, even now, with a match to light the flame. This tonic only makes the truth of it crystal clear."

I became very aware of a sizzle in the air, a growing intensity in the breath between us. My heart pounded in my chest.

I stalked toward him in anger, always my most accessible emotion. "You lied to me. You didn't tell me you were cursed. That you were dying." The word cracked on my tongue, sharp as jagged glass. "I never stopped hoping you'd find me. I never stopped dreaming of you." The admission cost me. I shook with the power of barely restrained desire and the rage of lies and loss. I grasped for hate, but it slipped through my fingers.

I advanced on him. Angry, wanting. He stepped backward into the bathroom, out of the confines of the door's threshold.

"I had never feared death until I met you," he whispered.

My hand flew up in a sign to stop him. I couldn't think of that. "We have allies and now we have weapons. When we leave here, it's to find your cure in the Nymphian Library. No more talk of death."

The space between us closed. "I want to touch you, but not like this." Muscles in his arms drew taut as he clenched his fists.

Hurt blistered through me. My emotions tangled with each other. Maybe we shouldn't act on these desires. Maybe it's all I wanted him to do. How dare he deny me. I shoved him further into the bathroom, then threw my affinity around him.

He acted as if he could see my magic flow through the air toward him. But that wasn't possible. Bars of ice flew upward from floor to ceiling, creating a cage so cold that vaporous smoke curled away from its surface. He turned in a slow circle, awe glinting in his expression. I scowled. I aimed to punish, not impress.

He gripped the bars, ignoring their sting. "You're radiant when you use your power." His shadows hovered lazily around him. "I don't want to touch you because I want you to know for certain, that when I do, it was not under any numbing influence. When I claim you it will be slow. And it will be thorough. And you will know, without a doubt, that you're mine."

My skin flared with heat.

"But... I do want to taste you." He pressed himself against the bars, my magic holding fast against his strength. "Release me so I can taste the cherry scent that haunts me." His eyes glowed with the force of his demand.

The urge to torture him turned me on as much as the thought of Dom's filthy mouth. Well, almost.

I stepped forward, grabbing hold of the ice bars. My fingers brushed his. Even that simple act had me suppressing a moan. But I had to know if there were any other secrets between us. The scar tissue Nolan left behind haunted me.

I thought of the dreki poster from downstairs. "Tell me what you know of Nolan's plans."

The braziers in the bathroom casted a flickering light, the metal holding the lighted coals quaked with his response. "He's building his army by recruiting and creating more drekis from the power of orphans. If a child seems promising to his cause, he will keep it, if it doesn't then the magic that has yet to manifest is drained. Raw magic can be turned into anything. Since you've left Haluma, children—girls—in your realm have been disappearing."

"How do you know this?"

He cocked his head. "Delah is a spy for us."

I gasped. "For how long?"

He held my gaze. "Since before I found you. She's safe now. We'll get her out in time."

Relief eased the tension in my chest. At least I was now on the right side of this conflict. Shards of shame stabbed into me, but the pain was less punctuated, less consuming. I could use it to fuel rather than whip.

Dom shifted closer, hungry. The boy who once offered solace had become the leader of a broken people who fought against the subjugation of a tyrant. I wanted to be at his side as he did it. I wanted to be his. Even if just for a little while.

My thighs clenched at the barely restrained desire radiating off of his body, clawing its way to mine. My heart broke anew for what time we'd lost and what violence lay ahead of us.

Dom's shadows curled out from his knuckles, reaching for me. He extended his arm, swiftly grabbing my wrist through the bars. Water magic swirled out of my fingertips, entwining with his shadows, enveloping us both in ethereal bliss. A serene calm surrounded us as our magics danced and responded. Time stilled for a heartbeat.

"You are my greatest temptation," he whispered.

He released me, forcing himself back. I didn't want to forget how he looked in this moment. He was intoxicating to take in. His eyes an eruption of violent amber. His hair a riot of dark waves. He was magnificent in stature and character, even if his life and his prophesied end were a tragedy. He was like an avalanche destroying the side of a mountain—both beautiful and terrifying. I understood the darkness that haunted him. And I witnessed the gentleness and hope he harbored in his soul. I couldn't let this curse win; I wouldn't let Nolan succeed.

"Have you changed your mind?"

I came back to myself, "About what?"

"Can I have a small taste?"

I did not contain the wicked smile that welcomed his request. A shadow flew out from him, snaking through the iced bars of his cage. It curled around my throat, searing my skin as it slowly, softly trailed up my neck, leaving goose bumps behind. My unrestrained moan had his shadows growing firmer as if they were Dom's very hands. Dom sniffed, his entire body stiffening.

I could no longer make out his topaz eyes with his pupils blown out. I arched into the feel of his shadows moving down my chest and across my stomach, toying with my waistline. The metal in the bathroom began writhing. The brazier shook, and sparks flew upward. I met his fiery gaze.

"Control your magic or you'll burn this place down." I released my magical hold on the cage, the bars evaporated into the air, water droplets glittering the floor. The only thing separating us was our own brittle restraint. I let it crack.

"The next time someone is giving orders it will be me." Step. "And you will obey." Step. "And beg for more."

He lurched forward and swiftly took hold of me. My back met the stone wall. He secured my hands above me, a subtle groan escaping.

His breath left a trail of heat as his lips grazed my jawline. Teeth scored my skin, straddling the line between pain and pleasure. I arched into his touch like he was a magnet whose pull I could not defy. I felt like a beggar, desperate for more of his teeth on my skin.

He spoke against my lips, "What I want to do to you is not the result of a bespelled tonic, *m'est kisertes*. It's the truth of my heart." My arms remained pinned above me while his other hand commanded my head, exposing the column of my throat. Excruciatingly slowly, he licked his way from my collarbone to my jaw, pausing at the scar from the Surveille parasite.

"*Foka*, I've wanted to do this for a while." He slowly traced a circle around the scar with his tongue. I sensed his magic washing over me. My skin flushed as he coaxed my blood to the surface, so every brush of air and breath on skin lit me on fire, sensitive in a way I'd never before experienced.

"Can you feel it?" His breath was warm against me and I shivered. My veins pulsed as he manipulated my blood, lighting me from within. Every sensation amplified where his magic flowed.

My affinity spooled out, seeking to embrace him. Ribbons of water streamed in recognition of his metal magic. He released my wrists and my lips found his again, starving. He bit my lower lip, then soothed the sting with a tender lap. His tongue found its place with mine and my soul settled even as my body charged.

"Liora," he groaned.

My breath hitched. "Say it again."

He paused, confused as my words battled through our desirous fog. His eyes softened. "Liora, my light."

His low tenor sparked an electrical tremor through my body. It sounded like a promise. From this point forward I only wanted my name, my real name, in his mouth. It kindled something within me—both terrifying and intoxicating.

I let my body and my magic say what my voice could not. We moved toward the bedroom, tripping on our boots in our haste. My hands could not have fathomed the feel of each rippled muscle as they roved along his body, mapping it. Letting my walls down, opened up a thread of connection that drew us closer.

The ground beneath our feet violently shuddered. The entire inn swayed. I paused, distantly recognizing this had nothing to do with our colliding magic. The sound of an explosion deafened. Our explorations ceased, and we both jumped into action, regrettably alert. Our connection flamed even though the moment collapsed around us. Perhaps Dom was right; the siren's spell was not the source of our desire after all.

I ran to put on my boots and secured my weapons. Dom did the same, stopping briefly to gently cup my jaw and give me one final, and very thorough, lingering kiss.

Bowen yelled for us, beating on our door. We opened it to both him and Evander. Evander tossed heavy furred cloaks to us, then pulled out gloves from a bag.

"We have to go now. There are dreki everywhere."

The blizzard howled outside as I pulled on the fur-lined cloak.

"The explosion came from one of my vials. I used it to disperse the group of dreki that swarmed the pub downstairs. They're searching for someone." Evander's gaze knowingly met mine.

I gathered the rest of my things, and grabbed the book I had been reading, dropping it in my satchel. We started toward the door.

"Wait. I can use the moisture in the air, and the blizzard outside, to map our exit. Give me two minutes." Bowen arched a brow, shifting on his feet, antsy to depart.

Dom assessed me curiously. I offered a crooked smirk before I sat down on the edge of the bed and closed my eyes in concentration. As Gemma taught me, I knew only my imagination could hold me back.

There was just enough humidity in the air to cling to. Quicker than my attempt in the Nereids, I projected my conscience into the vapor, a shimmering silhouette forming. I eased downstairs and found the crowd had thinned significantly.

I weaved through the people in the pub, noting the vertical

pupils of multiple dreki. I swallowed thickly, pushing away my anxiety, a rabbit among bloodthirsty hounds. The door opened to receive a shivering guest. I eased through the door into the darkness.

Outside, I noted where dreki crowded, passing them easily through the curtain of whirling snow. I sailed with the wind toward stables, marking the location of several horses. My presence fell easily unnoticed in the chaos of the winter storm.

I sucked in a lungful of air when I merged back into my body. Dom had positioned himself beside me, making long strokes down my spine as I slumped into him.

I blinked once, my eyes refocusing on the men around me. "Let's go."

CHAPTER THIRTY-SIX
THE SPY

The stairs groaned under the weight of our hurried steps. Apprehension settled heavy in the tavern. An explosion without destruction left confusion marking the faces of the few we passed still in the vicinity. The vibrating impact from the sound had toppled some glasses, but little else had been disturbed. The barmaid absently dried a tankard in her hand.

Dom's shadows raced ahead of us, silently forging a path toward our exit. We kept our heads down and our weapons readied. My skin prickled under the scrutiny of someone in the crowd, but I didn't attempt to identify the source. One foot in front of the other. Once outside, I could lead us to horses. My heart beat dimly in my ears, all my senses sharpened for any potential threats.

Several people swarmed back inside, the door of the tavern swinging outward into the night. We edged our way through the throng and met the biting lash of winter's fury. I leaned into the wind, holding fast to my cloak. Tears welled immediately at the corners of my eyes. My vision swelled with auras. Alarmingly, though not surprisingly, several were of the dreki variety.

There were too many of them to try and take on ourselves. We stuck to the shadows, avoiding those we could, and hurried on. I steered our group toward a stable. No one lingered around them, having sought safety and warmth in the nearby buildings. The stable doors rattled in our attempts to open it. Locked.

Dom's affinity encased the door's bolts and latches. With a *click*, we shoved inside amidst the scent of hay and horses. A boy of maybe seventeen approached us, offering to help. My senses flared.

An arm yanked me back and before I could respond, the blade of a shadow-sickle protruded from the young boy's chest.

Bowen cursed.

"Dreki," Dom stated, slowly removing his bladed shadow with an unnerving squelching sound. The boy crumpled to the floor. Evander swiftly dragged him to a corner and hid the body. I kicked hay into a pile to cover the bloodstains. This boy was too young to have been made a dreki, yet here he was. How many had Nolan sent, and where were they coming from? Disquiet rattled me.

Dom and Bowen finished readying the horses. When I approached, Dom pulled out the compass which glowed with a soft, reassuring blue. The sight brought me comfort. I would need to keep track of whether the glow intensified or not—a plan began to form in the event that it did. After identifying which direction was south, we mounted and silently began our late-night escape.

The blizzard allowed for sufficient cover from potential Nokts, and hunting drekis. Unfortunately, we could not avoid the brutality of its impact.

Dom set an intense pace through the storm. The burning wind and the sting of snow left my face numb and raw. Depending on how far the storm extended south, we might not make it through without consequence. I steadied my breath despite the jarring gallop of my horse and peered skyward. Filaments of my affinity reached toward the tempest.

Dom peered upward in the direction my magic flowed. Bowen and Evander remained focused, their heads bowed against the wind.

It took most of my concentration, but I used the visualization that Gemma had taught me and gathered the snow and ice into a barrier around us. I could not control the wind, but I could shield us from the pelting frost. It didn't stop my chills, but it offered reprieve.

One of Dom's shadows ghosted around me, caressing my face, then disappeared—a gentle thank-you.

The horses were able to pick up their pace with the lessened assault of sleet and snow. We rode south for several hours before the border line of the storm finally appeared. The blizzard's intensity decreased to soft flurries and I released my hold on my magic.

Dom stiffened at my slumping form. Lack of sleep and overextending my affinity had left me drained, despite my attempts to reabsorb. My dry mouth and chapped lips demanded water. The sky, no longer ladened with clouds, brightened in the early blush of dawn.

We veered off our path and ventured into a forested area of evergreens. Bowen tended to the horses while we constructed a rudimentary camp. We could only stay for an hour, but a rest was welcomed by all. I took a moment to drink deeply from the canteen Dom offered me.

Bowen made a small fire that we all huddled around. I leaned into Dom's side, his arm mooring me to himself. His shadows offered another blanketed layer of warmth that I nestled into.

"Can I see the compass?" I ventured.

Dom pulled it from its velvet bag presenting it to me. The soft glow had brightened just a little from a pale sky blue to a soft cornflower—evidence that Dom was headed in the right direction. I burrowed further into him, so grateful to have found him again, hopeful for his future.

Resolve at what I must do hardened within me. I inhaled his masculine scent, wishing things had been different. That I had been different.

Quiet sadness swathed me. I closed my eyes and reached for the snow around me.

CHAPTER THIRTY-SEVEN
THE GENERAL

Liora fell asleep against me. I secured her cloak around her, draping her in my shadows. The sight of the compass's strengthening glow had shifted something in her just as it had me. Hope alighted like the growing dawn around us.

Her body tensed with a swift inhale like she hadn't truly been breathing. It roused her from her slumber. She blinked up at me, eyes softening, and I watched as whatever plagued her dreams melted away. She was at once new and familiar. I knew her deeply, even as I wanted to know everything about her new life. If the compass was to be my lifeline, we would have time to catch up, to discover, because my cure awaited.

Evander poked at the fire sending sparks spiraling upward. "We should continue on foot. Let the horses go in case they have protections like Surveille parasites or other wards to track them."

Liora shivered against me at the mention of the Surveilles.

With the storm behind us, and Xuri and Finn likely making their way toward us, we wouldn't have long to travel on foot.

And Evander was right; the risk of keeping the horses was too great.

The temperature had warmed to a less tortuous sting, the winds having died down significantly. We grabbed our belongings and released the horses, turning again to the south, toward Aphellion.

Evander and Bowen walked together, eating bread and cheese, and speaking in low tones about elixirs and the art of dissolving sound affinity into different base liquids.

I kept pace with Liora, my shadows on alert for any threats. Liora removed the book I'd brought her at the inn from her satchel and began thumbing through its pages.

She filled me in on the information she had gleaned from it. I was surprised it made any mention of Nokts, considering I just learned the term a few days ago. Had Queen Thaleia not introduced the idea, I would have chalked this book up to mythical stories. But my interest was piqued.

Liora shared about the *couerdiae*. I repeated the word as she nodded. "Do you know what it means?"

I glanced toward the horizon. The word was Sarulien, and I had come across it before. Hearing it spoken from Liora's lips stirred something within me. My metal rings flared.

"It means heartbond."

"How do you think you form one?" She returned the book to her satchel and began rebraiding her hair. Two on the left, three on the right, like always.

"Did the book not say anything about it?"

Liora paused her braiding, thinking. "No. Only that it was required to access higher magic."

I didn't know much about heartbonds. I had never heard of anyone forming one in the last few centuries. It had become part of the legends of betrothed women and pining maidens.

Evander interjected, "I'm familiar with higher magic."

We both turned toward him.

"I was just explaining to Bowen how my tonics are made. The magic used is incredibly draining. I've bottled the sound of screams, of song, and various weapons. Well, those are my favorite ones anyway." He chuckled at himself. "I'm only able to make a few vials at a time, and then I have to rest for several days before attempting again. The nymph who taught me indicated the magic I required was a superior type of magic."

Liora adjusted the hood of her cloak to further conceal her hair, the silvery white now mostly faded to reveal a lilac-pink that I wanted to paint. "And this draining magic is different from the use of normal affinities?"

Evander studied her, nodding in affirmation.

Liora rushed on, "Do you know of Astrals and Nokts?"

Evander quirked a brow. "Yes," he ventured. "Knowledge is power in all places. Knowledge can also be dangerous if the wrong people find out it is spreading. Suppression is a very effective tool for people in power. They will do violent things to keep hidden what they deem threatening. Information related to Astrals and Nokts has been lost, and many people want to keep it that way. I'd use discretion when discussing it."

My ears gently popped as he threw up a sound barrier, shielding our conversation from spying ears. "Do you truly wish to learn more?"

There was no way in the hells he could stop now. We all nodded, angling ourselves further toward the sound wielder.

"What I know comes from information passed along by the nymphs. Astrals and Nokts both have higher magics. Astral magic descends from the ethereal firmament. It is light magic—moonlight, sunlight, lightning, starlight—which used to abound in our world. It disappeared at some point along with most Astrals and their sentinels.

"Higher magic requires stronger sources to be maintained. The ability to access higher magic has mostly disappeared. It can be harnessed in small quantities in the right conditions, but even then, it taxes the wielder. Legend says that a sign of Astral magic is strange coloring, not unlike your hair." He paused, assessing Liora. She blanched.

Her mother seemed aware of what the color symbolized. I wondered at who she must have been to have known about such things.

He continued, "Nokt magic is a distorted version of higher magic. It is light magic that has been stripped and deformed, turned inward on itself. Each type of magic leaves a signature. Light magic often leaves a glaze behind. A kind of shimmer, if you will. Dark magic leaves—"

"Char," Liora whispered.

He nodded in confirmation. "Some believe light magic hasn't necessarily disappeared, but rather lies dormant. Meanwhile, dark magic spreads." He shifted his gaze northward, undoubtedly in the direction of the glacial caves and the dying hinterlands.

"What are sentinels?" I asked.

"The original guardians of this world."

I retreated into myself at his words. I knew of the guardians, and had dreams of their return. They were massive beasts with scales and wings. Though, unlike Nokts, these were natural creatures, not a disturbing mimicry of one. Hearing someone speak of them left me strangely unsettled, as if the situation we found ourselves in held a history and a depth far greater than we realized.

We neared a small village, chimneys releasing opaque smoke into the chilly morning. Our conversation ceased when Evander dropped the sound shield.

A Lavender Starling circled overhead, stealing my attention. I leaned down to point it out to Liora. "This is the second time I've seen the elusive Lavender Starling. Do you remember what I told you about them? They are portents of hope, and as we venture into another unknown, I can't help but think you're the reason they're appearing. Their presence makes me think, if nothing else, we'll always have the dawn, *m'est kisertes*."

She preened under the nickname. "What does that mean, General?" she asked.

"One day perhaps I'll tell you, Spy."

She eyed me dubiously.

"Dom, ahead." Bowen pointed at a group of horses further down the trail, heading straight for us.

CHAPTER THIRTY-EIGHT
THE SPY

S wirling clouds of dirt erupted behind a trio of horses. Our group hustled into the tree line that bracketed the road. Weapons unsheathed, and magic coursed through my veins in preparation for the oncoming group.

Familiar voices hailed us. A man and a woman rode on two large steeds, with a third riderless horse tied to the back of the second. I smiled as Xuri and Finn dismounted, the sound of Finn's laughter singing in my ears. The other two mounts conspicuously missing.

"Where are the other horses?" Bowen asked, while Xuri mother-henned Dom.

She turned at the question. "Some dreki stole two horses in the night, along with a lot of our supplies. I never even heard them. At least we still have three to ride on, right?" she asked rhetorically, sheepishly.

Bowen assessed his options, quickly claiming Xuri's horse. She huffed without real bite to it. Someone had to share her steed.

Evander interjected, "My journey ends here. I have a friend in this town I want to check in with. I've given my stash of elixirs to Bowen for safekeeping, and I'll put together a larger supply to have delivered later. Bowen knows how to contact me."

I offered the soldier's sign of respect, as did Dom, and Evander quietly departed.

Finn returned his attention to the horses, then darted between Dom and me. He patted my shoulder, then spoke genially in my ear, "Good to see you, Rebby."

Dom cleared his throat, a dark expression cuing Finn to back away.

"I'm sure Finn and Dom have much to discuss. I'll take the third horse." I strode confidently in its direction.

Shadows coalesced in front of me, forcing me to an abrupt stop. I slyly glanced over my shoulder.

Dom glared down at me.

"You'll ride with me," he commanded, his body now blocking my path forward.

Stubbornness clamped down along with the desire to rile.

"We may not have time when we return to update your second-in-command. Now's your best chance, and we need to get going." I pushed past him, my hips confidently swinging.

A shadow grasped my wrist, spinning me around. Dom was beside me in an instant. "Such a menace." His fingers grazed my arm, lingering. It effectively disarmed me. "I would prefer if you would ride with me, Liora. Please." His voice rumbled like velvet gravel, meant only for me.

"If you reached the point of begging, then I suppose I can make an exception." I smirked.

His eyes turned molten. "Begging is nothing. For you, I would crawl. You've had me on my knees for a while."

His words lingered in the air, a sultry smoke curling around us. He brought my hand to his mouth, pressing a gentle kiss to my knuckles. I allowed him to lead me to our horse. Mounting first, he pulled me up to sit in front of him. His thighs caged my own. It was cramped and constricted, but his firm arm around my waist eased the discomfort.

Finn took the lead for our group, retracing the path he and Xuri had just arrived from. Plenty of daylight stretched before us to lead us back toward Lyrae.

We had traveled a few hours when a flock of vultures circled. Several dove down without returning to the skies.

We slowed our approach as we drew near. Finn, being the only one with a horse to himself, dismounted first and entered the grove of trees. We followed swiftly behind him, stopping short at the scene.

Several bodies were partially buried, the exposed flesh getting picked clean by the winged scavengers. What skin still remained was mottled and bruised. Dark, swollen veins stressed against ashen skin. I turned away, swallowing bile.

Finn pulled a smooth rock from his pocket, holding it tight. He and Dom exchanged a knowing look.

"You've seen this before." Not a question.

Finn waited for Dom's cue before responding. "Yes. At a Berine mining location. We believe there are experiments taking place. Though the aftereffects suggest they haven't been successful. We hope."

I forced myself to look at the bodies. They were too decayed and mangled to recognize identifying features. One appeared abysmally young. I squinted closer at its shoulder where the golden shimmer of Glint stole my breath. Frost crackled at my fingertips. This had to end.

"We need to move on. We don't know what might be hovering nearby, and I don't want to find out," Xuri stated. In silence, we returned to our horses.

The plan was to push through and make a quick stop in Aphellion for supplies and a true rest. Dom, Bowen, and I were working under significant exhaustion. From there, we would head straight to the Perellian Forest and the Nymphian Library.

The compass continued to strengthen in color and brightness the further south we drew, the closer we came to the library. I was confident his cure would be there. I sank into Dom's chest, enjoying what few moments I would have with him. He deserved so much more than his enemy's discarded puppet-weapon. But I would make it up to him.

The whisper of warm shadows caressed my body. And I didn't stop them.

CHAPTER THIRTY-NINE
THE GENERAL

The air grew warmer and more humid as we neared the city of waterways. We had stopped again for a brief break and to water the horses. I grabbed my horse's reins to lead it toward a gurgling stream.

Liora had moved up as a top priority, my duty to her rivaling my duty to the realms. The thought of distancing myself from her brought out an unsolicited, feral snarl to my lips. If she was fire, then I'd burn for her. I didn't care if I was left destroyed in the wake of her carnage, as long as I got to taste her in the process.

Then there was the issue of my bargain with Liora, and how I couldn't let her leave when it was done. And of course the fact that I was dying. I needed the cure to this curse. I could feel my blood thinning and time running through my fingers.

I knelt down at the water's edge, listlessly swirling the cool liquid with my fingers. One thing at a time. I had taken the correct tonic before leaving Vorkut so my blood wasn't actively poisoning me. It was happening more frequently, though, and I couldn't be sure how long I had between doses.

Xuri burst through the brush, her eyes searching wildly for me. "Dom. We have a problem."

I surged to my feet, assessing her for wounds, my senses heightened to incoming danger. My shadows sharpened into blades at my side. Xuri's stern tone caught the others' attention and they strode toward us.

She gave Liora a pained look before turning back to me. "One of the apprenticing oracles reached out to me." She tapped her temple. "Haluma sent a message."

Liora lost all color in her face. "What did it say?" she asked, dread infusing her delicate features.

Xuri turned squarely toward Liora, grabbing her hands. "They have Delah. Unless you return to Maripol, they will kill her."

Liora gasped, her head shaking in denial. I reached for her, putting a protective arm around her, wishing I could truly shield her. She leaned into me, her breathing becoming too shallow, too rapid.

I pulled her closer, gently placing my forehead against hers. "Listen to my breath *m'est kisertes*. Mimic it." Her eyes were glassy as she wrestled with her body's panic. We stared at each other until her magic stopped bucking against my own power. My lips brushed her cheek. "We will get her out. Together."

Liora paused, assessing me as if for the first time. Perplexity skittered across her meticulous appraisal. Her eyes lingered on my lips before inching upward to meet my gaze again. She stepped closer, tilting her head up. "Why? This is my battle, not yours," she whispered, her hand unconsciously twisted a lock of her hair.

I faltered, imperceptibly shaking my head in my own brand of disbelief. "Your battles *are* my battles now." She stared at me with surprised confusion, scanning my face for the lie. *Foka.* How could she not see the truth?

Her pupils dilated as she drew in a soft breath. "I—"

"Dom," Xuri urgently interjected. "We need to leave. Now." Her features softened in apology.

"We're coming, just give us a minute." I waved her off, fixing my attention back on Liora. "We can put off the library for a while longer. Let's get back to Aphellion and get a plan together. We'll figure this out." Her hands stilled.

"What about your cure? You're running out of time." She searched my face, fear mingling with hope.

"I have time," I lied.

A reluctant smile tugged at the corner of her lips. She grabbed my hand and brought me back toward the horse. The curse loomed heavy around me, but getting Delah out of Haluma mattered to Liora. So it mattered to me.

We made haste back to Lyrae. Liora relaxed into my chest, and the protector in me relished being able to surround her with my body. In this moment, there were no Nokts, or drekis, or King Nolan. Just the city of waterways ahead and the salty scent of the ocean wafting by.

As we neared the canals on the outskirts of the city, she twisted in her seat. I met her gaze, her doe eyes more lavender than blue in the afternoon light. "I'm scared," she confessed.

I fixed my eyes to hers. Shadows swirled around me unbidden, tendrils gently unfurling around her arms, winding upward toward her neck, and combing through her mesmerizing hair. The horse slowed down as I watched my magic tangle with her. She shifted to face me but the saddle restricted her movement.

"Hold my waist," she commanded. The horse slowed further behind the others, and I firmly gripped her in the narrow dip of her hips. Slowly, she made to stand on the saddle, then carefully turned around before reseating herself so that she faced me, her legs straddling my lap. It was decidedly my new favorite position to ride a horse.

With a hint of hesitation, she reached around my torso,

tucking herself into me on the crowded saddle. Her cheek rested against my chest. The trembling note of her released sigh was the only indication of her distress. I closed my eyes, relishing her weight against me.

Nolan dangled Liora's closest friend as bait. There was nothing she wouldn't do to try and save her and he knew it. I firmly encircled her body with my free arm, the other holding tightly to the reins, pushing my horse to catch up with the others. Rage at all that Nolan had stolen from her simmered under my skin. The metal on my fingers flared, ready to melt into a lethal weapon, yet no foe stood before me.

She spoke into my scaled leathers, "Thank you for helping me. I know it isn't a part of our bargain." She grazed her fingers along my vambrace. I manipulated the metal along it with my affinity, carving designs into the forearm guard. She traced them reverently. "I hope I don't wear out my welcome." A hint of insecurity weaved through her attempt at humor.

Water twisted out of her fingertips like living ribbons, iridescent in the warm sunlight, curling around me as my own shadows sought refuge around her. "Liora." My voice came out hoarse. I couldn't tear my gaze away. "*M'est kisertes*, you have made your way deep beneath my skin. I will do whatever it takes to keep you there. The bargain is over, you've completed your part. It is your choice whether you stay or leave." That last bit was true, even if it would kill me.

She shuddered against me. "I'll stay. As long as you want me to."

The pink flush across her cheeks turned on a switch that had me pulling her impossibly closer, as if an inch of space between us was too much. My thumb traced the smooth skin of her jawline. "This isn't a small thing to me, Liora. The choice is always yours. I will not be another man to cage you in." We studied each other, this moment suspended in time. The clouds above held their breath.

She appeared on the edge of weeping, eyes wide in disbelief.

I forged on. "I need you to understand that I want all of you. Because when you give me that, you will have all of me, and I will never let you go. I will be yours until my last breath." She nodded, her head heavy on my chest, her arms still encircling my waist.

I held her firmly against me as the horse cantered toward the city gates. I would give her space to process what I'd confessed. She didn't know that everything I had was already hers. She was everything I didn't know I needed. She was my light. *M'est kisertes.*

CHAPTER FORTY
THE SPY

I couldn't bring myself to release my hold on Dom, even when my back protested at sitting backward in a saddle, partially on his lap. His proximity stilled every internal tremor—my living shield of safety. His large hand rested comfortably on my lower back, gently tracing up and down my spine in an unhurried cadence. I wanted to soak it up before we dismounted into whatever chaos awaited. I couldn't recall the last time I had ever allowed myself to be held. I closed my eyes, steeping in this rare moment.

Too soon, we arrived, and I reluctantly peeled myself away. His stern expression told me he was readying himself as much as I was. The mask of a general preparing for battle. Xuri, Finn, and Bowen arrived a few minutes prior, and people were quickly gathering to bring provisions, care for the horses, and inform us of the communications from Haluma. Dom lifted his hand stilling the tumult around us.

"Give us a minute, and then we'll meet in the strategies room to discuss everything." He handed some bags over to someone before pocketing the glowing compass.

The closer we came to the Perellian Forest, the brighter it glowed. A beacon of hope for his curse's cure. Ripples of sadness washed over me that his search for a cure took a back seat to this current crisis. A crisis I created.

I sighed. He reached for my hand and I took it, letting him guide me through the throng of people.

He led me to an area removed from the main bustle of Aphellion. It was near the path to the lagoon Gemma had taken me on so many days ago, but veered closer to the Auren Mountains.

We approached a two-story home, thoughtfully designed from wood and limestone. A porch accented the front door, disappearing around the side of the home. Black metal, the same as the rings on Dom's fingers, reinforced the structure, making it both masculine and easily weaponized.

Beyond it, and slightly offset, rested a small building, almost like a storage shed but slightly larger. The roof was covered in rippling gold, reflecting the sunlight that shone through the leaves of a towering ash tree. A solid-gold Indigo Eagle, wings spread wide, peered over the entrance. The massive bird was the animal affiliated with the old rituals, with one of the gods.

Dom noted my wayward gaze, gesturing in its direction. "It's a private place of worship I built. To the Great One, Elyon. Took me a while to carve the eagle, but I think it turned out well." He released a spark of his magic and the outstretched wings flapped.

I gasped in delight. A soft chuckle escaped his lips. "I've always held a deep connection to Elyon. I'm attuned to him in ways even I don't understand." A shade of embarrassment colored his expression.

"How did you even learn of him? No one prays to the gods anymore. They have been silent for so long," I mused.

He softly exhaled, staring out toward the mountains, majestically keeping watch over Aphellion, his beautifully hidden stronghold. "I have no other explanation than I just always have prayed to him. I have had dreams of him. And I believe he watches out for me. Hasn't steered me wrong yet." He shrugged a shoulder, glancing down at me in amusement.

Dom was a man of deep intellect and purposeful confidence. Limp conviction didn't fit with his profile, and who was I to challenge his personal experience with a god who supposedly had long abandoned this creation? I never would have guessed the rebel general harbored a respectful devotion to the Great One.

I met those fathomless amber eyes, a grin fighting its way out of me as I delightfully collected new discoveries of this multi-faceted man.

He guided me back toward the entrance of his home. The dark wood of the front door swung open to a first floor sitting area replete with a welcoming hearth. Ornate art adorned the walls as if he were a collector. I peered closely at the different landscape depictions. Their shared style indicated the same artist. The kitchen sat back further in the home and the curved stairs presumably led to bedrooms.

"Make yourself comfortable. There is food in the kitchen if you want any. I'm going to change upstairs. There's a bathroom down the hall if you need it."

I padded to the first floor bathroom and washed my face. I used a rag to wipe off my arms and legs, but didn't have enough energy to completely bathe. I unwound my wind-tossed braid, combing my fingers through the traitorous lilac locks.

The coracite was nearly washed out and it was imperative I eliminate the pinky-purple color before returning to Haluma. My mother's words echoed in my mind, her warnings about my hair color impressed like a blacksmith engraving in my memory. And with the threat of Nokts in Maripol, and the connection between my hair color and a supposed Astral heritage, I didn't want to take any chances. Add it to my list of things to do. I massaged my scalp from the release of my tight plait.

I returned to the sitting area, nestling into a soft leather chair with a navy wool blanket draped across its back. The place was clean, but clearly lived-in. I closed my eyes, my body grateful to not be on a galloping horse. But my mind whirred on.

Ruin, the spy, took over and I entered task mode—forming lists, calculating risks, and mapping out routes. My exhaustion wore down my shields against anxiety and I struggled to rein it in.

Thinking wasn't distracting enough. Leaning forward, I channeled both my focus and my magic into one frozen dagger after another. Ice bent into filigreed detail on the hilt. Ancient symbols carved down the blades. My concentration distracted me from my tumultuous thoughts and feelings enough that I missed the sounds of Dom descending the stairs.

I startled when he placed a hand on my shoulder, breaking the silence of the space. "Those are amazing," he commented.

I looked up at him, noticing his hair still dripped. The scent of horse had been thoroughly replaced with warm leather and the freshness of the sea. "Are you ready?" he asked as he studied me.

I stood to face him, taking care to not knock the wool blanket on the floor. "Yes. We need to strategize, and we need to move quickly." His topaz irises glowed in the dimness of his home, emotions I couldn't name flashing across his features.

"Then, let's go."

THE BUILDING WAS A THREE-STORY BEHEMOTH, constructed with very few windows and several tons of granite. Dom explained the layout as we passed through multiple wards at the building's entrance. Polished granite floors greeted our entry along with two staircases that led to numerous offices and rooms. One staircase led to underground rooms several feet beneath the surface, meant for detaining criminals and presumably a few torture chambers.

We went up two flights, entering a large room with a circular table in the center, easily able to accommodate twelve people. It was a massive slab of black metal, one only a proficient metal wielder could have formed. My gaze instinctively veered to Dom. He locked in on me and heat warmed my chest.

Seated in several of the chairs already were Finn, Bowen, Xuri, Sieren, Xuri's apprentice Oralia, and several others, presumably higher-ranking soldiers and men in the rebellion. I took a seat between Dom and Xuri, despite my antsiness.

The door opened and Korin strode in, holding a large platter of food. Xuri narrowed her eyes at the young girl but didn't ask her to leave. She flashed a bright smile at me, and I responded with a quick wink.

Xuri gathered a few papers into organized stacks, then addressed our group. "We have a tentative plan for the extraction of Delah from the castle in Maripol. Bowen has offered his services in wielding sound tonics to use as a distraction when you enter the castle. For years, Sieren has attempted to mimic my ability to speak into others' minds." She gestured in Sieren's direction, respect tinged with amusement in the flex of her fingers. "She has succeeded in the last few months with an elixir that allows all who drink it to communicate by mind-walking." Gasps whooshed down the table.

"This elixir only lasts for a few hours at most, and works only when you're in close proximity as others. I brewed a small batch this morning. You ought to be able to focus your thoughts on particular people, and they will be able to hear and respond.

I've gathered enough of it to send out with the lot of you," Sieren concluded.

I spoke up, "They could have Delah in the dungeons or the Vestal tower. Though I am inclined to believe they have her in the tower, I don't think it's wise to focus only on it." The thought of the Vestal deception stoked my rage. "We should split up to make this efficient."

Finn, feet propped lazily on the metal table, his support rock clutched in his fingers, interjected, "Bowen and I can take the dungeons. You and Dom head to the tower. I've retrieved several of our own from within the castle's walls. I know where I'm going." His crooked grin reflected his giddy excitement and unhinged idea of a good time.

"I can rearrange the castle grounds. To disorient and sow confusion." The soft voice gained strength. All eyes turned to Korin.

"No." Dom's response was swift and final, brooking no argument.

Korin lifted her chin, brooking her argument. "No one has my ability. I would be an asset, a secret weapon. You can't go in there without backup."

Finn mock pouted. "What about me?"

Korin offered him a brief, conciliatory glance, then turned back to Dom. "Let me come."

Dom beseeched Xuri for assistance. She lifted her eyebrows, clearly leaning toward giving in to the young land wielder. He shut his eyes, pinching the bridge of his nose. "You'll stay here, Korin. You don't have enough training. This isn't the mission to start with, and Nolan has you on his radar."

She wilted in her seat, clenching her hands into white-knuckled fists. With a huff, she sprang up, exited, and slammed the door behind her. Dom released an exasperated exhale.

He raked his hands through his hair as he and Finn returned

to scrutinizing maps and outlining strategies that involved minimal exposure and a quick retreat.

We worked for hours going through all possible scenarios. As the daylight faded, I found I could not stop yawning, my focus waning. Our plan solidified, we agreed to take several hours to rest before heading to Haluma.

My heart raced in anticipation. This time tomorrow, Delah would be freed.

CHAPTER FORTY-ONE
THE SPY

"Where are you going?" Dom's low voice pierced my drowsy haze as I headed toward my room in the healing quarter.

Turning, I stumbled, confusion marring my brow. "To my bed. Where are you going?"

Shadows collected around his knuckles. "I had hoped you might stay with me tonight. Just so I know you're alright." He tucked his hands in his pockets. A lock of dark hair slipped across his forehead in response to hours of dragging his hands through it, his tell for both exasperation and deep thought.

I extended my hand. "Then take me home."

He tucked me into his side, my head barely reaching his shoulder. I didn't mind it when his strong arm wrapped around my waist. We were walking as though we were in a drunken three-legged race, which elicited a delirious giggle from me. He glanced down, a grin smeared across his own lips. The stars glittered above us, mirroring the twinkle of the magic in my veins. I didn't have to look behind me to know that with every step I took, I left sparkling ice in my wake.

Dom opened the thick wooden door for me, and this time,

the fire in the hearth was fully lit, casting a warm glow throughout his home. I followed him to the kitchen where he put water in a kettle.

I hopped on the counter, leaning slightly back to watch as he rolled back the sleeves of his shirt, exposing muscular forearms honed by years of physical training. He turned the heat up on his stove, and raked his hands through his messy hair that never ceased to appear artfully disheveled.

The silence between us grew heavy with the mounting tension of unspoken thoughts. Two warm mugs of spiced tea steamed with Dom's preparations.

He brought them over, his face a careful mask as he moved to stand between my legs. Never breaking eye contact, he relinquished the mugs, then began kneading the coiled muscles in my shoulders. A groan escaped me as I leaned into his touch, and he paused.

He opened his mouth to say something but thought better of it, resuming his careful movements. I shifted closer to him, aligning our bodies. Peering up, I stared at his lips. "I want you," I whispered.

He swept my hair away from my face in a tender, casual gesture. "*M'est kisertes.*" He appeared pained. "I brought you here because my heart and my magic are restless when we're apart. I cannot be at peace if you're not with me. I am a jealous man and once you're mine, I will not let you go. I know I told you that whatever you chose to give me would be enough, but I was wrong." He clenched his hand around the countertop, eyes blazing. "I want everything."

My magic purred.

Though I still sifted through programmed lies and distrust of myself, I wanted him to know I would give it all. "I didn't know how dangerous hope could feel." Fear still hovered in the background, but I could not deny how my hidden longing for a loving home, one that I had never truly had, found its culmination in this steadfast man.

His lips grazed my temple. His gravelly tone stoked the embers of my soul. "We can walk this path together. I will protect your heart with all my power and strength. With my very life."

He exuded quiet reassurance as my fingers skated across his forehead to push the persistent lock of hair away from his brow.

I summoned my courage. "You cut through my shields and awakened something I thought was long dead. You laid to rest something I thought I had needed to survive."

He reached for me then, twining his fingers with mine. "You have nothing to fear. Never from me."

His declaration and my acceptance of it clicked something final into place. My own possession erupted. I was in my body, and yet not.

A tug in my chest had my hand grasping at my heart, which had momentarily palpitated. Dom coughed, his breath mimicking mine, his own hand reaching over his heart with a wince. The gold rings around his eyes pulsed.

He peered closer to my face, imperceptibly squinting. "Your eyes..." He trailed off, surprise overtaking his features. We both stood on the knife's edge of desire, our bodies flaring and responding to our emotions.

Dom gripped my jaw, bringing my gaze back to his. "Tell me you're mine," he demanded.

I studied his face, full of everything I didn't know I needed. "I'm yours, Dominus. I think I've always been yours. I just didn't know it."

His fingers scored my scalp, tangling with my hair. He tugged on it, angling my head up as his other hand stroked down the side of my face. I licked my lips.

"You are mine, Liora, and I yours. As sure as the dawn." Reverently, he leaned forward, his lips brushing mine. I sighed into him, my hands snaking their way up his chest, savoring the wall of muscle beneath. Hope burned through the fear that tried to coil around my tentativeness. Safe. I was safe. The last vestiges of my resistance fell away. And I staked my claim.

Our lips touched, teased, pressed, exhaling their fervent prayers. His tongue caressed my softly parted lips. He was smoke and fire, honey and sharp edges. Our hands searched, gripping each other tighter, our bodies igniting. Our movements turned feral. For we were both starving.

Dizzy, floating, all of my senses zeroed in on the sensuous man before me—his masculine scent, his muscular arms, and broad chest—a firm, stabilizing presence. It was as if I were his precious metal, and I would let him melt me down in any way he pleased.

I ravenously felt my way around his mouth, savoring his tongue. I bit his lower lip as I fought to contain my moan. His forearms flexed, gripping my hips. He kissed down my jawline, nipping my shoulder while my hair twisted in his grip so he could move my head to the perfect angle. He mercilessly licked his way up my needy throat.

We grew hungrier, our bodies heating the air around us. If I was flint, he was the striker, and together we detonated. His teeth grazed my jaw. I leaned back savoring the drag, but I wanted more. So much more. He swallowed my moan with a devouring kiss as I rocked further into him. His arousal pushed against me, igniting every nerve.

My heart literally skipped, jolting me. It was as if time had stalled, and it was only us, only ever us, and the stars. We paused, staring into the galaxies of our eyes. When I finally came back to myself, refocusing, I gasped.

Our magic swirled around us in an ethereal ballet. His shadows and my water twisted, braiding around themselves. Bands of light shot out in glittering strobes from amidst the undulating waves of magic. Tiny pieces of metal and ice floated, suspended in the air like fireflies. The glow of the hearth reflected on their shimmering surfaces, refracting the tiny bands of light that continued to intermittently zip out. Dom and I intertwined our fingers, wondrously captivated by the strange magical dance unfolding around us, our physical explorations on pause.

In the midst of our enchantment a single magenta thread appeared, weaving its way around us. It encircled our wrists, and curled around our waists, cinching us closer. The thread separated, migrating to our collarbones. It curled and swirled around itself, morphing into symbols, where it silently embedded into our skin. A tender sting seared the delicate flesh on my chest, right below my clavicle.

I pulled down the collar of Dom's shirt to get a better look, but as I did the thread dissolved into nothing, leaving behind a small, faint, glimmering silver symbol right above his heart. It stood out even among the runic writing that now pulsed brightly beneath his skin. Thoughts would not form when feelings overrode me.

I was a furnace, insatiable when it came to the taste of him. I could feel the thump of his heartbeat as it synced to my own. I needed it all. His lips crashed back into mine. My hands devoured his body. His fingers traced every dip and curve of mine. Our magic writhed. Heavy and energized, soft and aggressive.

Not releasing his mouth from mine, he scooped me up off of the counter. I spilled my cup of tea as he whirled me out of the kitchen. Laughter burst out of me, but Dom growled in response at my attempt to break our kiss.

My arms wrapped around his neck and my legs twined around his waist. He cupped the back of my head with one hand, the other tightly gripping my ass as we ascended the stairs. I winced when he accidentally walked me into the side of the stairwell, a mumbled apology within the haze of our delirium the only response.

We entered his bedroom and I drew back for a gasp of air. I glanced around at his large room. Exposed beams framed the ceiling, and a glass door opened to a balcony facing the jagged mountain peaks.

Dom never took his eyes off of me, frustration pinching his voice. "You should probably know that Xuri had organized for a coracite paste to be dropped off, to lighten your hair. Though I like it as it is, she seems to be aligned with your mother that hiding its color is imperative." He followed my gaze out the window, then turned back to me, sighing. "And since we have to leave tomorrow, we should probably take care of that now. But the choice is always yours." His shadows grazed my body as he awaited my response.

I groaned at the thought of doing my hair at this very moment, when all my body screamed for was Dom. Or sleep. Or both.

"Xuri told me how it works; let me do this for you." He bit my earlobe.

"You want to color my hair?" It sounded surprisingly dreamy, if a little bit of a letdown.

He sat me down on his bed, then eased out of his shirt, exposing his chest and the silver filigreed mark now emblazoned above his heart. I reached out and touched it. I pulled my own top low to see the imprint on my own chest. They were identical.

"Do you recognize the symbols?" I asked him.

"It's Sarulien. I'll look it up later." His strong forearms flexed, drawing my eyes greedily in their direction. Gods, those were distracting. He gently tucked his arm around me, lifting me as though I might break. "We have matching tattoos now. The realms have conspired to mark you as mine." He carried me to the bathroom. Setting my feet on the floor, he handed me an oversized robe. It smelled distinctly of my general.

I removed my pants and top, leaving only my chemise on. I wrapped myself in the plush robe before stepping into the copper tub large enough for three people. My legs extended into the empty space. He grabbed a container filled with the coracite paste and sat on the edge of the tub. Scooping a glob of it in his large hands, he massaged it into my scalp, gently tugging on my hair.

I observed the luxurious space, draping my arm along the edge of the tub. The copper bowl rested in front of a window overlooking the snow-topped mountain peaks, their summits faintly glowing below the light of the twin moons. The window spanned the width of the far wall, extending from floor to ceiling.

Majestic hemlock trees stood guard with their fringed evergreen needles swaying to the tune of the wind. Matte-black, slate stone provided a decadent texture to the walls of the bathing room, complementing the smoothness of the black-marble floors whose white veining seemed to glow from the moons' illumination. Candles burned in ornate metal holders, hovering along the walls and countertops by the power of Dom's magic, lending a quiet intimacy. It smelled like Dom and reflected his personality perfectly.

His hands in my scalp were pure decadence. If I had the proper vocal cords, I would have purred. The windows reflected the concentration in his narrowed eyes as he methodically coated each strand. I sank deeper into the tub with his hypnotizing kneading.

When he deemed his work satisfactory, he twisted my hair up, securing it with a clip to give it the proper wait time for the lightening to take effect.

My eyes slowly shut in both fatigue and tranquility. Without opening them, I inquired, "How will I wash this all out?"

"I'll need to fill the bath with water." The silence lingered long enough that I opened my eyes. "Then, I will rinse it out for you." He swallowed. "If you wish."

My fatigue diminished as I studied this dark, intense man. "Your assistance sounds like a wise safety precaution."

Thank you, he replied. Oddly, I didn't notice his lips move, but my exhausted mind was still swimming from all that had taken place. I nodded in response. Dom held out his hand, offering me stability within his firm grip as I slowly stood, then stepped out of the tub. He opened the spigot, water filling the basin. I dipped my fingers in and agitated the water with my magic, warming it to my liking, bands of steam curling upward.

Dom respectfully turned away granting me privacy. Gingerly, I untied the robe letting it drop quietly to the floor. I removed my chemise, the soft *whoosh* of the material the same tone as Dom's intake of air. "Will you help me back in?"

He turned back toward me, his breath stilling. His eyes made a thorough, sweep of my body. He swallowed. Hard. "Beautiful," he murmured.

I glanced away at the intensity of his scrutiny, timid despite his words. I returned to the bath with the aid of Dom's warm hands, sinking into the water's lapping embrace as the tension in the air thickened. Steam rose languidly and my skin glistened with moisture.

He pulled down a basket of fragrant oils and colorful soaps. With a cup, he poured fresh water over my hair, rinsing the coracite out. His strong hands massaged oils and creams that smelled of honey and vanilla into my lightened strands. His brow furrowed in concentration as he methodically combed through my hair until all the coracite and travel grime had been removed and only clean silk remained. I closed my eyes, indulging in his tender attentions. His fingers teased at my scalp and I softly groaned in pleasure.

My magic escaped me, fingers of water entwining with

Dom's. Water exploded above me in fireworks of mist while parts of the copper tub melted and transformed into glinting metallic bubbles that hovered above the water, mingling with my sparkling iridescent drops. Dom's shadows swirled outward, leisurely grazing down my body. Goose bumps covered my skin as I relished the way my magic hummed alongside his. I squirmed beneath the water as his shadows moved downward, edging my hips, caressing my inner thighs.

Desire pooled, warring with fatigue. I wanted to weep at the injustice that my body demanded rest. The copper tub took on a life of its own as it softened under the weight of my body, firmly kneading the muscles of my back. I yawned as I peered up into Dom's glittering eyes.

He fisted his hands and his shadows disappeared. He leaned over my head, still playing with my hair, his breath softly brushing my cheek. I inhaled him, wishing my body wasn't so drained. "I can feel your exhaustion." He dragged his nose down the bridge of my own. I entwined my fingers with his, his other hand splayed flat at my shoulder, slowly, so slowly, moving downward. The water hardly covered the pink of my nipples. They hardened at his teasing touch.

His whisper sank into my skin. "I have extensive plans for your pleasure, and I want you wide awake to enjoy it all."

Oh.

"But if you aren't too tired, just say the word."

Oh.

The water swirled around me, my magic groaning for him. My heart swelled with a tenderness that, with anyone else, would have frightened me. I could no longer deny him.

CHAPTER FORTY-TWO
THE SPY

I tugged on our clasped hands, forcing him to stand and walk around the tub. He kept his eyes on me, moving slowly, a lion with his prey. His loose pants hung low at his hips, the arrowed muscles at his waistline drew my thirsty gaze. He used his free hand to release his pants; they pooled on the floor. Biting my lower lip, my heart raced in anticipation. His body did not disappoint. It would make even the most exquisite marble statues weep.

He kept his underwear on as he made to step into the gleaming copper tub, his large arousal unmistakable. I arched my brow in question. A half smile coerced a dimple to his scruffy cheek. "Your pleasure is my pleasure, *m'est kisertes*. I've thought about doing this for a very long time. My turn will come later." The words came out in baritone silk.

I scooted further back into the arms of the massive tub as he stepped inside. Desire and anticipation coursed through my veins. His patient self-restraint almost made me jump out of my own skin. I didn't want him to take his time. I forced myself to relinquish control and follow his lead.

I'd give him fifteen seconds.

He knelt down in front of me, water lapping at his thighs, as I opened my legs, inviting him closer. His broad shoulders blocked the view of the mountains through the window. Moonlight illuminated his body, forging him into a glowing god.

He softly held my jaw, along with my heart, in his sturdy hands. His eyes, heavy with want, overflowed with adoration as he tilted my chin, taking his sweet time searing me with his gaze. I wanted him to mark me. With his eyes, his hands, his tongue. I shoved a little encouraging wave of water at his back.

"So demanding," he chuckled. His hand curled around the back of my neck, bringing me closer. His lips crushed mine and I met him with equal vigor. My lips parted and he took his fill of my mouth. The sweep of his tongue flipped a switch in my body. Everything around us fell mute. Water curled out of me, and the tub sloshed with our movements. I arched into him, needing to feel the weight of him, my fingers grasping at every inch of his toned body.

He eased back onto his heels, pupils blown wide. Amusement crinkled his eyes as I whimpered in protest. "The dreams that have plagued me at the thought of your taste..." He shook his head, chuckling. "Don't let me drown."

Want lanced through my body, heating my core. His hands delved beneath the surface of the water, finding my calves, smoothly exploring their way upward. I could feel my desire warming between my legs as I leaned my head back, relishing in his command of my body. His fingers meandered to my knees, stroking upward as they splayed hungrily, stimulating the delicate skin at the top of my inner thighs. He edged to my center, leisurely exploring every dip and curve. Ice crystallized along the tub's edge where my grip cut into it.

I never knew connection until this moment. I didn't understand care before this man. I never felt so greedy and so generous. I'd never been so exposed and cherished as I was in this candlelit bathroom.

Dom dipped his head under the water, and I finally connected his previous words to his actions. Immediately, I threw my magic down, allowing him to breathe below the surface. I felt the curve of his smile against my inner thigh as he dragged his tongue toward my center, his teeth grazing the sensitive skin. I welcomed him into me. He gripped my hips, tugging them downward, urging my legs further apart.

The heat of his mouth coaxed an unbidden groan. My body begged for more, and his shadows answered as his tongue performed its own brand of magic. Ribbons of velvet shadow snaked up my stomach, teasing my nipples and tightening around my neck.

My skin flushed, and I could feel his magic beckoning my blood toward the surface, where his mouth sucked and teased against me. I was an inferno of sensations. Every touch of hand, tongue, and shadow scored into me, branding me as his. And I freely gave in to him. He could suck me dry and I would beg for more.

Each stroke and caress tuned a harmonious note to a collective symphony. My core tensed as the crescendo built. The metal candle holders dipped in their floating vigils. Light flickered against the copper bowl of the tub. My knees started to come together with my collective groans. Dom's hands forced them back down, opening me further. I would obey his every command.

Like a magnet, he found the throbbing pulse at my center, nibbling, then sucked on it, amplifying my ache. My back arched at the sensation. His satisfaction transferred to me through the hum of his approval. I bit my lip as my body tensed and thrummed in eager response.

"You're delicious," he spoke into me, the blow of his breath a different stimulation to my core.

My breath quickened as I buried my hands into the floating strands of his dark hair. He sucked harder as blessings and curses spilled from my lips, his attunement to my body its own form of worship.

My focus on anything but his mouth made my hold on Dom's air bubble waver. With an impatient flick of my hand, I parted the water around him, enclosing us in a giant bubble of the tub's water, effectively clearing his path to finish what he started. Water swirled with the iridescence of my magic, a mimicry of the transcendent colors my aura surely emitted.

Dom locked his eyes with mine as he worked me mercilessly. His fingers gripped my hips as he poured every ounce of tenderness and desire into his work. If he were an artist, this performance would be his masterpiece. The symbol above my heart warmed as a tsunami of emotions flowed into me. I wondered briefly if they originated from me or through Dom.

I peered down at the taut muscles of his sculpted back, flexing as he tore through all my layers. In this moment, everything in our souls aligned. This was where I belonged. This was home. I closed my eyes at the realization, the truth of it settling firm and immovable.

His fingers again moved inside me as if mapping every spot that left me writhing. "Eyes on me," he breathed. How could I not obey?

"Good girl." He winked, resuming his work ambitiously, thoroughly.

My body flushed as the pressure increased. I stood on the edge of oblivion and not one part of me gave a damn. I could almost hear him command me to come for him. He thrust his tongue inside me, unyielding, before replacing it with his fingers, his mouth again sinking onto the swollen, sensitive spot, luring every mounting sensation to the surface. It built and built. My mind fell blank, save for the beauty and passion of this moment.

Somewhere along the way, I'd decided that this type of love would never happen to me. This amount of raw desire, reciprocated, would remain an unfulfilled longing. As the candles flickered, the hinges on the vaulted door I stored my silent hopes in blew right off.

His name left my lips as my vision exploded in starlight. I unraveled. I reforged. This ecstasy pushed into the sacred, and Dom felt it too, his body responding to my own.

He rode my waves until the pulses melted away. My taxed muscles and waning euphoria left me dazed. I made room for him beside me in the cradling tub, and he shifted into the space, moving my back to his chest. Every point of contact left me purring in contentment. I relaxed against the safety of Dom's broad shoulders. In his arms, protection enclosed me.

He reverently tucked my hair behind my ear. I released my hold on the globe of bathwater still enclosing us. It streamlined down the drain. My magic sucked the water from both of our hair and bodies leaving a vaporous mist in the aftermath. The tub's copper surface remained soft and warm through the power of Dom's magic.

"You are magnificent," he whispered into my ear, leaving a shiver skating down my spine. A soft smile spread across my swollen lips, and a faint flush dusted my cheeks. He pressed languid kisses along my neck and shoulders. "You taste like life and hope and destiny. It's not that everything else hasn't mattered. It all led me to this. To you." I tilted my head granting him further access to my throat. I would never get enough of him.

"I never knew it could be this way." I turned toward him in the crowded space. He adjusted his arms, placing his hand behind my head to prevent it from knocking against the copper wall. I wound my legs with his, aligning our bodies. I brushed my hand down his face, his expression wiped of all the scowls he perpetually wore. In its place lay a vulnerability that suffused the fabric of the air with a tenderness so divine that words would only stain the threads.

Exhaustion clawed at me, shoving its weight through my limbs. My eyelids betrayed my desire to physically reciprocate. The softening euphoria, the warmth of the bath, and the multitude of extreme emotions from the day had pushed my fatigue over the edge. Staying conscious was an insurmountable task.

He stood from the bath, grabbing a towel. I rose to meet him as he wrapped it around my body. Though I relished my own strength and capability, in this particular moment, I let him take care of me.

He helped me out of the tub and back into his room, his hand refusing to relinquish my own. I didn't want to think about anything but this man in this moment. I shut the windows of my mind to all intrusive fears groping their way into my awareness. As I breathed Dom in, all residual turmoil stilled. My festering anxieties fell silent in the balm of his presence.

I pulled on one of Dom's shirts, his scent a warm sedative. The collar fell to the side, exposing my shoulder and the top of our shared symbol. It reminded me of something out of a Sarulien book, but it was more vines than the usual swirling script.

We held tight to one another as we burrowed beneath the blankets. He tucked me in the warmth of his hard body, his legs tangling with mine. "Rest, *m'est kisertes*."

"Will you finally tell me what *m'est kisertes* means?"

He inclined his head, debating his response. Amusement flickered.

"What do you think my greatest weakness is?" he responded, ignoring my demand.

I rolled my eyes. "I would guess it's your curse. Or the fate of the rebellion."

He reached for my hand, his thumb making circles around my knuckles. "What if it's you?"

"Then I suppose that's more a reflection of your poor taste in women."

His lip twitched in a barely contained smirk, "It means 'my temptation,'" he relented.

My magic languorously stretched, satisfaction filling my blood, at receiving the moniker. "Surely I can't be a temptation if..." I placed my palm against his chest. "If I'm already yours?"

He smiled into my hair, pulling me flush against his chest. He peppered my bare shoulder with languid kisses. I relaxed in the ensuing silence. In this small moment, everything felt right. Even if I knew it wouldn't last.

I registered a whisper, low and earnest against my temple, but sleep consumed me all too swiftly before I could make out what he said.

CHAPTER FORTY-THREE
THE SPY

A heavy rapping echoed through the chambers of my mind. The discordant knocks yanked me out of a dreamless slumber. Dom released my waist, rolling over to address the intrusion. He wiped his hand down his face, blinking focus into sleep-riddled eyes.

I threw my arm up, shielding myself from both sound and the burgeoning day with all of its burdens. Today we would portal to Haluma.

The knocking escalated into belligerence. Dom angled himself enough to peer down at me, an apologetic smile forming. "Finn," he rasped out, then cleared his throat. "I'll stall him, but it's time to get up. Did you sleep well, *m'est kisertes?*" Dom's morning timbre elicited a small collection of goose bumps.

I repositioned myself so that we faced each other. Ribbons of light illuminated his gilded irises. I gave in to the way they mesmerized me, like the moon pulls the tides ever closer.

I softly swallowed. "I slept more soundly than I have in years."

His smile could tame the sun. He traced my face with his fingers, brushing his thumb across my lips. "I would love to spend the next week in this bed with you. But we have to get ready to meet the others." His voice pinched, and he left the bed to throw on his leathers.

His steps rang solid down the stairwell. The creak of the front door morphed into Finn's bellowed greeting. I yawned, stretching languidly. I ran my fingers across the sheets, Dom's lingering warmth imprinted in their softened wrinkles.

Sitting up, I wished I could imprison this day within these walls, with only Dom and I. My magic could cage everyone out, and we would be free to just *be*. We would cook breakfast, explore one another, swim in the lagoon, investigate the silver symbol tattooed upon both our chests. We could make up for time we'd lost. I sighed.

This wasn't my reality. The last few days with Dom solidified my resolve. I would do whatever I could to ensure his success in finding the cure to his cursed blood and taking down the king.

I searched for my battle leathers. Dom had left them neatly folded on a nearby dresser. They were freshly cleaned and mended from our time in the ocean and our battle with the Nokt, another detail Dom must have orchestrated shortly after arrival. I reluctantly removed Dom's oversized shirt.

The curious scales from my armor glinted midnight blue in the brightening light of day. I rubbed the pads of my fingers down the overlapping scales, marveling anew at their collective tensile strength despite their seemingly individual fragility. I sensed that Dom's magic was the source of the proprietary armor. They mimicked what I had seen of the drekis, but instead of a bottomless black that reeked of death magic, these scales, made of magicked metal, glimmered in shades of silver and midnight blue.

Weapons holstered, I trudged down the stairs, steeling myself for the onslaught of the day. Muffled voices ceased their volleying at my appearance. Dom offered a tender greeting, a warm cup of tea in his outstretched hand. I gratefully accepted, moving to stand at his side. I glanced at the floor where I'd spilled my cup the night before, all traces of our passion removed.

"Sorry for the wake-up call," Finn stated, not sorry at all. "The others are gathering. As soon as we have our supplies, we will portal out, and perform a spectacular jailbreak. One they might even write songs about." More theatrical movement with his eyebrows.

I grimaced, shoving my face into Dom's shoulder. I was not prepared for his energy this early in the morning. Dom chuckled beside me, the rumble seismically shifting my organs. The silvered stamp below my clavicle tingled in response.

"Finn, how about you leave before she stabs you. We'll be right behind."

Finn tilted his head in curiosity but obeyed the request.

Dom leaned toward me, gently massaging my shoulders. "Thanks for not attacking my Second."

I nodded as we finished our tea. The last vestiges of sleep wafted away. At least Finn had shown up with a peace offering of warm pastries. We grabbed one each on our way out. Dom's magic locked the door behind us.

We stood outside, near the sparring fields. Our vials, weapons, and armor secured, checked, and rechecked.

Sieren extended a chalice containing a dark, viscous liquid. "This will open your minds to be able to communicate with one another. Take two large swallows." I downed the contents, stifling a gag at the bitter flavor.

The chalice passed around until all of us had consumed the necessary amount. Sieren offered a gracious bow. "May you return unharmed and successful."

"Wait!" Korin ran up to our group, her need for air overtaking her ability to speak.

She gave me a tight squeeze, then handed me a necklace.

"I made this last night. A true friend is one who puts the other first, willing to brave pain, willing to risk. You're a true friend, Rue." Tears from some faraway place prickled. I affixed the necklace, positioning it beneath my armor. A wide grin bloomed across her youthful face, and she flashed me her matching necklace. I kissed her forehead.

"Is everyone ready?" Dom asked, grabbing my hand. The portal opened, its inky blackness our entrance to the wood outside my and Delah's shared cabin. Dom twined his fingers with my own. He gave me a quick squeeze, then we stepped through.

The winds whipped my hair, but the experience compared to Belham's portals was gentler, a brisk fall breeze compared to a winter maelstrom. Dom and I emerged first, then Bowen and Finn. The portal shrank behind us.

A distant scream sounded, and Korin tumbled out of the closing portal, landing in a rolling heap in the dirt as if she pitched herself through without thought to the consequences. My mouth dropped open.

Dom turned away, a muttered *"Foka"* trailing him. Worry and anger at her stupidity knotted my stomach. She jumped up, the barest hint of remorse on her face. "In case you needed an earthquake, I wanted to help."

Dom stared at the sky, imploring the clouds to grant him wisdom. Not for the first time this morning, his hand dragged through his hair. "No one is to find out who you are." He glanced down at her forearm which partially exposed the tattoo of the red wolf. "Cover that up," he snapped. She quickly obeyed. I, too, tightened the hood of my cloak to hide my face.

Korin brushed debris off her pants. Finn came alongside of her shaking his head. "I don't know whether to be impressed or alarmed."

She smiled brightly at him, tapping his chest. "Impressed works just fine."

She turned toward Dom, awaiting his reproach. He looked down his nose at her, face stern. "You stay with Finn or Bowen. Stick to the shadows. Do not go near the Vestal tower. If Nolan figures out who you are, he'll drain you of your magic. Do you understand?"

She threw her arms around him. "Yes. Got it." He grunted in resignation, returning her embrace.

My attention turned to our immediate surroundings. Each step in the direction of my home brought mounting anxiety. Logically, I know Delah's not there, but if there was a sliver of a chance at finding clues or something of assistance, I had to try. The spindly trees that made up the forest had dropped thick mats of rust-red needles. Small animals skittered around us, disturbing the detritus of the forest floor, causing me to flinch with each unnerving sound.

When my small home came into view, Dom insisted he and Finn scope it out first. He released his shadows to swarm the corners of the cabin, allowing them to move with some obscurity between the shade of the trees. After several tense moments, we were afforded the all clear. Dom beckoned me to the front of the house, and I pushed open the front door.

Kaida leapt off the couch, her massive body bounding toward me. I yelped and instinctively ran toward her. She stopped just shy of tackling me with her giant paws. The familiarity of her presence eased some of the worry that cloaked me. I glanced up at Finn, his eyes dripping with horror and confusion. Dom stood ready to unleash every piece of metal at the fearsome beast now nuzzling me.

I chuckled, cracking the shell of quiet shock. I gave my good girl a hearty head scratch. She glared back at me. "I know, I know, I've been gone a long time. I didn't mean to be." She bowed her head, allowing me better access to her favorite spot.

Dom cautiously stepped forward. "You're friends with

wolvin?" His eyes still held a trace of alarm, but his curiosity won out.

"This is Kaida. We found each other a long time ago. We... have an understanding." How could I explain the relationship we had? It wasn't like I was an animal whisperer. Hers was the only mind I could inherently speak to and understand. "Kaida, these are friends. And there's more outside. Don't scare them." She scowled at me before returning to the couch.

The familiar smells of our home would have been a comfort if not for the fact that it was empty, and clearly had been for a few days.

Nothing appeared to be out of place. Perhaps Nolan had taken Delah while she worked with the elixists at the Keep. I continued my inspection with her bedroom, Dom following close behind.

Most surfaces were covered with vases of half-wilted wildflowers. The bed retained crumpled sheets from her final morning here. I twirled a dagger in my hand, wracking my brain for inspiration. An idea flashed as I focused on a discarded vial on the floor.

I got on my hands and knees, gently tapping on the floorboards around the headboard of her unmade bed. A hollow sound responded after several taps, and I pushed into it, dislodging a small plank. My hand rummaged inside the hole, my fingers grasping her journal.

I only knew of its general whereabouts after a night of too much bramblewine and her casual mention of the experiments she was privately doing that could get her into trouble. I ached at the memory. She had been trying for so long to drop hints of what was going on in Haluma. I willingly ignored them in the name of blind loyalty.

Dom's broad shoulders shaded the light coming in from the window as he peered over to see what I'd grabbed. I flipped through the journal, searching the worn pages for more recent entries. There were copious notes about the effects of Glint, describing it as a neuromagical-toxin, and ways the king was experimenting with it. I shook my head at what she uncovered all on her own.

I flipped back a few more pages. There were recorded times for shipments making it to the castle, all under the cloak of night. Berine shipments surged during new moons, when it was blackest. My breaths thinned as I inhaled page after page of damning evidence for the betrayal of Nolan against his own kingdom.

The weight of Dom's hand on my arm anchored me. I turned to the last entry in her journal. I closed my eyes in fear and tempered hope. I scanned her notes. She had done it. Delah had created an antitoxin that successfully reversed the effects of Glint. In Delah-fashion she had named it Steel. With a few doodles of flowers in the margins, she explained that steel, the metal, is harder than gold and also its opposite color. It also sounds like steal, which is what Glint was doing to magic, and what Steel would do to the power of Glint.

If Nolan knew about her antidote, she might already be dead. I clutched at the hope that she was still being held as a ransom. And I was the demanded payment. As deceptions piled, I increasingly doubted he would stand by his word for a trade. Me for her. I straightened my spine, not leaving any space for doubt that we would lead a quick and successful mission. Delah would be in Yarit by the end of the day.

Bowen entered Delah's room searching for Dom. They muttered in low voices while I unraveled the information that swirled in tornadic activity within my mind. I handed the journal to Bowen for safekeeping. After all, he could undoubtedly make sense of Delah's equations, ingredients, and shorthand scribbles better than anyone. He tucked the journal under his arm, while I started rifling through her desk, searching for secret drawers, or any place she might have hidden vials of the antitoxin. All my expected hiding spots came up empty. I tapped my foot, trying to think like Delah as I searched her room for any missing clues.

My scan paused on the wilted wildflowers. On a hunch, I lifted the vase and turned it upside down onto her desk. Three corked glass vials tumbled out alongside the dying flowers and murky water. The letters "FeC" scrawled on the side. I crinkled my nose in disappointment.

Dom held one of the vials, assessing its contents. Bowen leaned over his shoulder to see it as well.

"Your friend is tricky. For not studying under a Prime Chemist, like Gemma, she was aware of our elemental table. These are the symbols for iron and carbon."

I stared at him confused, waiting for elaboration.

"These two elements combine to make steel." His smile broadened as he handed me the vial.

There were three vials of the antitoxin. They may as well have been liquid gold for the value they held.

I handed the vials to Bowen to add to the leather pouch at his waist with the other glass containers. He tucked them away, along with the journal. We stepped outside, reuniting with Finn and Korin.

"There is nothing more here for us. Let's go get Delah." I allowed one last parting glance to the home that had been a haven these last several years. Kaida kept pace behind us, a monstrous wraith in the shadows. We walked onto the main road away from my quaint little home, perhaps for the final time.

CHAPTER FORTY-FOUR
THE SPY

We snaked through Maripol under the cover of Dom's shadows. Finn melted into the crowd to connect with a few rebellion spies that were stationed around the city, seeking any crucial updates that might hinder our mission.

The rest of us convened near the castle, observing the soldiers that patrolled the entrances. The overseers of Nolan's fortress exhibited nothing beyond the monotony of habituated patrols.

Korin hadn't showcased an ounce of fear. I worried my lip contemplating the risks she was taking at being here. I had no doubt her power would be coveted by the king. Her affinity would be helpful in this attempt to rescue Delah; I just wished she wasn't a young girl without much experience.

As if my thoughts nudged her, she met my gaze, stern determination hardened her soft youth. Perhaps I didn't give her enough credit. She regarded the Keep, the ground beneath us trembling in anticipation. Dom flashed a dark look toward her, and the subtle movement ceased.

Staff, soldiers, and visitors of the castle slowly trickled out as daylight waned into the bruised sky of dusk. Finn returned with food that we hastily ingested.

"It's time," Dom announced. We each retrieved plugs to put in our ears, shoving them in as far as they would go.

With a nod, Bowen receded into the darkness. He made his way toward the entrance of the castle, creeping just beyond the road that curved its way to the main gates. He removed two vials, verifying their contents. Briefly touching his own ear plugs, he tightened his cloak and pulled out his lucky pine cone. I stifled a laugh as he kissed it. What a special relationship those two had.

He fisted the two vials in his hands, extending his arms as far from his body as he could. His shoulders rose in a deep breath before carefully removing the caps, dripping the contents into the grass. He briskly retreated, dropping the evidence while keeping to the shadows.

Shards of glass scattered across the cobblestones. I counted the seconds between exposure and impact. The release of the elixirs oozed among the stone cracks. As the contents kissed the air, bubbles formed as if boiling.

The elixirs retracted the air around them. I braced myself. The sound of an explosion reverberated against the castle walls, followed by profuse gray and red smoke that billowed thickly outward in a menacing blanket. The threatening red haze indicated a noxious poison.

When Bowen explained the tonic's impact, he'd simply stated, "Run from the red, and you'll be safe," along with an unnervingly wolfish smile. None of us had any intention of being close enough to test his warning.

At the sight of the roiling smoke, we bolted for the entrance of the castle. The soldiers guarding it abandoned their immediate posts to investigate the uproar. We slipped into the Keep, our heads down, skirting through shadows, as our feet carried us purposefully to our assigned destinations.

Bowen infiltrated the grounds behind us, easily blending in among the crowd. He and Finn raced toward the dungeons after Dom shrouded Korin in opaque darkness as she followed behind them. My fingers readied to shape my affinity. I darted toward the Vestal tower.

The commotion at the gates triggered a wave of apprehension amidst the guards within the walls. Unsheathing blades sang with an icy hiss across the Keep. The soft clicking scales of a fortress filled with dreki prickled the hairs on my neck, unnerving me.

I sank into the space within myself that knew no fear. Dom would follow me once he saw everyone to task, but I didn't linger. Leashed rage came unbound, and I took gratifying sips of it. My anger hardened into focus propelling me forward.

I ceased blinking, allowing tears to gloss my eyes. The path ahead of me teemed with scurrying people whose auras surged in my vision. Many were filled with varying shades of colorful light, but others, clearly devoid of it. I tried to avoid those that emanated death magic, desperately hoping to evade their detection. My fingers itched to form an iced-out longsword. Not yet.

The sun retreated, leaving only torches and starlight to aid in the guards' frenzied manhunt. I stealthily approached the Vestal tower, noting the broad-shouldered man guarding it. The sound around me ceased and a slight pop in my ears gave me pause. A silencing shield warded the tower.

The scales of the dreki before me blended into the surrounding darkness—the power pulsing from him enough of a deterrent to warrant only one to guard the entrance.

His canteen met his lips, lighting my trigger finger. With a subtle gesture, the guard began choking. I forced the water he drank to climb back up his throat and fill his lungs. He doubled over seeking air, his hands clawing at his throat. His eyes watered as he slowly lost color in his face. Frantic gasps left his chapped lips and he slowly collapsed, his vacant vertical pupils still glistening in the scattered torchlight. My bloodlust raged on.

As I approached the door, I stalled at the iron lock. Perhaps freezing it would dislodge its springs and bolts enough to break it. Warmth crept up my spine a second before Dom appeared at my side. "There you are." I grinned.

"I'll always come for you." He brushed my arm. "Bowen and Finn are searching the dungeons right now. I tucked Korin away in a pocket of shadows." His eyes strayed to the lock on the door, immediately opening it with a satisfying click.

"I could have done that," I grumbled.

We walked through the heavy door, shutting it quietly behind us. "I know you could have, but it pleases me to do something for you." We stared at each other, the heaviness of our mission pressing down on my shoulders. His shadows spun out in a warm burst, grazing my arms before surrounding us.

I turned to lead the way up the winding staircase. Before I could take a step, Dom grabbed my arm, pulling me toward him. He swiped his fingers lightly across my forehead, from temple to temple, then across his own, whispering a small prayer.

"For protection," he muttered. His reverence confounded me, but if the great god Elyon listened to anyone, it would be Dominus.

"Thank you," I whispered. Dom kissed my forehead, and together we ascended the stairs.

The absence of guards lent an eerie quality to our urgent search. We passed several rooms on our quest, but all were dark and abandoned. There were no footsteps, no echoes of voices. It was as if the entire tower had been deserted.

We neared the top of the tower, the stairs revealing a landing with hallways opened toward numerous rooms. Dom spoke in my mind, courtesy of Sieren's mysterious tonic, *I can quietly unlock each door, but we need to be quick. I'll do two at a time; you take one and I'll take the other.* His apprehension filled my mind along with a tenderness he couldn't hide.

We positioned ourselves in front of our respective doors. *Now,* Dom instructed through the mind connection.

I held my breath in anticipation of what lay beyond and shoved against the weight of the door, peering in expectantly. Darkness and silence greeted me. Dom's room lay just as empty as mine. We exchanged glances, closing the doors gently behind us. Tension coursed through me.

The living quarters for Vestal Anchors were well-known, the "privileged" group large enough to warrant this massive tower dedicated to them. We continued down the halls, only to find each one as forsaken as the last. The abandoned rooms raised the hairs on my neck.

We ascended the stairwell once more. Small torches cast flickering light upon the stone steps. Only one door remained on the uppermost floor of the tower, nestled in a hall unto itself. Ominous. The door hung slightly ajar, a sliver of light peeking around the frame. We crept forward. A sense of foreboding sharpened my senses.

I nudged it further and sucked in a lungful of air as my body was yanked into the room by cold tendrils of power. The door slammed shut behind me in a cracking thud. Dom's screams flew muffled against it. No metal lock could be dislodged to gain entry, not when Nolan's magic had sealed it shut. Dom's hands beat against the unrelenting barrier.

The room sprawled out before me, spanning the entirety of the top of the tower. Beds lined the walls, at least twenty on each side of the room. Machines clicked and whirred upon tables littered with tubes and syringes, flasks and metal instruments.

At the center of the space stood the Supreme Vestal in his blood-red cloak alongside King Nolan. Vestal Anchors lay bound upon the beds, their bodies limp, their faces listless.

Some groaned on their exhale, but rope burns displayed prominently across all their wrists. I spared them all a cursory glance until I fell on Delah's familiar face. Bruises speckled her cheeks and arms, her eyes frantic as she attempted to scream through the gag in her mouth.

Nolan slowly clapped his hands as he sauntered toward me. Hollow mirth settled in his blue-black eyes. "Had I known what a pain in my ass you'd become, I would have handed you over to my esteemed Supreme Vestal ages ago. I'm glad you decided to respond to my message though." He shifted, annoyed, granting his attention to the beating from the other side of the door. "It's warded, so whoever is in the hall won't find their way in unless I allow it." He waved his hand lazily in the air.

Hold on. Dom's voice penetrated my concentration. I released my magic, an ice sword elongating to a double-edged blade, perfect for slicing through bone and tendons. And kings.

Nolan smiled, tsking me. "None of that." He released his shadows, which speared toward me, burning my hand and scalding my skin, the effect like tiny shards of glass. My sword disintegrated under his death magic, my hand spasming. Black flakes of char drifted toward the floor in its wake.

"Give me Delah," I gritted out.

Nolan motioned toward the cloaked Supreme, who began removing her gag and her binds. Delah scrambled away, bolting toward me on shaking legs. I ushered her behind me, pulling my longsword from its sheath at my back. "We're leaving." I walked backward toward the door, not trusting my blindside to the king.

Nolan cocked his head. "But dear, Rue, you haven't even met the special guest I brought in especially for you."

"Get to the door," I urged Delah as we continued our retreat. I staggered, feeling like my temples were on fire. Black spots speckled the corners of my vision.

Nolan's shadows swirled in an agitated tempest. Char accumulated in ashy mounds around us.

"It's still locked." Delah's panicked voice accelerated my heart rate as I thought through ways to get her out.

"I think you'll want to meet my esteemed friend." His eyes glittered with malice.

"He comes," the Supreme Vestal stated, his voice an unnerving tone that sounded neither male nor female. A ghastly shudder rippled down my spine. The black diadem embedded in his forehead glinted ominously in the torchlight, hideously captivating.

The door swung open, the force of it shoving Delah into me and onto her knees. We stumbled deeper into the cursed room. Maelic barreled in, dragging Dom by an arm, his legs leaving a trail of blood behind him.

"No!" I lunged toward him. Nolan's shadows wrapped around my body, hissing and burning everywhere they touched, arresting me. Surrounded in his frigid shadows, I found I could barely use my own magic, water dampened the floor beneath me, but little else.

"What do we have here?" Nolan's smile was all teeth and venom. He stepped toward me, removing a piece of paper from his pocket, slowly unfolding it.

My stomach dropped at what he held in his hands. Dom would know what I had done. Would he realize it was for him?

The back of the paper revealed the dreki recruitment poster from the inn, the same muddied footprint stamped on it. Dom held my stare, willing me to look at him. Fear flared in his golden eyes. He wanted to protect me. My heart began to break.

"I almost didn't get your message because of that blizzard," Nolan said, waving the paper in the air.

Dom's confusion morphed into betrayal as his bleeding body tensed with alarm. He shook his head, unbelieving. My heart shattered. He may not understand now, but I knew it was the only way.

Nolan read the paper with obnoxious theatrics, altering his voice in a pseudo-version of my own. "I will surrender myself to you. In exchange, release Delah, and call back your Nokts. I will be there by the next full moons." He finished with a flourish as I wilted at my own words. "Delah will be free, Ruin, but the Nokts are not up for negotiation." He crumpled the paper in his hands.

Dom's anguish lanced through me. *I'm sorry,* I attempted to mind-walk. It was all I could offer. I begged him to understand. He would be fine. The blood curse cure was in the library. He would be safe. He would live. Let him be angry. Let him hate me. I'd spent my whole life focused on vengeance. At least I'd be able to end it knowing the person that mattered most to the realms, and myself, would endure.

"You know better than to have come with others." Nolan gestured toward Maelic.

Blood trickled down the side of Dom's face as Maelic brought out a black dagger, dripping with golden syrup—Glint. Maelic locked his feral gaze to mine as he swiftly raised the dagger, then plunged it mercilessly into Dom's side.

Dom grunted as Maelic slowly twisted the blade before removing it. The metal now coated with Dom's precious blood and devoid of gold. Dom collapsed onto the floor, blood instantly pooling around him. A shriek exploded from a soul-deep space within me.

My legs buckled as the ghost pain of the dagger seared my own side. I threw my magic toward him, shoving against Nolan's restraints, trying to staunch the flow of Dom's blood. I knew his own magic would be stifled by the poison infiltrating his system.

A sharp sob hurled from the depths of my heart at the sight of this man who had become more meaningful to me than anyone in this world. I thrashed beneath Nolan's shadow-restraints. My soul bleated. The urge to protect Dom overpowered me, but I was restrained, impotent, no matter how hard I fought.

The telltale sign of Glint's effects illumined outward. A gold-flecked mist arose from Dom, curling out of his nose, mouth, and out of the hole Maelic had carved in his abdomen. A red-cloaked servant appeared with a container of vials. He raised thin, pale fingers, releasing a putrid magic that funneled Dom's power into the glass, sealing them as each became filled.

"Can't have the Rebel General's magic go to waste now can we?" Nolan taunted. He whistled as he waltzed around the room, hands in his pockets.

"Let them go," I pleaded. My hands gripped the stone floor, sticky with sweat, water, Glint, and blood.

"Unfortunately, that won't be happening, Ruin. While I do enjoy a carefully planned deception, I get cranky when secrets are kept from me. And you, my dear, have kept a very big secret." Nolan circled me slowly, a vulture ready to devour. His eyes shifted to vertical pupils, then flicked back with a blink.

Nolan turned to Maelic who had come to stand by his side. "Can you break down whatever illusion she has?"

Maelic's eyes turned milky. I had seen him use his magic, but it had never been focused on me. It felt like my insides were being boiled. I screamed in agony at his acidic power. My vision slashed white, my breath sucked from my lungs. All at once it ceased, and I gripped the wall, reclaiming air into my chest.

Maelic's face lit in cruel excitement. "You were right."

Nolan paled as he mumbled to himself, cursing. His composure slipped at Maelic's revelation. Forcefully, he beckoned the man hovering over Dom capturing his stolen magic. "Let's get to the real party here." He rubbed his hands together in eager anticipation.

There was too much for me to follow. My body shook from

the recovering shock of Maelic's intrusive magic. My mind couldn't grasp the reality that Dom lay bleeding out so close to me, yet too far to aid, renting my soul in two. The hollow in my chest widened. This wasn't supposed to happen.

Another servant stepped forward to resume harnessing Dom's escaping magic. I stared helplessly, willing him to wake up. I was still compelled under Nolan's magic, prevented from rushing toward my general.

Hold on, Dom. You have to hold on, I spoke into his mind. I hadn't realized until this very moment that I didn't want to do it all alone anymore. I didn't want to keep forcing penance on myself. I didn't want to sacrifice myself. I wanted a future. With him. *You have my heart. I will fight for you. Hold on.*

He lifted his head a fraction. Blood sluiced down every plane of his beautiful face, marred by the hate of the demons surrounding us. *This isn't my end, Liora*, he pushed into my mind.

I choked back a sob. My rage coiled and grew like an insidious viper at my helplessness to save him. I could do nothing but watch and cling to hope.

Nolan's shadows jerked my chin toward the cloaked man who had sidestepped around Dom in response to Nolan's signal. "Meet our guest, Ruin." He flipped his hand toward the servant. "Remove your hood."

The man obeyed, sliding it down, revealing a face that I knew hauntingly well.

Delah gripped me as dread, like a brick of iron, dropped into my gut.

The man before me was my father.

CHAPTER FORTY-FIVE
THE SPY

Grey, the man who appeared in my worst nightmares, blinked at me. His flat expression communicated nothing as he assessed me. He appeared older, and smaller, then I remembered. He was no longer a towering figure of torment and hate that my childhood-self cowered under. I returned his scrutiny with squared shoulders and an unflinching glare. Ice crept along the floor, emanating from my feet in response to him, despite Nolan's power seeking to suppress my own.

I thought he had died in the fire. Did that mean my mother was still alive? I remembered finding charred bits of her clothing, though. I did not find evidence of my father's demise, only the assumption they had both perished.

I swallowed thickly, trying to reconcile the truth standing mere feet away from me. Where had he been these last many years?

My thoughts were interrupted as the ground beneath us began to gently sway. The tools lining the tabletops vibrated and the bed frames groaned. We crouched, recognizing an earthquake might very well bring this entire tower down. I stared at Dom, willing him to open his eyes. His body slumped against the stone floor, his chest rising with shallow breaths.

Grey kept his gaze trained on me. For a moment, I thought he would reach out to hug me. I recoiled at the thought of it. The Supreme Vestal held up his hand and Grey's mouth shut. His eyes fell blank, entranced.

"What are you doing here?" It's all I could muster. My throat felt tight amidst the irrepressible waves of my emotions. Grey imperceptibly shook his head before his body fell slack, unconscious.

A sound echoed up the stairwell, spilling into the chamber. Glass shattered and a destabilizing boom resounded. I clutched at my ears as blood trickled out of them, trailing a path down my jaw. A high-pitched ring drowned out the sound of the chaos around me.

Nolan's shadows receded at the assault.

Finn and Bowen burst through the entryway. Bowen grabbed Delah who had collapsed somewhere behind me. As he pulled her out of the room, her feet slipped on the mixture of blood and ice that coated the stone floor.

Her screams barely registered, though her mouth gaped in anguish. Finn's eyes widened at the sight of Delah, a fleeting look of recognition before his attention darted between me to Dom.

I shook my head vehemently and pointed at Dom. "Take him."

Pain flashed across his face as he made the impossible decision of who to save. I managed to melt just enough bloodied ice on the floor to create a compact wave, shoving Finn toward Dom.

Maelic gripped my arm, yanking me back. He motioned toward the Supreme Vestal who clamped down on my magic, stifling it. I choked for air at the feeling.

Finn hoisted Dom up, retreating as swiftly as he was able.

His clothing darkened with Dom's rapid blood loss. I prayed to Elyon, Dom's favored god, my only sliver of comfort in this moment.

My shoulders incrementally relaxed at watching Dom and Delah hustle to safety. I faced my captors, thinking through every conceivable way I could escape. I thrashed against Maelic's strengthening hold. His nails cut into my skin leaving droplets of blood to bloom across the tender flesh of my forearm.

I whipped my head toward the sound of more footsteps. The ground continued to shake more violently than before. My eyes widened in horror as Korin ascended the final step of the staircase, her frantic gaze searching, then landing on me. "STOP!" she screamed. "Let her go!"

"No, Korin, get away!" My heart stilled. Korin, that brave, reckless girl. I instinctively lunged toward her. My skin shred further beneath Maelic's dreki claws, though I hardly felt it. He hissed in my ear adding to the increasing tumult swirling around me.

A portal formed in the corner of the room and Belham emerged in complete dreki form. His scales clicked into their final places as he surged forward. He awaited King Nolan's command, and at the tip of Nolan's head, he pursued the curly haired girl who had burrowed into my heart.

Each step slapped against the stone floor, leaving my heart thrashing wildly in my chest. I could barely follow the sequence of events as they unfolded too quickly for my mind to comprehend.

I threw up my arms uselessly in a meager bid to protect Korin. I lurched toward her, loosening Maelic's vise grip on my arm. Stones began to break as Korin bent the foundations of the castle to her will. She stood her ground with an otherworldly confidence. She focused on her link to her magic, her eyes tripping in and out of focus. The earth beneath us continued to shift. Plumes of dust and shards of rock floated in the charged air. My lungs involuntarily heaved.

Belham protracted his stinger, striding directly for the young girl. It dripped as if it could scent the host it yearned to impale.

No!

My stomach dropped in paralyzing dread. Time slowed. I heard nothing. I saw everything. Korin's panicked eyes. One hand outstretched toward me, the other controlling her tectonic magic. A building dropped out of my view from the window, collapsing in on itself somewhere below. Korin's urgent lips beseeching me to get away from Maelic.

But I couldn't. Maelic jerked me back, his claws drawing more blood. Nolan's shadows tore across my skin, slender ropes of darkness made of fire that twisted around my arms and inched toward my throat. Red welts flared behind their caustic touch.

Several shadows bolted my feet to the ground. Regardless of how hard I attempted to throw my body in Korin's direction, they wouldn't budge. Something about the shadows, aside from their rendering me immovable and burning, left my body as heavy as iron. My breathing shifted from jagged bursts of frantic escape to the rapid and shallow inhales of dreaded realization.

I could only bear witness.

Belham smiled a malevolent grin that leached every last thread of humanity from his twisted features. His reptilian eyes narrowed, intent on his prey. He outstretched the stinger that had formed from his hand, lunging into the air.

It happened so fast.

It played in slow motion.

He punched the stinger, like an arrow, into her slender throat. The throat that once emitted a laugh that could disarm even the foulest warrior. The throat that housed a collection of friendship necklaces, painstakingly made with the love of her very fingers. It was a killing blow, piercing major arteries. Her body jerked. Her fingers stilled.

"Look at me!" I willed her to hear me through the fray. I would be the last person she would see. A vision of someone who cared about her that she could absorb as she left this world. I forced my expression to reflect the love I had for her, pouring tenderness into every muscle in my face. Grief grew like a tsunami in the depths of my chest.

I didn't know if Sieren's tonic remained active, but I pushed my thoughts into her mind. *You are brave and beautiful. You are like a little sister to me. Rest easy, dear one.* Everything stopped as the vibrant light winked from her eyes.

Finn darkened the doorway in time to see her collapse. I didn't register the sound of her body hitting the stone floor. *I'll come back for you.* I didn't know if the words came from Finn or Dom; didn't know if I heard it through my ears or my mind. Finn folded back into the shadows as I loosed a guttural scream.

Dom.

Korin.

Grey.

Loss.

Death.

Evil.

Rage and grief battled over the slips of my shredded heart. A heart that was drowning in a pain so deep it viscerally assaulted me. My bones rattled like the lingering aftershocks of Korin's powerful tectonic magic. I keened. Nolan's shadows swarmed into my mouth as a choking, burning tempest, consuming all sound.

Then everything went black.

CHAPTER FORTY-SIX
THE SPY

My eyelids sluggishly opened, awareness sharpening. It reeked with the harsh scent of chemicals and mildew. I didn't know where I was or how long I had been here. Then the events that led to my current position came rushing back to me, slamming against my chest. Grief bellowed at the memory of Korin. Aching longing nearly stole my breath at the thought of Dom. Anguish crippled my heart.

Find me, I implored. But the connection we had shared from the mind-walking tonic must have worn off. There was no response. I was on my own. My mother's words whispered in the middle of my despair: *"Do not be shaken."*

Someone must have laid me down at some point, and I now sought to sit upright. Roughened rope restrained my body, and I fought against the shackles imbued with magic. Their power burned into my skin as I jerked my arms and legs against them.

My father leaned over me, double-checking the manacles. I grimaced at his proximity. His face held no recognition, no expression. It was like gazing into a soulless shell. The feeling of entrapment and the metal pressing against the scars on my wrist seized my lungs and my chest tightened. I clenched my eyes shut.

"It will be over soon," Grey whispered over me. The softness in his voice hung in sharp contrast to his mechanical actions. How was he here? Had he been working for Nolan this whole time? I didn't have time to make sense of all the questions and emotions steamrolling me.

My father retreated as the Supreme Vestal, in his horrid crimson robes, glided around the room. He paused at the sound of my clinking fetters, but did not respond. He lowered his hood as he continued his preparations.

When he finally turned around, I could not harness my breath, my heart stuttering at the sight before me. The Supreme Vestal was a Nokt. The obsidian stone in his forehead swallowed all light that entered it. There were no whites to his eyes, only a consuming blackness that shrieked violence. His jaundiced skin contributed a ghastly glow to his black hair which hung in stringy clumps. It fell listlessly and he didn't bother to shove it away from his brow. He grinned malevolently, sniffing the air as he strode toward me.

He raised his palm and my body immediately stilled. I could not move, utterly helpless. Again. Fear curdled within me. I emptied of all emotion, save rage. It surged to the surface of my being, its energy demanding I respond—flee or fight. But I could do neither, only watch and wait. I retreated into myself, to the old part that learned how to withstand torture and pain, disconnecting from my very body until the threat passed.

He held up a needle, examining it in the light. I started shaking uncontrollably. If evil had a smell, it was this creature. If violence had a face, it was the one before me. He licked the needle, then gripped my wrist with his cold, black, crusty fingers. A satisfied sigh left his decrepit lips as he shoved the needle into a vein. A tube connected the needle to a pouch of

Glint. It steadily dripped into my veins, warming my blood and numbing my nerves. Oblivion beckoned. My eyes rolled back.

∼

Muffled voices filtered in and out of my consciousness. I kept my eyes shut, grasping for coherent thoughts. Glass clinked. A finger traced my arm. The silver symbol in my chest pulsed, harnessing my attention. Dom's face flashed before my mind's eye. The anguish of my soul multiplied as I thought of his injuries, and his need to find a cure for his blood curse. I had to hold on for him. I had to fight against one of my greatest fears, the draining of my magic, my lifeblood.

Soon, I would likely become a husk. But I would fight until my skin turned to ash. My rage solidified into resolve. Delah and Bowen knew how to make the antidote to Glint. If I could escape, I could take it and avoid the deadly aftereffects of the addictive drug, escaping the fate that Xuri's mother succumbed to. I would have a chance to live through the withdrawal symptoms.

My eyes opened a fraction, slowly focusing on Nolan. His shadows churned around him in agitation. He muttered to the Supreme Vestal, gesticulating wildly. I barely grasped his conversation, though words like "prophecy" and "Astral" leapt out at me, begging my mind to sharpen further.

I became aware of a needle in my other arm, connected to more tubes. Water flowed into my body. They were replenishing my magic as they were simultaneously draining it.

The Supreme Vestal motioned toward me and they both pivoted, their discussion abruptly ceasing.

Nolan came to my bedside, his eyes maintaining their reptilian form as he had no reason to hide his true nature. He sniffed up my neck, dragging his nose up my throat, along my jaw, and into my hair. It left a trail of disgust and revulsion in its wake.

"How did you hide your heritage from me for so long?" he murmured in my ear. "Your own father didn't know, though he has been well disciplined for his ignorant oversight." He stood, adjusting his tunic. "I will not be killing you, Ruin, for your magic is too precious. Though, you might beg for death..." He condescendingly tapped my forehead with his index finger. I jerked away.

As the ghost of his touch lingered on my skin, I beheld a vision. My mind knew Nolan was a master at illusions, yet my heart still clung to the deceptive scene before me.

I sat on a blanket at the beach, laughing at something Delah had said. Her jokes were always so ridiculous they cut through my perpetual frown. She never did let me fully embrace my soldier status. She had always grounded me, one of the things I loved about her.

The sun glittered on the azure waters and the glow of heat warmed my tanned skin. A pelican soared overhead before diving and emerging with a fish in its bill. We clapped for it.

Delah lifted a glass, speaking a toast that was intended to encourage as much as it was to keep me humble. We giggled some more as our glasses met in a tinkling sound.

I winced at a jolting sensation in my arm. I assessed my forearm but nothing was there. Delah continued to laugh, unaware of my discomfort. I tried to remember what we were laughing about. I peered at her face, but I couldn't focus on it. I squinted to clear away the distortions. It kept shifting as though she were underwater.

My heart began to pound and my limbs felt leaden. I exhaled a reedy breath as the symbol on my chest tingled. Involuntarily, I went to touch it, but my arms would not lift.

Panic flamed through my veins, finding no outlet. I blinked and my vision filled with an obsidian stone. It sucked in the terror of my scream. The owner of the embedded stone smiled sadistically, relishing in the pain and fear that it consumed.

My eyes flashed to my bare legs, where blackened veins webbed a ghastly map under my pale skin. I didn't know who to pray to. I didn't know how to call for help. There had to be a way out of this.

"Do not be shaken."

A soft click sounded, and the Glint restarted its nefarious slow drip into my lifeblood. A tear slipped down my cheek. As it landed on the thin white tunic I had been changed into, I distantly registered its crimson color. More blood welled up, obscuring my vision.

Then darkness stole me into its anesthetizing embrace.

EPILOGUE
THE GENERAL

Xuri's melodic voice penetrated the fog of my consciousness. The sounds of rustling and hurried footsteps irritated the headache grinding into my temples. A cool towel settled on my brow. I flinched at the touch, pain lancing up my side. My eyes flew open.

Rays of sunlight swiftly replaced darkness, accosting my vision and sharpening the pain in my skull. Xuri and Sieren peered down at me, one with pity; the other with clinical assessment. I reached toward my left side, expecting to find a sword hilt protruding from my exposed abdomen. Nothing was there save for bandages that obstructed the view of my throbbing wound.

I sucked in a ragged breath, my body remembering before my thoughts caught up. Furious and frantic shadows speared out of me, every piece of metal in the vicinity levitated or trembled in unrestrained aggression. Xuri held up her hands to block the lashing magic.

Sieren flew against the wall, breath whooshing out of her. Finn bolted into the room, words coming out of his mouth that did not register in my agitated state. His hair whooshed back at the onslaught of my uncontrolled magic.

Everything honed in on her name.

Liora.

I had to find her. The urge to protect swelled from the depths of my bones to the point of pain. My last memory of her flashed—a dreki restraining her, Nolan's corrupt shadows spiraling. Much of the memory blurred. But the words she had projected into my mind were clear. *"You have my heart."* I could scarcely breathe.

Xuri propelled her voice through the din of my power. "She lives."

The intricate symbol over my heart strained, tingled, ached.

She lives.

My eyes darted about the room. My room. In my home in Aphellion, back in Yarit. I regained control of my magic as my three confidants reclaimed their balance. Kaida strode forward, somehow having blended into the shadows. She laid her gigantic head on my legs, her brown eyes downcast, as if she bore the weight of Liora's loss with me. I reached out my hand to stroke her fur.

"Where is she?" I croaked out. The pain in my side incrementally lessened.

Finn approached, sorrow mixed with resolve. "She was captured. I could save her or you. She demanded I save you." He momentarily looked away. "Kaida attempted to return for Rue, but we somehow convinced her to come with us and she followed us through the portal." His voice trailed off. Guilt riddled him for leaving her behind.

My heart raced. Every fiber of my being bellowed to rescue her. I felt like a leashed animal, feral and focused on escape. Nolan had awakened a beast that would rival the deadliest wolvin.

"You were stabbed with Glint. It penetrated multiple organs

and barely missed your lungs. It drained you of a significant amount of magic causing your healing to stall. We are doing everything we can, but with your blood already poisoned, it's taking longer to rid you of toxins," Sieren offered.

I nodded in understanding, barely suppressing the urgency to spring out of my bed. My muscles twitched.

Through gritted teeth, I leveled my stare to each of my friends. "I will find her. It's all I care about."

Xuri drew near, her outstretched finger hovering above the silvered symbol on my chest. "When did you get this?" Her inquisitive tone stole my attention.

"The night before we left for Haluma. Do you recognize it?" I grazed the symbol with my fingers as it tingled beneath my skin.

Her mouth twitched with a barely suppressed smile. "It's the symbol of the *couerdiae*."

My shoulders fell slack. That couldn't be right. "A *couerdiae*? But we made no bond forged from our blood. Could it be something else?"

Xuri tilted her head in thought. "Then the bond isn't complete. But it's definitely the Sarulien symbol for it. A *couerdiae*—"

I cut her off. "It's the source for higher magic."

She shook her head, a twinkle in her rich dark eyes. "It isn't just a bond for higher magic. It's a heartbond. A cord between two people. The highest form of connection one could only dream of experiencing. Her hair, the Sarulien symbol, it's exactly as my vision predicted. It means your magic is bound to each other, as are your hearts. It's a oneness that only the gods can bestow. Dom, you're heartbonded."

Her words sucked all the air out of the room.

My heartbond.

The weight of my previous declaration to rescue Liora slammed full force in my chest. No wonder I felt possessed by an insatiable need to protect and rescue her, to be near her, to touch her.

To claim her.

A knock on the door brought Bowen and Delah into my increasingly crowded room. As they filed in, Finn assisted me in taking a more upright position in bed. I motioned toward a robe. He handed it to me, and I wrapped it around my bare chest with its blood-soaked bandage and screaming *couerdiae* badge.

Delah bowed her head. "Thank you for your efforts to rescue me." Behind her gratitude, I could hear her unspoken pain at arriving here without Liora.

"I'm glad that part of our mission was successful." I clenched my fists to contain my impatience. Who knows what Nolan would do to her. The metal in my room flared.

"You'll go back for Ruin?" Delah asked.

A small smile cut through my distress. "I will. And she's no longer Ruin of the Scourge." *She's mine.*

Delah's eyes shone with a film of unshed tears, a tinge of silver reflected in them from the brightly glowing symbol on my chest. As if she remembered her purpose in my room, she extended her hand toward me. "Now that you're awake, you can take this antidote for the Glint. I came up with it myself." A small blush tinged her cheeks.

I accepted the vial, uncorked it, and threw back the contents. The fluid coursed thickly down my throat, tasting faintly of anise, a far better flavor than the bitter tonic I was used to taking to counteract my curse.

Sieren ushered everyone out. "Let him rest now. Close your eyes, General, when you awaken, you should be nearly healed. Then we can work on getting Rue back."

Finn squeezed my shoulder. "Try to rest. We'll need you and your magic at full strength."

The last of my friends exited, the door clicking behind Xuri.

I dropped my head back on the pillow. Delah's antidote warmed my insides and relaxed my muscles, bringing on a drowsiness I was almost powerless to fight against. I removed the robe and readjusted my pillows.

The *couerdiae* symbol shimmered with silvery filaments. I hadn't slowed down enough to study its design. It showcased intertwining vines that took the shape of an infinity symbol. Its shimmer never faded, unlike the swirling symbols and script that came and went along my neck when I used my shadows.

Another thought sprung forth, penetrating through the antidote-induced lethargy. I needed proof of a quickly formed theory, in light of the truth that I had a *couerdiae* with Liora. I leaned sideways toward the bedside table, fumbling to open the drawer. I hoped I didn't accidentally throw myself off the bed and into a disgraceful heap on the floor.

The drawer shimmied, creaking from the unbalanced drag I made to yank it outward. Still nestled in a velvet bag, I removed the compass. The night before we left to rescue Delah, I had put it in here for safekeeping. It glowed significantly brighter as we had traveled from Vorkut to Lyrae. I had assumed it was due to our increasing proximity to the Nymphian Library, where Queen Thaleia had distinctly reported we might find the cure to my blood curse.

The bag fell open. I released a tensely held breath. My fingers trembled. The compass was now as dull as a piece of driftwood. My theory proved correct.

The cure for my curse wouldn't be found in the library. The cure would only be found in completing the *couerdiae*.

In getting my bonded back.

∼

Dying for more?

Delah deserves love, too! Grab your copy of Delah's bonus chapter, available exclusively to email subscribers.

Get to know Liora's roommate as she uncovers the secrets of Haluma after a handsome rebel invites her to defect from the only realm she's ever known.

Get your Bonus Chapter Here
https://BookHip.com/SKJDSAG

Stay in touch with all things Astrals and Nokts

ACKNOWLEDGMENTS

The realms would not be the same without a number of wonderful people who shared their glittering magic with this book.

Thank you to all the therapists and teachers who poured into me over my lifetime, speaking truths over me and offering words of healing. My own growth arc and the opportunity to lead others on their paths toward wholeness, were the impetus to this story.

Thanks to my parents. This book wouldn't have been written as fast as it was without my mom loving on my children in the process and taking them to buy ninety-nine cent toy cars. Time is a finite resource and Mom helped me salvage some. To my dad, who separately asked me, completely unprovoked, why I didn't write a book. Thank you both for your support and encouragement, commiserating with me when obstacles arose, and celebrating every achievement both big and small.

I would be remiss to not list my sisters-in-love: Mel and Eliz. You darlings were there when I was wrestling with the "Will I be enough?" and "Do I have what it take?" questions. You held space with me and challenged me, and were my most precious cheerleaders. Look at us—pursuing creative endeavors and absolutely killing it. So glad I was grafted into this family tree.

Thank you, Esther and Lauren for being the ultimate hype girls despite my self-doubts and debut fears. Even when there were reservations about some of my artistic choices, you hung in there. You guys are total babes and I hope we can make it to another Romantasy convention together.

Thank you to my PA, Cassandra, who took over work for me so that I could breathe and keep forging forward with writing book two.

To my editor, Nicole, for bearing with me and correcting every single em dash I enthusiastically tried to use. I promise I think I understand how to use them now. Thanks for tracking with the story I wanted to write, and polishing it to a pristine shine.

To the authors in the ever-entertaining and informative Romantasy Authors Guild chat. Without you, I wouldn't have a blurb, or marketing tips, or people in the trenches with me to boost and laugh and hold my hand.

To my extraordinary friends and extended family—those in book club, my small group, and old friends near and far who have learned of my writing journey and jumped whole-heartedly into supporting me and this book. Your belief in my abilities, and the story I want to tell, astounds me. I am grateful for the gift of friendship in this life.

This book would never have seen the light of day without the ultimate support and love of my own fated mate. You have allowed me to follow big, vulnerable dreams, and I am forever grateful. Thanks for giving me countless weekends, for leaving your own work early so I can focus on mine, and forcing me to believe the praise I've been given, even when I want to doubt.

To my precious babies that have kept me grounded and distracted and inspired. You aren't exactly babies anymore, but you will always be to me.

And finally, I thank God, always, that I get to do the thing that makes me feel alive.

About the Author

Nika McKinney has always harbored the quiet dream of becoming a writer since she was a child. She collects words like some people collect stamps. Her happy place is writing magical love stories with gut-wrenching trauma, along with harrowing growth and redemptive healing. Words are her daggers and paintbrushes.

She lives with her own fated mate and their two children in the north of Texas where it snows entirely too little. She is also a board-certified mental health therapist and a firm believer in the power of faith and a frothy lavender matcha latte.

This is Nika's first book.

To keep up to date with Nika, follow her online at
www.nikamckinney.com

For the most immediate updates and sneak peaks on new releases, fresh art, and giveaways join the Readers of the Realms Newsletter
Nikamckinney.substack.com/subscribe

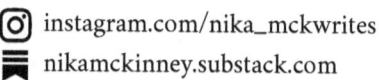

instagram.com/nika_mckwrites
nikamckinney.substack.com

www.ingramcontent.com/pod-product-compliance
Lightning Source LLC
LaVergne TN
LVHW040037080526
838202LV00045B/3376